IT TAKES A VILLAGE TO RAISE THE DEAD

Dagne Ekstrom

ISBN: 0998173304
ISBN 13: 9780998173306
Library of Congress Control Number: 2016916099
Green Dolphin Street Books, Eugene, OR

Dedicated to Lue Ethel Rhoads, *sine qua non*
and to Jillian Stanley, with thanks.

1

One of these days they were going to kill somebody, firing guns in the dark woods.

"Damn fools," Rey said. "What is it now? ATF? Bigfoot?"

The shooting was coming from halfway down the mountain, off to the north, somewhere between the Pear Sisters' house and Hoochville. She could guess who was doing the shooting. Eddy, for sure, and he'd drag his brewing cohort Hoot with him, convince Hoot there were trolls out there. And the other usual suspects, all armed as a well prepared militia should be, saving Cannibal Mountain and the US of A from One World Gubmint.

"Idiots," Rey said. The spotted kid nuzzled her leg and she gave it a reassuring rub on the sweet spot between its horn buds. "It'll be over soon."

She sat on the edge of her porch, listening. The sun set behind the peak and a wet chill rose from the ground. Women would have supper on the table, children would be finishing their chores, and the war games went on.

If only they were games. Unfortunately, it was just the targets that were imaginary. The bullets were real.

Eddy crouched behind a Douglas fir and sighted along the barrel of his shotgun at a shadow fifty yards downslope. He hadn't had but four or five drinks since yesterday, nine or ten tops, so he could trust his eyes. Yep. Dark tee shirt, slouchy hat: ATF, all right, look at 'em, trying to sneak through the trees. They didn't know who they was foolin' with. Never been a agent who could take Eddy's still. Never would be. These ones crashing through the bushes didn't know it, but they wasn't going to get as far as the still house. Their little outing was about over.

Two-hundred yards north of Eddy, Hoot squatted behind a salal bush, just above where the ground fell away. It was a noisy spot, with the water beating on the rocks way down at the bottom of the water-fall, and the heavy mist had soaked through his coat. But he liked this lookout. Trolls couldn't climb waterfalls to sneak up behind you.

Back home he'd been used to it, the old northern darkness, nights four months long. Twilight played tricks on you, turned everything into shadows. Twenty-five years at the lower latitude and his eyes had forgotten how to see through them.

That one there—moved with no sound, short and slippery. An animal? He pulled out a bottle of beer. Not his best batch. He uncorked it with his teeth and spat the cork into his chest pocket, keeping his eyes on the sneaking dark shape.

Animal? Waiting like that, like it watched him? Hoot took a pull off the bottle. There were no trolls down here. They liked more snow, more night. But every place had its monsters. He raised his gun.

Rey held the chicken coop door open as her flock filed in, muttering amongst themselves. The girls settled in and Rey said goodnight and fitted the stick across the door. They were nervous, chucking and rustling in their nests. The shots, sure, but something was in the air. It was still too early for raccoons. Cougar? Coyote? Nothing bigger than a mouse could get into the coop. A bear or a cougar might break the wattle walls, but there wasn't anything Rey could do about bears and cougars except hang cans around to scare them off.

Behind the house the goats rubbed the wall that formed one side of their shed. They smelled warm and pleasantly musky. As usual, they tried to sweet-talk Rey into staying out with them, but she settled them down on their fir beds and went indoors. She put a pot of beans on the stove to warm up, lit a lantern, cut up some early greens. The fire started right up. As it caught, a chunk of pitch exploded and shot into the room. A gunshot answered from less than half a mile away. Animals scattered and squawked.

"Okay, folks, settle," Rey said. "We're all tucked in for the night. We'll be fine."

Jacob Alder hadn't gotten very far into the woods when he ran into Crystal, and that was far enough for him. She rested her rifle butt on the ground, hand around the trigger guard. Jacob settled against the fallen log, as close as he dared get to her.

"And I'm getting cable TV and watch it all night," Crystal was saying. "Hot shower every night. And work in a makeup store. When the sun comes up the day I turn eighteen, I'm gone like a cool breeze."

"Yeah," Jacob agreed. "I'm never coming back to this hole, I swear to God." Jacob hadn't thought about leaving until right now, and he'd never taken the Lord's name in vain out loud until right now, either.

"Me neither," Crystal said. "I'm sick of being a fucking pioneer like my fucking parents."

"Oh, I don't know." Jacob took a chance on Crystal hating him again. "Your mom's OK. She plays pretty good."

"Maybe she'll play you a song, give you big ol' hillbilly kiss." Crystal put distance between them without even having to move.

Jacob blushed in the near-dark.

They were both fourteen. He'd promised his parents he would stay until he was eighteen, which was the same as forever, but Crystal wouldn't last four more months here, much less four more years.

"How are you going to do it?" he said.

"Do what?"

"Leave."

"Get a ride to Corvallis with Trucker John next time he makes a run to the valley."

She had it all figured out. Just when they were getting close—that is, just when Crystal had stopped thinking he was a baby—she was leaving. A jolt of panic told him he'd do anything to get her to stay.

Crystal twisted around and looked over the top of the log. "What was that?"

Jacob hadn't heard anything. He turned and peered into the trees just in time for a chunk of bark to jump off the log and bite into his cheek. Then he heard the shot and he and Crystal ducked down together.

Earl Alder took the uphill watch and El Duane Alder took downhill. Earl had claimed the comfortable stump which left El Duane, as usual, with the little brother's inheritance: the cold wet ground. Earl always got the easy road. Due to his strong Christian faith, Earl said. God's reward. But El Duane had Christian faith, too. He'd gladly lead the Wednesday meeting if Earl'd let him, but his big brother hogged it like he'd hogged everything else for the past thirty-nine years. Although in El Duane's opinion Earl hadn't been so lucky in the wife department. Yeah, El Duane had dodged a bullet there.

Mercy choosing Earl over himself had pissed him off—sorry, ticked him off—at the time, but it had been a blessing in disguise.

El Duane saw it the same second Earl whispered, "Look there. Between them two big firs."

"I already seen it."

Earl said, "FBI."

"Or UN," El Duane said. "Either way ... "

"They're here, brother. Time to take our stand for God and freedom."

"All right. That's it." Rey slapped her bowl down on the table. "Those morons'll shoot their own dicks off. Not that I care," she said, snapping up her coat. "But somebody's got to save them from their own stupidity." She picked up her .22 and put a handful of bullets in her pocket.

It was full dark now but the overcast was thin enough to see a white smudge of moon about a quarter of the way up the eastern sky. When she left the clearing around her cabin she switched on the flashlight. The guys were scattered over the northeastern slope, from the sound of it, having their little snipe hunt.

Muttering about men with too many guns and too much spare time, Rey kept to the ribbon of trail that circled north to Hoot and Eddy's place—Hoochville, where Travis had been staying with the two older guys. Hoot and Eddy would be fending off the ATF and maybe a troll or two. The Alder brothers would be taking out the scouts for the FBI, UN, One World Order forces, NSA, Satan and/or the Antichrist. Trucker John would be in on it just to look like a man for Sugar Agate.

Rey hoped that was all. The rest of the Cannibalites had more sense. Didn't they?

Earl had been looking at an FBI agent-shaped figure about thirty yards upslope. El Duane had been looking at a man with a One World United Nations hat downslope, trying to sneak away. Earl and El Duane did their duty.

Eddy held his fire until his gun stopped quivering, then squeezed the trigger real slow. When he opened his eyes, the revenuer was down.

Hoot didn't hesitate. These little ones were the meanest. He pulled twice and the troll, mountain demon, whatever it was, squealed and fell.

Crystal wasn't going down without a fight. Whatever it was shooting at her—government or terrorists or aliens or whatever, they weren't going to take New York and Los Angeles away from her. She flipped around to fire over the fallen tree.

Jacob rolled away and gathered himself into a running squat. Dad had been right all along. The feds were here to wipe them out, just like Waco and Ruby Ridge. He crabbed to the end of the log to get a good low position. This was it. Time to man up. Time to fight.

Trucker John intended to stay close to his trailer. He didn't much believe in bad guys on the mountain. Earl and Eddy and them told a lot of stories, but stories weren't always the truth. Sugar Agate had taught him that much. Her pretty stories lasted until she got what she needed, and then storytime was over.

Nope, he didn't hold with federales snooping around. Why would they? Nobody was doing much of anything illegal. Except Hoot, and Eddy, and Smokey. And hunting out of season, and not bothering with licenses. Most people had used to do various illegal acts before they moved to Cannibal Mountain. Some of them was wanted, no doubt, but the police had to have bigger fish to fry, in more convenient places they wouldn't get all tore up and muddy.

Bears were real, though. And wasn't that a sneaky, moving shadow of a black bear right there, up by the clearing? Trucker John closed in on it. Sugar Agate's angel face floated into his mind. He aimed his shotgun and fired.

A shotgun boomed on Rey's right. Ahead and behind rifles cracked. Rey proned herself into the ground, holding her breath while gunfire roared around her. Impossible to tell how many rounds were fired. At least fifty, coming from three directions, and closer than she'd thought. She was smack in the middle of World War III, too shocked to say oh shit oh dear, unless she was in fact saying it out loud but too deafened to hear her own voice.

When it stopped the forest was quiet except for the ringing in both Rey's ears, one shrill, one tolling like a church bell.

The ringing faded. She raised her head off the dirt, ready to duck even though by the time she heard a shot it would be too late.

"Hello?" she called. "Don't shoot."

She played her flashlight around.

Just dark, dripping trees, and more dark. "Who's out there? It's Rey. Everybody okay?"

In case it was police, she said, "I'm not armed."

I shouldn't have said my name, she thought, but then remembered she hadn't been Rey until she came here. Anybody looking for her would be after a name she hadn't used in four years.

She called out again and then got to her hands and knees. Nobody shot her, so she stood up. She knew she was a couple of hundred feet uphill from the clearing. Solar power was in short supply in these mountains so the flashlight was yellow and weak, but it lit the ground in front of her feet well enough that she made her way downhill, heading for the Pear Sisters' house. They lived closest to the clearing, which Rey figured was the center of the mayhem, and she was worried that bullets might have gone through their walls, or that Lacewing Pear would have a panic attack. Of course, Bee and Cricket would take care of Lacewing, and their walls were old growth timber logs a foot thick, so there was no real reason for Rey to go to the Pear Sisters except for advice and comfort.

But when she got to the clearing, she saw she needed a lot more than comfort.

2

The clearing was full of bodies.

None of them moved when Rey threaded a path between them. She stumbled on a leg and had to put a hand down on someone's chest to catch herself.

"Sorry," she said. The body didn't flinch or breathe. The face was obscured by dark stuff—blood, it looked like—but Rey recognized Trucker John's big belly and bushy beard.

The flashlight played around the clearing hesitantly, as if dreading what it might illuminate. The beam fell on Earl Alder and his brother El Duane, laid out in a vee with their feet together. Earl's shirt had exploded and El Duane's head wasn't much better.

Rey said their names. Quiet squatted like a toad. Picking between them, Rey had the sick surety that an arm would shoot out and grab her ankle.

Dollar Bill, originally Bob Doller but inevitably called Dollar Bill because he had the store down by the trolley over the river. His heavy-rimmed glasses stared into the dirt with their stems sticking up like dead bird legs.

Eddy, the smell of his product fuming from his body as if it were trying to escape and distill itself on the hard bowl of the sky.

And Eddy's cabinmate Hoot, less bulky without the Force of the Norse animating him.

Rey turned to leave. She felt queasy. Someone else had to deal with this. They'd figure out what had happened. She should get the hell out of here and go to the Pear Sisters' or her friend Jackie Tobasco's and get drunk on Eddy's moonshine while somebody else coped.

Then she saw Berry on the ground and knew Jackie Tobasco wouldn't be the one to deal with this. Berry wasn't a hunter of ATF or NATO agents or trolls or even bears, but just the same she was lying dead with an old rifle in her hands, and Jackie Tobasco wouldn't ever be the same.

Across the clearing, hanging over the downed tree, Crystal Hill's spiky hair curtained her face and her hands dangled down over the log. Rey felt Crystal's wrist but the skin was cold and empty.

On the other side of the deadfall Jacob Alder leaned against the log. His chest moved slightly.

"Jacob! Are you okay?"

Rey climbed over the log and touched Jacob's throat. His attempt at a beard tickled her palm. His chest moved again and Rey said "Jake! You're alive!" Something crawled out of his shirt and scurried to the trees.

Rey sat down on the log. She was not supposed to have to deal with this shit again. That's what Cannibal Mountain was for. It was as far away from group death as she could get. Never again, she'd sworn, and put fifteen-hundred miles and a century of civilization behind her, but it had found her again. At least this time it wasn't her fault.

She didn't care if a hand did reach out and grab her. She would have been grateful for any sign of life.

When she saw, at the far side of the clearing, Buck Hill's prone body with one arm reaching out toward his daughter, Rey did some cussing. When she was done she went around again and felt the carotid pulses of her neighbors—her family, not to put it too sentimentally, and Rey did not want to get sentimental just now.

They were all dead.

Rey saw the future of Cannibal Mountain unraveling. There would be publicity. They would bury their dead themselves, but eight sudden, violent deaths would be hard to keep secret, even for Cannibalites. Even if no one in the hollows had heard the shooting or thought anything of it, outsiders would find the mountain.

She would lose everything. They all would. On top of their personal losses, they'd be thrown back into the ugly world, even less fit for it now than when they'd first come, and some had been here twenty years, the Pear Sisters even longer. They were all different now, insulated from the world's lies and bullshit. And the world was different now, too—uglier, no privacy or even dignity. Most of them would be found, run through a database, and packed off to whatever punishment they'd been evading. Or they'd just end their days in a bad apartment in a gray town, learning how to die.

Rey could start over, maybe, in another off-grid place, but she was stronger and freer than some of them.

This wasn't something she could fix, no matter how lousy the consequences. That was the trap of it. You knew just enough to think you could fix it, but all you could really do was screw it up more.

While her mind was saying *No*, her feet took her back up the trail and into her cabin. In her hidden lab, she laid her hands on the silver case as if she were divining its contents, as if she didn't see it in her mind every hour of every day.

Why couldn't this have been a night when Travis had stayed with her? He wouldn't be much practical help, or even try to be, but his solid male body would have been a comfort, or if not a comfort, a delightful distraction. Thinking of Travis's perpetually tan skin and sun-colored hair made her forget how much she dreaded what was ahead.

She cut directly downhill, using the unfinished boardwalk that led from her yard to the upper end of the little road. The track was strewn with lobbets of wood and sour, rotting sawdust. At the bottom, where the road bent south toward the Alders' and

Hills', Rey stepped over the narrow ditch separating her walk-way from the dirt road. As she stretched her leg over, something big moved into her path. She jerked back, lost her balance, and stepped into the ditch. Water ran over the top of her boot and soaked her foot.

"Hey," the big thing said.

"Travis?"

"What's up?"

Rey stepped into the road. "I hoped I'd find you." If she hadn't been carrying the box, she would have thrown herself into his arms. "Did you hear the shooting?"

"Eddy and Hoot went out night hunting. They can't see in the dark worth shit. Sampling their wares too much, you know?"

He looked away from her, down the long leg of road. "Where you headed?"

She ought to do this alone. As long as nobody found out what she'd done, nobody would know their loved ones had died at all. And nobody could blame her if things went ass-up. But Trav would be the perfect companion. He wouldn't think too much about what she was doing, and the chances of his blabbing were about fifty-fifty. He wouldn't rat her out on purpose, but he was hopeless at keeping secrets. It would be worth the risk to have his help moving bodies. At the very least he could hold a flashlight.

"The clearing. Can you come with me?"

"Later, maybe. Let's go to your place. I don't like being out here with all those guns going off." He didn't mention why he was out in the first place.

There wasn't much time, but all Rey wanted to do was stay with him. Why not go back to her place with him, snuggle all night, and not think about this mess until tomorrow? It would all still be there in the morning, except for any parts animals might drag off.

She asked, "How'd you get over here from Hoochville? You must have walked right through where they were hunting."

"No, I was down the road. Uh, down at Dollar Bill's. For match-es. Couldn't find any in Hoochville." He threw an arm around Rey's shoulder and she closed her eyes for a second.

"Hey, what's that suitcase thing?" Travis asked.

"Tools."

"Kind of dark to be fixing things."

Rey said, "Were the Dollars up?" knowing that Bill Doller was sprawled out in the clearing. She didn't like to trap Travis that way, but he never suspected that she knew he lied sometimes.

"Nope."

Up close, Travis smelled faintly floral. It was a nice smell that was all too familiar. He turned up smelling like that sometimes over his own odor of man and forest. He might as well have worn a stick-on tag saying, "I've been with Sugar Agate."

"I've got to go," Rey said. "Wait at my place, okay? Stay inside."

"Why, baby?"

"I don't know what's going on out there. Just stay safe. I'll be back pretty soon." Travis would never feel the same about her if he saw her with the bodies. Travis liked things light and easy, clean and happy. That was the reason he was such a joy. Well, one of the reasons.

Travis pulled her up close and kissed her. For a few seconds Rey forgot about everything else. His kisses had that effect on her, even though she could taste Sugar Agate on his lips. The very fact that Rey didn't feel jealous was another way Travis made her happy. She couldn't keep her hands off him, but the way she loved him was the way she'd loved her big yellow lab when she was a kid. That dog loved everybody, and little Jillian Newhause loved other people to love him. Only there was this added dimension to Travis, of course, him being a human male, and made of sunshine and surf spray and guitar chords and warm lips and ...

No, Travis wasn't going to help her drag bodies around in the middle of the night. It wasn't where his talent lay.

"Go on," she said. "I've got matches up there."

"Huh?"

"Matches. You're out of them."

"Oh, yeah," Travis remembered. "Right. Later, then."

He cupped her ass and rubbed his thighs against her, and finished his kiss. That was where his talent lay.

She waited until Travis's footsteps disappeared up the walk toward her house, then turned left toward the clearing. The Pear Sisters' house sat close to the road, and the trail from the road to the clearing passed their side window. All the windows were dark; the Pears rose and went to bed with the sun. Rey tried not to make any noise. She had to do the deed in the dark, alone.

A gust of clammy air made her backbone crawl. *Alone in the dark* ... a memory hit her, something cold shoving her into an old abyss. She stiffened her shoulders and pulled her coat tighter around her neck.

When the log house was behind her she breathed easier. At the clearing, the bodies were still splayed where she had left them. Rey set the case on the ground and hunkered down in front of it. She shivered down into her coat, trying to hunch out the cold that reached for her insides. At least it wasn't raining. Lost causes were easier to take when it wasn't raining.

Bitter green light seemed to boil out from the seams of dark metal that never rusted, that an axe couldn't chop through. She touched the disks of the combination lock. The numbers had never left her. She turned the first disk to six. It rolled on its axis as if it were freshly oiled. Of course, this metal did not need to be oiled. Everything had been the best, newest, most sophisticated equipment money could buy, and the money had been limitless. A simple locked box was a work of NASA quality art: the art of protecting secrets, and the biggest secret in the history of humankind required the finest technology. Four years of sitting in a damp, scarcely heated cabin in a northern rain forest hadn't affected the tumblers.

The next disk rolled to four, the next to seven. Rey opened the antechamber of the box and picked up the electronic key. The green glow smelled like disinfectant and mushrooms. The key read her thumbprint and a strip of metal popped out of the end. Rey inserted it into a slot on top of the box. It turned like butter.

3

Bee Pear's hearing was not as bad as some people claimed. Right now, for instance, she heard somebody walk past her window, heard it as well as she ever had. She peered through the curtain, but whoever was out there walked without light.

Her aching knees and hips cracked loudly enough, she thought, to announce her presence to the passerby. She put on her glasses and got dressed over her nightgown, shivering when the air hit slivers of exposed skin. At Cricket's door she whispered, "Get up. We're going out."

Cricket said, "Have a good time," and pulled the quilt over her ears.

"Didn't you hear the guns?"

"They quit. Go away."

Bee said, "There's trouble and I'm not going out there alone. Don't wake up Lacey."

Cricket moaned and threw the quilt off her face. "How do you know there's trouble? You're just hoping there's trouble so you can stick your nose in."

"If we don't take care of it our own selves, outsiders will. You want the reporters here? We're not going to lie in our beds waiting for the police and the newspapers."

"Newspapers? You're thinking of 1959. The Internet might show up, maybe, if there is anything going on out there, which I doubt there is."

"We don't need any of them up here," Bee said firmly. "We don't need 1959 all over again. I'll light lanterns and meet you at the door in two minutes."

Rounded in layers of sweaters and coats, the sisters stepped carefully onto the stone walkway that led to the path alongside the house. Twenty years ago they wouldn't have bundled up in such fat layers, but skin thinned and muscles, if not spirits, lost their heat. Bee let Cricket lead the way. Cricket had better eyesight, but Bee had a better sense of what might coming up from the rear.

In the trailer just uphill from the Dollers' store, Jackie Tobasco flopped a leg over Berry's side of the bed, expecting to make a leg sandwich with Berry's warm, sinewy thigh, but Berry wasn't there. Jackie felt the sheet and came up empty.

"Ber—" She cleared her throat and segued into a full-scale hack attack. She was going to stop smoking for sure tomorrow. It was all the talking that made her so scratchy and phlegmy. She figured if she quit smoking tomorrow she could keep talking a few more decades.

"Berry? You home, sweetheart?"

Berry didn't answer. She was still out there. She would be freezing. There weren't enough wool coats in the world to keep her warm in this climate.

Jackie Tobasco got up and drew the blankets over the bed to hold in the warmth. She put the coffee pot on the propane burner and cranked a handful of beans through the grinder. Berry hadn't gone out at night for weeks, and Jackie had believed it was finally over.

"What are you doing, girl?" Jackie asked the coffeepot. "I told you it's more dangerous on the mountain than any city you've ever walked in. You could be layin' out there right now with a broken leg and nobody knowing and me here crazy worried about you."

Jackie dumped hot rocks out of the can on top of the stove into the bed warmer and tucked it where Berry's feet would go.

"Don't you have enough here at home? What are you looking for out there?"

Berry had tried. She stayed home and played poker and Scrabble. She repaired things that didn't need repairing; she gave in and let Jackie do her hair. She tried to read, but when Jackie would look up from her John D. McDonald or Phyllis A. Whitney, Berry would be staring at the door, not at her own book.

Tonight she'd slipped out without a word and a little bit ago there'd been the pop and boom of gunfire. Target practice with the boys, Jackie figured. Berry loved her guns. She could shoot the Cs out of a Coca-Cola can. That's why Jackie didn't go stark raving nuts when Berry stayed out at night. Berry could handle herself.

Jackie drank a cup of coffee, rolled a cigarette, and listened to the clock ticking. She poured a new cup of black coffee, poured it back in the pot, and said, "I'm coming after you, crazy woman," snapped her coat on and tied a scarf around her head.

Downhill, the Dollers' store and Trucker John's trailer were dark. Jackie's railroad lantern flung shadows into the bushes. She would run into Berry on the road and get an apology. Then hot tea and a warm bed to chase the chill off her island woman.

Lacewing Pear heard her sisters go out. She'd heard the gunfire but had chosen to let it drift. For the first seventy years it had been hard to let things go, but it was getting easier. Events flowed around her like warm honey, like summer water. Bee and Cricket let her float.

She didn't like being alone in the house. As soon as the door closed the dark got darker and rustly sounds rose into whispers. Lacewing knew it was only the wind, but she still didn't care to listen.

She said a Hail Mary and several Om Mani Padme Hums. Afterwards she felt clearer-minded. Her older sisters had sneaked out: there was something they didn't want her to know. That meant they were protecting her. There had been gunfire. Guns were dangerous. It followed as spring follows winter that Bee and Cricket thought or knew someone was hurt out there. Thus it was Lacewing's duty to go to the afflicted and use her gifts to heal.

She pulled on half a dozen gowns and shawls and dragged her medicine basket from under the bed, where she thought it hidden from Bee and Cricket. Basket in one hand and lantern in the other, Lacewing followed the smell of mint soap, and under that, getting stronger as she traveled, the tang of cordite.

The key triggered locks buried in a matrix of proprietary super fiber and Inconel. They opened with silent vibrations.

"You have to do this," Rey told herself. "Now cowgirl up and open the box."

An imperious voice said, "Hello, Rey. What are you doing?"

Rey froze.

Bee pushed forward. Cricket flanked Rey. The two were enough of an army to surround an average person.

Cricket raised her lantern. "What's all that out there? It looks like ... Oh, for heaven's sake. What have you done?"

"Me? Nothing!" Rey said. "They were like that when I found them."

Bee looked at the tableau of bodies. "Well, they've done it now. Killed each other dead. I presume they are dead? Did you check?"

"I checked," Rey said.

Bee said, "Cricket, go feel for a pulse."

"They're all dead," Rey said. "Guaranteed."

Cricket stayed put.

Bee bent over the box. "What's this?"

More noises and hubbub from the trail made Rey close her eyes. So much for secrecy.

Jackie Tobasco walked into the clearing and right into the boneyard. She screamed in her smoker's tenor gargle. Backing away, she stumbled over El Duane Alder's head. The scream gained altitude.

"Calm down," Bee told her. "Stop walking on people."

"They've been through enough," Cricket said.

"They're already dead, so I'm sure they don't mind," Bee said. "But you're messing up my crime scene."

"Ho-ly crap." Jackie walked toward the trailhead on her toes as if she were trying not to touch the ground. "What in the hell happened?"

"Yes, Rey. Go ahead." Bee sat on the big stump unofficially reserved for her, like a chieftain surveying her deceased subjects. "What happened?"

"I don't know. I heard gunfire and I came down to stop them."

Cricket tisked. "Walked into a shootout? And not a scratch on you. Interesting."

"And they were all dead. I haven't touched anything. And," Rey added, "We have no reason to consider this a crime. It has all the marks of a tragic, horrible hunting accident."

"Holy crap," Jackie said from a distance. "Holy crapping crap."

Bee said, "The question is, what are we going to do about it?"

"And the other question is, who's here?" Jackie Tobasco said. "Berry's not here, obviously."

Rey looked at Jackie.

"No matter who's here, what do we do? That box, Rey." Bee pointed. "It has something to do with this disaster."

Rey sat on the ground. If only it would swallow her up. She could almost feel a shuddering earth open its mouth for her. "I was just ... I was going to—nothing."

Rey was spared the choice between lying and giving herself away. Noiselessly, Lacewing wafted from the dark into the halos of lantern light, a vision of veils and shawls and dangling amulets.

"I am here," Lacewing said. "What creature needs my help?"

"Take your pick," Bee told her.

Lacewing walked closer and raised her lantern. She looked like a large firefly.

"How many are there?" she asked.

"Seven, no, eight," Rey said. "As far as I know."

Lacewing set her basket down and made several half-invisible gestures. She intoned bits of prayer and unintelligible syllables. Then she straightened her back and said crisply, "Right-o. We'll make a start then, shall we?"

"Oh, she's British now," Cricket said.

"She can accomplish a lot as an Englishwoman," Bee said. "If she's a nurse in the Blitz, we're in luck."

Lacewing crouched beside Rey. "Go on, then, open your kit. With the two of us pitching in, we'll soon have this lot sorted."

She didn't wait for Rey, but opened the nested trays in her basket. Rey had read a Robert Heinlein story about a room that was bigger on the inside than it was on the outside, and he obviously had taken the idea from Lacewing's healing basket. By the time she'd opened it fully, there were six stepped trays winging up and out on two sides and still plenty of room inside for colored glass bottles and little silk bags.

Lacewing kept tinctures and herbs for most things that went wrong. She had reset tibia and humeri, delivered the last three of Mercy Alder's babies, and soothed Trucker John's broken heart. She claimed viruses and bacterial infections as her dominion and had quelled a range of rashes. She had pronounced a man dead once, but to Rey's knowledge hadn't ever revived one.

Rey felt a rush of hope. "Can you bring them back?" Maybe she'd underestimated the woman's powers.

"Oh, probably." Cold air sank from the top of the mountain and animated Lacewing's cirrus cloud hair. "I've done my fair bit here for near on seventy years. Haven't lost a patient yet, except the one. We'd best get on with it. The longer you leave them the deader they get."

Rey suppressed an urge to kiss her. Let somebody else fix this and leave her out of it. The dead would live again, their families would never know how truly dead they'd been, and Rey's life would unspool peacefully. But how amazing that the great secret, the holiest of grails, had been here all this time, in an elderly lady's basket.

Lacewing squatted on the ground—a posture that Rey would understand forty years later was nearly impossible for a person of Lacewing's age—prowling, muttering through the array of bottles.

"What do you have? Something that performs miracles, I hope." *And does them better than I ever did,* Rey thought. *And with fewer side effects.*

"No such thing as miracles," Lacewing chirped. "And everything's a miracle when it's at home."

Rey caught a few muttered words: ember flower, gray mold, nettle.

The clothes of the dead stirred under the rising night wind and Rey's atheism slipped several degrees. A smell was already forming, a funk of new meat and dirty laundry.

Lacewing tapped various ingredients into a little jar and hid her nose behind the crook of her elbow while she stirred it with a spoon, the bowl as big around as a baby's thumbnail.

"Come along, then." She stood, pausing part way up for her joints to release. "Who's going to hold their mouths open for me?"

"Go ahead," Cricket told Bee.

"I have to supervise," Bee said.

Jackie said, "Don't look at me. I'm not your gal. Uh-uh. It ain't me, babe. Sorry. Count me out." She melted further into the background.

"I would, but I've been kind of queasy lately." Cricket patted her esophageal area and burped. "You've been volunteered, Rey," she added sympathetically.

Trucker John was the closest. Rey hesitated, then put one hand under his neck where sticky blood coated his skin and one hand on his thick jaw. She pulled his chin down, felt resistance, pulled harder. Rigor was already setting in.

"Mind that the powder doesn't blow away," Lacewing instructed. "I'm out of birdthistle so I can't make any more. I could try rubbing along without the birdthistle, but ... well, unpredictable results aren't quite the wanted thing."

"We don't have much time," Rey said.

"Right you are. Pull his tongue up and out."

Rey flinched, then got hold of herself and used a corner of her shirttail to pull Trucker John's tongue toward his nose. It felt as if it were pulling away, trying to get back into the warm safe place behind its owner's teeth. Lacewing dipped out a minispoonful of powder and shielded it with her hand.

"Here you are, poor lamb." She dropped the potion into the victim's sublingual tissue. Then, to Rey's horror, she spat in Trucker John's mouth. "Close him up," she trilled.

They moved on to Hoot and Eddy, Crystal Hill and Jacob Alder, the teenaged bodies as stiff in death as old bodies were in life. Rey held their tongues, Lacewing dropped in powder and spat. The hem of Rey's shirt was slimy. Not so long ago she hadn't been bothered by dead bodies, but the years had eaten through that callus.

Some bodies smelled worse than others. Sphincters had fully relaxed; congealed blood and urine produced a miasma of outhouse.

When all ten were dosed, the two women waited with the others. After a few minutes, Rey asked, "How long does it take?"

Lacewing said, "I've no idea."

"Too many variables, I guess."

"I suppose that is so. I've never tried it on humans before."

"How long does it take on animals, then?"

Lacewing stared peacefully into the lightless forest, smiled, and gently shook her head.

The bottomless pit yawned beneath Rey's feet again. "How long does it take on animals?" she repeated.

"I haven't a notion, dear."

Rey said, "You mean you've never used this at all?"

"One must begin somewhere."

Rey kept her voice calm. Lacewing didn't respond well to challenge. "Why do you think it'll work, then?"

Lacewing turned her translucent gaze on Rey, then back to the scattered bodies. "One must try, mustn't one? Can't sit back and do nothing."

Rey walked away. All that time wasted. True, her treatment allowed for some flexibility where time was concerned, but the watchword was the sooner the better. The total lack of signs of life from the victims made it hard to slap her frustration down.

Lacewing said, "I might try arnica. Or capsicum, or gold salts, if I had any gold salts, but I don't at all, none at all." Her voice tightened from cheery to subhysterical. "It won't fail, I'm sure. All the years, case after case—it's not all for nothing, is it?" She was audibly quivering. "I am our healer. If I'm not a healer, what am I?"

Bee cleared her throat. Cricket went to Lacewing and patted her shoulder.

Lacewing fluttered. "It takes time to die. It doesn't happen all at once. That's a Western prejudice. Everything has to be instant for us, doesn't it, especially out in the world, as I hear. But death is gradual. Fade in, fade out. There is still subtle circulation in the light body. We must learn patience. "

That was how Lacewing talked, as if she were the only person who'd ever heard of Eastern philosophy or alternative medicine and everybody else was an ignorant redneck. Lacewing was usually right about that.

Rey said, "If it's going to work, it needs to hurry up or they'll be too dead to make a full recovery." She paced from body to body, feeling death grow heavier, sucking them down.

Bee stood up. "Lacewing, is it working?"

"Not quite yet."

Bee said, "Rey, is it working?"

"No, ma'am."

"Will it work?"

"I don't see how it can."

"What do you recommend?"

It was too late. *No, it isn't. Yes, it is.* "Tell their families."

Bee took a lantern and beckoned for Cricket to follow her. If the village had a chief, Bee was it. She was the oldest and had more common sense than anybody else, and when there was important news to deliver, Bee always stepped up. She lifted a lantern and beckoned for Cricket to follow her.

But the elder Pear Sisters didn't have to go far to find recipients for the bad news. The remainder of the village pushed and stumbled into the clearing. Mercy Alder pulled a stairstep of children behind her: little Heaven, then Freedom, followed by Liberty, and almost-thirteen Ezekiel in the rear. Mercy stalked to the bodies and waved her flashlight around, then started praying, or cursing; the words were the same either way.

Fiddlin' Sue Hill and her other twin daughter Misty came next. Misty started crying right away, and Sue hollered, "Is that Buck? What happened?"

Bee stepped in front of Sue before Misty could see Crystal, but Mercy found her oldest son Jacob and her husband Earl and his brother El Duane, and the praying-or-cussing got louder.

Fiddlin' Sue looked to see what was tearing Mercy up so badly and saw Crystal. "What did your boy do to my little girl?" she yelled, and lunged at Mercy.

Jackie Tobasco came out of hiding to separate them, but got involved in the screaming and slapping and clothes-pulling. Bee pulled Sue off and fended Jackie away with one arm. When she got the yelling settled down, in the quiet they could hear Birdie Dollar at the trail mouth, saying, "Well, I never. I never, never did see anything like this." Her voice was so quiet and her manner so shy she was easy to forget about. Mostly people only recalled Birdie Dollar's existence when they went down to the store and Bill was busy so Birdie got what they wanted and took the money or the trade. Now she hung back, like always, remarking calmly on the carnage. Even while she was speaking, she was invisible except for her iron-colored hair.

"Now hush all that crying," Bee said. "You all stay back. We don't know who all's here or what their state is. Hold off until we get some facts."

Fiddlin' Sue stepped right past Bee's outstretched arm. "Are they dead? Are Buck and Crystal dead?"

Lacewing said, "Not entirely."

Mercy came forward. Bee took her arm and pivoted her around, frog-marching her back to the group.

"What the Sam Hill happened?" Sue demanded.

Rey stood up and helped Lacewing stand. "We're done here," she said, and told what she knew.

Sue knelt down by her daughter. "We've got to fix them."

"I treated them all," Lacewing said defensively. "They'll come around in a minute." The capable English wartime nurse was gone. "I did everything I could. They refuse to respond."

Bee made a little explosion in her sinuses. "I'm sure they would respond if they could. Maybe the problem is with your medicine."

The little kids goggled at the people on the ground, sniffling as much as they could get away with.

Jackie Tobasco asked, "Is Berry here?"

"She's here," Bee said. "Don't get all crazy. Plenty of time for that later." She moved her lantern around. "What is that?" She was looking at the box.

"Nothing," Rey said. "I thought it might help, but Lacewing had her med—"

"Let's see it."

"No, it's not anything. It won't do any good now." Rey flat hated herself for not handling this better.

Jackie Tobasco said, "Rey, whatever it is, if it might help, you have to try it."

Mercy stood over Earl. Her feet were on El Duane's arm. "Wake. Wake and rise up, in the name of Jesus, I command you!"

Earl and his brother sprawled on the ground, stubbornly unresurrected. "I'll get the Bible." Mercy hoisted Heaven onto her hip and went to the road.

Fiddlin' Sue said, "You thought it might bring them back, didn't you?" She turned to Bee. "Tell her to open up that box."

Lacewing let a long breath flutter between her lips. "Go ahead, Rey. It can't hurt anything."

It could hurt more than you know, Rey thought. *There are things more painful than death.*

She said, "I only brought it because I panicked." Rey clutched the case to her chest and stepped over a body, heading for the upper trail.

Bee blocked her.

Bee had never gotten physical with anybody. She ruled by personal power and divine right. She was vigorous and sharp—and eighty-seven years old, not that she admitted the vital statistics mattered. Now she gripped Rey's shoulders the way she'd gripped Mercy. The strong, bony hands were reassuring, the kind of hands that went with shoulders old enough and strong enough to cry on.

Bee steered Rey toward the box. Rey knelt down and opened the lid. Everything depended on her, and in the past four years she hadn't been able to fully revive so much as a chicken. Trying to revive humans in the middle of night in the middle of nowhere could only make things infinitely worse, but if she refused, she would have more or less killed half the village. She was screwed either way.

"If it works," she said to the living, "It might not be what you want."
Nobody said a thing.

Well, then. "We'll have to arrange them with their heads together, like wheel spokes."

It was heavy work.

"Feels like something got into them," Sue said. "I would've expected them to be lighter dead."

"Their sins are heavy on them," Mercy pronounced, setting Heaven down and brandishing a black square the size and shape of a candy box, its gilt sides glinting against the dark.

"Speak for your own kin. My family are no sinners." Fiddlin' Sue pushed Buck into position in the circle.

"Watch out for their necks," Rey cautioned. "We don't want anybody paralyzed."

The dead lay arrayed like the showgirls in a 1930s Busby Berkeley movie. Rey asked for light and the women shined their flashlights and lanterns on Rey's box of mysterious science.

She squeezed gel on every forehead, between the orbital ridges. It exuded its own blue-green glow and sizzled when it touched skin, as potent now as the day she'd stolen it. It had taken a long time to engineer a carrier that would never degrade.

She squeezed a dot on the throats and second cervical vertebrae, and when Jackie had removed all the shoes and socks, the corpses' feet pointed outward like clock hands, with their heels anchored in the dirt. The last in the circle was Hoot.

"Hurry up," Mercy snapped. Mercy had never cared much for Hoot. His drinking and his Norwegian-accented mumblings about trolls and goblins sent her into bouts of praying and defensive hymn-singing and made her pray out loud for God to heal the poor worthless wretch or take him to his reward, by which she meant punishment.

Rey stuck the tiny leads of the neuro-optic filaments into the glowing blue-green gel: white for the forehead, turquoise for the neck, purple for the feet.

"Hold your coats over them." Rey cursed herself again, this time for not planning on rain. Water was not a friend to the *NITR-6* in the gel.

The legs of the dead appeared to squirm in the quivering lantern light.

Rey squirted the genetically engineered fungus between the first and second toes around the circle. The Talypociadium cerevisiae-form Levinsis—which her team, in a rare fit of levity, had called Taily-po after the gremlin who stole mountain babies—was suspended in a matrix of DMSO boosted with a biological accelerant. It penetrated the skin in three seconds even in a body with no circulating blood, or with no blood at all, for that matter. The odor of skunk and antifreeze penetrated the shirt tail Rey tightened over her mouth and nose.

Rain splattered, pouring from a heavy cloud that blocked all moonlight. The circle of faces uplit in the quivering yellow lanternglow might have been a coven posing for a melodramatic group portrait. With one last, procrastinating look at the circle of bodies, Rey pushed the necessary keys and fitted her thumb onto the printactivated sensor. Cold tingled the whorls of her thumb skin. She pressed the button.

4

The neuro-optic wires glowed as purple, white, and blue light streaked to the bodies and from the bodies to the power pack, growing brighter with every pulse. Tiny lightning storms crackled on the foreheads of the dead. A stink of burning hair rolled into the open air before a shake of wind carried it away.

In the rhythmic, pulsing light skin knotted and writhed as current shot down the bodies. They began to glow faintly green.

The feet started moving first. Ankles flexed, knees jumped, thighs twitched.

"They're coming around!" Fiddlin' Sue cried.

Eyes opened. When Rey shined a lantern over them, the eyes still looked dead.

Dead fingers curled like starved starfish.

"I believe they're alive," Lacewing said.

Mercy and Fiddlin' Sue rushed to their teenagers.

"Wait up," Rey told them. "They've got to be disconnected right."

"Hurry up and unhook 'em," Fiddlin' Sue said.

Rey crabbed around the circle, working as fast as she could without getting things out of order. She wound up the wires, wiped off the gel, wiped off the gel again, and crossed her fingers.

"Okay. I've done everything I know how to—"

Before she got the words out, coats were flapping away over the ground in a low, cold wind and people were gathering up their relatives. The revived didn't say a word or even look around. They let themselves be handled and pulled along. When Fiddlin' Sue kissed her husband he didn't fight it but didn't kiss her back. Rey saw her frown before she took her brood toward the road and home.

Mercy bustled her family off but left El Duane behind in the rain with the other bachelors. Birdie Dollar came up without making a sound or a fuss and hauled her husband to his feet. Bill didn't lean on her, but looked down at her with about the same interest he'd paid her throughout their marriage, which was none.

Jackie slung Berry over her shoulder and staggered a few steps. "Oh, my big girl. I gotcha, hon. Hang on." She got her legs under her and left the clearing, calling back, "It's hit her hard, but we'll be all right. Don't worry about us. We're tough. Just need a hot toddy and a good night's sleep." Jackie's voice carried on, Cheshire cat-style, after she had disappeared into the darkness.

"I'm tired," Bee announced. "I think I'll go on home, now that the show's over. Come on, Lacey. Cricket and Rey can take care of things here."

Lacey fluttered an apology and followed Bee to the trail.

Rey looked at Cricket in the light of the remaining lantern and flashlight. They both looked at the inert moonshiners. Big Hoot and little Eddy were a mismatched pair, but they had more in common now: blank greenish faces, similar twitches—though Eddy twitched more than Hoot—and total, recumbent passivity.

When Rey and Cricket hoisted them up, the men stood swaying on sea legs. Cricket took El Duane and Trucker John toward the road and Rey turned uphill and north, taking Hoot and Eddy home to Hoochville. She opened their door and sat them down on their cots.

"So, you're good now? All set?"

Hoot stared in her direction, maybe seeing her, maybe not. Eddy explored his jagged front teeth with his tongue.

"Well, I'll leave you to get some sleep, then." Rey waited but got no answer. Travis could be useful here. They had let him stay in their cabin on and off for years and Travis hadn't done anything to pay them back except help test their beer and whiskey. As nice as it would be to fall asleep in Travis's company, when got home she would send him back to babysit.

"Just rest," she said, and closed the door behind her. She hadn't lit a candle or lantern for them. If they were awake enough to tend a fire of any kind, they were awake enough to light one themselves. Rey stumbled over a root and made herself slow down. All she could think about was wrapping herself up in Travis's arms and forgetting this night.

The house was dark. The fire had gone out and her bed was empty.

Rey lit an Aladdin lantern and lowered herself onto the bed. Visions of dead bodies and pulsing lights wheeled in her brain. After awhile her mind quieted down enough to hear the hoot owl up the hill and feel the goats bumping the other side of the wall. She got up and pulled off her boots, shoved the bar across the door, and blew out the lantern.

The goats bounced around the yard in the morning sunshine with an air of forced abandon, as if they knew how short-lived it would be. Rey ate a leftover biscuit and one of the three eggs the hens had left her and drank a cup of goat milk, no coffee. Travis hadn't come back.

The way Hoot and Eddy had slumped on their cots, limp as mud men, no moping from Hoot or cantankerousness from Eddy, gave Rey a mental kink. The rest of the revived must be all right after their dip into the big sleep. If not, by now someone would have come up the mountain to complain. No news was good news, right? Dying and waking up again might be an invigorating experience.

But that wasn't true.

No one had ever been the same afterwards.

Rey walked her half-finished trail down to the road. Off to the south, smoke streaked from the Alders' chimney; beyond that a cowbell rang in the Hills' pasture and the cow's calf bleated. The sounds carried clearly through the wet air. Cute little thing, the calf, with its big brown eyes and white blaze. It frolicked innocently through the spring days with no suspicion of its destiny. Rey followed the bell and bleating.

Fiddlin' Sue had made a pallet on the floor beside her and Buck's double bed and tucked Crystal and Misty in close. Buck lay inert, breathing regular and strong, on her other side.

"You go ahead and sleep, Misty," she said. "I think we're all right, but I'll stay awake as long as I can. Tell me if Cryssy does anything."

"Like what?"

"I have no clue. Anything."

"I'll put my arm around her so if she moves I'll know."

"Good girl. Get some rest now."

Buck's big-boned, lean body felt the same as always, except cooler. Sue backed against him and pulled his arm over her waist. He compliantly turned on his side, but the spoon was the next county over from a snuggle. Buck was an enthusiastic hugger, always grabbing her and planting big kisses on her cheek, or whirling her around in a western swing move and pulling her in tight. Never did he lay there like cold dough like he was doing now.

When she'd gotten them home she'd heated water and bathed Crystal. A lot of the blood on her came off, and the hole in her back was knitting up fast. Misty got her sister into a nightgown while Sue washed her husband. He didn't say a word even when she ran the washrag between his legs and over his ticklish feet, just stood in the tin washtub and let watery blood run down his muscles and knobby joints. Sue couldn't even find where the shot had opened him up.

She and Buck had been through a lot together. Drinking and fighting, living on the road, both of them cheating. That tramp trying to keep Buck for herself, Sue strenuously objecting and doing a month for assault. And having twins hadn't been any picnic. Losing the girls … Jesus, she remembered that scene like it was day before yesterday: the State car driving away with her blond angel babies in the back seat; stealing the babies back a year later, at the first opportunity after she and Buck had sobered up; driving eighty-five miles an hour across the desert and then up north to this place they'd heard about where Social Services would never find them. Buck cussing for miles on end. "Fine goddamn country where I got to steal my own children from the fucking government!" until Sue told him he couldn't swear around the girls ever again, and he never did.

But this night had been a whole new kind of trial. She reached down and stroked Crystal's cheek, smoothed the hair back off her forehead. With her hair washed soft and the black eyeliner wiped off, her rebellious daughter looked like her little angel again.

They'll come around, Sue told herself. Everything turns out like it's supposed to. And if they don't come around, I'll dive into Hell itself and drag them out. Nobody's taking my family away, not ever again.

"Rey. Wait up." Ezekiel Alder jumped off his porch and ran to the road.

"How're you doing, Ezekiel?"

"EZ."

"Sorry. EZ."

"Kinda weird, actually. It's pretty strange around here."

"Everybody okay?"

EZ frowned. "I don't know. How long is it supposed to take for them to wake up all the way?"

A cold rock settled in Rey's guts. "I couldn't tell you."

" 'Cause they're sleepwalking. I think Jake's awake, but Daddy and Uncle El Duane aren't doing their work and Jake's being a big baby. Mother and me and the girls have to do everything. I'm supposed to be bringing in wood now."

"How is Jacob acting like a baby?" This was a new twist, and not a good one.

"Just sitting, or when you tell him to stand up he'll stand up but he won't go anywhere. Mother made him start raking the barn and he raked all the straw out and kept going and raked up the dirt underneath so it's a mess. I told him to stamp the dirt back down hard and he's been doing that for a long time."

"I think I'll say hi to your mom."

"It's crazy," Ezekiel said. "Weird."

Ezekiel went off to the woodpile and Rey knocked on the door. Mercy's voice trumpeted through the walls. Freedom opened the door. She was about hip-high, wearing blue rubber boots and a prairie dress. Heaven tried to slip around her and get out the door but Freedom yanked her back in by her sash.

"Hi, honey. Can I talk to your mama?"

"Mother's talking to Daddy," Freedom said. "Daddy won't work."

"You look like you're working. Are you watching your baby sister?"

"She's supposed to stay inside." Freedom yanked on Heaven's arm and Heaven started whimpering. Mercy came to the door, hollering back into the house as she looked at Rey.

"What do you know about this?" Mercy demanded.

"I—"

"They're not right. None of them. I'm going to talk to Bee about this. Are any of the rest of them up and around? Earl would be the first one to put his hand back on the plow, he's a hardworking Christian man; if *he's* sitting in a chair waiting for Jesus then the rest of the ones you messed with I don't doubt are still laying in bed like drug addicts or night lifers. *El Duane! Go feed the cows, I told you!* How am I supposed to watch the children and cook and get my work done if I have to push grown men around? You tell me. You did this to 'em. When are they going to get back to normal?"

Mercy inhaled and Rey took the opportunity to say, "I don't know. I said I didn't know if it would work. Everybody wanted me to try." She stopped talking because it sounded whiny.

"Well, this is the week they mend the fences and plant lettuce and spinach and peas and to do that they've got to—*Earl, pick up the shovel and go dig up that garden like I told you!* Come in and see for yourself what your unwholesome act has wrought."

Mercy picked up Heaven and stepped back.

The inside of the Alders' house was spare and perfectly neat, as always. Mercy ran a tight household. No ship was more shipshape. The only sign that there'd been a glitch in her routine was an aroma of scorched eggs. Earl and El Duane stood at the kitchen table. El Duane held a coffee cup in his hand. Earl faced the window which overlooked the pasture and garden. Neither of them greeted Rey.

"Earl, El Duane, how are you?" Rey didn't expect an answer.

"They look pretty good," she said.

"Except for one little thing. Notice anything?" Mercy said.

"They're pretty quiet."

"They are *standing*. In my *kitchen*. In the *middle* of the *day*." Mercy was clearly outraged.

"It's still early. Wait and see." Rey couldn't sound as if she meant it.

"Alders don't stand around."

Rey thought of EZ putting Jacob to work. "Do you have anything that needs polishing?"

"Why?" Mercy looked around, ready to catch something being dull or smudged in her house.

"Maybe today they can do the polishing. Ezekiel can show them what to do. If Freedom watches the Liberty and the baby, you can get your work done."

"Thank you, Rey. I think I know how to manage my family. *Ezekiel! Bring Jacob in here!*" Mercy took the coffee cup from El Duane's hands and replaced it with a dry rag.

Rey left while Mercy issued orders for the day.

5

Rey turned north back up the mud road to where the it bent downhill to the right, toward the river. Sugar Agate's storybook house was just past the bend on the right, and then there was a long unpeopled stretch along the steep slope. Where the terrain flattened out, in view of the river, Jackie Tobasco's and Berry's trailer perched on the right side of the road behind bare flower beds. Not far beyond them the Dollers' store used the last of the flat real estate. Across the road from the store and hidden behind big firs and cedars, Trucker John's fifteen-foot trailer crouched in the dark.

Rey passed Sugar Agate's with her eyes straight ahead. Averting her eyes from that house had gotten to be second nature. Whether it was cowardice or common sense was an argument with herself she couldn't win. Rey fixed her attention on Jackie Tobasco's muralized blue and white trailer. The trailers, like the materials for the real houses in the village, had been moved onto the mountain before the plank bridge collapsed in the flood ten years ago. There'd been talk of rebuilding it, but arguments against it, based on expense and effort, were buttressed by the advantages of being unreachable. The only way into the village was by a hand trolley strung from a cable or, in midsummer, by crossing on foot over slick stones and unpredictable currents.

Jackie answered the door as Rey stepped onto the stump doorstep.

"Rey, honey, come in. We just got up. I was up late watching Berry. You know what, I don't think she ever fell asleep. Eyes wide open every time I looked at her. And cold? You could have chilled a beer on her belly, if you had a beer, which nobody probably will until the Norse Force gets back up to speed."

Jackie plumped a yellow satin pillow on the little couch and motioned Rey to sit. The tidy trailer house was filled with a carnival of gewgaws. Jackie abhorred a color vacuum, and Berry felt at home surrounded by bright paint and tropical prints. Our substitute for sunshine, they said. Every day Berry wore an aloha shirt over her fatigues.

Jackie, in a red and white housecoat and turquoise-jeweled slippers, her hair in juice can rollers, poured Rey a cup of coffee. "I mean, all you have to do is look at her and you know she's not right. Blue lips. The girl hates the cold. She should be stoking the fire, but if I hadn't bundled her up, she'd just sit there and freeze to death. Wouldn't you, Berry dear?"

Berry's wool socks were visible at the foot of the bed in the little bedroom at the other end of the trailer. They didn't move.

"Has she said anything?" Rey asked.

"Not a blessed word. Or a cursed word. You know she doesn't say much anyway, it's just the way she is, I don't know why. But not a peep out of her mouth all night or today."

How Berry would manage to get a word in edgewise hadn't ever bothered Jackie Tobasco. It was up to other people to work around her torrent of words.

"Has she done anything?"

"I dressed her, took her outside, brought her back in. Like a pet dog." Jackie shook her head. "Not herself. My little spitfire'll perk up pretty soon, won't she?"

Rey walked down the hallway and looked at Berry. Her spiky hair was the liveliest thing about her.

Jackie said, "Berry, look. It's Rey. Say hi, hon."

Berry blinked slowly. She could have been looking at a cement wall for all the interest she showed.

"Hey, Berry," Rey said. "How are you feeling?" For all the response she got, she could have been talking to the same cement wall.

On the sofa, Rey finished her coffee. Jackie made the best coffee on the mountain, too strong and too sweet whether you liked sweet coffee or not.

"I don't know how long it'll take. I'm trying to check on everybody. So far ... "

"Not so good?"

"They're all a little sleepy," Rey said. "Big night."

Jackie cinched up her robe and tucked her hands in the sleeves. "I'm worried, Rey. What if she doesn't get any better? I mean, is this it? This is as good as she's gonna get? Because I already miss the old Berry."

"It hasn't even been twenty-four hours." Time was probably not going to help. Time would probably only make it worse. Unless this was different. Conditions had been different; the subjects had been different. Maybe the outcome would be favorably influenced by the variables.

"Yeah, I'm worrying over nothing. Right?"

"Don't worry," Rey soothed. *Yet.*

"I think I'll get her up now. Take a walk. Go look at the river, see if those ducks are out. It's not raining, is it?"

"Not hard." Rey went to the door. "I'll look in on Dollar Bill and Trucker John. See ya, Jacks."

They hugged in a mist of Jackie's signature scent, a blend of makeup and rosemary hair rinse. Jackie was the person Rey needed to confide in. Jackie knew Rey's worries and problems. Not Rey's past, of course. Nobody knew much about anyone else's past. But Jackie Tobasco was Rey's best friend, and Rey had maybe screwed up Jackie's life bigtime.

Summerland Mission
Four years ago

The seven bodies lay in pools of lamplight, strapped to padded tables, looking more green than blue in the yellowish light. Their color would warm up after Jillian Newhause threw the switch that sent the signal through the tangle of neural threads and the bodies stopped being dead.

Six years of failure and finally, last week, a successful event. The resultant scion was still metabolizing and reacting to stimuli. This morning he had tracked a ballpoint pen with his eyes, and had vocalized; it was a hyena's howl, but still a step forward. Dr. Newhause had ensured the experimental subjects would re-enter life in comfort. The gentle rebirth would, she theorized, eliminate the unfortunate tendency toward violence.

Vital signs monitors came online. Four of the subjects showed cardiac activity. Jillian walked confidently to Number 578 and lifted his eyelids. Pupils still fully dilated and unresponsive to light, irregular r-s-t waves, no spontaneous respiration, no response to physical stimuli.

She frowned and returned to the console. The settings had been precisely calculated for each body. All the readings were correct, yet the treatment wasn't working. Prolonged low-power exposure didn't do the nervous system any good, and the only way to prevent low-power burnout was to increase power. She made the necessary adjustments.

"You may experience mild discomfort," she lied, and pressed the button.

Smoke curled from the skin of one, then three, then all the subjects. The smell of melting silicon fiber filled the lab and was replaced by the smell of barbeque. The EEG and EKG monitors flipped crazy patterns. 578's hair caught fire.

"Shit!" Newhause shut down the power and ran to smother the flames. She yanked the leads off the subjects. Deep burns blotched the contact points, but no blisters or redness developed, because the bodies were entirely dead. Up close, the smell evoked an unwelcome memory of her last vacation, a Hawaiian luau six years ago. For a split second she was there, dancing on the white sand with a nameless but unforgettable male hula dancer, while a pig baked in a palm leaf cocoon.

She turned off the alarm and turned up the ventilation. The monitors were not networked to any other display. No one would know what had happened until she reported it, but eventually someone would want the subjects for analysis and disposal.

She had planned such a comfortable observation period for her subjects. She would not hold them naked in cages. They would wear warm nightshirts, sleep on mattresses, and be treated like the heroes they were, advance troops leading humanity to eternal life, albeit lurchingly. Now they weren't going anywhere.

Staring at the smoke curling from their charred skin, Jillian Newhause swore again. The team would know her methods had failed. Her changes would be discarded; future subjects would be treated like stockyard animals, and her influence in the most important advance in history would be nullified. She would no doubt lose her position as co-leader and be demoted to support technologist.

But a demoted employee was a dangerous employee. What became of dismissed Mission workers? How could anyone be trusted to go outside, taking their knowledge with them? Even the Manhattan Project, even the deepest national secrets and most clandestine plans for global domination, employed less security than Summerland. No one had left, but two had died: one in a fiery collision on a dark desert road; the other, an energetic man of forty-two, had been electrocuted in a hot tub.

In the 72-degree air, Jillian shivered.

She locked the door, turned off the monitors, and shut down the control center. The damage was done; any attempt to revive them now would create, at best, vegetative subhumans with burned out internal organs, forced to produce brainwaves slightly more advanced than planaria until life support was disconnected.

As she pulled the sheet over the face of Number 573, the woman she'd called Mi, the door lever clicked.

Jillian froze. Only Roberts would try to walk in without permission. He was her colleague at the top of the command chain, but he didn't like being her equal. He believed he ran the project and his innate gift for bullying convinced everyone else of his power. He ignored half of her contributions and took credit for the other half.

And he hated her guts. Jillian could see his gleeful smirk as he made a swift end of her career—and maybe her life.

The door lever clicked again. If she waited any longer he would get suspicious.

As she opened the door she said, "Shh. I'm just starting."

He scowled, his version of a neutral face. "Why the delay?"

"What's the hurry?" she countered.

The marionette lines around his mouth sharpened. "What's that smell?"

"I'm right in the middle of set-up, Everett. What did you need?"

He leaned to see around her, took a ramlike step at her, but she didn't let him in. She wouldn't under normal circumstances. Protocol.

"You said this was a decisive run. I'm checking in. Did you hit a snag?"

"No, we're good, but I've got to continue now or there *will* be a problem. Want me to call you when I'm done?"

"Of course. What is that smell?"

"I'll come to your office in two hours." Jillian closed the door and set the security lock as it latched so Roberts wouldn't hear it. He knew something was wrong. Why else would he try to come in during an active procedure? How could he know?

Instinct was a tool and a curse. Her instinct right now was that Dr. Everett Roberts knew the trial had failed, and the only way he could know that was if he had personally engineered it to fail.

Cameras oversaw every centimeter of the hall outside her lab. She couldn't risk using the hall. There was no other way out of the complex.

Jillian slowed her breathing, then picked up the phone and punched 5.

"You kill 'em, I chill 'em. Got a pickup, Dr. Newhause?" the tech said.

"Just one, Carlos."

"Say when."

"Ten minutes. I'm going to finish up here and then meet with Doctor Roberts, so if you don't see me, just take the body. I'll put it by the door. Number 575. And I've got a pile of equipment to go to Facilities. Do you mind if I pile it on the bottom of the gurney? Just leave the gurney in the cooler and I'll come sort it out in about an hour."

"No problemo. Remember to leave the door unlocked if you're not there."

"Right. And keep this one covered. I'm not ready to share the results."

"Got it."

"It's very important."

Carlos paused, got serious. "I know, Doctor Newhause. Everything we do is important."

"Sorry. I have to take special care with this one. Hands off until I've done the exam, okay?"

"Be there in ten, Doc."

Jillian looked at the human beings she had killed. Number 575 reminded Jillian of herself: trim and muscular, brown hair that had been long like Jillian's before the prep techs cut it short. Jillian stripped to her underwear and put her slacks and shirt on the subject she'd thought of as Re. She propped the body at her desk, head on arms in a posture of fatigue and despondency. Using her desk scissors, Jillian cut off her long hair in five strokes and draped it over the corpse's shoulders. Locking the office door behind her, she rubbed off her lipstick, smudged eyeliner on her face, and smeared gel over that.

The equipment and her shoes went into a satchel and onto the bottom shelf of the rolling table. As footsteps neared, she covered the satchel with blue sheets, positioned herself on the gurney and pulled a sheet over her head, praying the person coming was the tech and not Everett Roberts.

Carlos entered whistling cheerily and smelling of soap. Turning the cart neatly around, he said, "Time to go, señora," and rolled her away.

She judged they had reached the doorway that led to the cold storage locker adjacent to the autopsy room when Carlos said, "Buenas tardes, Doctor Roberts."

Footsteps. The cart slowed.

"What's this?" Roberts' voice, suspicious.

"Storage. No, sir, sorry, but Doctor Newhause said this one's hands off until she finishes up with it."

"Why is that?"

"I didn't ask, sir."

Carlos pushed the cart ahead and turned into the storage anteroom. "Have a wonderful day, Doctor."

Carlos disliked Roberts, as did every other member of the tech staff, and liked Jillian Newhause, who treated the staff with courtesy and had a sense of humor, a rare trait among the senior staff. She was glad of an ally now.

Everett Roberts' martinet steps clicked petulantly down the hall. Carlos rolled the cart to a gentle stop. "Last stop, Cold Storage Station. Say hello to Jesus for me, señora." The cold storage door closed.

Dressed in blue scrubs from the supply cupboard, Jillian picked up the satchel and stole a coat from a locker—not Carlos's, she hoped. She wanted to gather a few possessions: her few photographs, papers, a change of clothes. But if Roberts had already found the body in Dr. Newhauses' chair, he would be in the cold storage room in seconds, and his next stop would be her own private rooms. Intuition and reason agreed. She had to escape the compound immediately.

The high speed car whirred up three floors to ground level. Jillian strode into the used drilling equipment shop that provided one level of cover for the labs, and out the back door.

Knee-walking low in the runoff ditch, she cut through the wasteland back of town, flattening into the dirt whenever a vehicle rolled by. Drivers around here weren't looking at the scenery because there wasn't anything to see. Their eyes were on the road, their minds on their business and a beer. Jillian was pretty sure no one spotted her except one crusty lizard and a turkey vulture floating in hopeful circles on the hot air. She made it to Black Springs' tiny downtown and stopped at the bank, then crossed the street and bought a baseball cap, sweatpants, and a flannel shirt in the general store and changed in the restroom. Before going outside again she scanned the street. A black SUV cruised by, tinted windows hiding its occupants. As she slipped out the door, two men walked slowly down the dusty sidewalk, scanning left and right. She kept her head down and went the other way, hoping her short hair and new clothes would be enough of a disguise. Summerland personnel seldom venture aboveground, and a smattering of rockhounds, UFO enthusiasts, and other strangers trickled through Black Springs— enough so that one more tourist could pass unnoticed.

A nervous hour in the bus stop café's restroom passed one heartbeat at a time, but the Greyhound bus finally came. It took her north to Moab, where she got off, found a downscale car lot, and paid cash for a quick deal on a small blue pickup truck with broken air conditioning. She sped west across the desert, heading for the Sierras and cover.

California was full of people. Monterey tempted her, but her money wouldn't last there, and the town had a high-profile beauty that made anonymity unlikely. Jillian sat in the library studying maps and using a computer until dark, then abandoned the blue truck in the Cannery Row parking lot. Craig's List had turned up a car even more unnoticeable than the pickup. She paid the owner cash and threw out the paperwork.

Hugging the coastline, northbound toward the empty mountains, one thought chased her: if she were caught, her life wouldn't be worth a nickel.

6

Rey Nickel set the chipmunk down. Someone had just stepped onto her porch.

Her lab was a space four feet deep and the width of the cabin: a secret room she had formed with a false inner wall. Outside, saplings and brush and a woodpile camouflaged the extra cabin length. Rey kept the cabin door locked when she was working so she could come out of the lab without being seen.

As she pushed the hidden door closed, Ezekiel Alder called out to her.

"Mrs. Nickel! You home?"

Rey opened the door. Ezekiel was petting two hens at once. He wore a turtleneck shirt too short in the sleeves; his hair was growing out long. Rey figured it was driving his mother crazy.

"Hi, Ezekiel. What's up?"

"EZ. Remember? Not Ezekiel."

Rey went outside. The lab was safely hidden, but she didn't take chances. "Right. EZ. Then you call me Rey."

"Cool." Ezekiel sat beside Rey on the edge of the low porch. The chickens ran around the yard chasing bugs. Ezekiel coaxed the hens to him with outstretched fingers. When they crowded around he dug a palmful of corn out of his pocket, scattered it on the ground and petted them as they ate.

Rey asked, "How's your family?"

"All right, I guess."

"Heaven walking yet?"

"Oh, yeah. She gets into everything."

Ezekiel had three younger sisters and an older brother. The Alders kept popping them out. Mercy Alder was looking disenchanted lately, though. In the time Rey had been on the mountain Mercy had gained wrinkles and lost weight. Rey figured she was through having kids.

They sat in the chilly morning sun without talking for awhile. Then Rey asked, "Does your mom know you're up here?"

Ezekiel shrugged.

"She's not crazy about you hanging out at my place."

"She thinks you're godless."

"Maybe I am."

Ezekiel stared out over the cleared yard into the trees. "Maybe I am, too."

"That's going to present a problem, EZ." Rey felt a duty to discourage the boy from abandoning his family's religion. She didn't share it, but life would be easier for him.

He said, "I'm not afraid of problems. Truth is more important than going along with the family."

Rey agreed with him, but said, "Your family is the most important thing you have. The only thing you have."

She'd lived without a family for a lot of years. She tried not to remember that.

Ezekiel stood up, following the red hen around the yard. The ground was just starting to sprout with wildflowers and big grasses. In the interests of reducing mud, Rey didn't walk on it until the plants had taken a firm hold, but she didn't stop the boy.

"What about truth?" he said. "I mean, would I be friends with my family if I wasn't related to them? Who they really are is more important than the coincidence that we're related."

"Don't let your parents hear you talking like that. And I'm not sure you're right. Maybe when you're older, but you haven't flown the nest yet."

"Because I can't," he said sourly.

"You don't want to yet." The poor kid was the rebel of his family. The rest of them seemed to toe the line, but EZ was headed for trouble. Rey couldn't give him any answers.

"Maybe you're asking for too much," she said. "They're good people. They take care of you. You're what, twelve?"

"No, I'm almost thirteen. Yeah, my parents feed my body, but that's it, and I do half the work, anyway. They're so—like they live in a box, you know? Now, who knows? They weren't very alive before, and then Dad and Uncle El Duane ... and Jake ... "

"How are they doing? Coming around?"

The boy shrugged. "They're different. I never did belong with them. I'm supposed to be with artists. Poets."

"How do you know?" He had never been off Cannibal Mountain. Kids here got some radio reception and watched parent-approved videos once a week, old ones bought by the sackful at a country trading post. That was the extent of their contact with the outside world.

"I got a book," he whispered. "It shows them. And they're me."
"What book?"

EZ glanced around. "Cartoons. But I know it's real. You'd know too. I can tell you're one of them, too. Different. Like me."

"I'm not an artist or a poet, but I know what you mean. When you're different, it's good to find somebody who's the same."

Ezekiel worked on his slouch, then reverted to his healthy country kid posture.

"Hey, I have something that would go with that turtleneck." Rey went in the house and dug in her box of clothes. On the porch, she handed EZ a black felt beret.

"Trucker John brought it nearly a year ago and I never wore it much. It's more your style."

EZ lit up. "Whoa. Ho. Oh, this is …" He fitted the beret on, pulled it to one side and low over his right eye. "Excellent. And Dad and Jake won't be grabbing it off me."

"You look great."

"Rey, thanks, man." He looked as if he felt completely dressed for the first time. "It's perfect."

In the narrow lab, Rey dabbed fungus on the chipmunk's tiny feet. Did chipmunks even have K-1 meridians? She rubbed gel in the fur, hoping to hit the right spots, hoping she used the right amount of gel. There was a lot of guesswork with chipmunks. This one had been dead a couple of days, probably, when Rey had found it in the woods. For some reason no animal had eaten it. With the power on its lowest and briefest setting, Rey said, "Good luck, little fella," and pushed the button.

There was no sizzle. No twitches. Rey felt for a heartbeat, found nothing. Failure. Then—the smallest of stirrings beneath the fur. It breathed.

Rey disconnected it from the apparatus, cleaned it off, gently stroked its spotted back.

"Good boy. How're you feeling?"

It opened opaque eyes. Its nose twitched.

Rey offered it water and seeds, but it wasn't interested. She observed it the rest of the night, getting up every hour to make sure it was warm, staying out of sight so as not to scare it. In the morning it was cold and still.

Rey carried it to the little burial ground behind her cabin and wrapped it in rhododendron leaves, thought a goodbye, and buried it in the humus.

"Well, we tried," she said, "and I'll keep on trying." She had to get it right. Maybe out in the world, down the mountain, in the cities, Summerland had already sold its secret. Maybe it was too late, but until she knew for sure it was all over, she was going to keep at it until it worked, at least on chipmunks. Then she could make sure no one country, no dictator, no lunatic owned it. Half the time she knew she was wrong, but the other half of the time she knew without a doubt that the only way big-C Civilization was going to make it was if everybody was in on the secret.

$$\mathcal{L}$$

Bee sharpened her pencil with a knife and swept the shavings into her palm, then into a potted cilantro.

After a few minutes, she called Cricket and Lacewing. They came in from the garden, Lacewing in a pair of cotton gloves that protected her from slugs and bugs. For someone raised in the woods, Lacewing was embarrassingly squeamish.

"One short." Bee whapped the journal with the eraser end of the pencil.

"What?" Cricket said.

"One body short. Where was Jobert?" She pronounced it the correct way and so did Cricket and Lacewing: the French way, not *Joe Bear* the way everyone else did.

"I didn't even see Jobert," Lacewing said, starting to flutter.

Bee said, "But you did. You and Rey gave him some herbs."

"Tinctures and extracts."

"Who took him home after the revival?"

Bee looked at her sisters. They looked at each other.

"I thought Rey did," Cricket said. "She was going up his way with Hoot and Eddy."

Lacewing pulled off her gloves and flapped them gently. "I don't think so. I saw her with Hoot and Eddy. Jobert's little, but I would have seen him. Is he lost, do you think?"

"You're flinging dirt," Bee said.

Lacewing stopped flapping.

Cricket said, "I suppose I'll have to hunt for him." It was always her for the big jobs. Not too old, not too delicate. Her curse.

"Well, just go to his house first, before you call out a search party. He's probably home. I just don't like him being unaccounted for, under the circumstances."

Lacewing stood at the door watching Cricket turn the corner of the house, heading for the clearing and path up the north side of the mountain.

"I suppose I should go with Cricky." She pulled her gardening gloves back on, though.

"Yes, go. But stop by Rey's on the way."

"Oh ... I ... " Lacewing clearly hadn't seriously planned to go up the mountain.

"Take your cane, and come back with Cricket."

"You sound like something's wrong."

"Not yet. I just don't want any more business like 1959. We were careless, and we had a thousand times more privacy then than we do now, and it was like trying to kill poison oak to get the newspapers out of here. So please go find Jobert."

Lacewing pulled off her gloves again and wrapped a thick red and white plaid coat around her bony shoulders. "My goodness, no. I don't want 1959 again."

She added a wool and sheepskin hat. "We almost had to leave here. Ah don't see how we could beah it now. Oh, my Lord, we'd be put in a *home*." She'd become a distressed Southern gentlewoman.

"Never," Bee said. "We'll be all right. The cave's blocked off now, and everybody's accounted for except Jobert. But I'll check before dark and make sure they're all safe at home."

Lacewing set off toward the uphill path and Bee pulled up closer to the stove, the journal on her lap. She could still see them, a dozen newspaper men, even a woman reporter, trampling her vegetable garden. Shouting through the glass, accosting them on the way to the outhouse. All because of those two misfits. Star-crossed lovers, they styled themselves. Fornicators, Mother Pear accused. Her son, Bee and Cricket and Lacewing's father, kept his nose out of it until someone had to clean up their mess. He'd taken care of everything—his daughters' hero. But the outside world got let in on the secret and the cave had very nearly been discovered. Even Daddy couldn't have hidden that. So he drilled the cave walls and welded an iron gate across it and camouflaged that, and eventually the whole thing died down. It wouldn't be easy to stay to themselves if word of this business spread. She closed her eyes, feeling the warmth relax her feet and arthritic ankles. Wood heat was a lot of work when you were in your eighties, but it felt like nothing else. Bee had a feeling the trouble wasn't over. They needed a plan B, in case things didn't settle down. That was her job: making plans.

7

Someone inside stepped on a squeaky board, brushed the wall, but nobody answered the door. The store was the front room, but there wasn't ever much stock in it, so Birdie and Bill lived mostly in the kitchen and back bedroom.

Rey knocked again and waited to hear footsteps. "Birdie?"

Sleeping, gardening, or in the outhouse. Bill wouldn't be getting up to answer the door, Rey figured, but Birdie ought to be around somewhere. Birdie didn't always answer her door, a habit that infuriated her husband.

As she crossed the road Rey glanced at the apex of the hand trolley cable support, visible above the bank, and river below. Mergansers chuckled and paddled in the quiet water by the shore. Rey took the overgrown track to the travel trailer where Trucker John lived. It was so hidden by vine maple and shadows she didn't see it until it was right in front of her, a damp box the color of dirt.

"John? It's Rey."

She hadn't expected an answer so she didn't wait long. When she turned to leave, glad not to have to see Trucker John alone, a tall shadow loomed at the corner of the trailer. Rey jumped.

Trucker John faced her. He didn't move. His dark clothes and beard smudged him in the murk under the trees. He stared at Rey. The expression on his face was either glowering or totally neutral; nobody could ever tell.

"Hey, John. I came to check on you, see how you're doing."

Trucker John stared some more.

"Need anything?"

Trucker John was essentially an all right guy, but his broken heart had broken something else in him, too, and he always seemed off-center and lurchy. Now he gave the impression of being two half-men stuck together at the waist, both halves angry.

"Coffee, breakfast? No?"

She backed away while she talked until the road was closer than Trucker John and she could stand to turn her back to him. She walked up the road faster than usual, trusting her heart to handle the twin loads of adrenaline and uphill marching.

Sugar Agate sat on a white wooden chair in front of her house, combing her hair. She lifted it like a heavy drape of dark silk, sliding an ivory comb through the strands. She wore her kimono, a garment which had a way of falling open. She had washed her hair this morning; she did this twice a week, which no one else did so often, she knew, not even the Alders or Pear Sisters, who had heated running water. It didn't matter to them if they went around with dirty hair, but their hair wasn't much, and they were old. A woman with hair like this would be a fool to waste it. Sugar Agate was an artist, and her medium was her own beauty.

The men in the village understood. Her hands were soft and clean, her nails buffed to the pink inner smoothness of seashells. Her clothes were delicate and fine, not the kind she could haul wood in. But this was no problem: men brought her wood and kept her kindling cut.

Sugar Agate was a busy woman. Bathing, dressing, tending her little flower garden, caring for her clothes, and decorating her home took all her time. It was a busy life if you did things right. Sugar Agate did things perfectly.

By the time Travis came along her arms ached from combing. She watched him walking dreamily up her path but pretended to be startled when he stopped in front of her. Travis did a doubletake, a little too slow to be genuine, when he saw her. He sauntered up close so she had to look up at him past his chest, which he bared under an embroidered leather vest fastened loosely with a large curved pin.

"That's a nice pin," Sugar Agate said. "Is it bone?"

"Bear claw."

Sugar Agate leaned closer to examine it. She breathed on the pin and rubbed it with a finger, which nudged the pin out of its holes. It fell on the ground and she leaned over to pick it up. It took a few tries and her kimono fell open further while she was down there, with her head nearly between Travis' legs.

But when she sat up she saw her moves had been lost on Travis, who was finger-combing his hair, fluffing up the front where it was getting a little thin.

"This doesn't look like a bear claw," Sugar Agate said. "It looks like a chicken bone coated with resin. See? You can see the marrow."

"Bear claws have marrow," Travis said. He refastened his vest.

She invited him in for tea. "I have honey," she cooed, playing on his sweet tooth.

But inside, she served him plain tea and when he asked about the honey, she said, "Just squeeze it out of the comb. While you're at it you may as well do the whole comb. Thanks." He might as well make himself useful.

"No can do. Take a look at my hand. It's not healing right."

"I don't see anything wrong with it." Sugar Agate suspected he was pretending to have a hurt hand so he wouldn't have to finish squeezing the honeycomb—or do any other work while he was here. She gripped Travis's fingers.

"Ow! What are you pinching me for?"

"They look fine. Are you sure they hurt?"

"I think I know if my fingers hurt or not. Why don't you put some more of that salve on them?"

"That wasn't me," Sugar Agate said, leaning back in her white-painted chair, taking her time sipping tea from a china cup. "That must have been your friend Rey. Maybe you should go get her to rub some salve on you."

"She's not around," Travis said.

"Off hauling tree trunks across the mountain? Wrestling bears?"

Travis shrugged.

"Is that why you came here, because you couldn't find Rey Nickel?" She was pretty sure her voice sounded cool, not jealous. Sugar Agate did not get jealous of other women.

She did envy what they had, though. Rey had enough of Travis that Sugar Agate couldn't have him all to herself, which went against Sugar Agate's principles.

Travis shrugged again.

"Well, I don't have any salve," she said. "If you want some dirty old grease you can go somewhere else for it."

Sugar Agate stood up and turned her back to Travis. She stepped across her bedroom threshold and dropped her kimono on the bed, calling back, "Don't look."

She put on her clothes slowly, twisting her hips and stretching her arms in postures proven to provoke any man to slavish lust. She needed a load of wood chopped and stacked, and the time to get it done was before the man got into bed. Afterwards, he lost all motivation.

When she turned around, though, Travis was examining the contents of the cut glass bowl on the windowsill. Irritating. Her invitation was irresistible, but he was fingering trinkets.

"What are you doing?" She failed to keep the snap out of her voice.

He picked up a thick silver chain and dangled it from his fingers, fingers that showed no signs of pain.

"This looks familiar," he said. "It's Jackie Tobasco's, isn't it?"

"No, it's mine. That's why it's in my house."

"But before it was yours, it was Jackie Tobasco's."

"She wasn't using it. She never wore it any more. It was laying around, hanging on a hook. If Jackie doesn't want it, somebody who appreciates it should have it."

Travis slipped the chain into his jeans pocket.

"Hey!" Sugar Agate protested.

"Hey, yourself. Come here."

"I'm awfully cold. There's wood out back, if you just want to—"

Before she could suggest what he might want to do with the wood, he showed her what he wanted to do with her, and it wasn't such a bad idea.

While Sugar Agate and Travis were occupied, a shadow peered through the side window. When the shadow heard footsteps crunching up the gravel and shell walk, it sank below the window and slinked away.

Rey didn't bother to knock. The men were where she'd left them, except Eddy was lying down, no covers, no fire going. Hoot rotated his head a couple of degrees toward Rey when she came in, less animated and less curious than a cow in a field. Or a tree stump.

Rey tried to get a conversation going, asked Hoot about his beer, asked Eddy if he wanted a drink of his moonshine, and got nothing. She made them drink water, sent them outside for a pee, brought them back in. They complied, slowly but without resistance. Rey fixed them a pan of cornmeal and a glass of milk and had to nearly feed them by hand, Eddy's gummy mouth sucking the mush down and Hoot chomping his big teeth at quarter-speed. They were like mush themselves: warm but lacking backbone.

She washed out the pan, banked the fire, and put blankets over them. Travis could watch them the rest of the day. The fact that he wasn't here now bothered Rey, but unless someone told him what was going on, it would be entirely possible for him to walk around the village and not notice anything unusual. He'd be writing a song in his head or reliving a long ride on a big wave, absent-minded and dreaming. It helped him avoid a lot of work.

The rest of the day she tended her animals and caught up on chores. She was running low on beans and rice and had nothing to read. With Trucker John out of commission, and he had sure looked out of it this morning, lurking by his trailer, who was going to go into the valley? As far as she knew, nobody else had a driver's license—though it was possible Trucker John didn't have one, either. It had been more than four years since Rey had driven a car, and that had been a sedan with automatic everything. On expedition days you could hear John's truck across the river as it rattled and spasmed, gears colliding like Flintstones ratchets. One of the living would have to figure it out. Or maybe Trucker John could do it with constant directions: *Turn. Clutch. Brake! Brake! Brake!* Maybe driving a stick was like cooking meat over fire or creative peeing, a skill hard-wired in men's lizard brains. Rey hoped so.

Sitting on the porch in the late afternoon, it came to her that she might have to spend the rest of her life babysitting zombies.

The word made her throw back her head and make a sound in her throat. The goats stopped chewing and the chickens huddled together.

Zombies.

8

Five years earlier

Everett Roberts passed the slicing and dicing on to another doctor. He hated getting his hands dirty, even with gloves on. Five corpses, four days, no answers. At the debriefing, nobody could offer a plausible reason for the failures.

Jillian Newhause had suggested several steps to make the process less traumatic for the subjects, but the others barely paused to acknowledge her presence. And she wasn't so sure it would make any difference. There was a fundamental flaw in their formula, but to voice that truth would be heresy. The Summerland Mission did not tolerate heresy.

The autopsy room no longer held bodies. It held piles of organs and body parts arranged by anatomy, not by former owner. When the doctors were done, the techs piled the flesh and bone into cremation troughs and fired up the burners. Even with the strong HVAC system, the smell made Jillian's intestines wobble.

The brains were studied again, flash frozen, filed, and locked away.

"The brain is all that matters," Roberts insisted.

But Jillian kept her theories, and her clandestine experiments, to herself. Life was not only in the brain. It sprang from the gut, the meridians, the solar plexus; it ticked in the heart and mitochondria and sensors in arterial walls. The body was not meat. Frozen brains would not tell them how to make people live forever.

This run had convinced Jillian that Summerland was both vital and possible—and that they were going about it all wrong. The five bodies had resurrected fully. Four of the subjects had spoken unintelligible words: one sounded like "Mother" and one sounded to Jillian like "Hell."

Or "Help."

Hearts and lungs functioned, if erratically. Feet and pupils responded to pain and light.

Number 298 sat up and gurgled, coughed up blood, and screamed. Kept on screaming. Eyes wide open, slavering foam from his mouth. Screaming. Doctor Mancusen prepared an IM sedative but Roberts, Newhause, and the other doctors said it would compromise the experiment. 298 was strapped down and placed alone in a room to scream alone. His voice became hoarse over the next four hours, after which he screamed soundlessly, but the team didn't notice because three of the other subjects were screaming, too. Number 297 opened her eyes and wept silently.

"She's not crying, for God's sake," Roberts barked. "Her tear ducts are leaking brain fluid. Stop fantasizing, Newhause."

297's chest heaved as brain fluid poured down her cheeks and into her grimacing mouth.

The horror lasted all night. When the subjects' larynxes were too damaged to produce any more vocalization, the exams began.

Cutting was minimal at this stage; only shallow biopsies and scrapings were taken. Body fluids were drained. 297's tear ducts were aspirated and the fluid was normal saline: tears.

Three of the subjects died within a month. They'd undergone procedures to paralyze their vocal cords to stop the disruptive screaming, so language tests were conducted using sign language and symbol boards, which was hampered by doubled disposable restraints on their wrists and thumbs. The first violent outbursts had cost one examiner her hand, and another was rendered brain damaged and partially blind.

The report labeled the trial moderately successful: two of the subjects had lived. If you could call that living.

9

Ezekiel Alder hunkered in his fort, peered out to be sure Jacob or the girls hadn't followed him, and took the rectangle of feed sack out of his pants. He folded back the wrapping and ran his fingers over the yellowed, cracked cover.

Trucker John bought hundred-book lots at a junk store on his trips to the valley. EZ had found this one at the Dollers' store a year ago and he read it every day.

He could see that it was meant to be funny. There were funny-looking drawings and a tone that said one thing but meant another. But he didn't care about the humor. The people in the book played jazz and painted and read poetry out loud in coffee houses. Every cartoon gesture and utterance was big, spontaneous, free; sometimes despairing, frustrated, and cynical. The cartoon people had long straight hair, wore turtleneck shirts and sometimes black berets. There were many guitars and wine bottles wrapped in straw.

They were his people.

With another survey of the pasture, he leaned back against a tree and settled in for his dose of hope and salvation.

It was Sunday night. Ezekiel's mother had spent the last three days trying to get her husband and brother-in-law to do some work, but even with Ezekiel overseeing his big brother and the bigger girls helping around the house, Mercy was worn out. The girls were wilting, too, whining and fussing over every little thing.

This morning had been the last straw. She'd gotten everyone up and washed and dressed. She'd put the Bible in Earl's hand and stood him up in the living room.

"Go on," she told him. "Just read that." She didn't expect him to give a sermon in his condition, but surely he could do his Christian duty and read scripture.

Earl stood there. He blinked twice. His color certainly hadn't come back. If anything, he was grayer than ever.

Mercy jabbed her finger on the verse. "Ezekiel 37. You know this one by heart." She didn't care if he understood one syllable, he was the head of the household and this was his job.

But her husband wasn't the head of anything today.

She stood beside him feeling her warmth leach into his body. He exuded an unwholesome smell, like a dead snake.

Earl was always busy. Mercy wouldn't allow anything less. But since God had put this trial upon them, she had noticed that El Duane did most of the hard digging and heavy carrying, and Mercy realized he always had.

Now, if Earl wasn't working hard at leading his family in the path of righteousness, what was his purpose?

She looked at El Duane. He always itched to lead the service, it was no secret, and Earl never would let him. El Duane sat still, staring at Earl.

"Now's your chance, El Duane. Go ahead and take over!" She said it more as a goad to Earl than a real invitation to El Duane.

His eyes slid to her, then back to Earl. He leaned forward and for a moment Mercy believed he was going to stand up, but he didn't go anywhere. She thought he sat up straighter, though, with a stiffer spine than she'd seen in him in three days. Or ever.

"Fine. I'll do it myself," she said. "Go on and sit down, Earl, if you can't be any help."

She had to push him to a bench. He slumped there while she started to pray.

Freedom looked at Liberty. "Can Mommy do that?"

Liberty shook her head, her mouth hanging open.

Heaven whimpered.

"Close your eyes, close your mouths, and bow your heads," Mercy ordered. "It's God's will. It's not for us to question it, no matter how big the inconvenience," she muttered, emphasizing the last word so God would for sure hear it.

This was one more thing she was going to have to do herself.

> *... The Lord set me in the center of the plain, which was now filled with bones.*
> *How dry they were!*
> *He asked me: Son of man, can these bones come to life?*
> *"Lord God," I answered, "you alone know that."*
> *"I will put sinews upon you, make flesh grow over you, cover you with skin, and put spirit in you so that you may come to life."*
> *... As I was prophesying I heard a noise; it was a rattling as the bones came together, bone joining bone.*
> *I saw the sinews and the flesh come upon them, and the skin cover them, but there was no spirit in them.*

As Mercy read, she wondered where Ezekiel was. He would be wandering the woods again, or up at Rey Nickel's, missing service. She would set him straight in short order. "Liberty, lead us in song," she said, and sat down, grateful to get off her feet.

After the service Mercy had asked God's forgiveness in advance for breaking the Sabbath commandment and made her husband

and his brother work until dark. She couldn't stand them hanging around all day, and anyway it took them five times longer to do any chore than it used to.

Now the dishes were washed and the kids were in bed. Jacob was lying there with his eyes open, but he'd been thoroughly prayed over and Jesus was just going to have to watch out for him overnight, because Mercy was done.

What a day. She poured herself the dregs of the coffee and sat by the kitchen stove, the lantern wick wound down low. There had to be a reason for this. There had to be a solution. If she could only see the signs, surely God would show her what to do. In the meantime, she could manage. She could lead Sunday services herself. She did a better job than Earl, anyway.

Rey found Travis by the river. As they walked to her place, she asked him to take care of Hoot and Eddy.

"You live with them. You're right there. Just keep them pottied and fed."

"They like you to do it," Travis said.

"They don't even know I'm there. They fed you and housed you for two years, now you can return the favor."

Travis pouted. On him, it looked sweet. His big innocent blue eyes, his broken nose, his flop of sun-streaked hair, got right under Rey's skin.

"Dude, I'm no good at taking care of dudes. I'm not a, you know, nurturer."

Rey wanted to nibble on his lower lip but forced herself to take a rain check.

"Trav, just make a little extra food when you eat and give them some. When you drink some water, give them each a slug. When you go pee, take them with you."

"Whoa, I'm not touching anything," Travis said.

"They can do it themselves once you give them the idea. And at night, make sure the fires are all out and door's latched. Then you can spend the night at my place."

"Can't you do it? I'm not good at that kind of thing. I'll forget and probably kill them or something."

"I've been doing it. It's your turn." He was too cute to argue with. God help her, something about the guy turned her insides warm and squishy.

But he had to step up. It was the right thing to do, and if she didn't help him do the right thing, he'd miss a chance to grow up some, and if he didn't grow up she couldn't let go and love him all the way.

"I'll walk you home," she said.

"It's early," he said. "Come on, baby, let's lie down for a little while."

For the next three hours Travis plied his great and unique talent for turning Rey into a mindless pool of melted butter.

Bee watched Sugar Agate leave her cottage and walk down the white path to the road. She was wearing her Indian princess dress, beaded cream-colored leather with fringe and conchos. Bee expected her to turn uphill toward Hoochville and Travis, but instead Sugar Agate turned downhill.

"Sugar Agate's going to the store," Bee announced. "I wonder if the Dollers are open for business."

"I haven't seen hide nor hair of Bill or Birdie, either one," Cricket said. "It's like they dropped off the face of the Earth."

"Don't be overly dramatic," Bee said. "We go months without seeing them."

"Maybe she's going to get her hair done," Cricket said.

"With what to trade? Jackie's not going to barter for a peek and a smile."

Lacewing came out of the kitchen, licking purple jelly off her finger. "I never got Mother's good pickle dish back from her."

"You won't, either, unless you do what she did to us and go into her house and take it. If more people did that, maybe she'd stop stealing things."

"Oh, bless her, she doesn't know she's stealing."

"Right. 'Well, nobody was using it. It was just sitting in their kitchen cupboard. They obviously didn't want it,'" Cricket mocked, using Sugar Agate's sweetest voice.

She didn't have to hide from Sugar Agate, but Bee didn't like to get caught watching people. It was better if her knowledge of her neighbors appeared to spring from the deep intuitive wisdom of a sage. If everybody knew it was the product of chance observation, everybody would be doing it. She picked up a throw rug off the floor and stepped onto the porch to shake it. As Sugar Agate left her sight, Bee walked to the road flapping the rug, not hard enough to attract attention. Sure enough, the girl slowed past Jackie Tobasco and Berry's place and looked like she was trying to see behind the trailer house. She didn't go to the door.

Seeing if anyone's home, Bee thought.

Sugar Agate went on to the Dollers', too far down the hill to see clearly from the Pear house. She turned up their overgrown driveway and Bee lost sight of her behind the trees.

As she gave the rug a last cursory flap, something caught her eye across from the store. A dark something shaped like a man, but moving slow, lurching like a bear walking on its hind legs.

"Cricket!" she called, just loud enough to be heard in the house. "Get the binoculars."

It crossed the road on the far side of the store, and then it was swallowed in the dark under the big firs.

Cricket came out into the yard. "Did you call me?"

"Somebody's down there. I didn't see who it was. He walked funny."

Cricket said, "Was it Trucker John?"

"Maybe. Small to be John, but it's hard to tell from up here."

"Maybe it was Jobert," Cricket said.

"It didn't move like Jobert." Bee folded the rug in half and turned back to the house. "Jobert walks straight up and cocky. He's got that little man syndrome. But if he's been alone, with nobody taking care of him … he could be hurt. Broken leg or something making him walk crooked."

"We never found him. Never saw him after that night."

Bee called Lacewing.

"I might have seen Jobert down the road. If it was him, he's hurt or sick. You better try to find him again and fix him up."

Lacewing offered several reasons why she should not do that, but Bee had an answer to all of them.

"Nothing to be scared of," Bee said. "He'll be happy to see you. He's been hungry and cold for four days. I heard they don't feed themselves or fix a fire. Don't have the sense to come in out of the rain anymore. You're the healer. Stop fussing and go help your neighbor."

"Cricket, come with me," Lacewing pleaded.

Cricket said, "I've got to hang laundry."

Lacewing made herself look defenseless.

Cricket sighed. Lacewing was going to owe her. "What the heck. Come on."

On the porch, Lacewing asked, "Are you sure it was Jobert?"

"I didn't see him. It might not have been one of ours. Could have been anything at all."

10

Jackie Tobasco hadn't been this happy in a year. Berry was sitting perfectly still while Jackie wound her hair in forty rag strips. Her head was an explosion of little pink, red, blue, yellow and purple bows.

"Hold still, now, honey," Jackie said unnecessarily. "I've got to get all this oil down into your roots. You're dry as toast. Ooh, you're going to be so pretty! Not that you're not already pretty. Gorgeous, gorgeous, gorgeous. But you're gonna love your hair. Beauty takes time, that's what you don't understand. Natural's fine, you know I love your natural hair, but once you see this you'll be begging me to do your hair every week."

Jackie chatted on. It would have been nice if Berry had responded in some way, but if she'd been able to talk back she wouldn't be sitting still for getting her hair put up in rags. Jackie had been longing to fuss over Berry for all the years she'd known and loved her but Berry would have none of it. She just pulled her hair back in a poodle tail, or made Jackie cut it down short like a boy's. Well, okay, Berry had the bone structure to pull that off, but when the rags came off she would look like a movie star.

"There, honey. Look there. Aren't you cute? All's you need is a little makeup."

And another bath. Jackie had bathed Berry every day, twice yesterday. She'd used the last of the good perfumed soap on her and still couldn't scrub off that mousy smell.

Jackie smoothed Mahogany Rose on Berry's forehead and cheeks. The foundation wouldn't blend right. Well, it was old; Berry had only let Jackie put foundation on her twice before and the little bottle had been sitting around for years. Jackie blended and wiped over Berry's chin and nose, around her eyes. A tiny bit got in the corner of Berry's eye and she twitched.

"You moved! You're coming back, aren't you? Oh, my sweet baboo is waking up!"

Jackie blotted the foundation out of Berry's eyelid. The more she blotted, the weirder Berry's skin got. The foundation soaked in. On her cheekbone, makeup stuck to a patch of spongy skin.

Jackie added a quarter sized dollop, feathered the edges.

A quarter sized piece of skin sloughed off.

"Oh-oh."

Jackie's eyes met Berry's in the mirror. Berry didn't look concerned.

There was no blood. Just a small blob of cheek mixed with Mahogany Rose.

Jackie took a deep breath. "Let's just fix that up, dear. A little more, not so much rubbing … There we go. Pretty as ever. Prettier! Now how about some eyeshadow? I'm seeing Gold Dust on your eyes."

It had been nearly a week since Buck came back to life and Fiddlin' Sue was still waiting for him to wake up. They'd passed the point in their marriage where she expected sex from him except on birthdays and full moons and anniversaries and Valentine's Day and Christmas Eve and cold winter nights when it was more a necessity than a pleasure, although it was a pleasure then too. But Sue did expect, on a daily basis, kisses and spontaneous hugs and bursts of song, and at least a few times a week for Buck to grab her and swing her around in a sudden, breathless dance.

They were a couple of romantics, even if the twins thought they were ancient. They had seen each other's every part and flaw. Sue was sorely missing the old Buck Hill.

In the eastern side of the mountain's early dusk, Sue straightened her back and brushed garden dirt off her hands. Buck was sawing firewood with Misty. Misty worked her end of the two-man saw nearly as well as Sue, but the new Buck would saw all afternoon and into the night if Sue let him. Crystal had been with Sue on rock-picking duty in the new garden bed. Sue had made her take breaks, but Crystal just stood there waiting to be told what to do next.

Sue wouldn't admit it to anybody, but the new Crystal was a relief.

Sue left Crystal in the garden and went inside to make cornbread and heat up the white beans she'd boiled yesterday with a soup bone from the last steer. In a month they'd have early lettuce, but in these early spring months they lived on milk, eggs, beans, and grain.

At the table she watched her husband and daughter pick at their dinner. They didn't look thinner, and they were strong enough to work all day, but they ate enough to starve a bug.

Buck licked his thumb and reached his hand into the steaming bean pot.

Sue shouted, "Buck! What're you doing?"

Buck fished around in the pot and pulled out the soup bone and set to gnawing on it. Mashed beans and bean liquor clung to his hand.

"He wants meat," Misty said.

"Best thing for healing," Sue said. "Builds up his strength. But Buck, honey, don't stick your whole hand in there."

Crystal stared at her father, watching his teeth scrape the leg bone, his lips suck the juice from the marrow.

🦢

Sugar Agate felt sure someone was in the Dollers' store. Birdie was tiptoeing around in back—or it might have been branches creaking. Where else would the woman be? She was always home taking care of her creepy husband and keeping the store open.

Dollar Bill gave Sugar Agate the squinks. He had a very bad vibe. Worse than Trucker John. Not like he merely wanted to get it on with her, but like he wanted to own her. If that was what he was like with Birdie, Birdie should have run off a long time ago. Or kicked him out and kept the business.

What if Birdie got sick of her husband and ran off and left Bill with the store? And what if he needed somebody to help him run it, and he asked Sugar Agate to marry him, and then they didn't get along, because Sugar Agate couldn't stand him and wouldn't let him touch her much less get on top of her, so Sugar Agate threw him out and had the store? And could still live in the pretty house Trucker John had built? It would be fun to own her own store.

She went around to the back, but Birdie wasn't hanging clothes or cutting kindling or gathering eggs. The back door was locked. Nobody locked their doors on the mountain. Well, used to nobody did, but she'd encountered some locked doors recently. People were getting paranoid.

Hanging on a leafless shrub by the back step was a cobalt blue bottle with a pink plastic rose stuck in it. Crazy old lady, hanging bottles on her trees. There was another blue one, and emerald and amber glass, each one dressed up with a plastic flower. Just hanging, nobody looking at them back here, and those tacky flowers.

Sugar Agate took the bottles down and dumped the flowers. They'd be lovely in her kitchen window with light shining through them. Birdie would be a little embarrassed by how Sugar Agate took Birdie's old trash and turned it into something really pretty. Creating beauty was Sugar Agate's gift, and old Birdie could just deal with it.

A shadow rolled between the trees, a big shadow for the small noise it made. Sugar Agate ignored it at first. Then she did a double-take.

"Hey," she said to it. "Is that you?"

The silence made her nervous. She put a smile in her voice. "John? I do care about you, you know." To make sure he knew this was not an invitation, she added, "I mean, we're broken up, but I always wanted us to be friends."

A shiver of salal leaves: wind, Trucker John, or someone—or something—else. An elk. A bear.

A similar shiver went through Sugar Agate. Trucker John scared her. Always had. Or this might be Dollar Bill, following her. He'd done it before. Gross. She started up the road, walking half backwards, keeping an eye on the shadows. Jackie Tobasco's and Berry's trailer was close, but was it near enough to reach if a bear was chasing her?

It could be one of those men, closing in after all these years.

Sugar Agate ran.

In a way, resurrection had not changed Earl and El Duane. They were more like themselves than ever. Earl leaned on his axe with the blade in the dirt getting dull, while El Duane pounded a wedge into big fir rounds, swinging the maul back and slamming it deep into the moist hearts. The ground shook with every slam. Mercy hadn't noticed how supervisory her husband's chores had become over the years, how the years had softened him and hardened his brother. In the past week the difference had gotten too big to ignore.

It was a sin to think it, but her husband was repellant to her, and not only because of his flaking greenish skin. Mercy had taken his youth and strength and muscles for granted. Now that they were turning to mush, she had the guilty thought that she might have fallen in love with his body, not his spirit.

El Duane stopped. Mercy took a step toward the door to tell him to keep on working. El Duane leaned the maul—fifteen pounds of steel head and five feet of tempered ash handle—against the splitting stump and peeled off his shirt. His skin was kind of green, too, but he had a tan from taking his shirt off when he got sweaty, and he sweated a lot, what with the digging and splitting and sawing. The tan turned him a GI Joe shade of army green that didn't look sickly at all.

That night Mercy slept in Jacob's cot. No way was she sleeping with Earl. Earl snored and farted and bruised her with his flying elbows. She hadn't wanted to share his bed for years, and this was the opportunity to make the change. Sleeping alone in peace was a blessing.

El Duane sat at the kitchen table, where he'd stay until she made him go to his bed in the lean-to he'd built off the kitchen when they first moved to the mountain. El Duane exuded sweat and sour feet. His hands were clean, but every other part of him was a disgrace to a Christian home.

"El Duane," Mercy said, "you need a bath. Do you think you can bathe yourself?"

He slowly turned his eyes toward her, the way a sleepy bull might. No flicker of understanding interrupted his expression.

"Of course you can't." Mercy filled the kettle and turned on the propane burner under it.

When the water was hot she got El Duane to fill the washtub.

"Take your shirt off." It seemed like her work had tripled since the resurrection. She tried not to resent it. *I am my brother-in-law's keeper.*

El Duane waited by the tub on the porch. Steam clouded into the cool evening air.

"Socks and shoes off, El Duane. Overalls, too."

He stood in the tub in his shorts and Mercy gave him a clean rag she'd hemmed by hand. He didn't move. Mercy took the rag and wrung it out in the warm water and put it back in his big paw.

"Wash." She put her hand over his and washed circles over his chest. *Just another chore.* "You're a child of God, El Duane, even if you're not exactly a man anymore." And yet, Mercy heard herself think as she washed his chest, his firm belly, his muscular thighs ... he was very much a man.

Crystal held her Spanish guitar where Sue had fitted it into her arms, making no move to play it. Just like her dad.

"Mom. It's no fun without Cryssy and Dad." Misty lowered her violin.

"We've got to get them up and playing, hon. It's the best thing we can do for them. Once we all play together again, they'll come around. It'll be just like before."

Birdsong floated through the open door and Sue answered it with four bars of trilling, convoluted scales.

"Play, Buck. Just lay down an easy E."

Buck stared blankly at the strings.

Sue put his fingers on the frets and pinched his right fingers onto a pick. She folded his left fingers against the frets and moved his right hand up and down across the strings. It sounded puny, but maybe it would get him started.

The silence in the house over the past nearly a week was just about unbearable. The family was all music, all the time. When they worked and slept, music ran through their heads and somebody was always singing; their fingers tapped on strings and twitched invisible bows. Without it, Sue was feeling like she was half dead, like Buck and Crystal.

"Strum, darlin'. That's the way." Sue kept Buck's hand moving.

"There, see?" she said to Misty. "We just need to get them going."

"It sounds like shit, Mom."

"No cussing." Sue counted six-seven-eight and struck up their old hit, "When Your Boot Heels Touch the Road". It didn't have a chord change for three-and-a-half bars. But when she and Misty moved on to the A, Buck and Crystal kept strumming E.

"A! A! Change!"

She stopped and moved Buck's and Crystal's fingers to the A chord and started up their right hands. But it was the same two bars later when they had to play B. They could strum, but they couldn't play music.

"All right. We'll just play in E. Keep a'going."

Without changes, there wasn't much to the music. It wound on and on, pointless. After a minute, just noise.

Sue lowered her fiddle. Misty stopped. They listened to Buck and Crystal strum the same stack of notes.

Misty laid her hand over Crystal's and her sister stopped swiping the strings.

Sue walked outside and stood on the little porch Buck had built onto the house. Fog rolled down from the mountain's peak, a cloud sliding down, fat from its trip over the ocean, too heavy to stay in the sky. She tucked her fiddle under her chin and stroked the strings with the bow. It got closer to what she felt than she could say in words.

Behind the fiddle's lament, Sue felt like she had when the county took her daughters and ripped her family in half. She and Buck had given up everything to make it whole again. Now they were torn in half again, first torn crosswise and now torn top to bottom. She didn't know what it would take this time to sew them up, but she was prepared to do it.

Lacewing dug her fingers into Cricket's arm. The man, or whatever it was, ran across the road not fifteen feet from them.

He was hunched over and crooked, enveloped in flapping black stuff. He could have been a gigantic crow, or a shaggy animal, or what he looked like, a bent man hiding under a hood and baggy clothes, running away but not fast, not afraid of the two elderly ladies who gaped after him as he melted into the woods.

Cricket peeled her sister's hand off but held onto Lacewing's fingers.

"What was that?" Lacewing's question came out with no breath behind it.

"I don't know. How would I know? You saw it as well as I did." Cricket turned around, taking Lacewing with her. She didn't want to have to drag Lacewing up the hill, but she also couldn't seem to let go of her hand.

"I think it must be Jobert. We ought to go get him. Help him."

"Go ahead." Cricket leaned into the climb, Lacewing a dead weight dragging her back.

"Stop, Cricket! He's hurt."

Cricket forced herself to let go of her sister. She felt lonelier without Lacey's hand to hold, but she wanted out of there. She plowed up the slope breathing hard. When she came even with Jackie Tobasco's and Berry's trailer, she turned up the footpath to their door and looked downhill to call her sister to hurry on up, but Lacewing was gone.

11

The revived Cannibalites were growing frisky. That's what people were telling Rey, anyhow.

"They're doing real great. Look, Buck's playing his guitar again!" Fiddlin' Sue had told her.

"And Crystal's an angel. A pure angel, like when she was a baby. No trouble at all. So don't worry yourself." Sue had walked Rey to the road and stood watching and waving—to be neighborly, or to make sure Rey left.

Mercy Alder said pretty much the same. Earl had about got the garden turned over, El Duane had put up half next winter's wood already. Jacob was in good shape, too. They were getting along on their own steam, no need to check up on them, thanks for stopping by.

As Rey left, she saw Jacob follow his little brother across the field like a cow following a dog, plodding steadily through the grass while Ezekiel danced circles around him.

Bee and Cricket Pear had nothing to report. Cricket asked if Rey had seen Lacewing and Bee jumped in quickly with a question about Jobert. Rey hadn't seen him.

"Isn't anybody taking care of him?" Rey asked. "I guess I thought he wasn't part of ... the incident."

"We don't know," Bee said. "We went up to his place to look in on him but he was out."

"House was dark, stove was cold," Cricket said. "And now I don't know where Lacey is."

"She's mushrooming," Bee said quickly. "Tell me if you see Jobert."

"Or Lace—"

Bee turned Cricket around steered her to the porch.

At the bottom of the road, Birdie Doller didn't answer the door. Rey had the feeling Birdie was in the back, but if the woman wanted to hide out now and then, it was a free mountain.

Rey peered into the trees around Trucker John's travel trailer and didn't so much decide not to go in there as notice that she was climbing back up the hill.

Jackie Tobasco showed off Berry's new look.

"She's always been beautiful," Rey said. "With or without makeup."

The old Berry would have told Rey to go chase her tail. This one stared blankly even when Jackie plucked at the waves and rolls of her hair.

"I just can't keep my hands off her now. Spent hours on her 'do and look how pretty." Jackie wound a ringlet around her finger. "I don't know if I even have time for anybody else now, not that anybody's been down to see me. Too busy with their honeys to get their hair cut. Like to get my hands on that Travis, though. He's gotten shaggy, hasn't he? A good looking boy like that ought to show off a little." She winked. "You, too, Rey-Rey. I'm just kidding about having no time. I've got a dayful of time every twenty-four hours. This one's no trouble at all. Come on down and let me shape you up. You're getting kind of flyaway."

When Rey got up to go she caught a glimpse Berry's cheek, the one that had been turned away from her. There was a thick brown smudge the size of a doorknob under her cheekbone, surrounded by a blotch of olive green.

"You missed a spot," Rey said, and gave Jackie a one-armed hug goodbye.

Jackie said, "Rey? You're looking kind of tired. Are you okay? You did a good thing, you know, hon. You gave me my girl back, and that means the world to me. More than the world. I don't want you feeling bad about bringing them back."

Rey made herself smile.

So if everybody who would answer their doors and talk was to be believed, the procedure had been one big smashing success. Rey passed Sugar Agate's house—no sign of intelligent life there—and took the path to Hoochville. Travis met her at the door.

"Hey, baby. Long time no squeeze." He hugged her, but it felt businesslike.

Eddy sat on his bed with a bottle and a cork. He twisted the cork into the bottle, twisted it out, and started over. Hoot was in the brewery, which was a cramped lean-to with a rough-sawn opening into the common room.

"Is he making beer?" Rey asked. Hoot tending to business would constitute evidence that the revived were getting better.

"I set him in there hours ago," Travis said. "We're out of brew. It's a desperate situation."

He ducked into the brewery and squatted down next to the big Norseman.

"How's it going, bud? Go ahead, hook that tube up. There you go!" He sounded like a first grade teacher helping one of his especially slow students.

To Rey, he said, "I know he can do it if he'll just keep trying. Kinda hard to get him going."

"Why don't you do it?" Rey asked.

"Can't."

"You don't know how?"

"Never learned. Never had to."

"You've been living with these guys for four years and you never learned how to make beer? As much as you like beer, you'd have to try *not* to learn how."

Travis shrugged. "Hoot wouldn't let me, anyway. He's the king of beers, aren't you, Hoot?"

Hoot's fingers fumbled with a piece of hose.

"How's Eddy doing?" Rey asked.

"He's a spry old dog. Eddy! Walkies in thirty! It's a full time job. I thought, hey, it's like having a couple of big old dogs, but it's more like having kids. A couple of old, wrinkled, dumbass kids."

He left Hoot and went to stir a pot of sludge on the cookstove. "They'll eat anything, though. They're not picky, I'll say that for 'em. I can't keep them full."

Rey brushed away a fly. The weather was balmy, in the fifties, and the early hatching flies were hungry.

"Good thing they have you," she said. In fact, she was amazed. All this time Travis had had a caretaker inside him, waiting to hatch out when the alcohol level in the environment fell below a certain point. "It's nice you're taking care of them after they took care of you for so long."

"They never took care of me. I just slept here. Anyway, I'm only in it for the booze. Gotta take care of my main men, right?"

Travis dumped three ladles of unidentifiable mush into bowls and added spoons. "Want to stay for lunch?"

"No, thanks." Whatever he was feeding them, he was eating it, too. They looked none the worse for it, but Rey had no trouble passing.

"Come on, boys, eat up."

The three spooned whatever it was into their mouths.

Rey left the house. Fresh air washed the funk away.

"See you, baby," Travis called. "Nuh-uh, not on the shirt, dude. Aw, come *on!*"

The trail to Joe Bear's A-frame crossed the creek and climbed a hundred vertical feet. Rey had been there only once before, but the trail was freshly walked on and even in the deep woods it was easy to follow.

His A-frame was made out of thick poles set on flat rocks, with a window in the front and a stove in the back. The door was closed. Rey called, "Hoo, Joe Bear," and got no answer except the griping of a crow. The door opened hard against the floor. He'd need to plane it off before next winter. The interior looked like its owner—everything compact, neat, and incongruously ornate in a shipwrecked Mississippi riverboat style. There was a loft over the entrance with a sloping ladder. Rey stepped farther inside to get a view of the loft. The corners weren't visible, but she cold see the bed, fringed bedspread drawn tight and flat.

The stove was cold and the air was already musty under the aroma of freshly cut wood. There wasn't any firewood by the stove or around the house, though. Under the window a row of seedlings wilted in dry soil. She dipped out a ladle of water from the plastic barrel and watched the dirt suck the water in. She went outside and called Joe Bear again, looked for bodies in the brush, then headed down to catch the Salt Creek trail back to her cabin.

Sue Hill called the tune. When the chord changes came, she said their names and slowed down while her husband and daughter moved their hands to obey. Forty or fifty hours of practice and they were getting better. Forty hours of playing the same pattern, twenty songs. It was no problem with the old-time music.

What's the difference between jazz and country? Country music has three chords and a thousand fans; jazz has a thousand chords and three fans.

The better they practiced, the more the family knitted together. Bonds of steel and nylon, woven song by song into unbreakable rope. That was why they called it chords, Sue thought. Cords tied people together.

Halfway through "Keep on the Sunny Side," played at dirge pace, something flew out of Crystal's guitar and hit the wall.

"Keep going," Sue ordered. "If you slack off, we all sound worse." An old lecture that hadn't ever done any good with Crystal when she was completely alive.

Misty strolled to the wall where the chunk had hit.

"Mom?"

"You've been doing real good, honey."

"Mom." Misty picked up something from the floor and stared at her sister.

Fiddlin' Sue followed Misty's gaze. Crystal held her guitar, her right hand draped over its waist. Gray gristle marked the stump where the end of her finger had been.

Mercy could feel the day plowed into her forehead. The lines got deeper every Sunday before prayer meeting when she looked in the mirror. Work and worry, all in service to the Lord. It was God's work but it was wearing her out some days, like this day.

And Jesus help them, they'd let the Devil in, letting Rey Nickel do ungodly science on those whom Jesus had called home. It was wicked, and now she was paying the price. Her back ached and there was no joy in her heart.

In her bedroom, her husband snorted and passed wind. His emissions were fouler than it seemed possible, almost-visible brown clouds of stench. And he was softer and fatter by the day, nothing but sloth.

We are all sinners. She herself had coveted what was not hers and that was a worse sin than sloth or greed. Mercy folded her hands and prayed for forgiveness for her failure of righteousness, past, present, and future. Future especially, because she felt her prayerfulness fade even now, pushed aside by the certainty that a massive, unforgivable, irresistible, and exquisite sin was moments away.

A creak of boards told her that El Duane stood on the back porch. The arrangement was that he did not come in the house after bedtime, but tonight he turned the doorknob and stepped into the kitchen. He was tall, muscular, and silent. He had taken to washing himself every day and he smelled of soap. The lantern light made his complexion ruggedly swarthy.

El Duane took a step toward Mercy. Mercy took a step toward El Duane.

In the bedroom, Earl trumpeted an elaborate fanfare of intestinal wind.

Mercy closed her eyes and had time to say, "God's will be done" before breaking one written and several unwritten but important commandments.

Two of the Pear Sisters walked arm in arm down the road. Bee used her cane and relied more than she would admit on Cricket's steadier legs.

"We really need one of these youngsters," Bee said. "A man to get into the brush and poke around."

"Not many men left," Cricket said. "Travis, and Ezekiel."

"Travis." Bee puffed out a snort of air with the word. "And Ezekiel's only a boy."

"Rey, then. Or Sue. Why don't we go get one of them before we go off half cocked ourselves?"

"If she's alive, we'll find her ourselves. If we can't find her, there's no hurry."

"Alive!" Cricket stared around her. "You don't think she's—No. Don't say that."

"Lacey's never been missing before. Face facts, Cricket. Something is wrong with our sister."

Cricket stopped walking and Bee was forced to stop, too. The village was quiet; not even the bleating calf or the sound of sawing interrupted the always-moving air threading through the trees.

"Why didn't you let me tell Rey when she came over?"

"This is our business. Not anyone else's."

"It's the mountain's business. Our community's business. We need help; you just said so yourself."

Bee tugged and Cricket followed, supporting her older sister without making a show of it.

Bee said, "We're the leaders. We are the strength of our village. If we look weak in public the fabric of our world will surely unravel. It'll be time to ask for help if we don't find her today. And I fear the worst, Cricket. The very worst."

"Well, damn it, let's get some help then!"

The argument continued down the slope, as the two elder sisters looked in backyards and sheds and in the many secret openings under ancient trees and inside brushy thickets, calling for Lacewing.

Mercy had bathed until her skin was sore. Prayer was merely hollering down an empty barrel. Getting in bed with the man who had been her husband was out of the question. She made a hard pallet on the floor and lay awake until dawn.

Before first light she got up and quietly set a pot of buckwheat to boil, portioned out vitamins, laid out bowls and cups and spoons. Ezekiel got his brother and daddy up and made them wash and sit down to eat. His tone was less than enthusiastic. He was tired of babysitting the men. For a moment Mercy felt sorry for him.

"The Lord gives us work that we might not fall into sinful ways," she said.

"What? Me? I'm not complaining," Ezekiel said. "And I'm not sinning particularly, either. Also, I'm working all day long. I'm losing weight. Look."

He pulled his cotton shirt tight around his torso, and sure enough, his ribcage stuck out. "How long is this going to last, anyway?"

"It is not for us to know, son."

Ezekiel snorted a barely audible puff of air that meant he was sick of his mother's Bible talk. Mercy didn't correct him. He had his troubles, too. But she couldn't do more than she was already doing, and son number two had to pick up the slack. It should be good for him.

Mercy said grace and helped Heaven eat. She didn't want to look at the men's end of the table. The three of them hung their big heads over their bowls and hoisted spoons into their mouths. She felt old now, the oldest living Alder, with all these babies to take care of. *Hold your tongue,* she chided herself. *You're as bad as Ezekiel, complaining.*

Heaven shook her head and cereal oozed out of her mouth. She hated buckwheat. Liberty tattled, pointing out the obvious. Mercy scraped the ooze back into the spoon and tried to get it into the baby's mouth. Freedom started whimpering: if Heaven was going to get away with not eating, she wasn't going to eat it, either.

A clatter from the men's end got Heaven's attention and Mercy sneaked a bite of cereal into her mouth. A chair scraped and there was a muted thump.

Ezekiel said, "Ma—!" and Liberty squealed.

Mercy turned around. Earl's face was covered with gluey cereal. His own bowl was in front of him. El Duane's bowl was still spinning on the floor. In slow motion, El Duane stood up and, with a glower at Earl, walked out the door. Earl sat there, dripping porridge.

Mercy said, "Ezekiel."

"Right. As soon as I'm done." He took his time finishing his breakfast before cleaning up his father.

Mercy heard sounds of shoveling and stake-pounding from the shed where El Duane was working. Her stomach rolled over and a feeling of feverish dread she hadn't felt since she'd been saved filled her. It had to be the sensation the Devil caused when he moved in.

Travis came by while Rey was gathering eggs. She was having trouble again with the speckled hen. Always a feisty redhead, this morning she was full of chicken energy, hopping around the door, hunting bugs.

"Hey, Trav. Want some breakfast?"

"What have you got?"

"Eggs. Pan bread. Dandelion greens."

"Aren't you ever going to kill one of those chickens and make a real chicken dinner for me?"

"Nope."

"It's been a long time since I ate chicken. Damn, baby, I'm hungry just thinking about it." Travis slid his arms around Rey's waist and nuzzled her neck.

"I don't spend my capital," she said.

"Hmm?"

"The eggs are more important than one chicken dinner. Besides, they're my friends. I like them. I don't kill people I love."

"I hate to break it to you, but chickens aren't people." Travis was heading for the hollow of her throat that he knew how to nuzzle until her blood hummed.

She extricated herself. "Help me herd Dotty inside. She's all wired up about some chicken issue."

"They'd be easier to eat if you didn't name them."

"It's going to rain," Rey said. The light was getting swallowed by clouds, dark and heavy with ocean water, scrolling over the mountain peak.

"No shit."

"It feels wet."

"Did you just get here? It always feels wet."

Rey went into the cabin, but Travis didn't follow her.

"Come on in," she said.

"Nah, I've got to get back to the guys."

"Really?"

"I swear, it's like adopting a couple of morons. Single parent of two droolers. But they're good guys. Can't do anything without Daddy Travis."

Rey stared at him. "Who *are* you?"

Travis shrugged. "Hey, you started it."

"I didn't have much choice," she said stiffly.

"Sure you did. You could have not told me to take care of them. You were doing it okay by yourself."

So he wasn't blaming her for the revival, just for telling him to pitch in. "Trav, you already live there. And you want to use the still and the brewery, you said."

"Yeah, we got a jug about ready to come off the line. Party on, my place, tomorrow night, if there's any left!" He waved and loped away. His gait was easy, his body loose and springy.

Rey had the same thought she always thought when he left: she hated to see him leave, but she loved to watch him go.

But she didn't love it as much as having him in her little house, wrapping herself around him for the night, lapping up the safe, satisfied feeling he gave her. She hadn't gotten much of that since the incident. As he reached the trees, a harsh cry arrowed up the hill. Rey saw Travis turn downhill. Investigating the sound? That wasn't like him. But he wasn't going straight home to his charges. Surely he wasn't going to Sugar Agate's.

Surely not.

12

Jacob looked up, then went back to his work. Mercy said, "What now?" As soon as she got off the porch she saw it on the road. Earl was already down, flat on his back, arms flung out, belly making a hill. The hill rose and fell. At his feet, El Duane leaned over him, the big shovel in his hands.

Blood started to run down Earl's face onto his neck. Mercy shouted and ran to the road, but before she got there El Duane raised the shovel and chopped it down on Earl's face.

Mercy grabbed Freedom and shoved her in the house and slammed the door. She ran to get the shovel away from El Duane, but he was already finishing the last blow.

The belly hill stopped moving and Earl's face was pretty much gone. El Duane leaned the shovel over his shoulder and looked down at his brother.

Mercy felt coldness like the hand of Satan moving up her back. "What have you done?" she said, and El Duane turned his head slowly, insolently she thought, and nodded once. Then he walked around the back of the house and Mercy heard him cleaning the shovel in the garden dirt.

It took Ezekiel an hour to round up the able-bodied and able-minded. No one answered at Sugar Agate's or the Dollers', which left Travis and the women. Bee said she would wait at home "in case." When they gathered at the Alders' they saw El Duane at the side of the house cutting up weeds with the hoe. He'd sharpened it so the metal shone like silver. Cricket promised the girls blackberry jam and took them to her own house. Ezekiel insisted on staying, but to keep him away from the scene, Rey told him he was needed to patrol the grounds.

"Are they all dangerous?" he asked.

"No." Mercy, Sue, and Jackie all spoke at once.

"Then why do I—"

"You're fast and you have good eyes and ears. If you see anything, run back here," Rey told him, and he took a kitchen knife and went to scout.

Earl's body was still in the road, covered with his blanket. After a week of close contact with Earl it had to be burned or used for the cows; it might as well end its life as a shroud.

With the kids out of earshot, the women could talk freely. It was a sensitive subject for Jackie Tobasco and Fiddlin' Sue, but they were willing to face facts. Travis sat on the porch steps, as far away from Earl's body as he could get.

"He just up and killed him?" Jackie asked, not waiting for an answer. "Brother against brother. I never thought El Duane had it in him. He was kind of jealous, but—"

Sue overrode Jackie with an elbow to her ribs. "Do you not see Mercy's right here? Shut up." She said conciliatorily, "He wasn't himself. None of them are. My Buck doesn't have a violent bone in his body, of course. We better face it, though. They're different now."

"Anyone could be next," Mercy said. Why had it started with her family? She was a God-fearing family woman, cleaving to the Way. "The Devil strikes first where innocence lies," she said. She made it up off the top of her head but it had a good Scriptural sound to it.

Sue said, "El Duane isn't the Devil. He's just ... not right yet. I'm awfully sorry about your loss, Mercy."

Jackie turned to Rey. "When will they be getting right again, Rey? It's been what, a couple of weeks?"

"Six days," Rey said.

"And how long until they come to all the way?"

Rey said, "I don't know."

Mercy started pacing, circling her husband's twice-dead body. "If you don't know, why did you do that to them? Your experiments ruined them. They aren't alive and they aren't dead. We don't hold with that Limbo and Purgatory nonsense, but if it existed, this would be it. How will they be resurrected? When Jesus comes, the righteous shall rise up, but these poor sinners don't have a chance of getting to Heaven. You did a bad thing, Rey. An evil deed."

"I told you I didn't want to. I told you I didn't know if it would work. You wanted me to try anyway. It was that or leave them dead. If you don't like it, you should have listened to me. I tried to tell you it might come out badly. Unpredictable results. You made the choice."

Jackie's warm hand on her shoulder made Rey aware she was shouting.

"You're right, hon," Jackie said. "You did say that. She did." She looked at Mercy and Sue.

Sue said, "Calm down, girls. We've got to make a funeral for Mercy's husband. Mercy's got to think of how to tell her kids about this, and get used to being a widow. Alls we can do is be good neighbors and sister up."

"I can work on it. If I have a subject ... " Rey started.

Nobody said anything.

"If you could hold off on the burial for just a day or two ... " She trailed off.

"You're not suggesting—" Mercy sounded shocked.

"Just wait a day, maybe two. I might be able to help him."

"Baby Jesus wept. You want to do your witch work on my husband's dead body? Again? I'll meet you at the gates of Hell first. Go on out of here, Rey Nickel. Don't come on my property any more."

"But it could save the rest of them."

"Go on, or I'll have El Duane come out here."

Sue and Jackie gasped, looked at each other and back at Mercy.

Before anything else was said, Rey saw Bee coming toward them, her slow, stately progress cueing them all to stop arguing and wait for her.

Bee didn't speak until she was with them. She pulled back the corner of the blanket covering Earl's face, tisked, and covered him back over.

"Cricket tells me El Duane did this."

Mercy answered. "Yes'm. I saw him do it."

"With a shovel?"

"With a shovel."

Bee said, "We're not going to stand around here. In my house, noon. We'll stay indoors until we know what's what. Who've you got to watch the children?"

"Misty can be in charge for an hour or two," Sue offered.

"Ezekiel can watch Jacob."

"But then who'll keep a lookout?" Rey said. "If there's a general change in the, uh, revived, somebody has to be on guard."

"Travis can keep a lookout. We can spare him at the meeting. I'd like to have Birdie there, if someone will get her."

Travis said, "Whoa, I'm not doing it alone."

"You can take Sugar Agate," Bee said, and dismissed him. "You'd best get Earl into the shed now. Remember to close the door so animals don't get in."

They trundled Earl to the shed in the wooden wheelbarrow and closed the door. Travis went to find Sugar Agate, with instructions to try to get Birdie to answer her door. It was early, around midway between sun-up and noon. Rey had about three hours to think of a way to convince Mercy to let her have Earl's body before the funeral.

Before that, though, Rey had a trek to make up and around Cannibal Mountain.

Something dark and low to the ground leaned against the back wall of Sugar Agate's house, breathing hard. The window was open and there wasn't any sound from inside. After a few minutes it stretched up and moved silently down the hill, keeping away from the road, and was swallowed in the trees.

Rey stopped at her cabin for her bear whistle. The shortcut took her nearly straight up to the base of the rocky peak where the trail ended. She'd come this way before. It was short in miles but long in energy expended and skin shredded. She was breathing hard when she finally reached the south side of Cannibal Mountain where the land fell away a thousand feet nearly straight down and she had to grab niches in the rock face to keep from sliding on the scree.

Scrambling over carefully placed fallen trees, she stepped on a tripwire and a bell clanged. At the same time an unholy screech raked her ears.

Rey shouted the *Whoo* they all recognized, called again to be safe, and the screeching stopped. Seconds later a brown streak of fur leaped out of the trees and thudded against her knees.

"Hey, Toasty!" Smokey's bobcat sniffed Rey's boots and pants legs, then leaped into the undergrowth, leading Rey home but staying out of sight and out of reach.

Smokey met her at the fence. Rey saw he had carved the cedar fence posts into human and animal faces.

"Rey! Far out!" Smokey leaned across the wire and hugged Rey hard, clapped her on the shoulders, and hugged her again. "Come on in, woman."

Toasty reappeared and stood on her hind legs for an ear rub. Rey said, "She looks good. Don't you, girl? Are you taking good care of Smokey?"

"She gets tired of me. She missed you," Smokey said. When Smokey made his yearly trips off the mountain, Rey looked in on the cat and spoiled her as reprehensibly as any grandma.

"What's that where your beard used to be? It looks like a face."

"Thought I'd try something different. Maybe one of these days I'll even cut my hair."

Rey said, "You look less like a Sasquatch." With the brush cut down to stubble, he was actually good-looking.

Smokey led the way to the peeled log that made a bench in front of his cob house. You couldn't see the house unless you knew what you were looking for. It was a wildflower- and brush-covered hillock with small windows obscured by tall grasses.

Rey accepted a glass of water and refused a smoke.

"I was thinking about coming down-mountain pretty soon. Gets lonesome up here after a couple of months. Busy time of year, though. Getting the seedlings started, making chickenshit tea."

"Farming's a lot of work." Rey inhaled a bouquet of sea air and turned earth, chickens and compost and wood smoke. On the other side of a screen of small pines the ground dropped away; an osprey sailed through the empty air.

Smokey didn't like to be rushed. They talked. After awhile, Rey said, "We could use you down below if you can get away."

"Trouble?"

"Yeah."

"Outside trouble?"

"No. Just us. It's not going to involve any outsiders. It can't."

Smokey listened while Rey told the story. She took an extra breath before talking about her part, but since the entire debacle was her doing, there wasn't any way to leave it out.

When she was done, he said, "Sounds like you could use an extra hand down there." He got to his feet. "I'll get the chickens in the coop and close up the house, give Toasty a good feed and give the seedlings a drink."

Smokey pulled camouflage over the doors and the chicken coop. He sat with the golden-brown cat for many minutes, talking and listening. The cat's purr was loud enough to hear twenty feet away. On the way out, he did things to some wires. Midday light broke over the peak and a fresh wind smacked the west side of the mountain. They took the long way around, curving west, then north and east to the village.

In front of Rey's porch, a fluffy pile of speckled feathers had been neatly parted from skin and bones. The bones and meat were missing.

"I liked that little hen," Rey said. "I should have put them all in the henhouse before I left. Poor little Dotty."

Rey called the flock and they came tottering into the yard, veering away from their eaten sister. Rey counted them. "Two more missing, but they could be off in the woods. I've only lost one before," she said, turning to Smokey. "I built their house extra strong."

"Sorry, Rey."

She picked up what was left of the body and couldn't think what to do with it.

"Cremation?" Smokey suggested.

"Later." Rey set the remains in the composting toilet shed and latched the door. There was no time for chicken funerals now.

"It's weird," she said as they took her walkway to the road. "Whatever it was took all the bones, too. Even the skull."

13

A little crowd of currently and formerly living people gathered on the Pear Sisters' walk, the undead looking at nothing, the living ready for Bee to tell them what to do.

"What do we do, Rey?" Jackie asked.

"Why are you asking me?"

"Bee's not here. You're up. What do we do?"

"Yeah," Sue said. "This is your ball of wax. Are they all going to go nuts like El Duane?"

"And what do we do about it?" Mercy said. "I prayed, and apparently the Lord's answer was for brother to smite brother."

Rey said, "Remember me telling you that you might not like the results? Every one of you said you accepted that."

"I was against it," Mercy said.

Rey shrugged. "You put them in the circle with all the others."

"Nobody's blaming you," Jackie said. "But we're scared. Bee won't know what to do without you explaining what's happened to our folks."

But they *were* blaming her, and Rey *couldn't* explain what had happened to the revived. The Summerland Mission hadn't been able to explain it. Unpredictable results, every trial. She had been so sure she'd found it that last time. What could have thrown the results so far off? Maybe she'd lost her edge, whatever spark of genius she'd had. Maybe living in a hut in a prehistoric forest was exactly what she was suited for.

Without the sisters animating it, the house felt unpleasantly ghostlike, as if nothingness was already here. After the semidead had been in it for a few minutes, though, the nothingness filled up with an almost-visible funk.

Rey said, "Do you want to wait for the Pear Sisters, which I'm happy to do, or get started?"

"Tell us what you know," Sue said.

"I don't know what the long-term effects are. I wanted them not to be dead, just as you did, and I let Lacewing try in case her method was effective, but it wasn't, and I did what I knew how to do."

"How'd you know what to do?" Sue asked.

"I used to work in a hospital. In the emergency room. I brought some medicine with me when I came up here." Hurrying past the quarter-truth, Rey said, "We just have to take precautions and watch them. Keep them calm, don't arouse the limbic system or archipallium. The parts of the brain that control the emotions and aggression. Routine, calm, and vigilance. Keep them busy at whatever they can do."

"El Duane was busy," Ezekiel said. "He was digging. With the *shovel.*"

"Don't give them access to anything that could be used as a weapon. And of course, they have to be watched constantly."

Sue said, "I'm not worried about mine turning violent."

Rey asked, "How did Crystal lose her finger, Sue?"

"Playing the guitar. It flew across the room and hit the wall."

"The guitar?"

"The finger."

Rey said, "Jackie, what's wrong with Berry's cheek?"

"Nothing. Nothing! I made her up, is all. She doesn't mind." Jackie smoothed Berry's forehead and left a streak the color of old mold where the foundation came off on her fingers.

"Berry lost some skin, didn't she? A piece of her face fell off and you used concealer or spackle or whatever to cover it up."

"It's called makeup. You should try it sometime. Seriously, come down any time and I'll fix you up. I'm not busy lately. You've got such a great face, hon, that bone structure, it's a shame not to play it up. I'd kill for bones like that."

"Anybody else have pieces of them sloughing off, decayed spots, sinking flesh?"

After a silence, Fiddlin' Sue offered, "Buck's okay, but he stuck his whole hand in a pot of stew and it was real hot. Didn't bother him at all. He's still got all his fingers." She held up her husband's hand to demonstrate. "I sure as heck didn't tell him to stick his hand in our dinner."

Rey thought. She said, "I think there are two things going on here. Their bodies are deteriorating. I don't know why. But their minds are coming back, in a sense. Not their rational minds, unfortunately. The more primitive parts."

"Jesus, that's got to be uncomfortable," Jackie said. "What do we do about it?"

"Watch them. Report anything unusual, good or bad. Don't assume they'll stay the same. El Duane changed; others might do random things, too. Stay safe."

"How are we going to stay safe?" Mercy demanded. "Keep them tied up? In cages?"

Rey grimaced, and nodded. "That might be the best way."

Jackie Tobasco asked, "What about Dollar Bill? The Dollers are right next door to me and I haven't seen hide nor hair of him. Birdie's always out back hanging bottles on her bottle tree or working in her garden. She's putting in something big this year. Maybe filbert trees? Digging up a big hole, anyway, and all by herself."

"She ought to take a firmer hand with her husband," Mercy said. "Bill would work if she made him. Husbands aren't much different dead than they were alive."

"And Joe Bear? Was he even fixed after he got shot?" Sue asked. "Did anybody go look for him?"

Rey said she'd looked in his A-frame and he wasn't there. "We should organize searches, in pairs, with guards. Trucker John hasn't been seen recently, either, as far I know." Her memory of him lurking in the shadows was as unpleasantly real as if he were standing in front of her. "We'd better keep them all together where we can watch them. Everybody stay together as much as you can. Get your folks secured."

"Tied up, you mean," Jackie said. "I'm not gonna—"

"Just until we know what kinds of changes are happening." Rey opened the door. "And keep an eye out for the Pears." She peered up and down the road, listened for noises from the woodpile or garden, heard nothing. The longer they were gone, the more nervous Rey felt. None of the sisters was ever away from home for more than a few minutes.

"I've got to have a funeral for my husband," Mercy said.

"You know we'll all help you, Mercy. First things first, though."

They left, leading their relatives by the hands, the living looking glum and unnerved, the semi-living blank-eyed.

"We'll be safe," Rey said to Sue, "as long as we all follow the plan."

Sue said, "That I'd like to see."

Cannibalites weren't much for sticking to plans.

She had told them not to go out alone, but Rey went by herself to look again for Joe Bear. His cabin was still empty and the stove was still cold. A sour wet-ash smell had settled into the walls. She had the feeling he, or someone, had been there and gone.

Rey followed the Sock Creek trail to Hoochville looking for fresh tracks. If anyone had come this way recently they had stayed off the muddy patches and hadn't stepped on any of the big rocks where a shoe would leave a print.

She found Eddy standing in the distillery holding a piece of pipe. He looked scrawnier than ever. Hoot was in bed, drinking brown liquid from a plastic Dasani bottle. Rey borrowed it politely and sniffed. Cold tea. She gave it back to him.

"Have you guys eaten?" she asked, but they didn't even look at her. She found sugar and buckwheat, lit a fire, and put a pot on the stove. While she waited for it to cook, she walked around outside the cabin. Birds chattered, small things rustled in the undergrowth. Even in the afternoon light, it was easy to get paranoid. Every sound could be a bear, a man, a monster. Any shadow could come to life.

Rey got the men settled with bowls of wheat gruel and banked the fire. "Don't touch the stove," she ordered, not getting any sense that they understood her

The cliff where Sock Creek fell down to the river was east-northeast from Hoochville, about an eighth of a mile north of the clearing. Sock Creek ran fast downslope and tumbled over small rock ledges before it fell off the side of the mountain. Anyone who didn't know the cliff was there could easily miss it, even in daylight, even with the crash of whitewater and cold mist giving it away; brush growing right over the lip of the chasm hid it from view. There was supposed to be a hollow behind the waterfall, but Rey had never been able to see it, and it was impossible to climb behind the falls, at least not without a technical effort. On one rare hot summer day, Rey had lain in the creek a yard from the drop-off with her head downstream, the shallow water damming in chilly pools at her feet and armpits. Now she walked the edge of the stream, then crawled on her stomach to see over the edge. No bodies sprawled on the rocks below. Rey stared at the cascading water until the waterfall looked motionless and the world looked as if it were rising.

14

"Did you check your bra?"

"Why would I be wearing a bra?" Bee snapped.

"Don't you get chafed?" Cricket asked.

"What chafes me is your personal, off-topic questions. I gave you the key."

"You did not." Cricket turned her pockets inside out again. "No key. You must have dropped it."

"Yes, into your hand."

Cricket stooped down and swept the cave floor with her palm.

"Be careful," Bee said. "You'll knock it into a hole. Then we'll really be in a predicament."

"I think we're in one now. Move back, will you?"

Bee stepped back against the damp rock wall until her sister pronounced the area key-free.

"It's not here." Cricket rattled the iron gate. It was rusty, but still iron. The sisters were locked on the wrong side of it, in the damp semi-dark, and no one knew they were there. Cricket turned around and felt the floor with the toe of her shoe, slowly moving to the back of the cave.

"Don't go any further," Bee warned.

"It's a ways back." Cricket kept going.

"The chute's only six yards back. Hold still. You don't know what you're doing."

"Do you want to get out of here? We've got to find the key."

"You're about to get out of here the hard way, feet first. Is that your plan?"

Cricket gasped and screamed, adding a dramatic receding-into-the-distance fillip at the end.

"Very amusing."

Cricket came back and sat down. "My back's sore. Too much bending and cold and damp. I think it's going into spasm."

"Tell it not to. Think warm thoughts." Bee massaged her sister's back. Chilly mist rode echoes of rushing water somewhere deep in the cave.

"I hate to think about what happened here," Cricket said after a few minutes. "Such a tragedy."

"Not so much a tragedy as the inevitable result of idiocy." Bee had never admitted to any sentimental feelings about the incident. "A couple of mental incompetents plus a fool adds up to a poor ending every time."

"They were in love, though. Love can make normal people into lunatics." Cricket paused. "Or so they say."

"Yes, you and I have been lucky. We were saved from lunacy. Moon madness. Our heads have repelled invasions of the heart."

"So far, anyway," Cricket said.

"I think, at eighty-seven and seventy-five, we're safe."

"Poor Lacey. Love got her when she was too young to know any better. Daddy should have stopped it sooner. Then none of that would have happened."

"Daddy put an end to it as soon as he found out. Daddy always did the right thing." Bee never said a critical word about their father. If she believed him to have been imperfect, or merely human, the suspicion was going with her to the grave.

Cricket said, "Lacewing was always soft, wasn't she? In the heart and in the head. In a good way, I mean."

"I hope you mean it well. We're likely to die where we sit in two or three days, so let's not end on a critical note."

Cricket sat down and Bee folded herself carefully onto the ground, using Cricket's shoulder to lower herself. Cricket leaned into Bee. "Our little sister will be all alone when we're gone. I don't see how she'll manage."

Bee didn't answer, but both women were thinking that Lacewing might do surprisingly well without them.

The light grew stronger, which meant the sun was moving to the west and its northernmost rays were striking the entrance to the cave. It also meant darkness was coming, and with it a cold night that would permeate thin skin and inadequate clothing.

Cricket broke the silence. "It's on the other side."

She pushed herself up and grasped the iron bars. "It's right there, on the other side. The key!"

Bee had nodded off. "What?" She wiped a drop of drool from her chin. She would have gotten up to look, but her joints were too stiff to bother moving. A wet, cold cave was no place for a mature woman.

"The sun's shining on it. I can see it ... " Cricket grunted. "But I can't reach it."

"You must have knocked it under the gate when you were swishing your hand back and forth."

"Or possibly you dropped it while it was in your hand after you unlocked the gate. Just possibly. Why in the world did Daddy install a self-locking latch on the gate? He was trying to keep people out, not in."

"He'll have had a good reason, I'm sure."

"Which we'll never know. Are there any sticks in here?"

There weren't any sticks, but the sisters did manage to knock the key six inches farther away by fishing for it with boots on the end of bootlaces. The end of a flung shirt sleeve touched it but wouldn't drag it toward them, even with a pebble tied in the cuff. As evening fell, the gap that had let sun rays into the cave made a path for the nightly marine wind.

"At least the wind's pushing the fog back," Cricket said. "I'm freezing, but it's slightly dryer, don't you think?"

"We'll be all right as long as we use our brains. And we haven't called for help yet."

"You said not to let anybody know," Cricket said. "I wanted to call for help, and you said no."

"We'll bundle up now before we get chilled to the bone, and then take turns hollering."

They pulled their collars up—Bee had a hood on her coat, which she said they would take turns wearing—and tucked all their shirts into their pants and stood close together at the rusted gate. Cricket started yelling "Help! We're trapped in the cave! It's Bee and Cricket! Heelllp! Come get us!"

"Are you delivering the Gettysburg Address?" Bee said. "Not like that. You'll wear out your voice and no one will understand what you're saying. Like this.

"*Help! In the cave!*" Pause. "*Help! In the cave!* Your turn."

"They won't know what you mean," Cricket complained, but she echoed the phrase. They traded off, waiting between calls. The night grew darker and colder, and the women tired.

"We'll sleep," Bee said, "and whoever wakes up first starts calling again."

"Everybody'll be asleep," Cricket said. "Nobody will hear us."

"Best time to raise an alarm, dead of night. You may sleep first, Cricket."

"No, you. I'll call a few more times."

"Well, keep it down. I can't sleep through all that racket."

"Keep it down? But—" Cricket didn't finish.

Bee curled up, as uncomfortable as she could remember being. "I'm grateful for having a roof," she murmured. "I'm grateful for being on the floor without having broken anything. I'll be even more grateful if somebody comes and lets us out of this miserable cave." When Cricket came to lie down and added her warmth, Bee remembered to be grateful for her sisters. It was a miracle they were all still alive. Lacewing, she hoped, was already home safe and warm.

Bee and Cricket had thought Lacewing might have come here for safety. She had run here before, long ago, inadvertently causing all the trouble. Shortly afterwards, their father had locked off the cave. Bee closed her eyes, wondering why their father had installed a gate that locked automatically from the outside.

Travis glanced up and down the riverbank. He saw nobody and turned to go, then caught a glimpse of ... No, it was only a shadow on a rock. The sound of rushing water covered anything that might have been moving around. No point in sticking around down here.

Back at the top of the road, he tried Sugar Agate's house again. The living room was perfectly neat, as always, although even Travis could detect a layer of dirt over everything. Sugar Agate tidied but she didn't clean. She waited for somebody to clean for her, and it didn't happen often. Travis had shown her early on that he wasn't going to be her slave like Trucker John and her other conquests.

One of her flowered quilts was smoothed over the bed, the oval rug centered beside it on the floor. Everything in place, everything pretty. Travis sat in the rocking armchair—also flowered, some kind of big yellow and white things—facing the door and rocked. He could live in this house very happily. Get rid of some of the girly stuff, maybe, but he didn't really mind it. He was sick and tired of shacks with holes in the walls, mice in the winter and spiders in the summer and other people all year long. This house, minus Sugar Agate, would be just right. Not too crowded, not too remote where you got nervous every time the sun went down. God, he missed California. He could live in a surf town, couldn't he? Be just another anonymous beach bum. Or get lost in Lost Angeles.

But they'd found him once. Just thinking about it made his testicles shrink. He'd had a headache for a month from the concussion, and peed blood. If he hadn't been so in shape from riding the board, not to mention so terrified, he never would have been able to sneak out of the warehouse. Jesus, he would have let them have their fucking dope if they'd asked, what was left of it. Their money, too. He didn't even mean to steal it, it just kind of happened. He hated cocaine, anyway. Not mellow at all. Took a dozen or two hits and started selling it off.

"Assholes," he said.

And now he was stuck living with a bunch of rednecks and weirdos in the fucking woods. The wet, dark, creepy, zombie-infested fucking woods.

Not that it was all bad. He had control of Hoochville now. And Rey and Sugar Agate were both good looking women. Rey was smarter, Sugar Agate was prettier. Rey was honest, a real girl scout; Sugar Agate would steal the teeth out of your head. Rey was generous, but she didn't have a lot to give away. Sugar Agate had this nice little house. Yes, Travis could see himself settling in here. Maybe Sugar Agate could move back to civilization. He'd convince her. *Why're you here living practically like an animal, a smart fox like you? You're wasting your time here,* he'd tell her. *Wasting your beauty years, your money years. Go find a rich old man, take you to South America, start over. I'll take care of the house in case you ever need to come back.*

Footsteps outside ended his daydream. Damn it, it was that Smokey guy. Travis went to the door.

"She ain't here, dude," he said.

"You ought to stick together," Smokey told him. Already issuing orders.

"Yeah, but she's not here. I was out looking around, there's nothing out there. You see anything?"

Smokey shook his head. "All quiet. When it starts getting dark, go home and lock your door. You have a lock on your door?"

"Yeah. No worries." You didn't operate a distillery and brewery and leave it unprotected, even on the mountain.

"So maybe we better look for Sugar Agate."

"I'll go. I was just seeing if she came back here." Travis stepped outside and closed the door behind him. He felt protective of the house. "You go ahead and make rounds. I'll find her. She's probably ... "

Smokey said, "What?"

In somebody else's house, borrowing their things, Travis was thinking. *All I have to do is see who's not home. That's where she'll be.*

"She's around." He pushed past Smokey, who smelled like a campfire and was surprisingly solid. He looked different, too. More human. A haircut? No beard, that was it.

"See ya."

"Yeah," Smokey said. "Take care, man."

No doubt. I'll take care of me, no worries.

But something had been bothering him. It was an unfamiliar feeling; not really a feeling, but a dissatisfaction. Like when he forgot something. As he wandered uphill, halfheartedly planning to look for Sugar Agate and Rey, the strange discomfort grew. The closer he got to Hoochville, the more uncomfortable it got.

Travis shook his head to get the strange sensation out, but it had already worked its way into his brain, sticky as a cobweb. The more he brushed at it, the more he knew what it was and the worse he felt.

He had to look after Hoot and Eddy. They needed him. He turned north for home.

Crap. This is what responsibility must feel like.

Jackie Tobasco and Fiddlin' Sue had started with mugs of blackberry tea, but quickly moved on to canned peach juice-and-moonshine cocktails. Berry sat with them in Sue's kitchen staring into her mug of tea. Nobody had discussed it, but it was understood that the revived probably should avoid alcohol. Misty was in the girls' bedroom reading poetry to Crystal, and Buck sat holding his guitar, tapping the strings at random times. It made a thin, hollow sound that twanged Sue's nerves.

"One of us ought to go get Mercy," Sue said.

"We got him tied up pretty good, but she shouldn't be alone with El Duane," Jackie agreed.

A few minutes and several swallows later, Sue said, "Well, we better go get her."

"Go get who?" Jackie asked.

"Mercy. Protect her from her dead relatives."

Jackie laughed. "Worse than in-laws."

Sue said, "I suppose we should brush our teeth before we breathe the devil's Kool-Aid on Mercy."

"Hell, no," Jackie said. "We'll take her a mug."

Jackie was more nervous than she let on. If Buck took a notion to do some damage, with his lizard brain or Olympic system or whatever in charge, she and Sue together would have their work cut out to stop him. Rey was right. They had to tie up the dead relatives, even Jacob and Crystal. Even Berry, as absurd as that was. Sweet Berry would never hurt a bug.

" 'I'll shut up my mug, If you pass me a jug Of that good ol' mountain dew,' " Sue sang.

"Jump in, Buck! Come on, baby," she urged. "Sing! I miss your sweet voice."

A gurgle of mud chugging down a sinkhole came out of her husband's throat. The gurgle turned into a howl that broke off into a phlegmmy rattle.

"Yay, Dad," Misty said quietly.

"Good, darlin'," Sue said, and didn't ask him to sing again.

15

Smokey made his third circuit of the village and surrounding mountainside. Passing the store again, he thought he saw movement behind the house and walked around to the back. "Bill? Mrs. Doller?" There was faint scrape of metal in dirt, the sound made by turning soil over with a shovel. This was a bad time to be gardening. It was too wet to dig, even in the river loam this far down the mountain, but people got anxious for fresh food and jumped the gun. It was a wasted effort. Gardens started in April, best case, or May.

The Dollers weren't in their garden. Sodden dirt clumps marked where someone had been digging; a muddy shovel lay across the back step. Clods of mud were strewn around a patch of soil the size of a sleeping bag. The gardener was using a lot of unnecessary effort, throwing heavy wet dirt around like that. Smokey shrugged. People gardened in their own unique ways. If the Dollers' way was the typical white man overkill approach, that was their business. He himself was a monoculturist, stingy with his materials and efforts. He had one cash crop, and one way of cultivating it. He tried knocking at the back door and sensed that someone was inside waiting for him to leave. He talked through the door, outlining the plan, and headed to the river again.

The light faded early on the east side of the mountain and Musket River was a shadow dividing a void, its surface catching cloud-colored highlights here and there. On the riverbank he felt freer, as if the current was scrubbing his insides, and at the same time confined, a thousand feet below the hundred-mile view from his home in the crags. Rey had invited him to spend the night at her place. He didn't think she meant anything other than spend the night. They'd started something once but it hadn't gone anywhere. He figured she didn't like the way he lived, and he didn't want to kindle a fire he couldn't stoke. They were both loners. She had some kind of thing with Travis, but she was too smart to take it seriously. And why shouldn't Rey enjoy a buff young guy? Smokey only saw her about twice a year, but she always seemed happy. Serious, but content and free. A real mountain girl.

Scanning the brush line, Smokey hummed a Grateful Dead medley and let the black river roll through him.

Birdie Doller stretched her arms out wide, extended one foot to each bottom corner of the bed, opened her mouth and yawned out loud. She had taken a long nap and used both pillows to do it. It was nice to lie in bed when you had the whole thing to yourself.

It was almost twilight. Time to get up and check the garden before dark. She slipped into Bill's boots and snapped her coat closed. The shovel was where she'd left it, dirt hardened onto it like concrete.

Who was that who'd called her name? The boy who lived around the mountain? Snoopy? Smokey the Bear, some silly name like that. The hippie who gave the village money every fall. He'd bought them a smokehouse last year, and tools like this ash-handled carbon steel shovel, $54.00 retail. She'd been afraid for a minute he was going to try to get in the house or poke around the garden, but he sensibly went on his way.

"Well," she said quietly. "I heard of crops growing fast, but this one's coming up a little too fast."

Birdie scraped around the arms and chest that had pushed up out of the dirt again. A knee had cropped up this time, too.

"Get back in there," she said. She pushed the arms down and heaved big clouts of sod over the torso. One hand flexed but she pushed it under the soil with her foot in her husband's heavy boot. She stood on lumps until they went flat.

"And stay buried, for cryin' out loud. Do you think I want to come out here and replant you two or three times a day for the rest of my life? Now good *night*."

For a dead man, her husband was entirely too frisky.

The clearing was empty except for a stray neuro-optic wire half-stamped into the ground litter. Rey wiped it off and coiled it into her pocket. If she hurried, she would have time to check on the Pear Sisters and Mercy before it was completely dark. Rey did not want to be out tonight in the dark. Not alone. Not at all.

Some kind of night bird cried, a chickadee or a sparrow. Good. More birds meant the mountain was healthy. Or not good. Birds were losing their habitats and taking refuge where they found room. She hoped somebody was studying that.

No one home at the Pear Sisters'. No lamplight in Sugar Agate's house. They must all be at Mercy's, having a wake for Earl.

But they weren't all at Mercy's house. The kids and some of the revived were crowded into Mercy's living room. Jackie T., Sue, and Mercy were in the kitchen cooking funeral food. Rey hung her jacket over the back of a chair and started washing pots. The house was warm and full of people. Lanterns lit the corners with a comforting yellow glow. If you waited a while, your nose got used to the dead-mouse funk emanating from the un-dead relatives.

Sue was setting a bowl of potatoes on the table when thudding and banging sounded outside. The women looked at each other, then at the kitchen door.

Splintering sounds.

Mercy said, "Don't let him get in!"

"The table," Rey said.

They each took a side and slid the laden table across the doorway.

"Is it El Duane?" Jackie asked.

"Who else would it be this time of night?" Mercy said.

"I thought he was tied up in the shed."

"It's him." Mercy's lips were so tight the words could barely get out of her mouth.

"It could be Joe Bear."

"It's not Joe Bear," Rey said. "He's too small to tear a shed apart."

"Or Trucker John."

"Or Dollar Bill."

"Or Birdie."

"It's not Birdie," Mercy said peevishly. "Making those noises? That's the shed being torn down." The crust in her voice sounded shaky even to her own ears. It was El Duane coming back for what was his. It was the curse of Cain, and she was Eve, Lilith, Salome, and the Whore of Babylon rolled into one big sinning troublemaker. It was too late to pray.

"Oh shit oh dear," Jackie said.

Rey hurried to the front door and waved everybody off the sofa. Misty and Liberty pulled inert Buck and Jacob off and helped Rey shove the sofa across the front door.

"What's out there?" Liberty's eyes were as big as teaspoons.

"Some kind of animal," Misty told her.

Rey said, "You kids make sure the windows are locked. Put something in front of them if you can, then stay in this room."

Misty said, "What about Dad and the rest of them? Are they going crazy, too?"

Freedom stuck her tongue out of side of her mouth and rolled her eyes. "I'm craaazy!"

"They're not crazy," Rey said. "But they are unpredictable."

Sue leaned against the kitchen table, staring at Mercy and Rey. "What do you think he wants?"

"In," said Mercy.

"Duh," said Jackie. "Why?"

Rey said, "We should have all followed the plan. Half of us are out there somewhere. Alone. We need to secure the revived people. Mercy, where's your rope?"

"On the porch."

"What do you have inside the house?"

Mercy had belts and suspenders and some pieces of brown twine and wire. They tied Buck, Jacob, Berry, and Crystal's wrists and put them in Jacob and Ezekiel's room. Sue stood at the bedroom door and apologized to the passive undead, urging them to be calm.

"Wish I'd brought my fiddle," she said. "Music soothes the savage beast."

"The savage breast." Rey added, "They're not beasts."

"I know," Sue said, "but some fiddling would soothe them anyway."

"It would pull my last nerve out by the roots," Jackie muttered.

Rey said, "I've got to find the Pears. And we need Smokey."

"We need everybody," Jackie said.

"Keep the house barricaded," Rey said. "I'm going to round the rest of us up. I don't like not knowing where everybody is."

"That's just dumb," Sue said. "You stay here. We need you, too. What we don't need is you getting clobbered by a crazy zombie."

Mercy gasped.

"You did not say that," Jackie said.

"Well, why not? It's what they are. Come on, I'm talking about my own husband and my daughter, too. What else do you want to call them?"

"The revived," Rey said. "Subjects. Victims. But I think maybe we're the victims."

"Consciousness-challenged," Jackie said.

Sue and Rey laughed.

"The dearly departed," Sue offered.

"The nearly departed," Rey countered.

"The dearly depart*ing*."

"The previously living," Jackie said. "Undead Americans."

"Stop it," Mercy told them.

"The Grateful Dead," Misty said.

"Satan's spawn," Mercy said, and fumed when everyone laughed. "I'm serious. It's not funny!"

"Oh, maybe just a little funny," Jackie said.

"Yeah, let's settle down," Sue said. "We don't want to rile up the spawn." She got a kerosene lantern from the living room and set it on the little desk in the boys' room.

"They like light," she announced. "Look, they're moving around a little. But it sure makes their eyes look funny. Glittery. Like marbles. Like a raccoon in the headlights."

The kitchen door thudded. Everybody jumped.

The doorjamb cracked, splintered, and the door bulged inward.

"Hold them off!" Rey said needlessly. The women were already rushing to push against the table. Against all their weight and muscle, the door slowly, jerkily, opened.

Jackie cursed loudly. Sue yelled at Misty to hide under the Alders' bed.

With a palpable crack, the door slammed open. Rey, Jackie, Sue, and Mercy were flung stumbling across the kitchen. They stared, their hearts stopping for an instant. Through the destroyed doorway lurched the massive, tattered shape not of El Duane, but Earl.

16

Mist crawled up from the bottom of Sock Creek Falls and searched like a wet gray ghost for warmth. Bee was sure she could feel her bones chattering. She backed into her sister, who always radiated heat. Cricket ran hot, Bee ran cold.

It was not a good idea to think about what the mist touched on its way up the chute. The fingers that felt Bee's face and slithered around the nape of her neck had touched things along its path that could give it no warmth. Not any more.

"Are you all right?" Cricket asked.

"Shh." *The ghost listened. It was best not to speak out loud.*

"You're cold," Cricket said. "We should be making noise, not being quiet."

"I'll go to the gate and call." Bee moved to get up.

"No, you stay here and keep warm."

"It's too late for that. I'm an icicle. I should move around."

Bee forced herself to straighten her knees and her back. Every vertebrae creaked and ached. She hobbled to the gate, feeling ancient. *Well, I am rather ancient. Eighty-four. No—eighty-seven. How the Sam Hill did that happen?*

She had to try twice to get any sound to come out. Deep in her lungs the gray mist had taken root. She coughed so hard she felt too weak to stand, but she hung onto the gate's bars and yelled.

Keeping her back to the chasm was frightening, but Cricket was here with her. "Help! In the cave!" she repeated, and repeated, and repeated.

⟡

Earl filled the doorway. Mercy shrank back behind the others.

"Oh, fuck," Jackie said. "He's alive!"

"He looks bigger," Rey said.

"But he still looks pretty dead," said Jackie.

Rey picked up a cast iron skillet from the stove. "Mercy, where's your shotgun?" she asked. There was no answer.

"Mercy?"

Earl loomed, leaning forward on the balls of his feet.

Rey heard the couch scraping the floor, Mercy gibbering orders to her kids, the front door opening. Sue said, "Mercy, no!"

Rey yelled, "Mercy! What are you doing? Don't go out there!"

But Mercy Alder and her three daughters were already out in the night.

"Oh, for shit's sake," Jackie said. Another big shape crowded in around Earl. "Earl must have untied El Duane. They're working together!"

⟡

Mercy carried Heaven on her right hip and Freedom on her left, dragging Liberty along by the hand. They veered off the road into the ditch once but Mercy stayed on her feet. Everything was dark. No lights shone from Sugar Agate's house, and Sugar Agate was never one to spare the kerosene. What was worse, the Pear Sisters' house was invisible. It wasn't even a darker shadow in the night. There should have been lamps in the front windows, or at least a gentle glow from the side bedrooms. As they neared the bend in the road, the house almost took form, but it was cold-looking and blind-eyed.

"Hurry. Get inside." Mercy set the little girls down with a push toward the dark porch. She looked down the road. No lights at all: not from Jackie Tobasco's trailer or the Dollers' store; no flickers through the trees in front of Trucker John's little trailer. The village might have vanished.

Mercy ran in and bolted the door. There were a lamp and matches on the table by the door. She pulled a quilt and blanket off a bed and made a pallet on the living room floor. When they were covered up together she blew out the light.

"Why are we sleeping here?" Freedom wasn't a whiner, since she wasn't allowed to be, but her voice was stressed.

"Shh. Whisper your prayers. No talking out loud."

Heaven said, "I want to go home."

"We will. Be very quiet."

"God can hear us," Liberty whispered.

"That's right."

> *If I should die before I wake*
> *I pray the Lord my soul to take.*

Mercy stared at the charcoal-on-black that was the front window and waited for Earl or El Duane to find them. Earl might spare his children, but they were El Duane's rival's offspring. Everybody knew what male animals did to their rivals' offspring.

"Find their guns!" Rey brandished the iron skillet in her left hand and pointed her revolver with her right. Sue came up with the shotgun and a deer rifle just as Earl and El Duane tossed the kitchen table across the room. Potatoes and green beans scattered.

"Mad, aren't they? Here!" Sue tossed the rifle to Jackie.

Jackie didn't take time to see if the rifle was loaded. She aimed at El Duane's ribs and pulled the trigger. The gun banged and jerked up. El Duane doubled over, then growled and started turning in circles, trying to see what had bit him.

The shotgun boomed and a bunch of holes bloomed in Earl's face and chest. It set him back but he didn't go down. Sue racked in another shell and shot him again.

Rey's .22 made a sound like a pea shooter, but the way her ears were ringing, she couldn't actually hear it. It didn't have much stopping power but it punched a neat hole in El Duane's face. When Trucker John had brought her the gun from town he'd said, "If you shoot somebody with this thing, don't let 'em know. It'll really piss 'em off." Proving him right, El Duane gave Rey a pissed off look and shuffled toward her.

"Get behind them," Rey ordered.

"Who?" Jackie said. "Me?"

"You. Be ready to go out the back door. Make noise. Call for help."

"They can hear us," Sue said. "You're telling them our strategy."

Rey fired again and popped a hole through Earl's sternum. She knew she couldn't count on another head shot, even at this close range. Earl swatted at his chest like he was after a fly.

Jackie sidled around the invaders, keeping the rifle trained on El Duane. "You got Earl in your sights?"

"Got him," Rey said, but the bullets were barely slowing him down. Jackie had to get out and get help. "Sue, get Misty and get out of the house."

"You can't hold them by yourself." Sue argued.

"Get your daughter and go." Rey gave her revolver to Sue and took the shotgun. "Go on. Get out!"

"Come with me."

"Okay. Right behind you."

Sue backed away across the living room and opened the bigger bedroom door, hissed at Misty to come out. "Get your sister and dad. Hurry."

Rey heard her. "No! Don't open that door!"

"I'm not going anywhere without my husband and both of my kids."

The shotgun boomed again and Earl staggered backwards. Rey pulled the trigger again—but he didn't fall down. She was out of shells.

She barely noticed the mammoth bell tolling in her skull, barely heard the rifle crack again. She shouted and felt the words in her head but couldn't hear them come out. "Run, Jackie!"

Earl tottered side to side, but El Duane slobbered unintelligibly and came toward her in low gear, slow but powerful. Rey's peripheral vision picked up Sue leading Buck, and Misty leading Crystal out the front door. Behind them, Berry dragged lopsidedly in wedding march-style, clawing at the gray skin filling the hole in her cheek. Jacob came into the living room, looked at his recently-dead father and uncle and emitted a cracked, adolescent groan.

Rey groaned, too. There was no way to keep these people together. Trying to corral them was like herding cats.

It was up to her. Jackie had to go for help. Mercy and Sue had families; Rey could hardly blame them for trying to keep their children safe. But big, sweet Buck might change into a monster like the Alder brothers. Moody Crystal might turn on her family. Sue's family was not safe. Mercy was so terrified she'd left two of her children—the revived Jacob and Ezekiel, who was unaccounted for, out patrolling the lonely forest.

Jacob was right behind her. Rey sidestepped. Earl and El Duane shifted their attention from Rey to the boy. Ezekiel scooted in the open door, said, "Where's—" and took in the situation.

"I'll get more guns." He ran to his parents' bedroom. Keeping low, Rey followed him and slammed the door. Ezekiel was disappearing under the bed.

"Time to go," Rey said.

Ezekiel handed out a sawed off single barrel shotgun. "Do you want this?"

"Yeah."

"The little one, too?"

Earl had some kind of arsenal under his bed, evidently. "Bring all you can carry. Let's go!"

A small rifle and a semiautomatic came out ahead of Ezekiel. Rey grabbed the bigger weapons and hustled Ezekiel into the living room, praying they'd slip under the attackers' radar.

No such luck. Father, brother, and son loomed in the path to the front door. Rey wondered if Ezekiel could shoot his relatives if he had to. Looking at their ravaged flesh and opaque eyes, she had no qualms about doing the shooting herself. She shoved the semiautomatic at the boy and raised the sawed off and fired straight at Earl. Having been pretty well ventilated and killed twice already, she thought he would be the easiest to take down.

A spray of pellets disintegrated Earl's face and chest. He slowly folded and sat straight-legged on the floor. El Duane and Jacob looked down at him, then back at Rey's gun.

She said, "EZ. Are there guns in your room?"

"I don't think so."

"You okay?"

"Yeah."

"Move!" Rey motioned to the two left standing with the barrel toward the boys' bedroom

They swayed a little, eyeing her.

"Kitchen," she said quietly to Ezekiel. "Aim high."

Ezekiel sidled across the room and stopped in the kitchen doorway. Rey bent her knees, keeping low, and shot El Duane in the chest. The big bell in her head tolled again. The man sucked air, leaked blackish blood

"Aim for his shoulder blades," she said. "Shoot."

Nothing happened.

"Now!"

A burst of fire from the semi pushed El Duane forward and to his knees. He looked as if he were praying, receiving a revelation. When Rey glanced at Earl, the bullet and pellet holes were already puckering together.

"Help me," she said, and Ezekiel, with a sidelong look at Jacob, took his father's feet and helped drag him into his bedroom. They dragged El Duane in after him. Jacob grunted and struggled, but he was still weak. Whatever was causing that weapons-grade power in the men hadn't kicked in yet in the boy. They tied hands and feet, winding rope tight around the bed frame. Rey envisioned the three angry undead males, with the bed still attached, ripping through the wall and lumbering up the road. "Tighter," she said.

17

Armed to the armpits, Rey and Ezekiel peered out the front door. The sound of violins wafted from the Hills' house. "I think they're all right for now," Rey said. "We've got to find your mom. And then I'll look for Smokey and Travis. We've got to get back together. Splintered apart like this ... "

"United we stand," Ezekiel said. "Divided we fall."

"We won't fall. You sure you're all right?"

"I'm cool."

They moved quietly to the bend in the road, where the shell and pebble path to Sugar Agate's door reflected cloud light. Rey crunched along it while Ezekiel kept a lookout. Rey opened the door. "Sugar Agate? Anybody home?"

When there was no answer, she said, mad that she had to say it, "Travis, are you here?"

They had to still be out patrolling, just what they were supposed to be doing—although Rey wouldn't put it past Sugar Agate, or even Travis, to play possum. She crossed the front room, its white-painted walls relieving the gloom a little, and into the bedroom. Empty.

When she turned to go, Rey ran her knee into the sharp corner of the armoire door. It swung open. Sugar Agate's white leather Plains Indian dress, fringed and beaded and as unsuitable for the rainforest as a garment could possibly be, spilled out of the armoire. Rey sucked air in and rubbed her knee. There would be a knot there tomorrow. She slammed the door shut but it bounced back, blocked by the bulky white leather spilling out of the cupboard, and by the body inside it.

Ezekiel was on the path, halfway to the door. When Rey came out, he walked confidently to the road, a scared kid acting brave who'd had to shoot his uncle and had watched Rey shoot his father with two different guns. He seemed to be holding up pretty well. Rey wondered how much more he could take.

"Nobody home?" Ezekiel asked.

"Nobody home. No one at all."

"Who's there?"

"Rey and Ezekiel."

"Are you alone?" Mercy kept her voice small.

"Just us."

The door opened. Mercy pulled Ezekiel into the Pear Sisters' living room and relocked the door. Rey filled her in on what had happened and didn't say a word about Mercy running off on her own or about how they should stick together.

"If any of them try to break in here, I've got guns," Ezekiel said.

"I should hope so," his mother said. Her voice softened. "You're the man of the family now, son. The only man I have left."

"Do you have a flashlight?" Rey asked.

"I didn't bring one, but I expect they've got one around here. It's not safe to show a light, though. There are more out there. And they're all getting riled up, aren't they? Coming to life. Life in death. No, death in life. Satan's alive and he walks this mountain."

"Stay calm, Mercy. I'll look for a flashlight and take it with me. I've got to find Travis."

Ezekiel said, "But you aren't supposed to go out alone."

"I'll be all right. I've got the shotgun and my handgun." To Mercy, she said, "Help me find the light and some shells."

Mercy left Ezekiel to guard the girls. Ezekiel and Freedom whispered together, Ezekiel with the drawl of a guy who'd been through the wars, Freedom all shocked and excited. Rey found a flashlight and Mercy came up with a box of shotgun shells. Rey loaded the shotgun and her pockets and slipped out the back door.

With no idea of where to look for Smokey, she turned uphill toward her own house to check on the animals and see if Travis was waiting there. Obviously he was not patrolling with Sugar Agate. No doubt Travis and Smokey were a mile apart. Nobody stuck together when the chips were down.

Jackie Tobasco shouted. Nobody answered. Where exactly was she supposed to go for help? For large animal trouble, she would go to Earl and El Duane or Trucker John. For personal problems, she'd go to Rey. When people in the village acted like assholes, she went to Bee. Where to go for zombie issues, she had no idea.

She heard more gunfire and her legs jellified. They wouldn't shoot Berry, would they? Berry wasn't agitated and dangerous. She was as sweet in half-life as she was before. As mellow now as the day they'd met on the island, Berry all milky brown and Jackie toasted by the subtropical sun, half delirious on warmth and rum and new love. Why Berry had loved her, Jackie couldn't understand. Loved her enough to run away to the cold, dark north woods, and stay. And now this. It was Jackie's own fault.

Running and stumbling toward home, the thought occurred to her that where Berry was from, this kind of thing was almost a tradition. Bringing the dead back to life, sometimes after killing them for just that purpose. It was too ironic: Berry might be the only person here who knew what to do about all these half-dead people, but being half-dead herself, she couldn't do a damn thing about it.

It felt like ages since Jackie had woken up to an empty trailer and the sound of gunfire, and now it was déjà vu all over again. She threw her and Berry's things together into a cloth sack, grabbed the railroad lantern, and went outside again. The gunfire had stopped. Jackie had promised 'til death them did part; now she couldn't tell if death had parted them or not. But the bottom line was, as long as Berry walked and breathed, however funkily, Jackie wasn't giving up on her.

The pleasure of seeing a light on in her house hit Rey hard. She had to swallow a lump in her throat and tell herself not to blubber. *Travis. Light. Safety, maybe. Home.* After all that darkness and all that violence, those four things lit her up inside.

But the door opened not on Travis, but Smokey. The smell of hot food and damp clothes filled the cabin, spiced up by Smokey's sour-but-clean woodsmoke odor.

"Two guns," Smokey observed. "What have you been doing?"

"Didn't you hear the gunfire?"

"Hard to miss. Who got shot?"

Rey leaned the shotgun against the wall, dropped her revolver back in her pocket, and sank onto the bed. "People who were dead enough to know better."

"Zombie battle, huh?"

"We won. For now. Until they untie themselves again. They're getting agitated. If I can't figure out a cure, we're in for serious trouble."

Smokey busied himself with cigarette paper and strands of tightly packed tobacco. "Hungry?"

"I will be. I just want to rest up for a minute."

"Smoke?"

"Pass."

"Mind if I do?"

"It's a free country."

"For a while, anyway." He torched the cigarette. Sweet fumes got in Rey's nose and made her sneeze.

They sat in silence for a few minutes. The ringing in Rey's ears had subsided enough that she heard the low crackle of the fire in the stove and Smokey's lazy inhalations. Smokey offered her the cigarette again, took a long pull after she refused, and tossed the butt into the fire.

"So how're you doing?"

"I'm a little buzzed. Second-hand smoke."

"It'll relax you."

"No, it makes me hyper and paranoid. Which might be a good thing, actually. Why are you here, anyway? I thought you and Travis and Sugar Agate—" Rey stumbled over the name. "—were out patrolling together."

"Sugar Agate never showed. When I went to see about her I ran into Travis. He went off to patrol between your place and Joe Bear's and Hoochville. I walked around a lot and then I heard all the shooting. Fiddlin' Sue said you were probably out looking for the old women."

"Did you check on the people at the Alders'?"

"I had a look-see. Quiet as lambs."

"The gunfire might have agitated them." Rey got up, stretched, broke open the shotgun and revolver, snapped them shut. "Let's go. Too many people are unaccounted for."

"Eat first. It's soup."

Adrenaline made her far from hungry, but Rey swallowed half the soup in the pan. It would do for food and water both. Smokey ate the other half, poured an inch of water in the pan and sloshed it around.

He picked up Rey's big flashlight. "I've got a little one here," he said, patting his vest pocket. Rey took her solar light, which gave off light as weak as the sun that tried to charge it. She took her own .30-.30 and loaded revolver and let Smokey carry the shotgun.

"Don't shoot it close to my ear," she said. "I've been deaf once already tonight."

They started toward the Alders' house to get a good look at what the zombies were up to.

Smokey said, "Zombies? That's what we're calling them now?"

"It has a certain ring to it, doesn't it?"

"I'm glad we can be casual about it. You know, without the scientific politically correct jargon. Makes it easier."

"Nothing about this is easy," Rey said gloomily.

She led the way into the Alders' house and to the boys' bedroom door. Smokey pressed his ear against it, looked at Rey and shook his head.

"Must be asleep," he half-whispered.

"Stay low and cover me." Rey put her hand on the doorknob, then a thought occurred to her. "Do you know how to use a gun?"

"Yes, ma'am, I believe I can manage."

"Huh." She looked at him for a moment and felt her lips lift in a slight smile. Then she opened the door, revolver at the ready.

Inside, Berry's slender form was turned away toward the window. The three males slouched on a bed together. Their unblinking eyes shone like motor oil in the flashlight beams. Rey stepped in and checked the ropes while Smokey pointed the shotgun.

"All secure, I think." Rey was glad to back out of the room. Even tied up, the revived gave her the creeps.

Smokey made sneaking-up surveillance signs with his fingers. Rey didn't understand them, but covered him while he double-checked. He tested the bed frames, which she hadn't done, to see if they'd been broken or chewed through. Then he said, "You folks have a nice night," and closed the door behind him.

They sat on the sofa, slanted across the middle of the room, facing the bedroom.

"So you think you can cure them?" Smokey asked.

"I screwed them up, I ought to fix them."

"Do you know how yet?"

"Not without a test subject. But it is clear that much additional work will be required before a complete understanding of this phenomenon occurs."

"That's a mouthful."

"It means, I hope somebody else figures it out, because I have no clue."

Smokey said, "I had an idea. You've probably already thought of it." He waited.

"Go."

"Well, some forms of THC impair visuospatial working memory, but mainly in infrequent marijuana smokers: if you smoked a handful of times in your life, or even up to several times a week, but not daily. And that's crucial.

"You know pot causes changes in mood and cardiovascular function, right? And those changes are concentration-dependent?"

"Sure." Rey unknitted her forehead and closed her mouth. "The more you use, the more stoned you get. And may I say I'm impressed by your academic science-babble."

"Thank you. The upshot is," Smokey went on, "cannabinoids slow you down and fuzz your focus. Common knowledge. And they erase bad memories. Good ones, too, of course, but very useful if you want to lose traumatic events and the learned responses that make you unhappy and angry. Like our friends in there. The beauty part is, it has those effects on people who don't smoke much. For your professional-grade smoker, no side effects at all."

"You astound me, sir."

"Me, too." Smokey pulled a small bag out of his shirt pocket. "I'm just a dabbler now. Once research was my work. Now I'm on the fieldwork level. But you gotta keep up."

"Yes, I know."

"Yes, you do." He was rolling another lumpy cigarette. "So what I'm proposing is, I'll go sit with our neighbors in there for a little while, and they'll slow down and mellow out and forget to be angry, and their heart rates will slow, and they'll get kind of fuzzy around the edges and not have very good aim. Meanwhile, I'll be the same as I always am. Then you and I can go take care of business without worrying about these guys."

"Secondhand smoke?"

"You got it."

"Well ... how long will it last?"

"On your average first-time user, a few hours at most. On this crew, who knows? It might not have any effect at all. Or it might be a permanent change. When you get your subject to experiment on, you can run some studies."

Rey shook her head. *Curiouser and curiouser.* "Might as well."

Smokey rolled up more fat cigarettes and lined them up like soldiers in his chest pocket. "Care to join us?"

"I'll wait here. Somebody's got to keep watch."

Smokey nodded and headed toward the bedroom.

"Smokey?"

"Yeah."

"You're not going to get all messed up, right? I need you compos mentis."

"Don't worry. My mentis is going to get more and more compos." He shot his cuffs, did some neck stretches, gave her a jaunty wave, and went into the bedroom.

Time passed. The sweet smell of burning weeds leaked through the walls. Rey wondered if the revived would react the way she did to the herb: hyper, paranoid, skittery. Too late to wonder now.

18

ricket sat straight up and instantly regretted it. Her spine felt fused and her hips were concrete blocks.

"We've been doing it wrong," she said, knowing Bee would hear even if she were asleep.

"What?"

They were huddled together again. Cricket didn't like the croak in Bee's voice. They all thought of themselves as hardy women, inured to discomfort and able to take a punch from nature. But eighty-eight wasn't forty-eight. Bee was getting sick. Pneumonia required a trip to the hospital, and that would open them up to questions from the outside. *Why didn't she have Medicare?* They'd want to set up a billing plan. *What, none of them had Social Security numbers?* That's how it would start. And if she couldn't keep her sister warm, that might be how it would end. Cricket held her tighter.

"We've been saying *Help, In the cave.* We should have been saying *Woo!* Our call. Woo!"

"Woo," Bee wheezed. "I'll start now." She flexed her knees and bit back a groan.

"No. I'm going."

"But it's my turn. Don't baby me. I'm not senile nor am I a helpless dodderer. Let go!"

"Bee, so help me, I'll tie you up with your own pants if you don't lie down. I mean it, I will."

"I know you will, you little pest. You did it before. I'm telling Daddy. He said you're supposed to mind me."

Cricket tucked her coat around and under Bee's shoulders. "I apologize. You're the boss, Bee."

"Glad to hear you admit it. I'll put in a good word for you before your spanking."

Something was wrong for sure. One cold night shouldn't make Bee delirious. She was tough, the toughest of them all. Bee didn't lose her head over anything.

Cricket stood at the gate with her hands under her armpits. She was glad she hadn't lost that thirty pounds. It was keeping her warm now. She wished she could give that thirty-pound lump of warm fat to Bee.

She opened her mouth wide and bellowed from her diaphragm.

"Whooo!

"WhoOO!

"WHOOO!"

"Listen," Rey said.

Smokey stopped and looked around.

"No, I mean I'm going to say something. I forgot."

They were approaching Sugar Agate's house from the back. The undead were nicely toasted and resting comfortably in their hazy bedroom. Smokey estimated the fumes would keep them happy for the rest of the night.

"Short-term memory deficit already? You said you weren't going to inhale," he said. "You're not going to get all paranoid now, are you?"

"I'm not paranoid. The woods really are full of crazed zombies. This is about Sugar Agate."

"Shoot."

"Sugar Agate ... I found her."

"Good. Can she handle a gun? Does she have one?"

"I don't think so. If she had, maybe she wouldn't be in her armoire, dead."

"Wow. When?"

"Just before I went home. I didn't want to say anything at first. It was too weird. I thought I'd just wait a minute and rest, but then we had to check on the revived, and it took you a while to, uh, sedate them. I didn't want to talk about it."

"A perfectly natural reaction. Do you think we should go and look at her?"

Rey wanted nothing less, but she said, "I guess we should." Somebody besides herself needed to see the body. Rey wasn't sure why, but she was sure that was true.

Sugar Agate was still there, still dead. Still beautiful and vacant and serene.

"There's no blood. She doesn't look banged up," Smokey observed.

"How do you think she died?"

"We'll have to examine her to tell that."

"I don't think we should take the time now," Rey said. "But maybe we ought to close the armoire door, if it'll close."

They pushed, Smokey readjusted Sugar Agate's cold and stiffening arm and leg, and shut her inside, safe from—what?

"Bummer," said Smokey.

"Yes."

"I wonder what happened."

Rey said, "I don't know. Who would do this?"

"A zombie?"

"She'd be torn up, wouldn't she? And would one of those zombies fold her up neatly and put her in her closet after he was done?"

"Well, as you said, we don't have time for it now. She'll keep."

They crossed the road. Rey asked, "What do you suppose would have happened if Earl and El Duane had gotten hold of one of us? We don't know they were going to kill us."

"Yeah, maybe they just wanted a hug."

"We don't know anything about them, actually. What they want, what they feel. What they're capable of."

"I'm happy not knowing. Oh, purely academically it'd be nice to know. But I'm not up for any primary research at the moment."

"I need a subject."

"You need two. One zombie, and one zombie victim. Hey, maybe we'll get some volunteers. For the cause, you know? Because Cannibalites are so socially responsible and group-minded."

Rey shot him a sour look, but it was too dark for him to see it. He must have felt it, though, because he said, "I kid. I'm one too." And in a spooky voice, "I'm one of youuuu. One of youuu!"

"Shush. You're going to scare the hell out of Mercy and the girls."

The female Alders and Ezekiel were all right, still huddled in the quilts in the dark. When Rey went out the door again, Ezekiel came close and whispered with urgency, "I'm coming, too."

"You need to stay with your family."

"They're fine," he hissed. "I want to patrol with you and Smokey."

"Next round, pardner," Smokey told him. "Hold the fort here for awhile."

Leaving Ezekiel frustrated with the females of his family, Smokey said, "Poor kid. Tough age."

"It's good for him to be needed, though."

"They don't really need him. They can work and hunt and defend themselves. Or Mercy can, anyway. He's got nothing going here."

"EZ's destined for bigger things," Rey said. "Just ask him. He'll tell you."

Mercy's back door was propped against the splintered frame. Jackie Tobasco inched up the lantern wick and picked her way through the mess in the kitchen. In the living room, blood and gore spattered the walls and pooled on the floor, but there were no bodies, living, dead, or in-between. Something smelled vaguely familiar, more pungent than blood or gunpowder. She listened. Shadows could be hiding awful things.

Mercy's bedroom was empty. Slowly, Jackie tried the knob on the other door. It turned but didn't open.

Locked. From the inside or outside?

"Berry?" she said quietly. "Berry dear?"

Was there a rustling, a creaking of old bedsprings?

"Berry!" she stage-whispered.

Getting no answer, Jackie went out the front door and sidled to the bedroom window. Darkness inside matched the darkness outside. When she raised the lantern, she saw a face—only her own rippled reflection in the glass. Jackie dug her fingernails under the window casing and pushed up, snapping a red nail she'd been cultivating for months. She ignored it and stuck her head inside the bedroom. The smell hit her: burning weeds and rotting clothes, snakes and mice, wet dirt.

"Berry! I've come for you. Where are you?"

In the yellow lantern light, eyes appeared, popping open in the dark like dull brass buttons. Jackie spied Berry, small and dark, closest to the window. With a cry, Jackie crawled inside and worked on the knots binding Berry's wrists and ankles.

"Who in the hell tied these? Hercules? Hold on, I'm getting a knife. First thing, a nice bath. Then we're getting away from here, my little blackberry. Someplace clean and warm." She talked soothingly as she sawed through the ropes around Berry's wrists. It was tight sisal that resisted the blade, and when she cut through the last fiber the blade jumped forward and nicked Jackie's thumb. Blood trickled onto the floor. Berry turned her head to look at it; the others started sniffing and shuffling their bound feet.

Jackie heard it, felt it, and kept cutting. She got Berry's ankles free of the bed frame and hauled her to her feet. "Come on, baby. You're free. I'll take you home."

Berry stood rooted to the floor.

"Real home. We'll go back to your island. Would you like that? Warm sunshine, rum and pineapple juice on the beach, long swims in the ocean."

Berry eyed Jackie blankly. Only it wasn't a blank stare, Jackie saw, more of an appraising, noncommittal gaze, as if she were waiting for something, or figuring something out.

"I shouldn't have kept you here. I admit it. I was so afraid for you, darlin'. You were into such scary things, you remember, and the scary people who followed you, I don't know what they were going to do to you. To us. But you won't do business with them again, not this time. You won't have to. I'll work, I'll take care of you. I can do hair and all like that. Come *on*, Berry!"

With a steady tug, Jackie pulled Berry to and through the window. They were fifteen feet up the road before Jackie said, "Oh, I guess I better close up. Keep those other ones in." She turned back, but Berry picked up speed, stumbling but making good time toward the bend in the road. Jackie ran after her.

"I don't want to get close to Trucker John again," Rey said, "but he's made himself scarce. We need to know his status."

"Bad guy?"

"Dead guy. More than that is anybody's guess."

"Why's that?" Smokey said.

"I get a bad feeling from him. He lurks. He looms. He glowers."

"Very disturbing," Smokey agreed.

The door of the decrepit trailer hung open, the bottom hinge torn off. Wisps of ancient insulation melted against the ripped aluminum siding. John didn't answer, and when Smokey and

Rey—she stuck close to him—did a walk-around, there was no sign of him.

No one's been taking care of him. Damn it, I should have helped him. I don't know why I didn't."

Smokey said, "You're afraid of him. If you're afraid, there's probably a good reason. Anyway, you aren't the only person responsible for him. He's got closer neighbors, and an ex-wife." He corrected himself. "Not anymore, though, I guess."

They pushed through the undergrowth behind the trailer, heading loosely uphill to intersect with the trail to Hoochville. Milky moonlight hinted at obstacles in the spaces between fir trees. Smokey walked behind, his flashlight lighting ten feet or so in front of Rey.

"Would Trucker John have any reason to kill Sugar Agate?" Smokey asked.

Good question. "That's something we're going to have to figure out. Once we get everybody secured and fixed up—well, I'm not sure. Bee'll have something to say about how to proceed. But we ought to be taking notes now, getting clues. So we don't forget anything."

"Apply a little method," Smokey said.

"Yeah. Priorities, though. There's not much investigating we can do while we're under attack."

"She broke his heart, didn't she?"

"He doesn't show much."

"The quiet type."

"Hence the lurking and looming." Rey stopped. "There's that bird again."

Smokey listened. "Where?"

"It's a whippoorwill, I think."

The call came again.

"That's no bird," Smokey said. "That's somebody using your call. The one you use when you need the trolley sent across the river."

Wooo. It was very faint, and had a raspy echo that made Rey turn around and step closer to Smokey.

"It's a human," she whispered. "I've been hearing it all night. But it's not coming from across the river. Or is it? I can't tell. My hearing's still messed up from the shooting."

"This way." Smokey stepped around her and made his way through the bushes.

"Are you sure we should go after it? What if it's ... "

"Bad guys? Calling to each other?"

"In code."

Smokey said softly, "Doubtful. But could be, so stay quiet. Step where I step."

The call rose and fell. "It sounds like it's coming from the bottom of a well," Smokey said.

"There aren't any wells up here. Oh, my god. I know where it is. It has to be in the cave." She steered them toward the clearing, skirted to the right of it, and clambered over fallen logs and around wet pits where storms had torn twelve-foot-high root fans from the ground.

"Isn't there a trail?" Smokey whispered.

"We're sneaking up on it."

The call floated through the air again, very close this time, then faded into eerie echoes.

Rey hunched down on her heels and Smokey did the same. When the call sounded again, raspier than before, Rey cupped her hands to her mouth and answered.

"Wooo!"

There was silence, then a louder Wooo! and a rapid string of words.

"We're here! In the cave! Hellooo! Help!"

"It sounds like Cricket!" Rey stood up and called, "It's Rey! We're coming!"

Branches slapped her in the face and snagged her coat. She would have missed the cave entrance, so artfully hidden was it behind drooping branches and screens of wild rhododendron, but Cricket called to them and Rey led Smokey in. The flashlight illuminated Cricket's form clutching the bars across the cave—bars that had not opened since Rey had been on the mountain, or ever, as far as she knew.

"Cricket! How did you get in there?"

"Watch where you're walking. The key's right there."

Rey took the flashlight and shone it around the ground. "You're locked in? How did that come about?"

A voice husked from the black interior. "Lacewing. Is that you?"

Rey looked at Cricket, aghast. "Is that Bee?"

Cricket nodded. "Hurry with that key. It's right under your feet. Don't kick it!"

"She sounds terrible. How long have you two been in there?"

"All afternoon. All night. We're cold. Bee's sick."

Bee coughed, a phlegmmy rattle that presaged respiratory failure. Rey got on her hands and knees and methodically patted every inch of the ground. Smokey picked at the lock with his multi-tool, then muscled the gate, but it wasn't budging. Rey unsnapped her coat and pushed it through the bars. Smokey handed his in, too, and his hooded sweatshirt.

"Go keep yourselves warm," Rey said. "Are you sure the key's here? We can go back and get tools to break the lock."

"It's there," Cricket said, her voice muffled as she wrapped Bee and then herself in the coats. "We almost had it a couple of times, but the rotten thing kept just out of reach. It's got a mind of its own, I swear. Do you have any water?"

"Sorry," Smokey said. "Hold on, ladies."

"Who is that?" Bee wheezed.

"The young man who lives across the mountain. Skippy something," Cricket said.

"Bee Pear, meet Smokey," Rey said. "Cricket Pear, Smokey. Sorry, I don't know your last name, Smokey."

"Good to meet you," he said. "Not under these circumstances, though."

"Are you going to get us out of here? We're very cold and my sister needs medical attention," Cricket said.

"Yes, we must ask you to hurry the hell up," Bee said. Cricket made a small shocked sound.

"You see," she whispered. "She's not herself."

"No problem. Rey, I'm going to go get a hammer and chisel."

"Right. I'll stay here." She kept patting the ground.

"In the little room off the kitchen," Cricket told him. "There are all manner of tools. Bring some water, too."

19

"What is that woman doing?" Jackie looked out the bathroom window into the Dollars' back yard. She was in a hurry to get away, but couldn't stand the stink emanating from the love of her life, and she was tired of trying to make Berry take a shower. She recognized Birdie Dollar's shape in the spotty moonlight.

"Digging again. At night? Come on, Birdie. Take a pill, brew some valerian tea, have some sex. Night gardening! 'Course, she could be digging night crawlers, but I've never seen her pick up a fishing pole." She looked again at Berry, who was naked and army green and not shivering at all.

"That's a lot of night action for somebody who's not even a zombie. Excuse me, honey, I mean a member of the revived juju sisterhood."

"Oo," said Berry.

Startled, Jackie said, "What?"

"Oo Oong."

"You're talkin'! Bless your heart. We're gonna be all right."

"Ooo Ooon."

"I will have to say you could use a little toothbrush action, especially if you're going to be saying things. You can brush 'em in the shower, how about?"

Jackie caught a last glimpse of her downhill neighbor working hard with an axe, chopping through roots it looked like. Jackie could hear the soft, squishy thuds of the blade. She turned her attention back to Berry.

"We've got to get the fuck off this mountain, baby doll. The whole place and all the people in it are going to blow to kingdom come, I don't know how, but it's all coming apart. You don't have to call a California Psychic to see the future here."

"It's Smokey. I need to get tools." He spoke before he knocked so as not to freak Mercy out, but got no response.

Mercy didn't like him. Didn't like his business, more specifically. Smokey got the impression there was a lot Mercy didn't approve of. She took his contributions easy enough—a solar generator, a smokehouse, tools. Now she didn't want to let him in to use tools he himself had probably bought and carried up the mountain. But if Mercy wouldn't let him in, the boy Ezekiel ought to. The kid liked him.

Smokey thought he heard rustling inside, but it could have been the wind. Maybe they couldn't hear him. The walls were thick, squared-off logs milled from probably three-hundred-year-old trees. He knocked some more, trying not to sound like a zombie at the door.

The doors were locked. *Great.* Now he had to worry about this bunch and the trapped Pear women, both.

Flashlight off, he traveled low and serpentine down the road to the Alders' house. Old habits. Good ones, too. There was something very creepy in the village, creepier than captive zombies and frightened women and children. Whatever the guys who'd started all this by getting shot up had been fighting, Smokey was feeling it.

The Alders' door was locked, the way he and Rey had left it. In the near-total darkness, it was only the familiar odor that clued him in that the window was open. Smokey played his light around the room, spotlighting tangles of rope and a dismantled bed frame.

Rey backed closer to the cave mouth and started feeling the ground again. Cricket's lantern was bright enough to light up anything metal, but there were only rocks, digging into Rey's knees.

"It's got to be there," Cricket insisted.

"Are you sure you didn't drag it to your side accidentally?"

"God, I hope not." Cricket felt around on the inside of the gate. "I'd die of feeling like a fool instead of from cold."

"It's only about forty," Rey said. "I mean, it's cold, but—"

"Wait 'til you're seventy-five and see how cold forty is."

"Right." Rey straightened her back, wondering how much worse her lumbar spine would get in thirty or forty years. "How did you get locked in the cave?"

"We were looking for Lacewing."

"She never came back?"

"Never hasn't happened yet."

"I mean—"

Cricket went on. "She's been known to come here, and I'm pretty sure she has a key of her own. I didn't want to come inside, but Bee did and I couldn't stay out and let her go in alone. This isn't a place you want to be alone. And Bee dropped the key."

"Did you check her pockets?"

"First thing I thought of."

Rey got on her hands and knees again. "Why would Lacewing come here?"

"Our little sister couldn't stay away. She got spanked for coming in here, but only when we told on her. She wanted to see what was down there. 'Old bones and monsters to eat you up,' we told her. I mean, we could not make up gruesome-enough stories to keep her away from The Crack. And then when ... well, she never grew out of it."

"I never heard the cave called The Crack."

"The crack in the ground. The Crack. Not everybody knows about it. Grandma said it fell straight to Hell, but of course it does no such thing. It's plenty deep, though."

"What's down there?"

"Nothing good."

Rey asked, "Has anyone gone down it?"

"Oh, yes. Several people."

"And what did they find?"

Cricket paused. "I don't know. Any luck with that key?"

"Did something happen here? What made her so fixated on it?" Cricket was either dropping hints or didn't realize how tantalizing a mystery she was spinning.

Cricket sighed. "Old-fashioned people, old-fashioned problems. Lacewing was disappointed in love. Every bit of it her own foolish-ness, but it hurt her just as badly as if she hadn't been a young idiot. There was a flap and a to-do, and the whole mess ended here. She never forgot."

"So the cave wasn't blocked off back then."

"Daddy saw to that. He took care of everything."

"To keep Lacewing out."

Cricket didn't answer.

A faint rustling, a snapping twig about fifty yards off, then quiet.

"It's just a critter," Cricket said.

"Shh." The sound had a deliberate quality a raccoon couldn't achieve. It wasn't Smokey. He wouldn't scare them like that. Rey gripped the butt of her revolver.

"Douse the light."

Cricket blew the light out and the outside world turned a paler shade of black.

A man-sized shape rushed across the cave mouth in two long strides. By the time Rey touched the grip of her pistol, the man was breaking trail uphill.

She shrank back against the gate and made herself breathe from her belly. It might be a poacher, or ATF, after Hoochville. DEA. It might be any of the agencies and individual crazies people here were hiding from. There was an off-chance it was Travis, finally patrolling the woods, although it was more likely Travis was home, alone this time, in bed.

"I couldn't see him," Cricket whispered. "He was fast."

"Not one of the revived."

"Are you armed?"

Rey nodded.

Cricket whispered, "You go. Run. We're safe in here."

Rey considered it. Running would feel good. Cowering with her back against a rock wall felt terrible. She said, "No, I won't leave you alone."

"They can't get us in here. Even if they got in, we've got a trick or two up our sleeves. Run while you've got a chance." When Rey didn't move, Cricket hit her with a pebble. "Idiot. Go!"

Smokey reconned the area around the Alders' house, then moved cautiously through the trees and rough pasture to the Hills'. Soft guitar chords accompanied a violin, the music plaintive and lonesome in the big quiet of the mountains. He could feel the Coast Range rolling west to east, south to north like massive Pacific swells, swallowing spots of light and music.

When Sue came to the door he had the impression she wanted to get rid of him quickly.

"We're fine," she said. "Don't worry about Buck or Crystal."

He hadn't asked about them, but she'd brought it up. "Are they restless? Agitated?"

"They're peaceful and relaxed, just like always. Well, Crystal's a handful. Not real relaxed. But my husband and girl aren't going on the attack."

"What's your plan for if they do?" Smokey insisted.

"They won't."

"But if they—"

"We're fine. The family is fine. We're going to bed now." She shut the door, not fast but firmly.

"Wait." He hadn't heard her walk away. "I came to borrow some tools."

After a moment, Sue opened up again. Smokey told her about the Pear Sisters locked in the cave. Sue came out and showed him the shed where the tools were standing in buckets of oiled sand. He took a hammer and chisel and an awl and jogged off.

The next one crashed boldly through the brush, making no attempt at stealth. Rey steadied the gun, aiming for body mass. As she put her finger on the trigger, he said, "Rey?"

"Who's there?"

"Smokey. Don't shoot me."

"Okay." She lowered the gun.

He eyed it, checked her face, then turned the light onto the gate lock. "Trouble?"

"A man ran by here. I don't think he saw us. He might be close by."

"Give me a minute and I'll have the ladies out of there."

The hammering of steel on iron was loud enough to alert anyone on the mountain to their presence, but in a few blows the lock gave way. Cricket went ahead with the light while Smokey and Rey carried Bee.

When they set Bee onto her feet in her home, she took one look at her living room and said, "Why is Mercy and all her begats all over my floor?"

"I'll explain it later," Rey said. "Rest first."

They got Bee and Cricket, who was more exhausted than she let on, into bed with hot food and warm blankets. Mercy sat up watching the elder women; Ezekiel was appointed babysitter again, about which he didn't hide his frustration. He grumbled until Smokey pointed out that one great measure of a man's worth was how well he protected his sisters, whether they were blood relations or not.

Smokey made another of those signals to Rey and she followed him to the porch.

"The zombies got loose," he told her. "The window was open, their ropes were cut, and they're gone."

"Shit," said Rey.

"I didn't want to tell you in front of the ladies."

"Right. So we've got to find them."

"Or maybe they'll keep on going. Make a break for freedom. Terrorize the countryside, et cetera."

"I wish I was sure it's our guys in the woods," Rey said. "The living scare me more than the undead do."

"Got a theory about who it is?"

"Several." She thought a moment. "Worst case, the one who ran past the cave is a scout, and there are a whole bunch of them down below."

"Like the law, you mean."

"Maybe. There are worse things than the law. Every person up here has enemies, and they're not all on the side of the angels."

Smokey said, "If there are more on their way to visit us, we've got to uninvite them. How can we keep them out? You know this side of the mountain better than I do."

"The river's too high to ford. There's only one way across." Rey felt galvanized. "Let's knock it down fast, before any more of them get in."

"You realize," Smokey said as they left, "we'll be trapping the zombies on this side."

20

"Twirl me around, Buck. Gimme a whirl."

But her husband wasn't giving her a whirl, standing up or lying down.

He let her twirl him—standing up, because there was no way Sue was going to do the lying down thing with him in his condition unless it was his idea, and that would mean he was pretty near close to his old self—but it wasn't the same. Still, a dance with half a man was better than no dance at all. She leaned against him and swayed, feeling him follow her lead.

"Do you still love me, Buck?" she asked into his shirt. "I love you." She looked into his opaque eyes.

Buck looked over Sue's shoulder as if the wall was deeply interesting.

"I've gotta know, darlin'." But really, Sue wasn't sure she wanted to know. What if the answer was No?

Sue stretched up and touched her lips to Buck's. Lips cold as clay.

Waited some more. Cold skin, cold as the grave, still as a stone. She was sorry she'd tried.

At least he could strum a guitar, and she could pretend he was really there.

Crystal had settled way down, Misty thought, almost back to her old self before she got rasty and PO'd about everything. Crystal hadn't been fit to hang with since they were twelve, a lifetime ago, so she had just as much of a sister now as in the past couple of years. Mom liked it better this way, that was obvious. Mom went around saying, "I've got my two beautiful daughters back." Misty suspected Mom kind of missed the spunk and spark, but Crystal was so pretty now, without the weird makeup and drawn-on tattoos, and so sweet without the attitude, so it was about even, all around.

Misty liked being the lively one for a change. She was the fun one now; she had all the spark. But she didn't want to take care of her sister forever. If the rest of her life was going to be babysitting her sister, Misty was going to take off. Crystal was always talking about—*had* always talked about, when she still talked—New York. Paris. Los Angeles. The opposite of Cannibal Mountain. Maybe she'd been right all along. Maybe this was no place to spend the rest of your life.

Mom wouldn't like it, but Mom would just have to get over it.

Maybe Crystal had been right about that, too.

"What I want to know," Travis said, hoisting a pint jar of new beer to his mouth, "is how you guys got together. Some kind of home brewers convention? I mean, you're not exactly twins, are you?"

No, they weren't. Eddy was worn right down to the nub, like he'd been pickled in his own brine; Hoot was a slab, some kind of Viking monster. Although now that they were zombies they were a little more alike. Quiet, both of them watching him. Well, they'd always been pretty quiet. Nice guys. Travis hadn't noticed that before, but they were pretty okay. Let him sleep in their house, gave him alcohol and some of whatever they were eating, didn't expect him to work it off or any Nazi bullshit like that.

"You guys are all right," he said, and they turned their gazes to him. With the jar upended in front of his face, Travis thought he caught them giving each other the eye, but it was through a glass of cloudy amber and he couldn't be sure.

"Drink up, boys. This one's on me." Travis filled a cup for each of them and helped them raise their arms in a toast. "Here's to the day's work, compañeros, compadres, campesinos. May the gods, what's his name, Bach, smile on us and not let the mash turn sour."

He pushed their arms down and bent their elbows. "Now you drink. Like this. Watch daddy. Chugalug."

They drank. The second time, they needed less help, and then they were flying solo. Travis smiled on them with pride.

"I love you dudes," he said, his heart warming with loose affection. "Another round?"

"You're a lot nicer to be around now, baby doll. You smell as good as you look. Better, even. No time to fix your hair, sorry, pick up that bag there and let's go. We'll find a little place, some corner of a college town or artsy fartsy downtown, maybe Portland, maybe San Fran, or someplace warm, I know you love the heat; Los Angeles! Nobody'll notice you. Notice us, I mean. We'll blend, a couple of women hermits. Nothing new there."

But in a city, Berry wouldn't be able to roam. The police would find her, or very bad men, or a speeding car. How she would tolerate being an apartment captive was a problem they'd have to deal with when they got there.

In truth, Berry was looking worse, skinwise. On the other hand, she looked strong. She'd always been a wiry, tough little bird, but lately her muscles bulged up on her forearms and her belly had developed a six-pack.

"That bag there. The red one. Pick it up. Pick it up. Oh, here. Carry it, okay?"

The bag dropped from Berry's slack hand. Jackie slung it over her shoulder and pulled Berry out the door, onto the stump, and to the road. It sure felt like Berry could be keeping up better if she wanted to.

"Ooh," Berry said. "Oh. Ohne. Zz."

"Let me do all the talking when we get out there. You'll be fresh off the boat from Trinidad or somewhere, Tonga maybe, no English. Okay, here we are. Don't get your fingers caught in the pulley."

They had reached the hand trolley.

Jackie said, "Oh, Christ on a crutch. Dammit!"

The trolley was off the wire, sitting on the ground beside the toppled tripod of thick logs that supported the cable, and the cable had been pulled over the river and lay half in the trolley, a useless anaconda-like pile of steel.

Jackie stared.

"We're stuck. Fucking stuck! You and me and all the monsters, all one big happy stuck-together family."

Jackie set the bags down. "What now, Berry dear? What in Hell's little acreage do we do now?"

Berry didn't have any answers, but something caught her attention down on the riverbank. She went after it, suddenly surefooted and quick. Thinking she was going into the river, Jackie shouted after her, but Berry disappeared into the vine maple and giant sword ferns.

A scuffling in the bushes, a high-pitched squeal, and a grunt told a short-short story about some creature's last moments on Earth. Then the fuss was over.

"Berry?"

Fearsome sounds, oral in nature, emanated from the thicket.

"Berry?" It sounded horribly like dear Berry had been attacked by ... what? One of the hideous undead had found her, sweet and succulent Berry, warm and delectable woman, and, oh God, it sounded as if he was feasting on the flesh Jackie Tobasco adored, flesh she had only recently been able to adorn to her heart's content.

"Berry!"

The bushes rustled. Jackie backed away. Up over the lip of the riverbank rose a dark head, a face smeared with red juice, and Jackie could tell it wasn't blackberry or salmonberry juice; it was too early for blackberries or salmonberries; no, it was the juice of something bigger and warmer than wild mountain fruit.

In Berry's hand dangled the freshly-opened carcass of a large nutria. Berry rounded the top of the slope and brought the red-furred body to her mouth.

"Oh, Berry. Oh, Berry, dear," was all Jackie could say, and the words didn't do any justice to her feelings.

EZ pulled the twine tight. It hurt his fingers so he slipped a green stick into the loop and twisted. That did it. The deerskin tightened around the gallon bucket. It made a satisfying hollow *bog* sound. He trapped the drum between his knees and patted the middle, the edges, used his fingertips and palms. A rhythm bopped down his arms and the drum skin hopped to it, making a tune of high and low notes, skinny and fat sounds, rain and falling rocks and heart-beats, and sounds he'd never heard before. He played his bongo in his fort, closed his eyes, and saw the turtlenecked, beréted people around him, nodding to EZ's beat, grooving to it, snapping their fingers. They were in a café, the world going by outside, smoke and wine fumes and other imagined exotic elements hanging in the half-light from candles in drippy wine bottles that were for some reason wrapped with straw.

The trouble at home didn't matter at all. It wasn't his real home, anyway. *These* were his people. He'd be playing bongos with them someday for real, and maybe someday would come sooner than he'd thought. Home seemed to be falling apart fast, and it couldn't fall apart fast enough to suit him, now that he knew his destiny.

☙

The rich stink of the beer penetrated Travis' nostrils and burrowed into his brain. Drunk on fumes but thoroughly wasted on three pint jars of brew, he hoisted Eddy up and aimed him at the bubbling pot of mash.

"What now, Eddy? Point or something. I know this thing goes in that thing."

Eddy was mute on the subject of creating whiskey. Eddy was mute on every subject.

"Doesn't it? Come on, man. Help a dude out." Travis had a feeling the longer they waited, the more Eddy would forget how to distill spirits, and what a tragic waste that would be. The whole set-up rusting away, an endless string of sober days trailing off into a gray old age. Or someone else taking over the still operation, snatching Travis's chance from his hands when he was so close to the first, best chance he'd ever had in a lifetime of cruddy luck and blown opportunities. He couldn't think of anything worse than having to give up on moonshining.

The beer was probably going to work, and beer was good. But moonshine—that was the Monster Board, the pipeline, the Ride of the Year. There was something ultimate about it, like turning lead into gold. Not that Eddy's whiskey had ever been golden. But Travis's would be.

"Here?" He poked a tube at a hole in the heavy lid on a blackened pot.

Eddy didn't dissent. Travis stuck the copper tube through the hole.

"How about this thing?"

Another tube, another hole, a fitting and another fitting. "There sure are a lot of parts, pardner. You sure this is right? It's not going to blow up or anything, is it?"

Travis was pretty sure Eddy shook his head No. It was hard to tell for sure, with the swimming feeling his own head was experiencing, but hell, he had to do something, and ol' Fast Eddy wasn't talking.

Travis lit a fire under the kettle and inspected the outfit. He didn't see any parts that could cause any harm. Mash, check. Tubing draining into pot, check. Fire, check. Lid on tight, check.

"It's all copasetic. All systems go. Okay, brother, let's have a brewski to celebrate and forget our troubles, whaddya say?"

Some time later, Travis opened his eyes. Apparently he'd taken a nap.

"Hoot? Good beer, man. We make a good team." Travis didn't expect Hoot to answer. Hoot wouldn't have answered before the accident; he was a quiet man, a great, strong, silent man from the frozen north. "You're a good guy, Hoot. And you, too, Eddy. Curly and Larry. And I'm Moe 'cuz I'm the boss now."

Travis rolled over and sat up. The bunks were empty. The door was open.

"Guys?" He pulled himself to his feet and looked around the mud and scrub surrounding Hoochville. They were gone.

A persistent hissing rumble came from the distillery, like a stopped-up teakettle with rocks inside it. The pressure cooker jittered and rocked on the stove. Now that he was standing up, Travis could feel its heat on his face. Somebody, maybe him, must have stoked the fire before he fell asleep on the floor. Alcohol fumes rode the heat waves and set off a small but fierce storm in his saturated brain.

The guys were in no condition to wander around in the woods; if they were half as drunk as Travis, they'd no doubt fall off one of the cliffs or find a way to shoot themselves all over again. He grabbed his coat and took an unsteady step toward the door, planted one foot outside, and stopped. *The hissing.* Shouldn't he put the fire out or take the lid off the pot or something? But wouldn't that ruin the product? Where would another batch of grain come from? Town, that's where, and who was going to go get it now? Travis, that's who. Travis would have to drive the truck, without a license, without his brain, which hadn't been that great to start with, not knowing where to go or any damn thing about buying grain including what kind to buy, or how to get money to buy it with. He had to save this batch.

The guys could walk around for a little while without him, couldn't they? Eddy would want him to save the liquor.

No, that was bull. Eddy would want him to save Eddy. Hoot would want him to save Hoot. The big guy loved that spot up at the head of the falls. He went troll-spotting there, hanging half over the cliff looking for the buggers to come out of a cave supposedly hidden behind the waterfall.

The kettle hissed and jumped on the stove. Hot metal groaned.

Travis turned back. *Save the liquor, then go get the boys.*

A voice howled from far away—some animal getting eaten, or a half-man left alone to die?

Hell with the liquor, go get your boys.

The boys.

The booze.

His guys.

His moonshine!

"Fuuuuck!"

This felt suspiciously like responsibility.

Daybreak came so gradually Rey slid from dreaming to awake seamlessly, riding the incoming tide of gray light. Her companion's warm shoulder supported her cheek and the condensation of his breath made a cloud with hers.

"Mmm." She burrowed into his side. He was wearing a shirt. Odd. He never wore clothes to bed. "You cold, Travis? I'm freezing."

He pulled the blanket up under her chin, so she knew he was awake, which woke Rey up a little more, and when she was nearly all the way awake she felt, smelled, and sensed something unTravisy.

"Smokey?"

"Hey."

"Oh!" Rey pulled away and rolled onto her back. "Sorry."

" 's okay."

"We slept? How long has it been light? Were you sleeping?"

"No, but I could use a nap. If you're awake, give me twenty winks. It's been quiet all night." With that, Smokey turned away from her and in a minute was snoring genteelly.

Rey went outside. Rain spattered desultorily. They'd gotten wet in the night, chilled by the air that blew up off the river. Taking down the trolley had been harder than she'd expected. It was repairable, but not anytime soon. Nobody was coming across the river until the trolley was fixed or summer lowered the water level.

She set out a three-day supply of feed for the goats and hens and opened the pen and coop doors. She took a cold outdoor shower, put on clean clothes, and went inside. Smokey opened his eyes.

"Hey," he said.

"Good morning again. Let's eat something and get going."

"Yep." He swung his legs over and stood up in one easy move-ment. "Sorry to surprise you."

"Sorry I called you Travis."

"No problem. I thought you needed some sleep. I did, too." He yawned big, scratched his belly. Rey told him where the facilities were and put some food together. They ate without a fire. She told the animals to be careful and she and Smokey headed to Hoochville to collect Travis. She led the way, wondering why it had felt so good to wake up with Smokey, whom she had known for years but barely knew at all. She missed Travis. It had only been a few days but already she missed sleeping with him. Today it was a different kind of missing. There was plenty to worry about, enough to keep her mind occupied until they got within sight of the moonshiners' cabin, when it blew up.

As soon as the door closed behind her, Berry wanted out again.

"Hold still! You're a bloody mess." *Jesus.* Jackie struggled to wash the blood and bits of flesh off Berry's face and neck and hands. She was up to her wrists in it, smears to her elbows. Good God, the woman's forearms were muscular. And she was scary strong.

The foundation makeup came off with the gore and Jackie saw that the hole in Berry's cheek had sealed over.

"Well, that's good, at least," she said. "But you're not sleeping in my bed until you take a bath."

Berry walked out, leaving the door open behind her, and in two seconds was in the trees and out of sight.

"Oh, what the rosy round hell?" Jackie sat on a kitchen chair and put her forehead in her hands. Berry had been so sweet lately. Not her old self, with all her feist and fire and general adorability, but Jackie had enjoyed the peace and harmony. Now Berry was restless again, worse than ever.

Jackie sat for a little while, then found herself tidying up the table, and that led to cleaning off the beauty station, and in two hours she sat back down at the table in a clean trailer drinking a fresh cup of coffee. Then there came a scuffling sound on the door-stump, a scratching at the knob. Jackie opened the door.

A small carcass lay across the stump, oozing blood. Judging by the remaining ear and hind foot, it had been a rabbit. Now it was basically a fuzzy dishrag. The expression on Berry's face could only be described as proud. She looked from the carcass to Jackie, not smiling, but pleased with herself, clearly expecting Jackie Tobasco's approval.

"Well, *hell*aluliah," Jackie said. "Look what the cat dragged in."

⟐

"Oh, my God." Rey and Smokey reached Hoochville minutes after the boom. Choking smoke hung in the ruins. Rey stumbled toward a blackened corpse half covered in charred debris, then drew back. "Is it Travis?"

Smokey turned her away from the body. "Hard to say. Don't look."

"I've seen dead bodies before," she said, pulling away. "I have to know who it is."

But it was more charcoal than identifiable human.

"He must have been right on top of the explosion." She nudged debris with the toe of her boot, looking for anything that might tell who it was: more importantly, who it was not. *Not* sweet, bad, innocent, golden Travis.

A scrap of metal lay on the black ground. Rey picked it up and brushed it against her jeans. Under the soot, a formerly white length of bone appeared, spearing through two holes in the metal clasp.

"It's Travis's pin." She brushed at it. It was something to look at besides the ruin at her feet. "I guess that IDs the remains."

"Maybe. I'm sorry, Rey," Smokey said. "Really, don't look."

"It doesn't matter. He's not there. It's just physical detritus now." Rey sighed. "His body looks so small. Death takes a lot away from a person."

"That it do," Smokey agreed. "That it do."

21

Bee whacked her hatchet into the big stump, scattering kindling a dozen feet around. "All of them?"

"Even the kids. Jacob was gone when Mercy woke up this morning, and Crystal probably snuck off after breakfast." Rey dodged spears of flying fir.

"But we don't know about Bill Doller." Bee splintered another wedge of dry fir. The smell of split wood got right into her brain, and that hollow *thwack* was the most satisfying sound in the world. "We'll have to insist Birdie opens her door. Enough is enough."

Rey gathered up the kindling, staying out of range. "I'll go."

"Fine. Any sign of Jobert?"

"Not as of yesterday." Rey started toward the Pear door with the kindling, then paused. "Sue's pretty worked up. She's not so surprised about Crystal—"

"But she didn't expect Buck to run off."

"No. And Misty's acting odd. It's shaken Sue up."

"Current events are throwing us all for a loop. Sue will have to keep her hand on the plow and hold on, teenagers or not."

"I hope she doesn't lose them all," Rey said. "I don't know how she'd survive that."

Bee straightened up slowly, giving her back time to adjust. Rey could hear the older woman's knees cracking. "Whether any of us survive this is the question, Rey." Bee scooped up the sticks on the chopping block and went toward the house. "We need to have a meeting."

"I think we've lost control," Rey said.

"Not I," Bee snapped. "Not you, either. There's no time to lose control. Also," she added in a stern voice, "there's the matter of Sugar Agate."

"Yes."

"It's a very serious thing, no matter how you may feel about it. It's murder, whether by someone not in control of his actions, or by one of us."

"How I feel about it is the same way you feel about it," Rey managed to say, caught off guard. "What do you mean?"

Bee stood in the doorway and gave Rey one of her penetrating looks. "None of us particularly liked Sugar Agate, or none of us but two or three of the men here. But not liking isn't killing. It takes more than not liking to commit murder."

"Sure."

"I'm not blind nor senile yet. Even if I were, it's been in all of our faces for years that you've had a rival, or Sugar Agate had a rival. I'm not saying you're the only one who'll be better off with her gone. Even my sisters and I will benefit a little, getting some of our parents' things back, not having to lock our door. But we've kept that problem to ourselves, not displayed it with our laundry."

She held out her laden arms and Rey, speechless, tumbled the kindling she'd gathered onto Bee's pile. Rey opened her mouth like a fish a few times, waiting for words to produce themselves, but she settled for turning away without making a fool of herself.

Birdie still wouldn't answer the door. Rey could hear her moving around inside—she was sure it was Birdie from the soft footfalls and the tentativeness with which objects were touched. The front and back doors were locked; all this locking of doors was a new thing that felt alien and lonely. As Rey left the back yard, she heard something and turned, half-expecting Birdie to come out of the trees, but there was only a vague after-image of movement in the freshly turned garden soil, a bird hunting for worms or a wary squirrel.

She found Smokey up the hill looking for signs of Hoot and Eddy and Travis: two out of the three, since one of them, and surely the carcass was not Hoot, was now thoroughly burned up. The cabin was destroyed; only the brewery end had any standing walls, the glass and crockery shattered. A fine mist drifted over the smoking ruin. Rey kicked at hot spots until they were all exposed to the moisture. It was good to kick things.

I'm a suspect?

I've been airing my dirty laundry for years? I'm gossip, I'm a fool, I'm a scandal.

So much for my secret life on Cannibal Mountain.

It wasn't much of a meeting, with more than half of them gone. Bee started where she had left off with Rey: the murder of Sugar Agate. Even with the ineffectively revived, as she put it, running around loose, the fact was that Sugar Agate had been killed neatly and cleanly, with no gnawed bones or missing flesh. That pointed to a fully living person as the culprit.

"We're not safe in each others' company," Bee said. "That's why we need to attend to this problem before we can think about what we might do about the other matter."

They were again in the Pears' living room. Jackie paced by the Pears' door, opening it every thirty seconds to peer at the road. Misty squirmed and hunched, trying to get out of Sue's white-knuckle grip.

As nobody else spoke up, Rey said, "Finding everybody's relatives and neighbors is more important. We don't know where they are and we don't know what they're doing. They might be hurt out there, alone and helpless. Or—I'm going to be honest, sorry—they might be dangerous. You know it's true. You've seen them be dangerous to each other, so they might be dangerous to us, too."

Bee looked as influenceable as a boulder.

Rey looked around for support. "We can investigate Sugar Agate's death when we've got the bigger issue cleared up. Plus, we've seen strangers in the woods. We're in a state of emergency. There's no time to play detective."

Mercy said, "It won't take long to solve the girl's murder. We can clear it up in five minutes." Her eyes stayed steadily on Rey. "We know who wanted her out of the scene and why."

Rey felt as if saying she was innocent was an admission of guilt. "Yes. She broke Trucker John's heart. She stole things from everybody."

"Trucker John's an abomination created by the Devil's science," Mercy pronounced. "You said there's not a mark on her. None of our walking dead did that. I know. I've seen how they kill."

"To be fair," Jackie said, "Travis and Trucker John aren't the only men who were sniffing around her."

Mercy and Sue begged to differ.

Jackie said, "Not all of them did anything about it, so relax. I'm just saying that girl played with a lot of hearts. And maybe other parts, if you get my drift."

"Disgusting," Mercy said. "And no truth in it."

Sue raised her head and said dully, "Oh, there's truth all over it, Mercy. People on the mountain are special, but you know what? People are people. Men are men. Even a good man'll catch afire if a woman holds a match to him."

"You think Buck—?"

"No, I don't think Buck. But a lesser man might not control himself as good as him."

Mercy reared back. "Are you saying my husband paid any mind to that tramp?"

"I didn't say it," Sue said. "You did."

"If either one of those brothers was disturbed over Sugar Agate," Jackie said, "it would be El Duane. He was—is—a big old lonesome bull and Sugar Agate was a prime heifer. Hell, El Duane would have had any female here."

"Hush your lying mouth," Mercy hissed.

"There are children here," Cricket reminded them.

Bee took over. "Rey's point is taken. More than one person had bad feelings about the victim. But we're not only speculating about motive. Who had a strong motive, who had the opportunity and the ability, and who would have done it that way?"

"Not Buck."

"Not Earl."

"Not Berry."

"Not any of the zombies," Ezekiel said.

Mercy squeezed his head.

"Correct. One of us right here in this room," Bee pronounced.

To Rey's horror, every eye in the room turned on her. She opened her mouth, but before she could speak, the door opened and Smokey came in.

"*Now* it's one of us in this room," Jackie said thoughtfully.

"One of us what?" Smokey asked.

"Killed Sugar Agate."

Smokey ran his eyes over the gathering of women and the lone boy, then looked questioningly at Rey.

The breath of air that had followed Smokey in through the door stirred the pages of the tablet Bee kept at her side. He nodded to Bee and Cricket, then to everybody else. Then he said, "I'm not part of your community, I know. I've kept apart up there on my end of the mountain and I think we're all satisfied with that arrangement."

Mercy nodded emphatically.

"So I hope you'll forgive me for butting in. I maybe have earned the right to say a little something in the past two days."

This time is was Bee who nodded.

"You need to drop this detective work for now and save yourselves. I can't put it any plainer. You're in grave danger. It might already be too late. Me flapping my gums could be the last sound you ever hear. If the next hours or days or minutes don't show you your murderer, and I think they will, you might or might not have another chance to figure it out."

"What do you recommend we do?" Bee asked him.

Smokey looked at every face. "You're going to have to stay together, and I mean more than just being in the same house. I know you're a bunch of wildcats, can't stand rules, you all came here to get away from law and order, but laws were made so people could protect themselves, and you need to protect yourselves now, so you're going to have to get behind order."

"Your orders, I suppose," Mercy said.

"Damn near anybody's. And damn soon."

Cricket made tea and Sue followed her into the kitchen to help. Smokey said they should eat and hydrate now; nobody knew when they'd have another chance. Jackie Tobasco doubted things were that dire and Smokey allowed that she could be right. Cricket brought out bread and apple butter.

They listened to Smokey more than they ever had to Rey. When he said they needed to round up the escapees, there was a general consensus. The only debate was about how to accomplish that.

"Just call them in," Sue said. "If they love us, they'll come home. If they don't, we have to let them go."

"Oh, horse pucky," said Jackie. "Even Berry's beyond that stage. She's lost her mind. First she was eating rabbits raw, then she dragged them home and left 'em on the doorstep, and now she's probably out catching deer with her bare hands. No amount of me calling her's going to compete with that kind of fun."

"No," Rey agreed. It felt good to agree with someone for a change. "They won't come when we call. I think we could lure them back, though. Find out what they want and let them know we have it."

Someone said that was the problem, the undead already knew what the living had and they were no doubt out there in the trees plotting to come take it. And what was that, somebody else wanted to know, and depending on who was speaking, it was food, their brains, wanton and rampant sex, to kill all the living and take over the village, to be left alone with their own kind (Ezekiel said), or unconditional love and understanding.

When the debate quieted down, Rey said, "I think they want bones. Meat and bones, but mostly bones."

Rey told them about the deboned chicken, and Jackie remembered how Berry had eaten the bones right out of the rabbits and nutria; Fiddlin' Sue said that Buck had fished a beef bone right out of the pot.

"But why?" Cricket asked.

Rey shook her head. "I don't know. And it might be incorrect. It's just a hypothesis."

"How does that help us catch them?" Bee said. "Does anybody have a bunch of bones lying around? And if they do, wouldn't the unliving have gotten to them already?"

"Three words," Smokey said. "Bar B Que."

22

"No chickens," Rey said. "Not even one."

"We're all making sacrifices." Smokey tried to reason with her.

She knew she was being selfish, but that didn't change how she felt.

"Sue said we could have the calf if we needed it."

"Good. If we barbeque the calf we won't need any chickens at all."

Jackie said, "That calf is a lot more valuable than a whole flock of chickens."

"Sue always meant to eat that calf, anyway. I'm not killing my hens."

"You feel sorrier for a dumb chicken that a sweet little baby cow?" Jackie said. "With those big brown eyes, that follows his mama around? She licks his forehead. She loves him. Nobody loves a chicken. Except you."

The calf, as usual, had no idea how close it had come to death; the chickens never knew what hit them. Mercy said the boy had a natural knack with a chicken neck.

"All set?" Rey said.

"Ready for action," Smokey said.

Smokey manned the barbeque and waved meat-perfumed smoke into the woods around the clearing. Jackie watched the trailhead to the Pear Sisters' house and the road. EZ and Rey positioned themselves one on each side of the fire pit with EZ closest to the cage.

"What if a bear smells it?" Jackie called.

"Get out of its way," Rey told her.

"Don't get between a bear and his barbeque," EZ said.

"Remember to sound the alert when we get a bite," Smokey said. "I wouldn't want to be standing between a zombie and his barbeque, either."

It didn't take long. Jacob shuffled out of the trees and headed straight for the meat without a glance at the people guarding it. When he got within range, Smokey and Rey threw a net over him. He went down in a scramble of arms and legs, still trying to get to the food.

"Don't let him rip it!" Smokey warned. "We've only got two of these."

"The kid can fight," Rey said, dodging a clawing hand and getting kicked soundly in the thigh.

They gave up getting him to his feet and carried him to the cage, where EZ had the job of removing the net.

"There's no way," he said. "I'm going to have to give him some chicken."

"Give the poor boy something to eat," Rey said. "He's skin and bones. And some big time muscle." She rubbed her thigh, where a knot was bunching up.

EZ stabbed a chicken leg off the grill with a stick and carried it to his brother, who settled down instantly. By the time the net was recovered, another form came lurching into the clearing. Rey and Smokey netted Crystal, who was barely recognizable through mud and blood and forest floor detritus. Smokey said she looked like she was wearing full forest camo. She fought and spat for a minute, but once she had a chicken thigh in her hands she didn't care what EZ did with her.

"That's the easy part," Smokey said. "The rest of them are a lot bigger."

"I hope they're okay with sharing the meat," Rey said. "I don't know how satisfied El Duane's going to be with one piece of chicken"

"Incoming!" Jackie yelled, and the sound of her scrambling out of the way was followed by the sound of many feet on the dirt path.

Rey glanced at Smokey. Could they handle a mass attack? She'd only counted on one at a time, for some moronic reason. Smokey pointed to himself and held up one finger, at Rey and held up two fingers, signaled to Jackie and EZ with three and four fingers. Rey hoped he meant he'd take the first one and Jackie would take number four, if there was one, because she couldn't imagine what else all those hand signals meant. At least he seemed to have a plan. He threw a bunched up net to Jackie and moved toward the noise.

The net fell over the first one. It batted its arms and said, "What are you doing? Get that offa me!"

"What—?" Smokey said. "Sue?"

"I'm no zombie, if you hadn't noticed. Turn me loose."

Smokey took the net off, untangling it from Sue's hair clip and a long-handled wooden spoon. "You're not supposed to be here."

"Move up," Mercy said from behind Sue.

Rey looked behind her, saw no arrivals from that side, and turned back to Sue and Mercy. "You can't be here. Go back indoors. It's dangerous out here, and there's a plan. Follow the plan!"

Holding a black dutch oven, Mercy crowded past Sue, who was untangling netting from her boot hooks. "Come on, girls. We'll set our blanket over here out of the smoke." Heaven, Freedom, Liberty, and Misty paraded after Mercy, carrying a length of toweling, a blanket, a basket, a big wooden bowl, and a violin.

"Ladies, this is no picnic. I insist that you—"

"Is it a barbecue or is it not?" Sue demanded.

"It's not that kind of barbecue," Smokey said, his voice getting a little higher. "We're catching zom— catching your revived families. Go on home now. Don't you understand this is dangerous?"

Mercy humphed. "It's no more dangerous with us here than with us trapped inside that house."

"Yes," Sue said. "You go on catching zombies. We brought baked beans and potatoes to roast in the coals and a jug of sweet tea. We'll be fine."

Rey heard a noise from behind and whirled around, but nothing came into the clearing. "But you might be scaring them away. It's working great, or it was. Look, we've got Jacob and Crystal already." She pointed to the cage.

"How are they?" Sue asked. "I bet they're hungry."

"They each had a piece of chicken."

"Well, that's not enough. Fix them a plate, Liberty," Mercy told her daughter. "If this is to be the last time we eat together, I aim to give my children a nice time while I can. Now you"—looking at Smokey—"better turn around and get one of those nets ready for Buck before he eats all that meat."

They barely got Buck ensnared in time to save him from diving into the fire pit. They gave him half a chicken breast and packed him into the cage, which was rapidly growing crowded. EZ took food from the girls and poked it cautiously through the bars. The zombies grabbed and growled, but they were too focused on gnawing chicken bones to fight each other.

It took three people to subdue Earl.

"I think we've got the hang of this," Rey said. "I believe I'm ready for the big one."

"Bring on El Duane," Smokey said. "Then there's your moonshiners, and the store man. And that little guy, Joe Bear, and Jackie's gal. But they should be easy enough, unless there's more fight in them than I think there is."

"Don't underestimate Berry," Jackie said. "She's a spitfire. I don't think she'll fall for this trap. She was doing fine on her own, hunting like a puma. She always did like to get out of the house."

When Bee and Cricket came up the path carrying fresh bread and a jar of preserves, Rey just sighed. "Sit out of the way," she told them, "and don't say I didn't warn you if the going gets rough."

"I've seen rougher," Bee said.

"Not recently, though," Cricket amended. "This is quite exciting. I sure wish Lacey were here to see it."

"Maybe she will be. I don't feel her being dead, Cricket. I think our little sister is running with the pack. No doubt she'll be along soon, hungry and footsore. I'm preparing her a plate right now."

When a new rustling came from the near-dark path, Jackie hesitated before throwing the net, for which Birdie Doller was thankful. She entered shyly, her glasses and aluminum-colored hair catching the firelight. "I smelled the food."

"You're risking your life being here, but that doesn't seem to bother anybody else. Help yourself." Rey resigned herself. They'd catch who they could, protect the living as best they could, and chalk the failures up to life with renegades and scofflaws. The more she thought about it, the less difference she could see between the living and the undead. They all followed their own lights, even if those lights led them off a cliff.

Birdie tore into the meat and beans like a woman who hadn't seen food in a week, or ever. She sucked at the chicken bones, asked "You going to eat that?" and took them off of other people's plates.

The next shadows stumbling into the clearing made Rey do a doubletake.

"Travis!" Rey ran to him and grabbed his arms. "You're not dead!"

He had on Eddy's old leather hat, and in the near-dark Rey could hardly see his face. "I thought you were burned up." Eddy and Hoot swayed behind him, positioned like a couple of bodyguards.

Travis's lopsided grin was completely alive. "What's cookin', good lookin'?"

"Trav, I thought you were dead. Who was that in the cabin? Where have you been? What happened?"

"Did our invitations get lost in the mail?" Travis motioned to his entourage and they moved toward the food. When Hoot and Eddy got close, they were netted, fed, and caged. Travis protested, but after he saw they were happily occupied with eating and protecting their dinner from the other inmates' poking and heavy breathing, he let Freedom feed him.

Sue tuned her fiddle to Misty's and they launched into "Will the Circle Be Unbroken." Bee and Cricket's pure, wavering harmonies blended in. Mercy sang the melody. *When I saw that hearse come rolling For to carry my mother away.*

Rey hated that song. *Undertaker, please drive slow, for the body you are hauling, I hate to see her go,* indeed. How anybody could sing it without breaking down she didn't understand, but she cut off her old grief and decided to hear the music as a sign of life and togetherness that they had been missing of late.

Then Travis wiped his hands on his jeans, which didn't do anything for his hands or his jeans, and picked up Crystal's guitar. He strummed chords better than Rey remembered: nothing fancy, but keeping up with the changes. Sue eyed him with that seriousness musicians share. The music went on, gospel and honky-tonk and tunes older than the mountains. The little girls drew the outline of a jail in the leaf litter and played Undead in Jail. Liberty made her little sisters shake invisible bars and gobble invisible food while she threatened them with a twig. EZ turned over a bucket and drummed on it. He got some impressively unbucketlike sounds out of it.

"I'm Satan's Spong," Heaven mooed, rocking from side to side in her jail. "Satan's Evil Spong."

Succulent *umami* molecules of roasting flesh mingled with the good loamy smell of potatoes and beans and fresh bread, with sweet dismembered wood and smoke, and the mixture rode the rising western wind. It roamed down the road until cold air on the river blocked it, and there it was inhaled by the hungry forms on the riverbank. It was a painful temptation, that rich meaty aroma, but it would have to wait.

"I'm not sleepy," Bee said. "I'm having fun. Leave me alone."

"I'm having fun, too," Cricket argued, "but you darn near got pneumonia in the cave. You can hear the music from your bed. I'll build a fire. Be sensible, Bee."

"You go. I've been sensible. Now I'm going to party a little."

Cricket put her wooly shawl around Bee's shoulders. It never did much good to try to persuade Bee to do anything she didn't want to do. Younger sisters learned to use an indirect approach. "Do you think Lacey will smell the food and hear the music and come home?"

Bee patted her hand.

"Got one," Smokey called out.

Berry ran toward the fire, growling, her feet barely touching the ground.

"Told you," Jackie said. "Like a puma."

Berry spat and scratched in the net, all nails and teeth and shiny eyes. Jackie fussed over her—"Don't be so rough!"—but finally allowed her to be caged and fed with the others.

In the music and excitement, Rey hadn't noticed, but the undead had gone quiet. They gazed through the weave of branches, an individual occasionally vocalizing in gutturals or swaying unsteadily. She had a half-seen impression they had their heads together, but when she looked back they were staring out at the living, as dull as waxworks.

Freedom was trying to bargain her way out of jail with shell casings she'd found on the ground. Misty was the jailer now, strutting around the imaginary cell smacking her stick against her leg.

"The prisoners will not speak!" she barked.

"We're just talking," Liberty said. "We're not saying secrets."

"No," said Freedom, big-eyed with innocence. "We're not plotting our escape."

23

In the pale bedroom the armoire loomed like a dead tree. A breath of aromatic wind lifted and released the ruffled hem of a pillowcase and coaxed the armoire door open. Clothes swung on wooden hangers, moving as if enjoying their freedom now that the bulk in the bottom of the cabinet was gone.

Birdie Doller didn't go so far as to stand up and sing, but she clapped and swayed to the music, a grin stretching smile muscles that, if not actually virgin, had never gotten further than second base. Her dull silver hair frizzed out of its tight curls. Nobody had ever seen her have a good time before; she looked like a different person. When Sue and Travis played "In the Sweet Bye and Bye," Birdie actually sang the chorus with Mercy and the Pear Sisters, but it came out *We shall meet on that beautiful sho-eEAA!* Mercy frowned at her. Too much personal enjoyment when singing gospel music was a sacrilege. The EEEing got louder and Mercy followed Birdie's staring eyes.

Bill Doller hove into the clearing. Rey and Smokey got ready with a net, but Bill passed the barbecue pit and went straight for his wife.

"Well, I never thought old Dollar Bill had any feelings for that poor woman," Cricket said. "It just goes to show you there's romance where you least suspect it."

But Birdie, far from opening her arms for a sweet reunion, was scrambling backwards, kicking over glasses and plates with her husband's heavy boots.

Slippery and muscular as a marlin, Bill shook off Rey and Smokey. Jackie flung her net over his head but he kept going, dragging her behind him. Birdie backpedaled fast, but Bill gained on her without making any show of exerting himself. Smokey came at him again and the two nets slowed him down, but he plunged ahead, driving his wife backwards, nearer and nearer to the cage.

EZ grabbed her arm to pull her aside but Birdie flailed and knocked him away. She crawled back another foot until the cage stopped her. Bill kept coming, straining hard against the nets. Hands reached out from the cage unhurriedly, and in half a second had Birdie's frizz of hair in their fingers.

Rey jumped on Dollar Bill's back and he fell over, landing on Birdie's legs. EZ hit the arms sticking through the cage bars with his bucket but the blows didn't stop the plucking hands. Tufts of metal-colored frizz floated downwind. They finally pulled Birdie free and Rey removed the remains of Birdie's hair from an army-green hand that had separated from its owner's arm.

"Hell," Jackie and Mercy said, meaning quite different things by the same word.

Jackie put an arm around Birdie. "Don't worry, darlin'. You come with me down to my shop and I'll fix you up so you can't even see the bald spots."

Birdie gasped and sniffled while Jackie chattered. "What in the world got into him, going after you like that? You without a mean bone in your body, all the grief he gave you and you as patient as a saint, some people said a doormat, but never mind them, and he takes after you like a drunken prospector, that's the thanks you get. Well, you always hurt the one you love, it's the sad truth."

Birdie looked back. Her teeth clacked. She stammered and pointed.

The cage of undead had started rocking side to side. The undead were rocking it together, lurching with a single rhythm left, right, left, swaying farther with every lurch. As the cage creaked and its bars snapped, the things inside grunted in time to their agitated dance with one voice: *Uhh*, Uggh. *Uhh*, Uggh.

"Tie them up!" Rey shouted.

"It's not holding," EZ said. "There's no time!"

Smokey worked one of the nets off Dollar Bill and left him incapacitated on the ground. He threw the free net to EZ and ran for coils of rope he had stashed by the fire pit. A heavy thud broke open a body-sized gap in the cage. As Jacob wriggled through the opening, EZ netted him. He and Rey tied Jacob's ankles and arms like a rodeo calf, got the net off just too late to capture Berry, who had pushed the bigger undead out of her way and was halfway across the clearing.

Smokey tackled and hog-tied her, then ran to help Rey and EZ. As Earl bulled his torso out of the hole, the rest of the undead lurched hard to the right, left, and right again. The cage teetered, hung at a diagonal, then crashed onto its side. Its inhabitants sprawled in a pile, snapping and clawing at each other. Somebody's arm stretched through the hole but was pulled back in.

"Push it over! Put the hole on the ground!" Rey said. They tried but didn't have the strength to roll the cage over.

"Use the meat," Smokey said. Rey got his meaning right away. She speared the remaining chicken pieces and waved them in front of the cage. Once Sue and Mercy got over their shock, they came closer, ready to help if they could. The caged things reached for the meat where Rey dangled it just out of reach. EZ and Mercy guarded the break in the cage with sticks, whacking anything that extruded. Rey waved the chicken on a stick closer, farther, closer, farther, and the knot of hungry bodies surged after it. The cage rocked. On a forward surge Rey shouted, "Push!" The cage toppled over, sealing the broken place against the ground.

"What now?" Mercy asked.

"They'll come up with something else in a minute, I bet," EZ said. "We better get them all tied up while we've got a chance."

Rey shot him a smile. The boy seemed to be growing up by the hour. A good thing, too, in the circumstances.

Cricket had hustled Bee home and taken the girls with them. Smokey, Rey, EZ, Travis, Sue, and Mercy pulled and roped and fought and did their best to avoid getting clawed and bitten. Berry was the worst, spitting and snarling and trying to shred everything in reach. In what felt like hours the zombies were individually tied up. They sprawled and hunched docilely on the ground, only their eyes roaming restlessly.

"Something's changed," Travis observed.

"Yeah. They're not the sweet little deadheads we knew and loved a day ago." Smokey took a pull off the flask Travis handed around the circle of wranglers. "What's up with that, Rey?"

She felt like saying, "You're asking *me*?" but instead said what her subconscious had been thinking while her conscious mind was playing zombie rodeo.

"Good question. I'd say they're now capable of acting together. Whether they plan or just respond the same way to stimuli and problems, like a flock of birds, I don't know. They're evolving, though, and fast."

"And they're fucking strong," Travis said.

"Yeah," EZ said.

Sue and Mercy said, "Watch your language."

"They've become physically powerful. I don't understand where this strength is coming from. I haven't seen this effect before. The single-minded rage, yes, that has precedent, but ... " Rey trailed off. She remembered, too late to avoid curious looks from Smokey and the women, that she was supposed to be new at this revival of the dead business.

"Stronger, and capable of concerted action. Could pose a problem." Smokey reached into his shirt pocket and pulled out a bulging cigarette, glanced at Mercy, put it back and licked his lips.

The group of humans stood and sat with their backs to the embers, facing the bound undead. The air was cold and the sky dark between ghostly clouds.

"If they could follow orders ... " Smokey said.

"I doubt it," Rey said.

"But if they could. Since they're getting smarter and all. Maybe they're getting well. The strength is a good sign."

"Don't forget this." EZ held up the hand that had been attached to Earl. "And there are some other extra parts around here, too. I found a couple of fingers and some teeth."

"Not so strong, after all?" Sue wondered.

"They're dying again," Mercy said.

"No, no ... let me think about it. I don't know what it means. All I know is what you know: they're dangerous to others, to us and to each other. They're strong but fragile. As to their mental status, I need to put them through some tests."

Smokey gathered up rope. "Let's put them to bed somewhere for now. I'm ready for a solid two hours' sleep myself."

They decided to put them in the Dollers' house. Birdie probably wouldn't want to sleep there tonight, if ever again; Mercy refused, saying her house had already been a jail for the unholy once and once was enough. So they trooped down the hill by flashlight and cloud light. Rey brought up the rear, walking with Travis.

"What happened?" she asked him.

"Blew up the still."

"You did?"

"Yup."

"How?"

Travis shrugged. "I had to go after the boys. If I'd known it was going to burn the place down, I'd have let them run off. Now the liquor's gone, the house is gone, and the boys are locked up." He threw an arm around her shoulder. "I'll stay at your place."

Rey leaned into him. He felt so damned good. He would feel even better wrapped around her. She knew just how he would smell and how his hair felt between her fingers, how his skin felt as golden as it looked. He was her peach, her California nectarine. She would always be in lust with Travis. Who wouldn't be?

"I don't think so." Rey kissed him on the cheek. "I'm so relieved that you're all right. Whose body was in the distillery?"

"No clue. Joe Bear?"

"Whoever it was had your pin."

"Sugar Agate has my pin. Had it, I mean. Hey, maybe it was Sugar Agate."

"It wasn't Sugar Agate." Unless Sugar Agate was trying to steal Travis even after she was dead. Rey wouldn't put it past her.

"We need you at the Dollers' store tonight. I'll bring down more bedding if there's not enough." When Rey pulled out of his casual embrace the night breeze made her shiver.

The undead were settled and secured, tied tighter and well-separated from each other. No one wanted a repeat of the cage-rocking action. Smokey and Travis took the first watch. Rey took Sue with her to get more blankets. Jackie contributed a sleeping bag—"If the zombies sleep in it, just keep it"—and they continued up to Sugar Agate's house for more.

"Look. There's a light on," Sue said.

The glow of a low-wicked Aladdin lantern shone in the window. Keeping off the shell and pebble path, they went to the door and listened. Through the door they heard a steady creaking: a drawn-out squeak, a pause; the sound of scraping bark. Rey wished she hadn't thought about Sugar Agate's ghost.

She opened the door. Facing them square on in the yellow gloom, Trucker John leaned back in Sugar Agate's wicker rocking chair, then leaned forward, in no hurry. At his side was a tattered sack with a shirt sleeve hanging out the top. The little table had been cleared of stolen objet d'art, replaced by a pile of John's big, grimy possessions.

"Should we ask him for some blankets?" Sue whispered.

"Maybe not."

Trucker John's glassy eyes rocked into and out of the yellow light. Rey remembered the way the revived could move now, lazy and sudden as alligators.

"We'll go now," she said.

At the Dollers' house the night passed slowly, even with a two-hour sleep break in which Rey managed to doze for twenty minutes. The undead lay still but not asleep. In the dim light their eyes blinked out and back like poison fireflies and their raspy exhalations overpowered even their body odor. Travis slept next to Hoot and Eddy. He looked like a sandlot angel, dirty and pure.

Smokey and Rey took third watch together.

"What do you think?" Smokey asked, talking quietly to let the living sleep.

"I think there's hope, if they don't fall apart. How far this disintegration will progress worries me. Flipping the cage over caused a lot of damage."

"I don't suppose reattachment would work on zombies," Smokey said. "Excuse me, but I've been waiting for this all day." He pulled a fat-bellied cigarette out of his shirt pocket and swiped a stick match across the wood floor, brought the flame to the paper.

"Oh, God, that's better." He held it out to Rey with the universal facial expression that said, Want a hit? She shook her head.

"You know, as long as I'm awake and they're awake, I might as well do some verbal acuity tests. I'll take them outside individually."

"No can do," Smokey said. "You can't go out with one of them by yourself, and Travis and Sue have to sleep. It'll keep 'til morning."

"Morning's a long way away," Rey said.

"It'll get here." He took another toke, firing up the end of the blunt to a cheery red, a tiny warm light like a campfire a long way off.

24

They were intelligent cretins. They couldn't tie their shoes or talk and they wouldn't follow directions, but they knew how to feed themselves. They possessed a disturbing ability to act in concert: not as cleverly as a pack of wolves, but better than, say, a couple of goats. And they watched each other. They watched Rey while she tested them. Their eyes were always roaming, gathering information and storing it away.

If I test them again this afternoon, they'll be entirely different.

When she'd learned enough, Rey took Smokey aside.

"Check their hands and fingers."

After a long look, Smokey nodded. "Huh."

"You see it, too. Good. Because it's impossible. Only certain amphibians and a very few reptiles can do that, and it takes them longer than ten hours."

"Well, these folks are something special."

"And not special-precious. Special-freakish."

"Too bad we can't bottle it and sell it. Regeneration. It'd be worth a fortune. More than a fortune. It's almost the fountain of youth. Legs, spinal cords, hearts, kidneys—"

Fountain of youth, indeed. Smokey didn't know the half of it. "It stays here. Right?"

"Sure. No way we'd use this to make money."

"Anyway, they're only growing nubs now. It might not go any further."

They fed the regenerating revived, then ate breakfast. Travis had gotten pretty adept at making porridge, and he added a jar of Birdie's marionberries to the human chow. It didn't take him long to spot the growing tendrils of Hoot's broken-off fingers. They looked like worms, skinny and pink and blind-ended. Travis held up Hoot's hand to show everybody.

"I've got to check on Crystal," Sue said. "Her thumb might be coming in. Hey, they get new teeth, why not other parts?"

"Don't get your hopes up," Rey cautioned.

"Sure. Baby hands, then permanent hands. I wonder why God didn't think of that. Probably because He's not a mother."

"That's the trouble with patriarchal religion," Smokey said.

"That's the trouble with evolution," Rey said. "If you can still reproduce, the errors stay in."

Sue said, "Well, God shoulda fixed that, too."

Which made Rey wonder, with repulsion, if the revived could reproduce. She shuddered. Taking dirty dishes from Sue at the sink, she said, "We've got to segregate Crystal and Berry from the men."

"Why?" And then, "Oh, Lord. Yes. Yes, we do."

They assembled in the clearing to have room for everyone. The regeneration of appendages caused a lot of ooh's and ahh's, but the salient point, Rey repeated several times, was their ability to work together. It was dangerous, but it might mean they were becoming more human. "Social regeneration," Rey termed it.

"But it's only good if they're working together on our side," Bee said. "If they're plotting to overthrow and eat us, we're worse off than before."

"So we have to control them all at once instead of one by one," Cricket said. "That's a lot harder. What are we going to do, put them in a big harness?"

"That'd be a lot of horsepower," Sue said.

"We've got us a tiger by the tail." Jackie tucked a stray gray curl into the flowered scarf Birdie wore. Birdie kept her eyes on the ground and off the undead.

The consensus was to build two sturdier cages inside the Dollers' house. "I don't care if I ever go back there," Birdie said about it. So the damaged cage was rebuilt stronger and a smaller one made for the females, and by late afternoon the whole caboodle of them, including Trucker John, who put up a fight when extracted from his reclaimed house, were in their jail within a jail, docile and watchful and unsleeping, with new, pink arms and hands and fingers, muscles straining against their shirts, and growling stomachs.

"Ohn," they moaned.

"Buh. Ohzz."

They could learn. Rey demonstrated that the next day, after three hours in the Dollers' back yard using simple behavioral techniques. Even Crystal followed simple directions if she got a treat afterwards, which was more than she'd done before the shooting. El Duane sat and stayed as often as you told him to so long as the jerky bites held out. The revived even learned from each other: take Trucker John aside and teach him to stack wood, bring in Jacob to watch him, and pretty soon Jacob could stack wood, too, faithfully replicating all Trucker John's mistakes.

"I'm gonna teach mine to play music again," Sue said.

"Can you teach Berry to stay home?" Jackie asked.

"If you know how to train a dog, you can teach your revived just about anything." Operant conditioning wasn't exactly intelligence, but it would do for now. Tomorrow, who knew? "They're healing," Rey said, and wondered how long it had been since the last time she'd smiled.

They weren't ready to be turned loose, though. When they heard this, Mercy and Fiddlin' Sue and Jackie T. opened their mouths, and just like that, Rey was back on their shit list.

"You said it was just like training a dog," Jackie argued. "Which is kind of insulting, but we're all capable of training dogs. Or kids."

"You don't have a dog *or* kids," Mercy retorted.

Rey explained about uncertainty, volatility, unknown disease progression, and the history of violence, particularly in El Duane's case.

"Then keep El Duane in a cage," Mercy crabbed.

"Just give it another couple of days. You could all use some rest, anyway. Mercy, you need help getting your house cleaned up. We can look for Lacewing and Joe Bear. I'll help you retrain your folks so when you do take them home it'll be a smooth transition."

Sue gave it one more shot. "How do you know they'll learn better, later? You can't teach an old dog new tricks. This could be the only time we've got to get through to 'em."

Rey shrugged. "Maybe you're right. Or this could be the worst time, and they'll learn easier and easier every day. The important thing is, they're under control now and they seem to be healthier. I really believe they're finally coming back to life. I had no idea the process would be so gradual, but it's happening. Let's not ruin it by rushing, okay?"

"Well," Jackie conceded, "all right, I'll go along with it. One more day. Then I'm taking Berry home. She's looking kind of peaky to me."

"Maybe tomorrow she'll be able to tell you how she's feeling herself," Sue said. "Me, I just can't hardly wait to be playin' again. I'm going to go tune up Buck's guitar right now."

In the blasted Hoochville ruins, Rey stood over what was no longer even a vaguely human form. With the bones gone, there wasn't much to examine. Rey found a stick and poked at the crumbling charcoal: a few thick shreds of possible leather and a pile of small black disks, another loose trail of smaller disks scattered where the torso had been. Rey gathered a handful of rhododendron leaves and used them to pick up the blackened disks. The disks turned out to be four metal buttons bearing undecipherable marks, and sixty-two cents in change. Did any Cannibalite carry coins? Rey doubted there was sixty-two cents in hard currency on the entire mountain.

Uphill at Joe Bear's cabin, Rey looked under his few furniture pieces, beneath the cushion on the ornate rocking chair and foot-stool, in the pots and jars and rusting fancy tins and plastic containers. In the loft, the brocade coverlet was still smooth, the pillow fringes hanging straight and still, Joe Bear's extra boots clean and precise at the foot of the bed.

Rey headed south to her own cabin. Where the trail veered away from Salt Creek and the gurgle of the swollen creek faded, she stopped. Loud sounds in the forest were always worth stopping and listening to. The first years on the mountain had been full of false alarms—birds that sounded like bears in the brush, deer that sounded like stealthy stalkers. She had learned the sounds by now, and the one she'd just heard was no deer. Not a cougar, either; you'd never hear a cougar until its teeth clicked around your cervical spine. This was something big, ursine or human, and it had just taken another step.

Home was three- or four-hundred yards away. She moved quickly, not trying to be quiet but not panicking, scanning for climbable trees. Not all bears were good climbers. She wished she had brought a more serious weapon. A bear wouldn't pay much attention to a .22 unless the bullet hit the nose or an eye. She stopped to listen again and heard prolonged brushy sounds in the trees downslope, then another crunching footstep up on the other side of the creek. Branches rustled and there was no wind to blame. She forced herself to send out the Cannibal Mountain call and was met with absolute quiet. Even the birds shut up. Whatever was out there was not one of her own patrolling the mountain. Rey ran for home, hearing through her own ruckus branches crashing and snapping behind her, closing in from right and left.

25

"They sleep with their eyes open."

"I'm not sure they're sleeping," Smokey said.

"They sleep standing up."

"Maybe they don't need sleep."

"Creepy," EZ said, for the fifth time that afternoon.

"They're different, all right." Smokey patted his shirt pocket, pulled out a match and lit it one-handed on his thumbnail. The caged insomniacs swiveled their heads toward the flare.

EZ didn't like the way their eyes reflected the flame. He was about to say "creepy" again but it was beginning to sound repetitious even to him. "When's Rey coming back?" he asked instead. "Not that we need her. We're okay on our own."

Smokey nodded.

"I mean," EZ said, "we're armed and alert, and they're not getting out of that cage. Are they, Smokey?"

"Nope." He flicked out the match.

EZ watched every move Smokey made. He didn't think Smokey noticed. The guy didn't really look like the heroes in videos, but he did have that rugged outdoor skin and he was pretty big and strong even if he wasn't so muscly, or if he was you couldn't see it under the layers of clothes. He had a faraway look in his eyes sometimes, like he was seeing trouble a long way off, before it got here.

"You be okay if I step out for a minute?"

"Sure," EZ said, but when Smokey went out the back door, all the comfort in the room left with him and EZ was alone with eight slow-moving, dusty weirdos and sixteen quick yellow eyes. The fact that they were in cages didn't make him feel much safer. He stiffened his knees and hoisted the rifle higher.

All the heads turned in unison, in that slow way that made a person sick to the stomach to see. They were following a sound outside. It had been such a small sound EZ hadn't paid any attention to it until the zombies showed an interest.

"It's just an animal. Or Rey coming back." He said it to them and to himself. "Probably Smokey checking the perimeter. Relax."

But they kept staring as if they saw right through the wall.

By the time Smokey came back in the zombies were shuffling, feeling the cage bars, quietly pushing each other out of the way to get their turn at fumbling with the locks. EZ's rifle stock was wet under his palms.

"How's everybody?"

"Fine," EZ said. He cleared his throat to get rid of whatever was making his voice squeaky.

"You hear a noise?"

"Wasn't that you?"

"Some of it, probably."

"Where were you?" EZ asked, getting perturbed that Smokey had left him all alone but willing to die before he admitted it.

"A leak and a look."

"Did you see anybody out there?"

"Nope. I thought the noise might be Rey or one of the others."

"It must have been an animal. That's why they were so interested. They hunt now. Mom found dead, eaten animals behind the house. Some of our chickens are missing."

"Yeah, well, we're feeding them now. They won't have to catch their own dinner any more." Smokey went to the front window and peered out around the cotton curtain.

EZ said, "It doesn't seem like you should go out by yourself. We're supposed to stay in twos, Rey said."

"Rey's right," Smokey said. "But until our relief comes, we might have to bend the rules a little."

EZ sniffed the peculiar wet-smoke odor that followed the man, a stink of bitter herbs and old campfire. Smokey coughed from down in his chest and gray vapor puffed out of his mouth.

"Were you smoking?" EZ asked him.

"I grabbed a short one, yeah."

"It's bad for you."

"Yes, it is. Don't start, son."

"You roll your own, don't you? I've seen those before." And EZ recalled where he'd seen skinny, lumpy hand-rolled cigarettes: in the cartoons of beatniks in his secret book. "It's marijuana, isn't it?"

"Busted."

"I want to try it," EZ said firmly. It was the missing element—that and New York City, Green-witch Village, and San Francisco. He had the drum, he wrote poetry. He hadn't drunk red wine out of a bottle with straw and candle wax on it, but he knew things and he had plans.

Smokey said, "Forget about it. I'm a professional, I know what I'm doing. Seriously, forget you saw that."

"I have to. It's my future, man."

" 'Man.' Herb is your future?"

"I'm moving to New York. Or maybe the West Coast. And I didn't see it, I smelled it. I figured it out. I'm not dumb, just because I live in a dumb place. I'm better off trying it now with a professional like you than out on the mean streets, right?"

" 'The mean streets.' Wow. Where do you come up with that stuff? And by the way, you're already on the West Coast, and this place isn't dumb. It's fucking awesome. It creates awe. It's one of the last accessible old growth forests in North America. You've got more freedom here than any place I've ever been."

"But—"

"You do have a limited family, I grant you that. Your mom's not dumb, but let's just say her worldview is provincial. When you grow up, get out there, see the world. You'll come back scratched up and saddle-sore, build yourself a cabin and settle down in God's country."

"Never," EZ said hotly. "I'm a poet."

"Cool. Tell me a poem you wrote."

Wishing he'd never confessed his secret vice, EZ said, "You wouldn't like it."

"I love poetry, dude. I know a few by heart. I've written some songs. Go ahead, tell me one of yours."

Great. Smokey was no doubt thinking of crude rhyming junk, song lyrics, maybe Longfellow at best. EZ's surrealistic free verse would go over like a fart in Sunday service.

But EZ wanted Smokey to hear his poetry. Hear it and understand it. God, that would mean a lot, Smokey *getting* what EZ meant. Smokey thinking he was intelligent. Smokey seeing him as the adult he was inside. "Well, one, it's not my best—" he started.

The things in the cage growled. Smokey looked at them, followed their stares, and peered around the curtains again. EZ heard it then, a purposeful but clumsy rustling.

"What is it?"

Smokey put his finger to his lips, then pointed at the inmates, gave EZ a meaningful look, and slipped silently out the front door. The zombies shifted from side to side and EZ slapped the bars to keep them from getting too organized about it. "No noise," he told them. God, he hated this. Since the gun battle in his own house, he'd gotten more afraid of guns. They were horribly loud and not very effective against nonhumans. And who knew what was out there? Any crazy thing seemed possible.

The first blow landed on the outside wall behind his head. He bounced forward, stumbling into the cage and careening off of it before any of the undead hands could grab him. The second blow bowed the door inward above the latch. Ezekiel raised his rifle and aimed at the door, panned to the window, back to the door. Behind him the undead scuffed and grunted. In the back room, glass shattered. He whirled and forced himself to edge around the cage. A pair of shots cracked outside. They were followed by the crunching of glass. EZ crouched low, looked into the kitchen, and aimed high.

A body folded itself over the windowsill, arms and head dangling inside. A futuristic automatic weapon, all cutouts and angles, lay under its hands. A slick red rivulet crawled from under a black watch cap. Then another blow thudded against the front door. At the same time the front window broke. EZ turned his rifle to it.

Behind him the door flew open. Smokey shot a short burst that spun the figure coming through the window around, knocking the intruder back and down. Smokey ran around EZ and jumped through the window, threw the inert form inside, and jumped in after it.

"Watch the kitchen. Stay in the corner. Keep low."

"Low. Got it." *Go low* would be his position in all future activities, EZ figured, maybe his street name if he ever got to the streets. Go Low was even better than EZ. He took a shooter's stance to the side of the back window and waited for the next attack.

Rey pushed forward, knowing someone could be ahead, waiting for her to come to him. She was being herded to the killing floor.

They might be in her house and the thought of it enraged her. With a jolt of will power she stopped in her tracks to listen. The pursuers slammed through the brush, but she had a few seconds on them. That advantage wouldn't last long. Rey turned right, straight uphill, toward the rock peak of Cannibal Mountain. The route was familiar and there was a chance she could lose them on the way up.

Breathing hard, she cut along a zigzag trail no wider than a footprint. A male voice shouted behind her, telling the other where to go. They weren't trying for secrecy. Rey cut the corners off the trail and clambered through heavy scrub and boulders, choosing speed over quiet. Ahead, light opened where the trees stopped, not timberline but a jumble of massive stones that were the bald mountaintop. What she was looking for was close ... here ... no, farther up ... a desperate moment wondering if the winter had buried it—but no, it had been so well hidden by grasses and scrub trees she had crawled past it. Rey wriggled into the fissure fast and quiet, turned in the cramped space and held a steadying hand on the branches, thankful for the cover of wind flung up from the coast as it reared against the rising land. She backed up on hands and knees and opened her mouth wide so she could catch her breath soundlessly.

The first time she had found the fissure there had been two rattlesnakes in it. She could only hope the snakes were out for the afternoon. Rattlesnakes hated company.

Overhead, feet scraped on boulders. Engineered plastic gadgetry clunked. The crevice was dark but not lightless; all one of them had to do was look straight down as he passed over her. She kept her face down and held still. A footstep fell close to the entrance and a black-booted foot stopped. It pivoted until the man was facing the crevice. Abruptly the foot rose into the air and the man yelled, "Shit!"

"Say again," a voice said from a dozen yards away.

"Goddamn rattlesnake!"

"You bit?"

"No. Fuck, I hate snakes. Son of a bitch!" Rey heard a firearm being cocked.

"Put your fucking gun away. You want to kill it, cut off its head. No gunfire unless necessary."

"Jesus, I hate those fuckers." The man's voice receded.

Rey listened to the search party move off up the mountain. It wouldn't take them long to see she wasn't there, and then they'd be back in the woods and on her trail again. She peered out around the brush and saw nothing, heard nothing. No men, no snake. They had scared each other off. Rey threaded through the branches and ran low downhill, cutting cross country away from the trail. She got about even with her cabin, above it a good quarter mile, when a rabbit cut across her path and disappeared under a bush. Running from what? Rey half turned and saw movement in the trees, something large and tree-colored, coming uphill fast. She sped ahead. The man in forest camouflage was a good runner, but he was large and weighed down by a pack and a long gun.

She ran for the cliffs on the south side of the mountain. The drop-off was well east of Smokey's farm, but the terrain was similar. She had sat on the dizzying edge with Fiddlin' Sue and Jackie Tobasco, looking out at the world they planned on never seeing up close again, drinking just enough beer to make loitering on the cliff dangerous. Treetops masked the drop-off. Like the Sock Creek falls on the north side, even in broad daylight you could walk over the edge and not have time to wonder where the land had disappeared to.

The camo'd man called out to her.

"Stop! I'm not going to hurt you." He had to gasp the words out.

Unlikely, Rey thought, and kept running. The cliff was close. She focused on the trees. When you saw branches and no trunks, you were there—or past there, taking a shortcut to the bottom. You had to look closely even if you knew where the edge was.

"We just want to talk to you."

Not far to go. She put on speed.

The light expanded. Rey scouted desperately for a stick, a stone, found none, skirted uphill away from her pursuer and at last picked up a short, rotting piece of fir branch. Through the dense forest she heard him getting closer, running full speed for her, in a hurry to "talk." Rey threw the branch into the light and dropped and rolled into a salal thicket. The branch swished through floating fir limbs, cracking wood against wood, raising a protest of crows. The man ran after the sound, full speed ahead, and made a garbled sound of surprise as he lost the ground and hurtled down the air express elevator.

She knew once the adrenaline wore off she would be too exhausted to move. She had to get down the mountain before that happened. If there were more of these men, they would find the others shortly. Rey had to warn them, hide them somehow, get them armed and ready to fight. As she got to her feet, something shot by her and lodged in the tree bark. She jerked in the opposite direction and realized what the object was and what the filaments trailing from it meant: one of them was shooting a taser at her.

She hadn't been hit, but the surprise slowed her down. At the cliff's edge a man in camouflage, smaller than the other but just as well-armed, rushed at her. Rey remembered in a flash the slow evenings with her friends sitting by the cliff's edge, savoring the panorama, looking down like tipsy goddesses on the ospreys and eagles. She turned. The man advanced on her slowly and deliberately.

"Drop to the ground, arms out."

Rey took two sideways steps downhill. He made a businesslike noise with his weapon. Rey knelt. He stepped forward.

Gunfire from below made him turn his head. It's starting, Rey thought. They're in trouble.

She pushed herself backwards, fast. The first push took her legs over the edge, the second carried the rest of her body with them. Only her forearms clung to horizontal ground. Her hands grabbed at root clumps, fir cones, dirt.

"Help me!" she said. "Please!"

The man came forward cautiously.

"You want me alive? Take me before I fall! I can't hold on. Help me!"

Training his rifle on her, the man bent and gripped her wrist and pulled. He was stronger than she had thought he would be. She used his strength to let go of the root she had been clutching and grabbed his wrist, then let go with her other hand and fastened it on his arm. He was all that kept her attached to the mountain.

She drew up her knees, planted her feet against the cliff face, and yanked her arms downward. She pulled him so hard something in her shoulder popped. It had to be hard. He had to come with her.

"Hey—!" he started, and Rey tugged him down with her.

26

It was one of those dark phantoms that look like a tall man in black lurking in the corner of your eye, those dark phantoms that always turn out to be nothing. Mercy turned away from the window without another thought. She and Sue had stopped in at the Pear Sisters' to check on them and the children. It was supposed to be a flying visit, but naturally the girls didn't want to let their mothers go, and Bee offered fresh biscuits with honey and Mercy realized how hungry she was. It was probably hunger and fatigue making her eyes play tricks on her. And she *was* fatigued. Exhausted. It was Rey's fault, even if nobody else would come out and say it. Rey had done the unholy act and now they all paid the price. Mercy wished there were something the opposite of a prayer to say for Rey. Nothing so ungodly as a curse, just a word in the Savior's ear that a little justice would be welcomed.

"Who's out there?" Cricket asked. "Is that Travis or Smokey?"

Sue looked. "Doesn't look much like either of them."

Mercy returned to the window. A tall man, and wide, dressed in mottled black. Dark forest camouflage, carrying a large gun.

"Get down!" She grabbed her nearest child and ran to the bedroom. "All you kids get under here. Now!"

Sue took up her rifle; Cricket picked up her father's shotgun. She opened her mouth to demand he identify himself, but Sue shushed her.

"Don't let him know there's just women in here."

"He'll be less likely to kill us if he thinks we're no threat to him," Bee said. "And we don't know that he's a threat to us."

"Oh, come on." Cricket took on a tone that made her sister look at her in surprise. "He's not the Avon lady."

"Door to door gun salesman, maybe," Sue said.

If the man saw the gun barrels pointing at him, he paid them no mind. He walked to the porch and stood in front of the door. His voice was deep and steely.

"Jillian Newhause, come out."

The women looked at each other, then resumed aiming their weapons.

"You've got the wrong house, mister," Sue said. She didn't sound quite like a man, but she did have a set of pipes that played effectively in the bass range. "Go on about your business."

"Where is she?" the commando demanded, sounding dangerously at ease.

"Never heard of her. Go on, now." Sue worked the rifle's lever.

"Open the door, ma'am. I just need to speak with the head of the house a moment."

"Who you callin' ma'am? Go on, I said. I'm not openin' this door for you."

Cricket pumped the shotgun. That got the man's attention, but he didn't step back. Instead he changed his grip on his big ugly gun. Getting ready for something. Up to the challenge.

Mercy came out of the bedroom and asked, "What does he want?"

"Somebody named Jillian."

"Who's that?"

"We don't know. Do you?"

"No idea."

"We got no idea who you're talking about, but I do know if you don't go down off this mountain I'm going to have to make you go." Sue put everything she had into it. She longed for Buck so badly her eyes watered.

"Don't create trouble," Bee said, looking at Sue and Cricket.

Shots streaked the distance from the road's end to the Pear Sisters' house.

"Trouble's already here," Sue said.

For a terrible moment Rey thought he would never let go of her wrist, but he flailed wildly, then his training kicked in and he grabbed his black gun with both hands and fell into space, firing at her as he went down. Chips of mountain hit Rey's face. The cliff face was less than vertical at this spot. She spread-eagled, sucking up every bit of traction and resistance. It was crucial not to gain too much momentum here or she would overshoot and it would all be over. But then her feet touched Deadman's Ledge where Jackie had won the pumpkin seed-spitting contest, only seven feet down but it felt like a mile, and Rey dropped to all fours and cowered and shook for a few minutes. The men might be dead or seriously broken, but they could have snagged a branch on the way down, too. In that case, they would be back.

Another cluster of shots echoed from the village. Rey took deep breaths and got herself oxygenated. She could feel her legs starting to wobble and powered through a set of squats to get the blood circulating. With the shot of strength, she climbed the root and rock holds in the cliff face until her head was almost to the lip. She tossed a pebble overhead onto the ground. Hearing no response, she peeped over the lip, saw no one, not even a shadow in the trees. She hoisted herself over the edge and made a crow's flight down-mountain, trusting her quiet feet and the deep woods to hide her.

※

The man at the door backed up one step. "Last time. Open the door."

"Last time. Get out of here," Sue barked.

Mercy pulled Bee with her back to the bedroom. Cricket and Sue aimed.

His bootstrike bowed the door inward. The latch was made of sturdy stuff but worn; the wood was dense old growth but tired from damp and age. The wood splintered, the latch cracked. The commando raised his foot again.

Another shot, closer this time. The foot came down but it failed to hold the man upright. He knelt in front of the door as if begging to come in. Then he fell onto his side.

"Don't shoot!" Rey's voice said. "Open up, quick."

※

In the front room, Smokey said, "EZ."

"Huh?"

"It might not have been wise, our shooting right off the bat that way. Force of habit, brother. I should have sent you into cover, not made you shoot at people. I apologize."

"You couldn't do it alone," EZ said. He sounded more relaxed than Smokey had hoped for.

"All I can say in my defense is, there's a time to think before acting. In this situation we've got down here, overthinking does not pay off."

"Let God sort 'em out," EZ said, quoting from a WWII video.

"I need you to board up the windows. Can you do that?"

"Can do, Smokey. Can you watch the front and back by yourself?"

"Can do, bro."

EZ found a hammer and broke up the kitchen table. The windows did need boarding up, but Smokey didn't know how intensive the interrogation would get, and it might not do the kid any good to witness it. He was better off keeping busy.

In the front room, Smokey folded the man's watch cap over his wound. EZ's shot had glanced off a rib. It would hurt like a mother, but wouldn't kill the guy for quite a while. "Come on, chum. Wakey wakey."

A few slaps opened the man's eyes. They were hard eyes, as hard as the face under the green and black paint.

"Who are you?"

The eyes closed.

Smokey poked him in the torn rib meat and didn't wait for him to quit flinching before repeating the question. The mouth set harder.

"I don't really give a shit who you are. You don't want to tell me, I'll just call you Jerkwad. What do you want here, Jerkwad? Why are you breaking into my house with such a great big gun?"

The man looked away, bored, contemptuous. Smokey aimed a finger at the ribs again and the man got interested in the conversation.

"Doctor Newhause. Tell us where she is."

Smokey said, "You got the wrong address, Jerkwad. No doctors here at all."

"Jillian Newhause."

"Nope. Don't know any Jillian Newhauses. Don't you feel like a fool, busting in on folks when you got your directions wrong? I wish I could send you on home, but that ain't happening. What are you really after?"

Jerkwad smiled. It was a weak smile, but had a hard crust to it. His chest rattled as he spoke and Smokey decided he might have overestimated the man's health.

"Whatever she calls herself."

"Can't help you, man. You wasted your time."

Jerkwad raised his head a fraction, took a deep breath while he set his jaw muscles against a wince. "It's urgent that she be found." Breath, wince, jaw set. "National security. You have to hand her over."

"National security. Wow. I wish you'd just said that right off, man. Sure, I'll go get her. Oh, wait. I can't. Because there is no Doctor Jillian Newhause here."

"She must be found. We have questions only she can answer."

"I hear ya. I feel your pain. Who wants to talk to her?"

Jerkwad relaxed his head and breathed shallowly. A little peace crept through his muscles. His hard eyes stayed on Smokey.

"Who do you work for?" Smokey waggled his fingers over the intruder's face. "Another poke help you remember?"

"Fuck you."

"No, fuck *you*." Smokey dug his thumb into the wound. The man strangled a cry.

"Who?" Smokey demanded. He had to do it again. It had always been his least favorite part of his job, one of the big reasons he'd quit. *Maximum result with minimum damage* had been his motto. It was something he hadn't had to think about in years and he would have happily gone another twenty without it. Yet it all came readily back: muscle memory. It was in the brain forever like a fungus.

"Tell me who sent you." The question was followed with a deep pinch. Typically answers flooded out with the screams. Smokey wanted to get this shit over with.

It worked. "Summerland!"

"Means nothing to me. Explain."

The man's lips clamped together.

Smokey sat back, wondering how to proceed. He sighed, bound the man's wrists and feet, bandaged his wounds with dishtowels, and dragged the guy next to the zombie cage. The undead reared and fretted like horses passing a corpse.

"Is the other one dead?" EZ asked.

"Yeah. Sorry."

"They were going to kill us, weren't they?"

"I believe that to be true. I doubt if just two came up here."

"What do they want?"

"Some doctor. Newhause. Anybody you know?"

"Never heard of him. Maybe he wants a doctor 'cause he's hurt."

Thinking *He should be wanting a priest*, Smokey fed the zombies and EZ, gulped stew straight out of the Mason jar, and made them all drink water. The zombies were due for hygiene breaks soon, if they in fact eliminated waste. He tried to figure out who else would be out there and what they really wanted up here on Cannibal Mountain, but there wasn't anything to go on.

A faint rustling alerted him and he took a sniper position by the side window.

"Smokey!" It was stage-whispered, but he recognized Rey's voice.

He opened the back door enough for her to slide in and she crouched down, going from window to window.

"Did they follow you?" Smokey asked her.

"I don't think so, but they're hard to see. I heard gunfire. Was that you?"

"Two men in the wrong place. You look like you've been dragged through the woods and put away wet."

Rey told him the pertinent parts of her encounters up-mountain. "There's at least one more up there, a slight chance two more are climbing back up. You only saw the two here?"

"There's no sign of any more. Either they're waiting for something or we got all of this outfit. More likely they're planning the next offense, flanking us, calling reinforcements."

"How do we protect ourselves? We're spread all over."

"The only way is to capture or kill them. We need at least one alive to answer questions. I don't know how long that one's going to last." He thumbed in the direction of the cage.

"I need you and Travis to cover me while I bring the others down," Rey said.

"Is Travis up there?"

"No. I thought he was here."

"Haven't seen him," Smokey said.

"You and I can do it, then. Or I'll get Jackie and Birdie."

They settled that Rey would conscript Jackie, leave Birdie in Jackie's trailer, assign EZ to guard the undead, and hustle the other women and kids downhill through the woods. They might as well all stay together, Smokey said, until they could implement a plan.

"Good luck to us with that," Rey said.

"Of course, we might get them all before we have to fight any more. Unless ... "

"Unless they call for more," Rey said. "They probably have satellite phones or something."

"First let's round up the good guys. Then we'll see what kind of goodies the bad guys brought."

Smokey escorted Birdie to the store. Rey and Jackie approached Sugar Agate's house from the back and peered through the window. Travis was stretched out on the bed with his shoes on. Rey knocked on the glass. Travis snorted and turned over. Rey hissed his name and Travis jerked awake.

"Get your gun and climb out the window," Rey instructed.

When he had joined them, she told him to guard the other side of the road and for god's sake, stay low and out of sight.

Mercy led the kids out the back door. Jackie took point, the Pear Sisters and children in the middle, Rey and Travis flanking. They threaded silently through trees until EZ opened the door at the Dollers'. One look at his face told them they had not left their troubles on the road.

27

"I couldn't stop them. I told them there's food. I gave them food, but they wouldn't stop."

"It's all right, EZ. Let's take a look." Rey pushed the boy gently to his mother.

The revived huddled together, one member at a time glancing out of the scrum at the humans. It was impossible to tell if they wore expressions of guilt, or fear, or satisfaction, or any emotion at all, because their faces were smeared with blood and strings of gore. Pink fluid dribbled down their chins. Some gnawed on meaty bones, sucked at the marrow and licked off the juice. In the smaller cage, Crystal and Berry shrieked, stretching out rigid arms toward the feast they couldn't reach.

"Damn it, I wanted to interrogate that guy," Smokey said.

"I fed them. I did," EZ whimpered.

"We know, son," Mercy said, stroking his hair. "Smokey should never have left you alone with them."

"Who was it?" Jackie asked.

"One of the attackers." Rey told them the story, with Smokey and the shaken EZ filling in their events. "And now we don't have a source of information."

"Well," Jackie said, "we'll just have to catch another one. I suppose that one's dead?" She pointed at the body in the kitchen.

"Anybody searched him yet?" Getting a yes and then a no to her questions, she knelt beside the body and started emptying his various pockets and pouches.

"It happened so fast." EZ sounded steadier. "I don't think the guy even knew what was happening."

"I'm sure you're right," Mercy said. "Right, Smokey?"

"There was nothing you could have done, son."

"Don't *son* him," Mercy said. "Who locked him in there with the undead? You did. Any fool would have known what would happen."

"I won't argue with you on that," Smokey said.

Rey said, "They ate the bones first. Clearly, the revived want or need bones more than meat. Whether it's a taste they've developed or some biological need, a deficiency, I don't know."

"They do look happy," Travis said. "Don't you, Eddy? You happy, Hoot? My bros were hungry!"

Sue said, "Crystal wants a treat, too. And Berry. Hello, ladies. It's coming. Keep your hair on."

Jackie looked for an available piece of carnage to share with the females. Mercy followed her to the kitchen, the girls tagging behind like ducklings.

"Somebody get this body out of here!" Mercy called. "Just as soon as Jackie Tobasco's through digging for buried treasure."

In the living room, Rey regarded the mess in the cage. "What I don't get is how they reached him. I mean, they're tied to the bars. El Duane and Jacob and Trucker John could have gotten to him, but the others were too far away. Yet they have pieces of him, too. And they're still tied."

"They're sharing," Smokey said.

"Cool," Travis said. "They're getting along."

"They're getting along, but I don't know how cool it is." Smokey looked at Rey.

"Altruistic cooperation," Rey said. "That's an interesting development."

They thought about this for a minute, homey clinks of food preparation from the kitchen syncopating normality with the mayhem in front of them.

In the Dollers' bedroom, Bee and Cricket lay on the double bed listening to scraps of talk.

"I haven't slept in any bed but my own in sixty-odd years," Bee said. "I don't care for it. Its lumps conflict with my lumps; where I dip, it pushes. I don't know how Birdie sleeps on this thing. I'd rather have straw."

"Still … " Cricket admonished.

"Yes, it's a bed and we get to lie down and I'm grateful. I just like to speak out about things sometimes."

"I know."

They listened a little more. Then Cricket asked, "How do we know how many are out there?"

"We don't. Just have to wait and see if any more come around, at which time we'll be outnumbered and outgunned."

"Well, we've had a very nice life, haven't we? I feel bad for the young ones. We got to enjoy this mountain and live a long time, and we had privacy and lots of peace. What's in store for the others?"

"Oh, horsewash, Cricket. 'We've had a very nice life.' You're giving up now? The men in black come and that's it, we lay ourselves down and die? Give me a break."

"They're in camouflage, not black, and I do not plan on lying down and dying, I foresee that we may be shot. At that time I will lie down and die, yes. Unless you think you can organize us out of this fix."

"I might."

Cricket turned her head to look at her sister. "Really?"

"I *might*, really. I'm still thinking. Why are they here?"

"They want that Jillian person."

"And why do they think she's here?"

Cricket thought. "Maybe it's Sugar Agate. That would be convenient, since Sugar Agate's dead. We can give them her body and off they'll go. They could have followed her or something, whatever detectives do. Something with the internets."

"If Sugar Agate was a doctor, she was also the best actress since Joanne Woodward. But the doctor might well be here. I don't think it's Fiddlin' Sue because she and Buck were famous. I think I heard them on the radio not too long ago. And I don't think Jillian Newhause is Mercy, because Mercy would not lie about her name for fear of being damned to eternal fire. Jillian Newhause is either not here, or she's Jackie Tobasco, Berry, or Rey Nickel."

Cricket raised a hand. "All right, stop talking for a minute."

Bee closed her eyes, breathing loosely. She was too tired to sleep, but sometimes imitating sleep brought it soft-shoeing in through the mind's back door.

Cricket said, "It could be anybody. We don't know. But we ought to find out."

"And turn her over to those thugs and get back to our lives," Bee pronounced.

"Do you think so? Whoever she is, she's one of our own. We should protect her."

"And die for our trouble. No, I take your point. Lacewing would agree with you. I do, too, in my heart. Yes, you're right; I wouldn't turn her in. I'm not heartless. But if Jillian Newhause is here, and I don't say she is, it's her moral duty to give herself up, and if I discover her identity, I will do my utmost to show her where her moral duty lies. My utmost."

When the undead relatives had been pottied and washed and re-fed, there had been time for the band of exhausted people to claim comfortable spots in the crowded house and think about next steps.

"When are we taking them home?" Sue, Jackie, and Mercy wanted to know.

"How are you going to guard yourselves? I don't want anybody winding up like our commando friend," Rey said.

That was pack mentality, the women argued. Once in the bosom of their families, the revived would grow new human personalities the same way they grew new fingers and arms. They would take their nearly departed home with them first thing tomorrow.

"But we have to stay together," Rey argued. "There are more invaders out there. You don't have the firepower to protect yourselves individually."

"Sure we can. You did it," Sue pointed out. "We've got guns. We'll be fine."

Jackie said, "I think we're safer spread out than lined up here like carnival ducks."

Smokey spoke quietly. "They can cooperate with each other. They can follow orders. They're strong and they seem to be getting smarter. They can regenerate body parts. They don't appear to be afraid of much, certainly not of killing. Those are exactly the qualities an effective fighting force has. Why don't we give them a crash course in guerilla warfare? We stand a much better chance with the whole population engaged."

Looks were exchanged, eyebrows raised, lips compressed.

Then Jackie said, "Well, they were fighters before of one kind or another. Only thing is them following orders. I haven't seen it yet. Alls I've seen is a man torn apart and eaten raw, and no remorse shown. Hey, I didn't mind when Berry did it with rabbits and like that, but humans is bringing it awful close to home."

"Yeah, we don't even know if we need them. The bad guys haven't been back in hours. It looks like they've cleared out. Respect is due to Smokey and Rey and EZ for that. They had the wrong address, wrong mountain." Sue said it and everyone except Smokey and Rey agreed with her.

Mercy heard fretting in the second bedroom and went to check on the girls, muttering, "Last two people in the world I'd give a loaded weapon to is El Duane or Earl."

Jackie was sitting on the floor with one arm through the cage, trying to hold hands with Berry. Berry kept squirming and Jackie kept finding her hand again. "I think Berry could do it. I don't say it's necessary, but she'd be a fine warrior. The girl's got eyes like a hawk and nerves of steel. She ought to have been a Marine." At the sound of her name, Berry slid her opaque gaze to Jackie's mouth. Her own mouth moved silently in imitation.

"Well, yeah," Sue said, "I didn't say Buck couldn't fight. I just don't think he's going to have to. And he shouldn't. He's a lover not a fighter, and he's been through enough, I'd say."

Smokey's hand stroked his shirt pocket where he kept his cigarettes, but he left them where they were. "The kids shouldn't be part of it. We'd leave Jacob and Crystal out of it. What if we do a little training just in case?"

"Preparedness," Rey said. "Better to have it and not need it than need it and not have it. And there are two more of those men out there. At least two more."

Bee and Cricket had gotten up and were sharing the old loveseat in the corner with a spare blanket tucked around their ankles. Bee cleared her throat. "First, a shooting war here, we're not going to have. Let's get that straight right off."

"But if they shoot at us—"

Bee cut Smokey off. "A few shots here and there will be ignored. But there's been too much lately, and sometime, those shots are going to draw attention. Cannibal Mountain is isolated, nicely so. But there are people in the valleys and up the next mountains, and gunshots are good at echoing. So no more shooting.

"Second, I intend to find out what's at the bottom of this invasion and likely that will be enough to end it. But until then, we're going to have a well-trained, armed militia even if we don't need it, as Rey said. If anyone has a good counterargument, I'll hear it now."

"We can't trust them," Mercy said from the bedroom.

Bee looked at Smokey, at Rey, back at Smokey. "Well?"

"We'll make it so we don't have to trust them," Smokey said. "Safeguards, close observation, constant backup."

Mercy sighed loudly enough to be heard in the living room. "You're begging trouble," she said, "and don't say I didn't warn you."

"We won't," Cricket said cheerfully. "We never do."

Bee said, "All right, then. When does the training start? After the invaders attack again, or before?"

"Right now, ma'am," Smokey said, smiling at her.

28

Human bones were the best incentive.

This made the humans nervous, but nobody thought their own revived were a danger, and they didn't like to openly accuse others' relatives of evil designs. So bits of pelvis and femur left over from the zombie feast were retrieved from the waste pile outside and put to use in guerrilla boot camp.

"He made himself useful after all," Smokey said. "Thanks, fella."

While the others rotated sleep and guard duties, Smokey took Travis, Jackie Tobasco, and EZ as his assistants and drilled the recruits. Hand to hand combat resulted in a shortage of one thumb and one hand, but adjustment in grip technique prevented further manual losses. Just like riding a bicycle, Jackie pronounced. It was hard to reinstill the appropriate fear of getting shot, though; it didn't hurt them much and they recovered faster with every hit. Observation and caution were an even harder sell. Looking to the leader for orders was going to be all but impossible, although the brighter ones grasped the basics of team formation.

"From hunting," EZ said. "They like to gang up on the deer."

By the time they had covered evasion, dawn had moped in and Smokey was dead on his feet. "I know how the walking dead feel. Am I turning green?"

"I don't think it's catching," EZ said. "It's not, is it?"

"No, no. But if you start growing body parts, give me a heads up." Smokey nodded toward the naked hand and thumb stubs, already nubbing out into usable appendages.

"That was pretty fun," Travis said. "I never did that kind of stuff before."

"You never played war when you were a kid?"

"Naw. I was rippin', rocking out with my buds, stokin'. You know."

"Well, it's no boot camp, but it's better than nothing," Smokey said. "Welcome to the Cannibal Mountain Tactical Team."

"Cool," said Travis.

The training crew, desperately in need of sleep, woke the women. Jackie and Sue argued about taking their folks home right away, but Smokey convinced them to hold off at least four hours.

"We'll have them forever," Mercy said, disconcerting everybody by agreeing with Smokey. "Let him keep the responsibility a few more hours. He trained them to fight, not that they didn't already know. I'm going to make a pot of tea and fix pancakes, if anybody wants to help."

Smokey and his drill sergeants ate the first batch out of their hands, then slumbered like downed trees.

"You know what I wonder?" Sue said.

"What?" Rey said.

"Why did they attack the store?"

"I've been thinking about that," Rey said. "They must have been after our revived."

"So they must have been watching the house. And so they must have been watching all the houses. And either they thought that doctor was here, or they lied about that and they just wanted our revived."

Misty stepped into the living room, licking jam off her fingers. "They keep asking for Doctor Newhause."

What?

Sue said, "We told the one who tried to get in the Pear Sisters', there's no Jillian Newhause here. He didn't believe ... "

Rey didn't hear the rest of Sue's sentence. So it *was* her they were after. It was the Summerland Mission. They'd found her. They were shooting at anybody, everybody, to get to her. Rey was hurting these people again. She was getting them killed. There was only one right move.

"Doctor Jillian Newhause?" Rey repeated.

"Does that mean something to you?" Jackie asked.

She was going to say it, but the words were too bitter.

Lying was foul. It sneaked up fast on easy feet until you felt its jaws snap your will. Like an alligator. Like the undead.

"They're going." Rey nudged Smokey's foot. She roused Travis but let EZ sleep on.

Most of the newly minted army lined up at the back door. The line wasn't quite straight and their posture wasn't quite erect, but they wore a purposeful, almost intelligent expression. The same expression, all of them. Sue led Buck and Crystal out and across the yard until the trees swallowed them. The rest followed without fuss, melting into the green.

Birdie refused to stay with Dollar Bill so Jackie took her home with Berry. The Pear Sisters consented to wait a while before going home alone, even though Rey volunteered Travis to go with them for protection.

"We don't have any place to go," he told them. "Hoochville's mostly burnt down, and there's a gnarly dead guy in it. I guess me and Eddy and Hoot will be staying here."

"You can stay in Sugar Agate's house with Trucker John," Cricket told him.

"Dude scares me," Travis said. "And I'm pretty sure he's not up for sharing that house. Especially not with me."

Bee proclaimed eighteen hours would tell: if the invaders didn't return during that time, odds were good that life could go back to normal.

"I think normal's on vacation," Travis answered. "Normal's on a warm beach somewhere sipping a cold Corona."

In the afternoon gloom, Rey was the first one to hear voices outside. Smokey went out to check and slipped back into the house at double speed-double quiet. He held up two fingers, pointed toward the road, and slid the cage against the door. Rey moved the small one to block the back door.

"One out here," Smokey said.

"I've got one out back," Rey answered. "Travis, you see any more?"

"Can't see. My guys are getting foamy, though. Could be a whole army of them out there."

"Are they the ones from upmountain, or new ones?" Smokey asked Rey.

"Different clothes."

Something like a battering ram pounded the front door. The cage bars rattled. Rey hunkered beside the door and aimed where she guessed the invader would be when he smashed in. One more blow cracked the wood around the doorknob and the third strike blew the door inward, pushing the cage back a foot and a half. Rey pulled the slack out of the trigger but the doorway was empty.

A brown metal can sailed through the ruined doorway into the living room. Rey flinched, then grabbed for it, but it landed inside the cage. There was just enough room to pull the cage door open to grab the can and maybe have time to throw it back out, but that would have placed her smack in the sights of the attacker.

She yelled, "Take cover!" and rolled away. Huddling beside an overstuffed chair, she waited for the explosion to rip her apart. Instead, air hissed out of the can and a thick white cloud swelled into the room. The breath she took scoured her mouth and throat, but she used it to shout "Tear gas!" Then she pulled her undershirt over her head and took aim at what she hoped was the doorway, unable to open her eyes against the burn.

There was noise at the cage, a grunt, some thumps. Something thick fell over Rey's head—a blanket. She clawed at it but it pulled tight around her neck. She heard Travis call something—maybe "Hoot," maybe the mountain call—and confused sounds from outside the door.

Amazing how fast Hoot got away. Travis had the Y of Hoot's suspenders in his fist and then he just wasn't there. Before Travis could say Get back in here, you're going to get shot, the tear gas flew in, Travis dashed for the door, and there was Hoot, pushing the camo guy's throat into the ground through his backbone with the Terminator-looking gun in his other hand. Good old Norse Force, a freaking Viking. The big guy hoisted camo man by his collar and dragged him into the house. The tear gas didn't bother Hoot at all, but even outside it was making Travis miserable.

When the second camo man came around the house, Eddy was up in the guy's grill like a pissed off monkey, and just that fast the guy's gun belonged to Eddy. Eddy pointed it. Camo man ran off serpentine into the bushes. He was damn fast, but not as fast as Eddy.

Travis heard two-thirds of a scream, some bush breakage, and then Eddy was dragging his prey back into the yard, his face blank and clay-colored but with some self-satisfaction showing through those flat eyes.

"My boys." Travis teared up with emotion, or maybe that was the tear gas. "I am so fucking proud."

Rey's eyes burned and streamed tears. First tears I've shed in years, she thought. The tear gas permeated the wool blanket but she knew it was worse on the other side. Her nasal passages were on fire; her sinuses frantically deployed mucus to wash the chemicals out. Something pulled at her and she clutched the blanket as she was dragged across the floor. Once she was outside it was easier to breathe, but the pain didn't stop. The blanket was yanked off and she collapsed gasping and retching, face down in the sweet forest mulch.

Smokey's voice was a hardly recognizable rasp. "Wash it off. Travis, stay here." He drew Rey to her feet and they stumbled to Jackie's trailer, every breath a punishment.

"What the hell?" Jackie pulled them inside.

"Tear gas," Smokey said. "Shower."

"Right here. I'll get towels. It won't be very warm. In fact, it's going to be cold. You ought to go up to the Pear Sisters'. They've got hot water."

But Smokey was stripping Rey's shirts and pants off and bundling her into the little shower. He tore his contaminated clothes off and squeezed in with her under the freezing water. Rey shivered and let the stream wash the chemicals off her skin, opened her eyes and tilted her nose and mouth to the spray. Smokey's body felt as chilled as she was, but as the pain lessened she leaned into him, feeling for warmth under his skin.

Water streamed over his contours. He was built of chiseled muscle and heavy bones. Good to lean on. Sturdy, efficiently engineered. Rey felt his internal heat, his heart pumping under his chest. She rested her forehead there.

He wrapped his arms around her. He was lightly furred, a comforting animal presence giving her shelter from the frigid water, from the poison, from so much that was wrong in her world lately.

"Turn around," Smokey said.

"I'm freezing," she said.

"You can talk. Good." His voice was hoarse, like hers.

"Thanks for pulling me out."

"Get your eyes and mouth, your face."

She obediently turned her face to the stream again, opened her mouth and sluiced the irritants out until she couldn't stand the cold any more. But she stayed. Smokey was behind her in the little shower stall and she didn't want to lose the feel of his body pressed against her back and thighs. He was entirely different from Travis. More solid, and not merely physically. As long as he was there, nothing bad was happening.

And something nice was happening involving pressure and heat and more of that animal presence. Rey pressed back.

His hands on her shoulders, his mouth against her hair ...

"You guys must be a couple of icicles. I warmed up towels. You get all the tear gas off?" Jackie peered through the bathroom door. "Come on, polar bears. You get pneumonia and we're down two marines. Here you go." She held out towels and slid her gaze over the naked bodies filling the stall, then made the suggestion of a wink at Rey and left them alone.

Bee plunged the knife into the slab of dried venison loaf. "It's just a feeling. She's close. She's coming back soon."

Cricket didn't want to talk about it. If Lacewing was all right, Cricket didn't want to jinx it. And if she wasn't all right, Cricket didn't want to talk about it at all.

"Don't you feel it?" Bee demanded.

"I'm not superstitious."

"Well, neither am I, which is why this is noteworthy."

"I hope you're right." Cricket sighed. "I miss Lacey."

"I don't understand why she flew off. Oh, I suppose I do. It was too much pressure. She has a position in this community and she let everyone down. So off she went."

"I'd forgotten," Cricket said. "How she unattaches. How loosely tethered she is to the earth. To us."

"To herself," Bee said, and put the sliced loaf on the table. She joined Cricket at the table set for three. Per long habit, they sat in silence for four seconds, remembering they were alive despite the thousand things that could have killed them singularly or together, six and seven and eight decades of close calls, both noteworthy and unnoticed.

One of them was still alive. Smokey didn't like the way Hoot had pawed at the one he'd dragged in. Travis seemed pleased. He was finally playing war. Smokey was glad he was having a good time. He only hoped the surfer boy would cowboy up when the time came.

Eddy's captive was still breathing, and Smokey had to credit Travis with this fortunate turn of events.

"I was like, No, Eddy, bro, leave him be! And Eddy had the dude's gun, ready to shoot him up. He listened to me, though. Didn't you, Ed-Man?"

"Keep him away from both of them," Smokey said. "I need him conscious and talking. Preferably in one piece."

Smokey wore Dollar Bill's clothes with the pants belted up. He cleared up the debris and put Travis to work managing air-clearing and furniture-covering; he loaded weapons and watched for attackers, but his mind was in Jackie Tobasco's shower stall.

Those thoughts he firmly stowed away for later. Now it was time to have a chat with the one living invader.

29

Jackie looked at the floor, out the window, then at her chipped nails, and finally at Rey. Rey looked miserable, even aside from her red eyes and nose and the hair plastered to her head. Birdie was sleeping; Berry sat at the table cleaning her Winchester 30-30 from which Jackie had taken the bullets. Like riding a bike, Jackie thought, sniffing the ripe scent of gun oil. You never forget how to clean your gun.

"Say something," Rey pleaded.

"Something," Jackie said.

"Come on, Jacks."

"What are you going to do?"

"I have to go." Rey covered her eyes with her fingers, whether from emotion or pain Jackie couldn't tell. "Don't I? I have to leave."

"Do you want to leave?"

"No."

"Really? There's plenty of times I want to leave here. Right now, for instance. I and Berry would have left already but the sons of bastards took the trolley down so we're stuck like flies on flypaper. Even without armed men shooting the place up and my girl getting turned into Predator, there are days I'd give up anything or anybody for a thermostat and Chinese take-out."

"And a hot shower," Rey said, smiling faintly.

Jackie tried, but she couldn't smile back. Sure, everybody on the mountain was hiding something or on the run from somebody, but this hurt.

She said, "You're sure full of surprises."

"I don't want to be."

"I knew you were smart, but you're a damn doctor. Huh. It makes me wonder how come when I had the flu or food poisoning or whatever it was, you didn't fix me up? And Liberty broke her ankle and Lacewing Pear futzed around and lucky thing the ankle fixed itself in spite of her. I mean, we weren't going to die. Maybe you knew that so you didn't have to give yourself away."

"I'm not that kind of doctor. I did research. I've never set a bone. I've never treated intestinal problems."

"Research, huh?" Jackie said. "Researching what? What makes those terrorists want you so bad?" She wondered if Rey would tell all the truth, or any of the truth, about that little question.

And sure enough, Rey shook her head. "The less you know, the safer you are."

"Oh, jeez. You're yanking my chain, girl. Spy versus spy. Being in the dark doesn't make you safer."

Rey stood up, paced the five steps to the other wall and back. "I'll tell you as soon as I can, Jackie, I promise I will. And I'll turn myself in to them. But ... "

It was the right thing to do, but thinking about Rey going with the armed men gave Jackie a whole new level of hurt.

"I'm going to wait until I know it'll do everybody some good. I'm leverage."

Jackie stood, made eye contact with Berry out of habit but got nothing in return, walked to the door. "No offense, I love you, ReyRey, but we're safer without you right here in the house." She pulled her red and turquoise robe around her stomach and cinched it tight. "The hell of it is, you made this whole mess happen, but I do believe you're the only one who can clean it up. So don't run off too soon."

" 'Don't go away mad, just go away.' " Rey tried another smile. "I'm sorry, Jackie. Please don't tell anybody yet. I'll take care of it. Please?"

Impulsively, Jackie pulled Rey in for a hug, made up for it by opening the door, then made up for that by zipping her lips.

"Get dressed," Rey told her. "Be ready."

Jackie watched Rey lope over the spongy ground, seeing her own clothes from the back for the first time. She could have been watching herself.

A nest of worries had her too confused to think in a straight line. She was losing Berry or had already lost her. Now Rey. Maybe her home, maybe her life, maybe the end of the world as she knew it. If Jackie's experience was any guide, there would be more fighting and a world of hurt, coming soon to a theater near you.

Stripped down his underwear, the enemy wasn't so bulky. Smokey let him keep his skivvies, having no desire to see genitalia unless it was absolutely necessary. He said so to the captive, who stood beside the bed while Smokey took his ease in the straight chair.

"You brought a lot of toys." On Birdie's lumpy quilt Smokey laid out an assault rifle, a semiautomatic pistol, knife, a bigger knife, a water bottle, compass, waterproof map case, tear gas grenade, three MREs, rolled poncho, and various pouches and straps. "But I don't see a phone. How do you talk to your boss?"

The time of refusing to answer had passed. Smokey had spent half an hour putting the guy at his ease before making him strip, and Markowski's tongue was loosened. He said, "I don't."

"They leave you out here alone, making your own decisions? You show up when you show up?"

"I don't have a boss."

"How do you talk to the other mercs? Bird calls?"

"What makes you think I'm private army?"

"You're GI? I don't think so. No insignia, for one thing. You got caught, for another."

"We're not government issue, but that's all I'm going to say. You got my name and sosh and I don't have to tell you any more."

"I don't blame you," Smokey said sympathetically. "You looked like a fool, getting caught by a bunch of civilians. I wouldn't want that getting back to the guy signs my paycheck, either."

Smokey propped his feet up on the bed. They left dirt on the quilt; he almost removed his feet and brushed off the quilt but stopped himself in time. Disdain was better for his image. "Okay, fine, a mysterious agency sent you. To do what?"

The man smiled.

"Markowski. You're caught. I need a few basic facts, just background to what we already know. You need your clothes back and to get out of here and go home so you can tell your girlfriend how heroically you performed. Let's make the trade. Your clothes and most of your equipment back, straight across for twenty-five words or less. Let's get this over with."

"I ain't telling you nothing."

Hostility leaked around the words. Not contempt; anger. The guy was getting irritated. Good. He wasn't trained in interrogation resistance. He was resisting, but not in a sustainable way. Still, Smokey really did want to get this over with. He still felt bad about poking the open wound of the man who got eaten.

"As long as there's time, I don't mind much. I got to be here anyway. Of course, if things get hairy ... well, we'll worry about that when we come to it." He lowered his eyelids and ran his gaze over the man's mostly naked body. "Hey, you party?"

"What?" A gratifying shift in posture: the chest sinking, the eyes widening.

"It'll relax you."

Markowski couldn't mask his horror.

Smokey swept the collection of tactical gear to one side of the bed and patted the quilt. "Get comfortable."

Markowski stayed where he was.

"Sit." Smokey put an edge in his voice that would have made him sweat if he'd been in Markowski's shoes. Which Markowski didn't have.

If the interrogatee called his bluff, Smokey did have another way to twist the scenario, but he didn't need it. The man was terrified. Clearly *Deliverance* scenes unspooled in his head. Smokey went with it.

"I realize we're only a ragtag bunch of hillbillies. No fancy formal training, no government gadgets. But we enjoy life. What's the point of living if you can't share a little fun with others? You're not too good to party with me, are you?" Suspicion crept into his voice.

"No." It sounded weak. "I don't party on the job."

"But you're not on the job. I punched your time clock for you. Sit down." Steel in his tone.

Markowski sat. Smokey smelled fear sweat. He stood up so he could tower over the prisoner. This was like shooting fish in a barrel. Maybe he hadn't hated all of this part of his job. Any job well done was satisfying. You could take pride and pleasure in it. Living on top of Cannibal Mountain all these years, Smokey had forgotten about that aspect of it.

He unbuttoned the top of his—Dollar Bill's—shirt and sat beside the prisoner, leaning sideways against the headboard. The old bed sounded as if it were disassembling, heading toward the floorboards. Markowski had been slumping, but he sat up at attention, his hands on his knees, ready to defend his honor. Smokey reached in his shirt pocket and pulled out a joint, resealed it by sticking it all the way into his mouth and drawing it out again, moist, through his lips. He made sure Markowski saw him do it. He scratched the match on the headboard—he'd make it up to Birdie later, after they'd lived through this—and fired up. He hotboxed the blunt so fumes filled the small room, making sure to blow clouds into his prisoner's face. When it was down to a roach he licked his fingertips and pinched the lit end. The fire sizzled against his skin.

"Now this here was my special blend. Mostly good homegrown sensimilla flowers. Potent shit. You feeling it?"

He leaned forward, peering into his prisoner's eyes. "But I added some other ingredients. It won't hurt me, I've got a tolerance built up. This won't kill you, but it does have an effect on the brain. Minute but widespread frontal lobe seizures. Then your neurotransmittors bottom out. What really gets us to home plate, though, is the digitalis. It comes from foxglove, which happens to be a weed in these woods. You can't go to the outhouse without tripping on a bed of the stuff. That's what's making your heart slow down now. The combo's a very effective disinhibitor. More effective than sodium pentothal. It can kill a healthy young man like yourself inside three minutes, but you're more use to us alive. Not indispensable, but useful."

Smokey patted Markowski's knee. "The beauty part is, your bosses can't hold you accountable for anything you say when you're drugged. Even if they find out, which is totally up to you, you're off the hook." He gave Markowski's kneecap a friendly squeeze.

If he hadn't been with Jacob and Earl—or, as EZ had started calling him, Zombie Dad—EZ would have been mortified. For the past few years, when he'd run into Crystal or Misty on the way to or from the outhouse he had hidden, or at least looked at the ground on the theory that if he couldn't see them they couldn't see him. But with all that had happened, and fortified with the excuse that it wasn't him using the facilities but other people, not even human people, EZ forgot about being embarrassed and called out to Misty.

She waved. Crystal walked behind her, an identical twin until you saw how big Crystal had gotten through the shoulders and arms, and her lichen color, and her heavy way of walking. Misty opened the wooden door and closed it behind her sister and came through the saplings to the wire fence between their properties.

"Zombie-sitting?"

"Yeah." EZ came across the pasture. Jacob had gone inside their outhouse; Zombie Dad waited by the door scratching his buttocks.

"Pretty weird about the army guys, huh?"

"They're not in the army," EZ said authoritatively. "They're terrorists or mercenaries."

"Do you think more are coming?"

"More are already here. Out there." EZ cocked a finger vaguely upmountain.

Misty looked behind her and up the mountainside. "We shouldn't be out here, then."

EZ shrugged. "I'm not too worried. I've got a weapon. I already shot one of them." It felt so good to say it he said it again. "I got him in center body mass, Smokey said. A clean shot."

"You're lucky. Mom won't let me fight. I just get to take my sister on potty breaks. Whoopee."

"At least you're armed."

"Well, sure. Mom made me bring the revolver. But she said if I need to fire it, run away instead. She forbid me to fight, if you can believe it. Forbid. Her word. I said, 'Mom, we're having a war, in case you didn't notice. We need all the fighters we can get.' And I know how to shoot; I've been shooting since I was six and I'm good. Why was she and Daddy teaching us how to shoot? For this right here!"

EZ gave her a cool, knowing nod.

The Alder family outhouse door creaked and Jacob came out. EZ called, "Your turn, Dad. Jacob, wait by the door." EZ watched as they switched places, then turned back to Misty.

"They follow directions pretty good," Misty said.

"I helped Smokey train them."

Talking with Misty felt as unreal as all the other stuff that had been going on lately. EZ knew he was a kid to the grownups, down there with Liberty and Freedom. But talking with Misty over the fence, both of them with their weapons ready, on the lookout for danger, with their lives on the line, and Jacob out of his big brother spot—they were equals now.

"You can fight," he said. "No one can stop you. We need everybody, not just the old people."

"I've got really good eyesight. And I'm fast." Misty glanced at the Hill outhouse. "You know what burns my cookies, is I was the good kid. Mom trusted me when Crystal went all crazy. Now she doesn't trust me to protect us. Just to babysit. Well, I'm not doing it. I mean, I'll watch out for Crystal when I'm around, but she's Mom and Dad's kid, not mine. It's not fair."

"I know. All of a sudden I'm supposedly the man of the house but she uses me more like another mother." EZ lowered his voice and leaned closer. He inhaled Misty's scent: something soapy and foreign. "I'm moving out tonight."

"What? Where are you going?" Misty looked around, as if searching for anyplace a person could escape to.

"I'm moving down there with Smokey. We're a team. The Cannibal Mountain Tactical Team. You know what?" The words burbled out without the benefit of thought. "You should come, too! Be more than a babysitter."

"Sure. And your mom and my mom will march right down there and haul us home by our ears. End of the adventure of the great tactical team."

Misty looked around. "Did you hear that?"

"What?"

"Some animal."

"A wolf?"

"There aren't any wolves in the mountains, stupid."

A low baying crept through the trees. The sound soaked up light and frosted the air. EZ gripped his rifle.

Crystal stepped out of the outhouse and cocked her head, riveted.

"It sounds like some kind of dog," Misty said. "I think hound dogs sound like that. I better shut in our chickens and cows."

Baying broke loose, low-pitched, mournful and owl-like, a siren winding down into the cellar of human hearing. It came from the north and east and from somewhere close at hand, starting low and getting lower until it was more vibration than noise.

"Wolves." EZ's heart thumped his budding Adam's apple. He was terrified of wolves. You could say there weren't any left all you wanted, but that was the thing with wolves. They were good at hiding until, too late, you saw a pair of yellow eyes at the edge of the trees, then another pair, and then the pack was on you.

"Not wolves," Misty said. "I don't know what it is, but it's not wolves. Don't worry. I'm not afraid of it."

"Me, either." It had gotten turned around somehow, Misty telling him not to worry. "I'm a trained fighter."

30

"Who sent you?" Starting off easy.

Markowski closed his lips, but the glaze over his eyes said it all.

"What's your story, man? Out here in the tulies loaded for bear, looking for a doctor." *Deep down, everybody wants to tell their story.*

"Is somebody sick? Are you sick?" Showing concern.

"I'm not sick."

"But you're feeling funny."

Markowski shrugged. It looked like it cost him an effort.

Smokey pulled out another, fatter blunt and dragged it under his nose, savoring its aroma like a cigar.

"So you're private army. Who signs your paychecks? Wouldn't be an enemy of the United States government, would it? A spot of terrorism to fill out the family Christmas Savings Plan?"

"I'm no terrorist. I love my country." Markowski's lips were dry and cracked.

"And yet you break the law, make a living via screwing over your homeland. Homicide, assault, kidnapping if you were to find this doctor. If someone were to turn her over to you. Hard to reconcile."

"I'm fine with it."

"Good, good." Smokey leaned in again, checked the prisoner's pupils, smiled. "Here we go." He settled back against the headboard. "Who hired your outfit?"

More shrugging, embellished by a working of Markowski's jaw muscles.

"Take your time. I'm in no hurry unless more of your guys show up, in which case I'll just cut off our discussion. If you get my meaning." Smokey let it percolate a second. "Who came with you, Markowski?"

"Fuck you. Two of us walked off a cliff, you got one, and the freaks out there ate one."

"Who else?"

Markowski blinked so slowly Smokey raised a hand to slap him awake. Then Markowski pulled his eyes open with his forehead muscles. "One unaccounted for."

"Who sent you into this mess?"

"Poindexters. Bitch stole company secrets, they want her back."

Smokey played nice, offered him a glass of homebrew, and Markowski gave it up. What the poindexters would do with Dr. Jillian Newhause he didn't have specifics for, but they'd encouraged extraction by any means necessary. His whole outfit hated that asshole Roberts, who thought he was a major player but was a little weenie. Not that you mountain hicks were such pleasant company, either. Yeah, the guy left alive up here, if he was alive, had a sat phone and he no doubt had already used it to call headquarters. As soon as they got clearance from Roberts, they could be here in six hours. Maybe less. And no, he didn't have a radio himself and couldn't countermand the order anyway.

And what were these company secrets that were worth dying for? Fuck if I know, was Markowski's answer, but it was a very big deal. Fate of the world stuff. Or so Roberts said. Some kind of mission. Knowing Roberts, he was puffing it up.

Did he know anything about a bunch of these mountain dwellers dying? Markowski said no, and this time Smokey couldn't tell if he was lying or not. The weed had gotten inside his own brain, too, in spite of his superman tolerance, and it dulled his acuity more than he'd counted on.

Who would answer the call to arms? Whoever the asshole honcho said to send. Markowski was a mere grunt; troop deployment was beyond his pay grade.

Smokey was pressing for a better answer to the last question when a sound ripped up his backbone and rattled his ears.

Markowski looked at him, his face open in surprise and fear. "What the hell was that?"

"Sounds like our time's about up, bud. Bye."

"I told you everything I know!"

"Except who's on the way. How many and when, Markowski? Our chat's coming to an end." Smokey stood up, all business.

"They'll send another six at the most. That's all we have. Six like me. ARs, sat phones, be here inside six hours." He stopped talking and listened to the nearly subsonic moaning coming through the walls.

Smokey opened the door and told Travis and his boys to put Markowski in the small cage. "Let him wear his shirt," he offered.

"Uh ... " Travis looked around. "No can do right at this moment, Smokes." He peered out the front door and whistled, got no response. "Hoot and Eddy ran off."

The mountain wasn't big enough for the both of them. She'd lived in the same house with him for fifty years, it felt like; now next door was too close. When she'd told Jackie she didn't want her husband staying in the trailer with them, Jackie had been only too glad. Just us girls, she said, looking relieved. So as far as Birdie knew, Bill was in Sugar Agate's house with Trucker John. Or out in the cold and wet. Or in Trucker John's cruddy trailer. She didn't care. The nasty old goat wouldn't stay buried, but that didn't mean he was going to stay above ground.

A bullet wouldn't do the trick, and if she cut off his head she wouldn't put it past him to grow another one. Bill couldn't swim, but Birdie doubted she could hold him under long enough to drown, and drowning probably wouldn't last, either. Birdie could only think of one other way. She hoped Bill was in that little trailer. She hated waste.

Outside, some big animal was in heat—or it could be a Sasquatch, which was absolutely real, no matter how Bill laughed at her. Nasty sound, like all the devils on the mountain singing. Bill would have to wait. This was no time to go out.

"It's me. Don't shoot." Rey came in through the kitchen door and saw there was a new man in the smaller cage, wearing camo underpants.

Travis told her, "Hoot and Eddy ran off. They heard that howling and *ptchoo*, outta here."

"I think it's them," Rey said. "talking to each other. This house reeks of pot."

"No extra charge," Travis said happily.

Rey found Smokey in the living room and let him tell her about the interrogation. She looked at the floor, trying to spit out the words she had to say, but then he said they had six hours, tops, before more invaders reached them, and the moment passed. A minute after that EZ and Misty came streaking across the yard.

"That howling," EZ panted.

"It was the zombies," Misty said.

"They all started doing it and then—"

"They all ran out of the outhouse."

"They went north and up. I never saw anybody move that fast," EZ said. "We'll never catch them."

Travis asked, "Were Eddy and Hoot with them?"

"All I saw was Dad and Crystal and them take off," Misty said.

"How about Trucker John?" Travis said.

The kids shook their heads.

Jackie steamed into the kitchen, a small tornado of frustration in her wake. "Berry ran off again! Those other ones started in, I know it was them, and they made her up and run off right when I had her clean and settled down and now she's out there with that, that, that pack of hyenas. What's she going to come back with this time, a deer in her mouth?"

She passed by the half-naked man in the cage without a glance, brushing the kids and Travis aside on her way to the front door. She stuck her head out and screamed, "Berry Ann! Get back here! Berry, come home! Don't leave me," she called more quietly, and leaned her head on the broken door frame.

Rey pulled her away. "She'll be back. But there's another man out there, so don't make yourself a stationary target." Rey sat Jackie down in the big chair and let her cry. After a minute words replaced the tears and Rey listened to her friend talk and curse. Then she smoothed Jackie's hair back and let her pull herself together. Rey joined Smokey by the front window.

"A new development," she observed. "It's a thrill a minute with this crowd."

Smokey said, "Where do you suppose they're coming from that takes six hours to get here?"

"Hm. Anyplace by air, if they have a private plane. Where's the nearest landing strip in the mountains?"

"Can't say. Maybe as far away as Corvallis, depending on the size of their aircraft. A small plane could land a lot closer. Florence or even Waldport. Estimate as little as an hour and half driving time, less by helo."

Rey did the math. A trip from Arizona worked out about right.

"You know we can't fight them all off indefinitely," Smokey said. "Guerilla warfare only works as long as you've got a supply train and guerillas."

"And we're short on both."

"What do we have a lot of?"

"Trees," Rey said. "Shadows and places to hide. Knowledge of the terrain. Four or five people who can fight. That won't be enough."

"It could be," Smokey said. "We also have the zombies."

"Do we? They all seem have run away."

"I trained them to come back to our call."

"Okay, let's get them back. Although I don't see how they'll be enough of an army to make the difference if a fresh set of fully living, fully trained troops land on us. They're going to have a tough time reaching us without the trolley. There's no place to land a helicopter. The clearing, maybe, but it's pretty small and has trees hanging over the edges. The peak is too rocky and jagged."

"They could descend from a helo on lines. They could do a technical ascent of several mountain faces, and they could probably get across the river using lines if they wanted to bad enough. They're not military and I don't believe any mercenary has the strength, organization, and training to carry out an invasion using those techniques, but we can't count it out. And some of these guys might be ex-SEALs, ex-Rangers."

Rey rubbed her face with her palms. "They just want Jillian Newhause. If they get her, they'll go away."

"But we can't give her to them, so we've got to convince them they're wrong before they kill anybody. So far, they've been shooting first and asking questions never. We've got to use whatever stopping power we can get."

Rey nodded. "There's no more time to mess around, then. The few hours I have left I want to spend honestly." She forced herself to look at Smokey straight on, and lowered her voice. "I'll tell everybody else as soon as I can, and say goodbye. It's me they want. I'm Jillian Newhause."

She waited a beat, and couldn't stand it anymore. Turning around, she tried to smile at Jackie, then went into the kitchen. She wondered if Travis and the kids had heard her, but the kitchen was empty except for the caged man. Rey went back to the bedroom and picked up his pants and socks, pushed them through the cage bars and went to the door. He said something, but she didn't catch it or stop to listen.

The remaining goon might pick her off as soon as she set foot outdoors—but they wanted her alive. Alive, so Everett Roberts would feel safe. Alive, so the Summerland Mission could extract information from her. Rey did not want to stay alive for that.

However, there were responsibilities to shed first. The goats and chickens needed new homes. There were items to burn and things to bury, people to say goodbye to. Rey stepped outside into a thick, windless rain.

"Wait."

She looked back. Smokey was moving toward her. The look on his face was grim.

"I'm sorry, Smokey," she said. "I'm going, and this will all be over."

"Stop."

Something in his tone lassoed her.

He said, "Where are you going?"

"I've got to close up the house and see to the animals."

"Why?"

"Because I'm responsible for them."

"Then don't leave them."

Rey stared at him. The old beard was reasserting itself as fierce stubble. The dark circles under his eyes no doubt matched her own. "This is my fault. All of it. I turned all those people into freaks. I have to fix it. I have to go with the soldiers." She was ashamed to hear her voice tighten and she bit the wave of emotion back.

"Yes, you have to fix it." He moved closer, clenched her upper arm. "You have to stay and clean up the mess."

"But—"

"*But* we need you here, fighting with us."

"What part don't you understand? They'll leave you all alone as soon as I give myself up." She shook her arm free.

"They'll never leave us alone. We're found. We're on their map. If we roll over, the mountain turns into a tourist attraction. A Ruby Ridge, a Waco, an Oregon Standoff. You won't be able to throw a stick without hitting a Feeb or ATF or reporter. You will have given yourself up for nothing."

If she wouldn't feel despair, she could let herself feel anger. She bit out the words. "So I can't fix it. I fucked us up royally and that's the end? I don't accept that, Smokey. I'm going to do whatever I can to save my friends, and if it's not enough, at least I will have tried. I don't give up."

"That's exactly what you're saying you'll do: give up. It's suicide and it's stupid. You're not doing it."

Her anger wasn't backing him down. Funny that she'd always thought of Smokey as a passive, laid back pothead, an overly mellow holdout from a never-was utopia, but now she was having trouble summoning the strength to walk away from him.

"Me staying is murder."

Smokey's stare drilled into her.

Rey said, "So we're just screwed, then."

His expression stayed stony, then the smallest tell of a smile covered the distance between them. "Looks that way, doesn't it?"

31

Travis shooed the kids off, but they wouldn't leave, sticky and excited like spring flies, talking about fighting. Travis didn't want to fight, he wanted Hoot and Eddy to get back to making beer and moonshine. No doubt he'd find them huddling in the beer-end stump of Hoochville, but for now he was only going as far as Sugar Agate's house. She'd been his girlfriend and as selfish as she was, now that she was dead she definitely would want him to have the house, but she was going to have to vacate before he moved in. Just as well the kids were along for the ride. They could help him take out her body and carry the clothes and trinkets to somebody else's house.

When he went inside, though, the first thing he saw was big sloppy Trucker John hulking over him, the first thing he heard was Misty shouting, and the first thing he felt was a log landing on the side of his head. He stayed conscious, looking at the smooth floorboards and a pair of boots like tree stumps planted within easy kicking distance of his face.

Instead of double-teaming Trucker John for him, the kids ran out of the house. Some fighters.

"Don't kick me, dude," Travis said. "What was that for?" If one of the boots moved back to plant a kick, Travis planned to grab it and yank hard. The guy should go down like timber.

"My," Trucker John roared. "Myyyyy!"

"Jeezus. What are you, Frankenstein?" Travis's head was starting to throb. "No offense."

The boots rolled and shoved him until Travis scrambled on hands and feet out the door. "It's not yours," he yelled. He noticed short purple flowers pushing up by the doorstep and remembered how Sugar Agate fussed over the flower garden in the summer. No way was dumb zombie Trucker John going to keep the garden up. Hoot would, though.

"At least let's bury her before we get all twisted up over who gets the house. And that's me." He added in a lower voice, "What does a dirty zombie want with a sweet little deal like this?" With mounting righteousness, Travis yelled again. "After you drag dead animals inside and throw their guts all over the place, don't expect anybody to clean up after you!"

Trucker John moved in the doorway and Travis trotted quick-like to the road. The door slammed and he turned his head, expecting the zombie had gone inside to claim the territory and, who knows, probably the body, too. But Trucker John was loping down the walkway. Travis yelped and ran. In what seemed like two steps the zombie was right behind him, exhaling that foul dead snake odor. Travis dodged away but Trucker John kept on going, disappearing uphill into the trees.

"I'm coming back with Hoot and Eddy!" he yelled at the bushes where Trucker John had melted away. "Then we'll see who owns the house. Me, that's who!"

Bee craned her neck through the doorway. "What's she saying?"

"Trucker John punched Travis," Misty repeated.

"No doubt Travis deserved it," Bee pronounced.

"He's a trained killer now, and he's on the loose."

"Travis is hardly a trained killer."

"Not Travis. Trucker John. He punched him hard."

Cricket said, "They all ran past here. There must be a meeting."

"The undead don't have meetings," Bee said. "Civilized people have meetings. But they are up to something. I don't like it."

"We can follow them," EZ offered.

Misty looked aghast.

"You'll do no such thing," Bee said.

"I'll find out what they're up to. Misty and I can spy on them."

"Misty and you can go on home," Bee said. "That's where you belong, with your families."

"Yes'm," Misty said.

EZ protested, "No, come on, are you kidding? I'm going even if you won't. I'm not scared. I'm a great tracker."

"You're a great cracker," Misty said to him. "We're going home now, Ms. Pear." She all but curtseyed before she left.

Out on the road EZ snorted disgustedly. "Could you be a little more of a wuss?"

"I could, but then how would people tell us apart?"

EZ scowled and came up with nothing.

"They're probably watching us," Misty said. "Follow me."

She led him behind her house, crouching under the window-sills, sneaking around the cow barn and up through the dense, dripping trees. They came out south of Rey's cabin. A pair of white hens looked at them expectantly and rattled their feathers in disgust when no feed was forthcoming.

"So you lied to Miss Pear," EZ commented.

"Yep."

"I didn't know you lied."

"I didn't want to worry her. Crystal used to do it all the time." Misty looked at EZ. "It's not a big deal. Everybody lies sometimes." She looked at him closer and laughed. "You never lie?"

He shrugged. "I don't know. I mean, I don't always tell the truth, but you don't have to if you just leave things out, change the subject. You know."

"Too much religion."

"It's not my religion." They climbed over a five-foot-thick fallen log cushioned with bright moss and nursling trees.

Misty pushed giant ferns aside; the ferns bounced back and sprayed EZ with rainwater. "Don't you believe in God?"

"Sure I do. But not like Mom and Dad. Or Mom, anyway. Do zombies still believe in God, you think?" He wiped his face with his cuff, which didn't help. He was fairly dry inside, but the outside of his jacket was drenched.

"I don't think they believe in anything. They don't think about anything. They're like … " She gestured loosely into the woods. "Like trees with legs."

"And teeth," EZ said.

"And guns."

Misty gave him another fern shower and suddenly gasped, "Oh my God, what's that? It's – it's a tree with fangs! And it's aiming its branches at us! Run!"

"You're so funny I forgot to laugh," EZ said. "You ever hear of the boy who cried wolf?"

"You ever hear of the girl who cried tree? It's a tall tale. It's be-yond be-leaf."

"Shut up and listen for zombies," EZ said.

Jackie, Smokey, and Rey confabbed in whispers so the captive couldn't hear them. Now and then one of them walked past him to look out the back of the house. On one pass Rey gave him a tin cup of water, watched him drink it, and made him give the cup back. He didn't say a word.

Jackie said, "I never thought you should turn yourself over to them. You're not the bad guy. You maybe didn't know what you were getting us all into, but you had good intentions. Yeah, good intentions pave the road to hell, but to heaven, too. I'm not telling anybody and don't you tell them, either. Not you either, Smokey the Bandit. It stays right here." She pointed at the floor. "Right here."

Gratitude and dread formed a mixture of overwhelming guilt. Then Rey gave herself a mental slap and they talked strategy and tactics.

Smokey went outside, crouched in a salal thicket, and let loose the Cannibal Mountain call. Immediately it was echoed back. It was low and guttural, but it had resonance that went right through human skin. Pretty soon a jagged file of formerly dead came out of the trees from behind Trucker John's trailer. Earl was in front, with El Duane on his heels. Jacob and Crystal slouched after them, in no hurry but covering ground.

"Look at 'em," Jackie marveled. "Just like soldiers. I'll hand it to you, Smokey, I didn't think you could really train that bunch." She was craning her neck, looking for Berry.

"Yes, good job," Rey said. "They're practically in formation."

"Like drunk ducks," Jackie said.

"They're too orderly," Smokey said. "I've got to remind them how to move serpentine and use cover." He stood up and motioned *down* and *serpentine* with his hands. The zombie squad complied surprisingly well, bending their knees and veering side to side.

"We've got us a team," he said. "I think our boys and girls will do all right."

Then Trucker John appeared. He held a pole over his shoulder, his body blocking what was behind him until he serpentined to the right. Then Rey could see the pole's other end on Hoot's shoulder. Hoot was trying to veer the opposite way from Trucker John. The opposing motions made what was suspended from the pole sway wildly. At first Rey didn't recognize it, but when the pole-carriers moved side-on to her, she got a good look at the black carcass from Hoochville. Flakes of charcoal drifted from the body to the muddy road.

"Uhh ... " Jackie said.

"Oh," Rey said.

"They brought the burned corpse," Smokey said. "Maybe that's the guy Markowski said was out there."

"No," Rey said. Eddy came out of the trees several paces behind Hoot, and he had the end of a pole over his shoulder, too. He tilted sideways under its weight. Berry carried the back end of the pole, and trussed in the middle of it like a slaughtered pig was a man in camouflage and heavy boots, his head hanging back, caked mud and blood making the camo suit unnecessary.

Rey said, "*That's* the guy."

They made the dead hunters take their catches around the house and deposit them by the back door. Jackie got the shovel and started cleaning out the grave-sized depression in the vegetable patch, right where she had seen Birdie gardening in the dead of night.

Oh.

That would explain why Bill had been so mad at Birdie.

Well, it hadn't done Birdie any good, had it? She'd lost the hair on top of her head and now her house was war headquarters. Jackie kept meaning to get answers from Rey—what was this all about?—but somehow the question kept getting lost in the pressing matters of the moment. At this moment she was occupied with hiding the hideous burned up body in the ground, out of sight and out of her mind. She didn't ask any of the muscle-bound undead for help. Smokey could train them until Jesus came and Jackie still wouldn't trust them any farther than she could throw a Chrysler.

And that one poor son of a gun looked like the troops had snacked on him all the way home. Smokey and Rey were trying to figure it out now: who'd done the eating and who'd put a stop to it, with rewards and punishments to match. Berry was in the clear, of course. Berry hunted animals, not human beings. Earl, now, or El Duane or Trucker John—especially Trucker John—wouldn't hesitate to fill up on anything, friend or foe. Once they knew how to gang up, what if they didn't know the difference? What if they didn't care?

Rain drizzled under Jackie's collar and crept under her sleeves. She was cold and wet and her back hurt like a mother by the time the hole was redug. Then when she went back to the house to get somebody to carry that awful thing to its grave, she walked straight into a big kerfuffle of snarling undead and Rey shouting and Smokey pushing zombies back with a rifle butt and flying clumps of charcoal. Smokey was yelling and Rey was picking herself up off the ground where she'd gotten thrown down. In a minute the fuss died down; the outcome was three partly dead chewing on a leg and butt of the burned corpse and two more eating an arm each.

Jackie said, "I guess I dug that big hole for nothing."

Rey said, "I wonder why they didn't eat him before they got here?"

"Well, Berry brought her kills back before she ate them. Like a mother cat. It's some kind of instinct, I guess."

Smokey said, "Let's get this one inside before they eat him, too."

Markowski looked worried when they laid his compatriot out beside the cage.

"Who's your friend?" Smokey asked.

Markowski shrugged.

"We'll just call him Lucky. Rey, would you look him over, see if he's salvageable? Jackie, keep a lookout in front, okay? I'll watch the Zs."

Jackie took one more look at the chomping undead and shook her head. No amount of etiquette training would teach them even the most basic table manners. Not even Berry.

She still loved Berry, always would. Who wouldn't? Beautiful, wild, warm woman, designed to dance on hot beach sand, made for joy. The passion was still there, but it felt more like a song she remembered and less like her heart busting open. What was worse was that the thought of the distance didn't panic Jackie the way it would have a week ago. It was sad, but sad like a song. She hoped things would turn out all right. Maybe they would. If they lived through this, and it was looking like it might happen that way, with Smokey and the zombies—which would be a great name for a rock 'n roll band—on the job, she and Berry might not be together anymore. Could be nobody would be together anymore. Kids separated from their parents, husbands from wives, sisters from sisters, lovers from lovers. Bits of Bible verse and poetry from another life skittered across her mind: things didn't hold, and men took against their fathers, and the dead got up and fought in their naked bones.

32

"You lost an earlobe and a few pinches of skin from your exposed areas. Other than that, you're intact. How is it they didn't eat you entirely?" Rey squeezed a thin film of antibiotic on the last of Lucky's flesh wounds and taped squares of toilet paper over them, saving the few sterile bandages in the first aid kit for her own people, just in case.

Lucky cursed.

"No painkillers, sorry. Didn't you guys bring your own?"

"I don't need no drugs. Just keep those creeps away from me!" He squirmed and Rey called to Jackie to help tie him down.

Jackie talked while she bound his ankles. "You are one lucky man, Lucky. You've still got your lips and eyes and all your important dangly parts. How'd they catch you, a big tough soldier like yourself?"

"Bite me."

"Poor choice of words. Don't say things you don't want to come true. I had a friend once took an illegal mind-altering chemical on a camping trip, cracked a joke about giant rabbits, and they found him the next day nibbled to death by big blunt teeth." Jackie stood up and pressed her hands into her lower back and stretched her spine. "I need a hot bath and a massage. You a masseur, mister?"

Lucky did a groan-curse combo. Rey put the medicinal supplies away and left him trussed and tied to the bars. He and Markowski muttered together, sliding mean looks at Rey and Jackie.

In the back yard, Smokey mustered the troops, pushing them into shape, making them clean themselves after all the gnawing and slurping.

"They didn't finish," Rey observed. "I thought bones were their main thing, but they've consumed most of the softer tissues and only started on the bones."

"Smokey made them quit," Jackie said.

Rey doubted that was the reason. "They'd keep on eating no matter what he did. They're single-minded that way. I must have been wrong about the bones. Or else they've evolved again."

Jackie said, "Or they prefer their meat less than burned to a crisp. I like a bit of char, myself, but I'm not one of the walking dead, and I don't eat the bones. Maybe getting overcooked makes them bitter. I'm going back to the front window. Not that there's anybody else out there. I guess we've got them all. Right, Markowski? Right, Lucky?"

"Don't taunt them," Rey said. "They'll talk to us before long."

"Just making conversation," said Jackie.

Soon Smokey led the cleaned, slightly less repulsive undead troops into the kitchen and lined them up against the wall facing the captives. It was easy to pick out the ones who had not been able to resist tasting the live prey. Crystal's teeth chattered at the captives like a cat's jaws clacking at a bird, and a string of drool spooled from Jacob's open lips.

"Teenagers," Jackie said. "No control whatsoever."

"And always hungry," Smokey said. "As far as I can figure out, Earl and Buck made them stop. Exerted a little dad power."

Lucky whimpered. Crystal stepped toward him. Smokey said, "No," and she looked at him out of the corners of her muddy gold eyes, slouched back into line.

"They want more," Rey said. "They like the warm ones, the raw ones."

"Keep them away from me," Lucky whined. "There's something wrong with them."

Smokey laughed. "You think?"

"No, I mean really wrong."

"Shut up, asshole," Markowski barked.

"I'm off the job. You can't tell me what to do! Those freaks—"

"Shut up or I'll fucking kill you. *I'm* on the job. You need to take a sick day just 'cause you got pinched a little? Who gives a shit? Grow a pair and stop fucking talking."

"Sore spot," Smokey said. "What's wrong with our guys, Lucky? And hey, Markowski can't touch you. I'm your boss now. I should warn you both I don't guarantee I can control our friends. They're good people, but they're hungry, and the porridge and beans we serve here isn't sticking to their ribs. It takes a lot of energy to hold them back and I'm up way past my bedtime. So tell me, friend Lucky, what's the problem with my outfit?"

Lucky sneered. "Your shirt doesn't match your pants."

"Good one," Jackie said.

Rey said, "Your compadre already talked."

"At length," Smokey said.

Markowski banged his shoulder against the bars. "He drugged me! He blew poison in my lungs. I gotta breathe, don't I?"

"Yeah," Lucky said. "He forced you to inhale. Maybe he forced you to swallow, too."

"I'm going to kill you when we get back, motherfucker."

Smokey addressed Lucky. "Let's see if your answers match your friend's. You can walk. Get up." To the women, he said, "We'll be in the bedroom."

The same homophobic alarm that had worked on Markowski did its work on Lucky. Smokey prodded him toward the bedroom and closed the door.

As soon as the men left the room the undead army grew restless. Jackie gave them flatbread spread with a little canned corned beef. They swallowed it and licked their fingers, sniffed their neighbors for more, and were quiet for all of five minutes. Then slowly, with sidelong glances at Rey, they insidiously encircled the cage.

"Hey, back in formation!" Rey tried to sound commanding, but all they did was step out of her reach.

She called Smokey and he came out holding Lucky by the collar. Lucky got a look at the scene and started whimpering. Inside the cage, Markowski stood in the center, turning and turning.

Smokey yelled orders and drew his weapon. Rey and Jackie already had their guns drawn.

"Line up! Attention!" Smokey ordered, and all except El Duane shuffled back to the wall. Their line had a temporary look.

El Duane made noises. As speech, it was unintelligible, but he communicated his proposition effectively. *Lucky*, he gestured. *Lucky, no eat. Markowski, eat!*

"Well, no way," Jackie said. "You all can go catch deer and rabbits. No eating humans! Bad zombies!"

"I suppose he feels they caught Lucky fair and square," Rey said. "They can hunt, but then they'd be running loose. You know they won't stop at rabbits and deer. We've got to contain them again."

"How are they going to fight for us if they're in the cage?" Jackie asked.

At the word cage, the line dissolved and the hungry dead surged without any obvious effort toward the big cage. As if there had been a memo, they grabbed the cage and shook it. They wrenched, pulled, slammed, and twisted, and in a cacophony of cracking and grunting the cage fell into a pick-up-sticks of poles and splinters.

In the kitchen, Markowski was crying. Jackie cowered in the doorway between the rooms, pointing her rifle at one, then another of the crazed undead. Lucky gibbered, "I don't want to be eaten alive. Shoot us all now, lady. I'm begging you, shoot me now."

Smokey took out El Duane's right knee and he went down. Rey knew it wouldn't last long. Smokey shot at Trucker John's face but the big zombie ducked and the bullet merely tore a gouge off the top of his scalp. He didn't seem to mind.

"Don't," Rey said.

"Get out of here," Smokey told her. "You and Jackie run."

"Come on, Rey," Jackie pleaded.

"No. Stop shooting. It's not helping." She could barely breathe, but they were all doomed if they didn't get this under control. "They won't die and you're just making them angry and defensive."

"They're a little past defensive."

"They're hungry and they're scared of being locked up again. You'd be mad, too." To the revived, she said in soothing tones, "We won't tie you up or put you in cages. I promise. Are you hungry?"

Trucker John took a terrifying step toward her. Rey stood her ground, swallowed the wad of fear in her throat, and said, "What do you really want? It's not meat, is it?"

"Meee," Trucker John gurgled, and others echoed him.

"Don't say m-e-a-t," Jackie hissed.

"It's all right. We'll give them food. The kind they really want. But you have to wait just a little, folks. I'll get you some food and you can help. If you try to eat us, we can't help you get the food you want."

They looked at Rey as blankly as only the less-than-living can.

"Deal?" she asked.

"Ohn. Ohnz," Berry moaned.

"Meee," Trucker John growled.

The peckish monsters agreed. *Ohnz* and *meee*, absolutely. And soon.

EZ went in first. The rocking chair swayed in the draft and he jumped, remembering Trucker John, but he squared his shoulders before Misty saw him being afraid—he hoped.

"Where's her body?" Misty asked.

"In that closet thing." He went into the bedroom, so different from the bedrooms in his or anybody else's house. This probably was what bedrooms outside were like: pretty things set around catching the light, bright rugs dotting the floor, colored pictures on the walls. He gripped the handle of the carved cabinet.

"Don't be afraid. It might smell bad; it needs to be buried pretty soon." There hadn't been any deaths on the mountain in his lifetime, or none he remembered. That wasn't counting the shootout, or the temporary re-death of his father, or numberless animals. A dead human body up close was a thrill.

"Go on, open it," Misty said.

With a flourish, EZ flung the door open.

"Where is it?" Misty asked.

EZ moved the clothes aside and stuck his head inside. "It was here. In that Indian dress. She was right here!"

"Maybe she got tired of waiting and went and buried herself."

EZ was stumped.

"Was she really in here or what? It's too small to hold a body," Misty said.

"Yeah, she was in here, folded up. Somebody must have buried her already."

"Dead people don't get up and move themselves." Misty stopped. "Unless ... you know."

"Yeah." EZ looked over his shoulder to the front room. The rocking chair was still. The only movement in the house was swaying, empty clothes hangers. "Unless they walk again."

"But somebody would have to do the science thing on them, right? Like Rey did. Maybe she did the science on Sugar Agate."

"I don't think so. She didn't say anything about it. She could have. Maybe she did." He had himself halfway talked into it.

Misty looked under the bed and out the window, then passed EZ on her way to the door.

"Wait up," he said, walking sideways so he didn't have to turn his back to the bedroom.

"I thought I told you two to go home." Bee frowned at the children. Lovely when they were good, inexplicable when they were being recalcitrant. "Ask your mothers if one of them moved it. My sister and I are not in a condition to dig any large holes, nor would we bury any person without some sort of ceremony, to which all would be invited. The idea is farfetched and born of desperation. Otherwise you would not be coming to us with this. Instead, you would be at home where you belong."

"But you're afraid to go home," Cricket said, "Because your mothers will make you stay at home. They need you. You are both being irresponsible leaving them alone."

EZ glanced at Misty, who had a ready response. "We are going home. But we wanted to make sure the, you know, the not-dead hadn't gotten into the house because Trucker John was in there, and he must have done something with her body. He might have desiccated it."

Cricket raised her eyebrows. "Desecrated it, do you mean?"

Bee sank back into her chair by the wood stove. "My feet are almost warm but my knees are still cold. Spring is worse than winter. I can't seem to store enough heat to get through to summer. Cricket, can you make us some tea, nice and hot? Misty, Ezekiel, would you like a cup of tea? While we're waiting for it, you can sit here by the fire with me and rub my knees. Then help me put my boots on and I'll walk you home."

The children thanked her and excused themselves. Obviously they had important business to attend to, which Bee said she fully appreciated.

When they were gone, she threw back the crochet afghan she'd covered her lap with and sprang up. "Cricket! Never mind the tea. Oh, well, go ahead. Maybe it'll settle me down. This worries me a good deal. I don't like it at all."

"Yes. It looks bad."

"I doubt if anything will come of it, but I wish we could stop it somehow. It could turn into a bushel of trouble."

Cricket set out mugs and crumbled dried leaves in the pot. "There's a lot of inconvenience any time you lose a body."

"You know this is bound to be worse than an inconvenience."

"Not necessarily," Cricket said soothingly. "Maybe with all this other, people will forget all about it."

Bee sat at the kitchen table, feeling as weary as she'd pretended to be two minutes ago. "Lord, I hope so." She caught herself rubbing her knees. She'd lied to the children to get rid of them, but actually, her knees were badly chilled. *One day I'll freeze from my neck to my toes,* she thought, *and, looking back, merely having cold, stiff knees will seem like the golden summer of my youth.*

Strategic planning was short-rationed for the duration. They watched the revived melt out the front door—quiet, purposeful, totally disregarding the humans and their irrelevant plans.

Jackie picked at a chipped pink fingernail. "I hope they come back when we need them."

"They'll come," Smokey said.

"You know or you hope?" Rey knew their hope of unkillable, obedient soldiers had leaked off into the shade and dark of the forest with the hulking forms, an undisciplinable ragtag disaster of loose cannons, unstoppable and insatiable.

"They'll come," Smokey repeated. "I trained them. I know my troops."

"As long as they find something to eat," Jackie said. "You know what, even if they do come back when you call them, I don't want them back until they're stuffed full of meat."

"I promised to help them find food," Rey said. "I didn't help them. I'm not convinced they'll leave my hens and goats alone."

"You can't exactly go hunting with them," Smokey said.

Rey said, "That's exactly what I have to do. I'll get us back by dark." She checked her ammunition and put on her coat.

"Are you completely insane?" Jackie blocked the door. "Your goats will be little appetizers and then they'll eat you, you moron!"

"I don't think so. Anyway, I promised. I owe them."

"Oh, for God's sake," Smokey said. "They're fine. They don't need you. And they very likely will eat you. Maybe not all of them, but you saw what they did to Lucky."

Lucky groaned and swore from the kitchen.

Markowski called out, "Hey, let her go." He sang "A-hunting we will go, a-hunting we will go, we'll catch a little bitch and eat her with a stick—"

"Shut up," Smokey spat.

Rey gently but firmly moved Jackie aside and said, "If I don't come back, don't go out looking for me. Stay safe. Fight hard." She turned away. "Overly dramatic. Sorry."

33

Rey was a hundred yards up the road when a hand grabbed her arm and turned her around hard. Rey raised her rifle and had time to wish she had brought her handgun for close quarters defense before she saw that it was Smokey on the other end of the grip. He brushed the rifle barrel aside.

"Let me go," Rey demanded.

"You're not going," Smokey said.

"Let me go!" She yanked her arm away but only succeeded in bruising herself against his grip.

"No. You're acting crazy. It won't work, anyway, and you'll get torn apart and eaten alive."

"They're not going to eat me, damn it. I would think you trusted them, of all people. You trained them."

"I trained them, and I know them, and they will kill you, and it will be in a way I don't want to think about. Go ahead and get shot, but don't make me live with knowing you were eaten alive. I won't let you." His jaw was clenched, his mouth hard, but his eyes blazed with feeling. His expression intrigued Rey. Then outrage took over.

"A minute ago you said they'd obey you, you're such a superior drill sergeant. 'They'll come back.' What happened to that?"

"I stand by it. But they're going to eat before they follow my orders, and for sure before they follow yours."

"Smokey, I hate to break it to you, but I'm not one of your recruits. You don't get to tell me what to do. *Let go.*"

He hung on, his face as determined as his hand, holding her back.

"I promised them," Rey said, trying to make him see reason. "They'll fight with us if I earn their trust. What happens when they see I've lied to them? How obedient will they be then? I've got to go—" she twisted away and pushed at his chest with the rifle barrel. "—while I can still catch up with them. Damn it, let me go!"

In one fast move Smokey had the rifle in his own hand and Rey was sitting on the ground. She raised herself to one hip and kicked at his knee but hit his shin. He stepped back and made calming noises, which infuriated her. Scrambling upright, she lunged at him, going for a roundhouse to his face, which he handily sidestepped. He got an arm around her shoulders and held her rifle out of her reach.

"Okay, okay," he said. "I apologize. You're right. Keep your promise, not that they'll remember, not that they ever understood it in the first place. But I'll go. Not you. They're used to my authority, and I stand a way better chance of surviving a zombie hunting expedition than you do."

Rey refused but Smokey rolled right over her.

"Take this." He passed her weapon to her and tightened his hold on her shoulders. Later, when her fury settled into what was a normal level of agitation, she realized it had been a hug.

"If I don't come back, don't come looking for me. Stay safe. Fight hard." He crossed his right arm over his chest and thumped. "Overly dramatic." He winked, turned, and ran up the road.

Rey hated it, but he was right.

The hayloft wasn't a good hiding place, but it was the only hiding place they had. Rey pounded another nail in the board across the high window. Fiddlin' Sue had agreed to be ready to hide for a few days. When the invaders couldn't find anyone and figured they'd all run off, life could get back to normal. Rey would be gone by that time, but Sue didn't know that. No one did.

They hoisted food and blankets and lanterns up to the loft. Sue left a hammer by the barn door, ready to seal herself and Misty inside.

"Not that it'll come to that," Sue said.

"I hope not. But they are coming."

"Maybe they're here already, watching us right now. Out in the trees."

The cow and calf shifted restlessly, their gentle footfalls thudding through the floorboards. Their smell permeated the closed space: warm hair and manure, sweet hay and cow breath.

"No," Rey said. "When they get here, they won't waste time spying on us."

"I don't get why they won't believe us. We don't have their doctor. I wish we did have a doctor. We could use one. Maybe if we had her we'd hide her, keep her, not let her go. Why are they so stuck on her being here?"

"Bad information, I guess. Sue, I'm going to try to find you a better hiding place. Are you sure there aren't any caves you haven't told me about?"

"Just the big one over the falls."

"I know of a crevice, but it's not hidden enough, and it's too small for you and Misty. Will you promise to think about going off the mountain? Head west. You'd have a better chance away from the village."

"What about Crystal and Buck?"

Rey hesitated. The other half of Sue's family was running wild out there somewhere. "I don't think you could keep them corralled and quiet. Anyway, they've gotten good at hiding and running fast. Better than any wild animal. They'll be all right, if anyone will be."

"I wish Misty would get back here. I hate being all alone, not knowing."

"If I see her, I'll send her home," Rey promised.

"Buck'd fight for me. If the terrorists come up on us he'd fight for his family."

They went back to the house so Sue could keep a lookout for her daughter. The rain dug into the dirt and penetrated the long grass. Sue said, "It'll take a week to dry out without a fire. More than a week. 'Til next July. I believe I'd just as soon stay in my comfortable house and have another shootout as hide in the barn like a mouse."

Rey said, "There are old mice, and bold mice, but no old bold mice."

"I've met some pretty bold ones, and by their size they weren't any spring chickens. But come to think of it, after I met them I killed them."

Mercy said they would be fine, didn't need a hiding place, their hiding place was in the Lord. His mighty sword would smite the devils down.

"Okay," said Rey, "but aren't you supposed to help yourself, too? The kids need you as much as they need Jesus."

She got Mercy to admit, finally, that if plan A with the Lord didn't work out in time, which wasn't unheard of, Mercy needed a plan B. "Like the Ark," Rey suggested. "It's all part of the plan."

"We'll go in with the Pear Sisters," Mercy said. "In their root cellar."

The root cellar was news to Rey. She urged Mercy to get ready fast. There were five hours at the most, and maybe a lot less.

On her way to the Pears' Rey went into Sugar Agate's house. Already it felt cold and damp. The sparkle was gone. The armoire door hung slightly ajar. Sugar Agate's remains were not inside.

There was no blood and tissue trail on the floor, no scuff marks, nothing but mud crumbs that could have been left by Rey's own boots. Sugar Agate had disappeared as neatly as she had lived. And, just as she hadn't lived by her own efforts, she hadn't disappeared by herself, either.

"Not to point fingers, but you're not the one to be telling us how to survive this crisis. As for Sugar Agate's body, you have to admit it's odd that you're the one who found it, and now you find it missing."

Cricket jumped in. "But Bee, we already—"

"Thank you, Cricket." Bee cut her off. "What do you suppose happened to the remains, Rey? Since you're making all these discoveries about the deceased."

Rey wanted to protest, but she moved on. "We don't have time now. Mercy said you have a root cellar you can hide in."

"Well," Cricket said dubiously, "we have a hole under the kitchen. I don't know if it's a cellar, exactly."

"You don't expect us to live in a dirt hole until the invaders decide to leave, do you?" Bee let her outrage show, but Rey could see a more primal fear under it. Bee feared being trapped in the cold and wet, and probably dark and worm-ridden, space that was in effect a grave.

"Maybe there's someplace better you can go? You don't have to tell me where it is." *Since you don't trust me.*

"I'm not hiding," Bee said, and walked away. She hadn't invited Rey inside, and Cricket was left at the door to relay the conversation.

"They're killers, Bee. They won't care that you're our elder."

"They might kill us, Sister," Cricket said over her shoulder. "They don't care if we're old and harmless."

"My home, my mountain, and those thugs can go hang."

"She's not going into the root hole," Cricket said to Rey. "I can't really blame her. It's a disgusting place."

Mercy and her brood climbed the porch steps. "Well, here we are, as ordered. I'll get the beds made and help get food prepared. Are we going to use a chamber pot down there, or do you think we can risk climbing out for the necessaries?" She brushed by Rey and Cricket, the three girls following her inside with scowls on their faces.

Cricket translated to Rey. "Bee wonders what they're doing here."

"I heard."

Mercy bustled and talked simultaneously. "Rey told us to stay in your cellar. But I've seen your root cellar, and it's going to be like being buried alive, if you don't mind me being frank."

"Why should I start minding now?" Bee said. "Rey told you to hide in our root cellar, eh? Is that right, Rey?"

"No."

"You certainly did," Mercy said.

"I told you to hide. *You* said the Pears had a root cellar."

"And then you told me to bring the children and hide in it, and I did. Problem, Bee?"

"Of course there's a problem. That little cellar won't hold all your lot. It's barely going to be big enough for my sisters and me. I don't like to be ungracious, Mercy, but it's impossible. Rey has steered you wrong."

Mercy whirled on Rey. "Thanks very much, Rey."

Rey tried again to explain the need to have a hiding place, just for a day, maybe two. Three at the very most.

"And my family, not owning a root cellar, and who in the world has a cellar in this climate? It's probably full of water. My family can get mowed down and tortured by evildoers because we had the sense not to dig a water pit under our house?" Mercy stamped her foot. The girls whimpered.

"Mercy!" Rey whispered. "You're scaring your daughters."

"Oh, they're not scared. Are you?" She turned her glare on them and the whimpering stopped. Then she addressed Bee, with one or two quick glances at Cricket.

"You're sharing your cellar, *if* the evil ones come. It's the Christian thing to do."

If Mercy's brood and the Pear Sisters jammed themselves in together, as they would probably wind up doing, what about the rest of the Cannibalites? Jackie Tobasco. Birdie. Travis and Smokey, and herself. Smokey would likely be all right on his side of the mountain where he could elude bad guys indefinitely. In a pinch, and this was a pinch, Rey would try the crevice she'd used before. It wasn't watertight or even sight-tight, but she could use branches to conceal herself inside it. For the rest of the living, though, there was only one place Rey could think of. She checked on Jackie first, collected a flashlight and rope, then slopped north by northwest through the dripping forest.

The afternoon sun didn't penetrate the clouds, much less the mouth of the cave. Rey flicked the button on the flashlight and pushed open the iron bars. She waited for her pupils to dilate.

There were no stalactites or exotic formations visible in the isolated cone of light, only damp rocks decorated with green moss and ghostly lichen. Cold, wet air pushed her gently but steadily, urging her to go back.

Somewhere ahead was The Crack. Examining the ground before every step, she moved against the soft, clammy hands of mist. It would beat getting killed by the invaders, but she wouldn't want to spend the night here. Bee's night in the cave could have killed her. Rey felt it as a living thing: soft, murderous air and cruel stone, and a hole to swallow the victim when the cave had done its work.

Her foot met six inches of space it didn't expect and she stumbled. The ground became treacherous, uneven, fragmented with fallen rocks. It was slow going. The little beam of light pointed out a bit of ceiling; searched the cave floor a body length ahead; highlighted the ground where her next step would land. The mist sparkled in the light.

After what felt like an hour, the light skidded over a smooth patch of floor and the ceiling opened up into a shallow dome. A breath of drenching air covered her face. It was all that warned her that the smooth black patch was not floor. One more step would have swallowed her. The Moro reflex grabbed her from the inside, convulsing her arms and cramping her chest. She'd found the Crack.

By inches she crawled toward the hole in the ground. If the lip of the hole was unstable she would fall in, and no one knew she was here. She had to go back. But first she was going to get at least a peek into the abyss.

34

Smokey came back alone. The undead hunters hadn't eaten him, but neither had they obeyed his command to come back to the Dollers' house. They were quite firm about it, he reported. Nothing doing. Hunters? You could say that. More like natural born killers. Crystal and Jacob had shared something that might have been a squirrel and El Duane just about knocked Smokey out when his noise spooked a deer. No harm done, though: a young buck came along minutes later and swiftly went to that great unfenced garden in the sky.

"As long as it keeps them occupied and full," Rey said. "As long as they're not hunting humans or goats."

Smokey said, "They have lousy manners. They can do their own after-dinner wash this time. I'm not squeamish, but it grossed me out."

"Did they eat the bones?"

"They sucked the hooves dry and spit out the hair."

"But they ate the bones."

"Yeah. Why?"

"They eat some bones but not others."

"They like animal bones. People bones, not so much. Too much alcohol, maybe."

"Maybe." Rey filed the information behind more immediate issues. "We should hide. It's really our only hope. Who knows how many goons they'll send, what kind of weapons they'll have, how soon they'll get here? We can't hope to fight them. Especially if our revived are out of control."

They were at the back corner of the house, keeping watch over each others' shoulders.

"Where will they come from, do you think?" Rey asked.

Smokey gave it a minute's thought. "Everywhere. If they come in by helo, we'll know. If they choose stealth, we won't know until somebody gets nailed."

"There aren't many places to hide on the mountain."

"Leave, then."

"Too risky," Rey said. "Here we know the terrain."

"And you know there aren't any hiding places."

"Not none. Just not many. Anyway, these people aren't going to leave. No way."

"So that leaves fighting," Smokey said.

"Or the cave."

He gave her a skeptical look. "You can see right into the cave. It's impossible to hide there."

"There might be a way. Come on."

The sudden tapping on the window startled Fiddlin' Sue so much she dropped the water jug she was carrying. The jug cracked and water seeped across the boards. In the window was a small hand. Her daughter's hand.

She lifted down the board that was holding the door in place and held the door upright so Misty could slip in.

"Who's that in the yard?"

"EZ," Misty said.

"Well, have him come in. It's not safe out there. And where have you been? I've been worried sick. Are you all right?"

Misty beckoned to EZ. "I'm fine, Mother. Everything's fine."

"Where have you been? Hello, Ezekiel."

"Hi, Mrs. Hill."

Misty said, "We followed them. We watched them hunt. They're real good at it."

Sue felt the hairs on her arms tingle. "You followed the undead? Have you gone crazy?"

"They ran off and I was trying to get Crystal and Daddy back. Then the other ones joined up and they caught a rabbit and Crystal caught a squirrel and a deer."

"Cryssy caught a deer?"

"It screamed."

Sue said, "I'm about ready to scream, myself. Ezekiel, how could you let her go off after them like that? They could have torn you two apart. You'd be a lot easier to catch than a deer. I'm surprised at you. What will your mother have to say about this?"

"I don't know, Mrs. Hill. She did tell me I'm the man in the family now. I figured that meant I had to make my own decisions."

"The idea. You're thirteen, aren't you? You don't know how to make a decision, obviously."

"Mom—"

"He's not the man of *this* family, that's certain and sure. And Lord God, you don't go following him off into the woods spying on the living dead and terrorists!"

"Mom!"

"Anyway, get your things. I packed them up; they're by the door. We'll need more water. And a pee bucket. Everything else is ready to go to the barn."

"Why?"

"We're hiding. The hayloft's the only place we've got. The men will be here in a few hours, Rey said. Ezekiel, you go on home to your mother and sisters. I don't know where you all will be staying.

Good luck." Sue hugged Ezekiel briskly and ushered him out the door.

"Hiding? No! I'm not hiding," Misty said. "They'd find us. The hayloft would be the first place they'd look, anyway. EZ and I are going to fight with Smokey and Rey."

Sue shoved a bundle of blankets into Misty's arms. "The heck you are. Get those up the ladder and come right back."

"No, Mother! We're going to stay and fight!"

"You're going to hide and live through this, is what you're going to do. You think I want to lose my remaining daughter?" Her voice got tight and loud. "We're all we've got, you and me. Maybe your daddy will get well, maybe your sister will, too. I don't know. But I'm not losing you. Get out to that barn!"

"I'm staying and I'm fighting."

Sue puffed air between her lips. "What a notion. A fourteen year old girl. 'I'm going to stay and fight!' You'd fight an army all by yourself, I guess, and not bother to leave me a note. Get ahold of yourself and get out to that barn."

Misty didn't move, but the defiance had gone out of the air. She stood holding the bundle of blankets, watching her mother bending over the broken jug, picking up the pieces. Misty set the blankets down on a kitchen chair and took a rag to the puddle on the floorboards.

"Watch out. That's sharp," Sue said. She put the shards in the sink and took the wet towel from Misty. "Thanks, honey. Ready?"

Misty put her arms around her mother. She was nearly as tall as Sue now, and in a year or two would probably be even taller. Buck and Sue both came from tall people.

"Mommy," she said gently. "I'm not going to hide."

Before Sue could grab her, Misty was gone.

35

The cave felt less ominous with Smokey beside her.

"Clammy," Smokey said, "but refreshing on a hot day."

"Whatever that is," Rey said.

"A little more global warming and people will be fighting for this cold fog." Smokey shined his flashlight at the Crack. "How far down does it go?"

"I can't tell. There are ledges and then it's too dark to see." Rey lay prone on the cold ground and squirmed forward. "If we could tie a rope to something, we could get down there."

"What you mean 'we', white man?"

"You know you want to."

Rey held the light while Smokey fastened rope ends together. "Guaranteed to stay tied," he promised. "This should get us to the bottom of the hole, or China, whichever comes first."

"Me first," Rey said.

"No way."

"Yes, because if I get in trouble you can pull me up better than I can pull you up. You would be able to pull me up, wouldn't you?"

"A challenge to my manly strength?"

Smokey took off the rope Rey had wrapped around her waist and put it back on in a sling that went under her thighs and around her chest. His hands lingered a bit longer than necessary.

"Don't talk. You'll drop your flashlight," he said. "Give three tugs when you want to come up, in case I can't hear you. Stay as close to a shaft wall as you can."

"Is the rope going to break? Won't the rocks abrade it?"

"I'll put my coat under it. But if you find footholds, use them. I'll belay you. Just don't let go of the rope."

"Oh, *don't* let go. Got it." All of a sudden she was afraid. *Thank God for epinephrine. The coward's friend.* "Don't leave." She stuck the maglite they'd fetched from the house in her mouth and backed over the edge.

She felt catastrophe in every sway, every lurching inch, in the abrasive force on the rope. Staying vertical took all her concentration. The translucent mist blowing against her legs and seat felt thick enough to float on. Clamping her teeth tighter on the maglite, she bent her neck and looked down past her feet. The bottom was invisible.

Shallow shelves of rock made handy toeholds, which took strain off of the rope. The top of the shaft was a widish oval and opened out about two body-lengths down. As her eyes adjusted, the pitch blackness lightened to gloom, but in another ten feet even that twilight was extinguished. The maglite picked out ledges of glistening stone, some scant finger-holds and some shelf-sized. Rey lowered herself inches at a time. Her jaw was sore and the rope tore thin layers of skin from her palms.

Still no bottom. The Crack was too deep: a dead-end unusable for hiding people. With one last look down, Rey planted her feet on a wide ledge and tugged on the rope. Before she completed the second signal tug, a loose chunk of edge rolled out from under her feet. Her jaw clamped onto the flashlight as the thing she had stumbled on bounced into the abyss. Hanging in midair, she swung from side to side, bashing into the jagged shaft walls. In a fast glimpse she saw the unmistakable shapes of bones resting on a stone platform. Broken skeletons of mammals piled one on another, skittering as her body brushed them. She was no stranger to skeletal remains, but she recoiled just the same.

The rope swung her to the other side of the shaft and her light slid over more jumbled bones, among them the arresting shape of a human skull.

"Smokey!" she yelled.

He heard her and pulled her up.

"Well?" he asked.

"No good. It's a long way down." Rey massaged her thighs where the rope had pinched her. "My feet are numb. I could barely climb up even with you pulling me."

"What did you see?"

She stamped her feet to get the circulation going. "Not much, but enough. There's some pretty heavy stuff down there."

"Like what? Treasure? Old prospector skeletons?"

"How did you know?"

He waited a beat.

"Yeah," she said. "Skeletons. A human skeleton and other bones. One human for certain, skull intact, mandible and all."

"Wow," Smokey said. "But no treasure?"

"I'm sure it was treasured by whoever was using it when they died." Rey flexed her hands, rubbed her jaw muscles.

Smokey coiled up the rope.

Rey asked, "You're not going down there?"

"Later. If they can't hide there, we've got to keep looking." He looked her over. "You sure you're okay?"

"I'm fine. Just sore. Someday we'll have to find out whose body that is."

"Someday."

"If there is a someday," Rey amended.

"No way people could crouch anywhere in the shaft for a day or two?"

"I really don't think so."

Smokey slung the coiled rope across a shoulder. "What will they do?"

"I hope one of them has some ideas," Rey said. "I don't have a clue."

If Travis hadn't had Hoot and Eddy to back him up, Trucker John would have ripped him into six pieces. Travis knew that just from one look at the big zombie's face. But his boys were behind him this time and that was a damn nice feeling. When had he ever had that kind of brotherly love on the outside? Never. Even with big bad John growling at him, Travis knew he'd live through this. Maybe he'd even win.

Like they'd read his thoughts, Hoot took a step forward and to Travis's right. Eddy did the same on his left. Eddy was still a little, wiry guy, hadn't taken in an ounce of nutrition in probably twenty years, but in his zombiehood he was all fast-twitch muscle fiber, ornery as a rat and loyal as a wolf.

"It's my house now," Travis said. "My boys and me live here, so you go on home now."

Trucker John took one giant step at him and Travis backed up. Hoot and Eddy didn't. The three undead were smeared with blood and gobbets of flesh with hair stuck in it. Travis took another step back to get out of their stink.

"It's your house, boys. Anybody tries to take it away from you, you fight for it. We'll move the brewery and rebuild the still." On an impulse sparked by the promise that they were going to keep him alive for the next minute, he added, "And you can take the bed for yourselves."

Hoot grunted softly. It was about the most he'd said since Travis had known him. "Oos mit," it sounded like.

"Yeah. Oos mit," Travis agreed. "Right, Eddy?"

Eddy gabbled something fast and whiskey-scratched in his ru-ined voice. It sounded pretty supportive. The guys stepped toward Trucker John. Growling ensued. Travis could see Trucker John's big teeth, his jaw muscles working, his yellow eyes clouding and flash-ing. He saw the hair on Hoot's and Eddy's necks stand up. Instinct told him to back the fuck up. *Dogfight.*

There was an eruption of snarling, punching, clawing men. Their teeth gnashed and fresh blood flew like red shotgun pellets. Somebody screamed, another one yowled, maybe in triumph, may-be in pain. Who could tell, with zombies? Trucker John went down. The other two made a lot of noise from down in their guts, sound-ing like it came from someplace a long time ago. Uncut aggression. No thought involved. Impressive.

The chaos quieted down a little and the number of fists and feet flying around dropped to ten or twelve. They fought hard and fought fast, his guys. Eddy and Hoot got down over Trucker John ...

... and took big bites.

"Hey, whoa, whoa! Hold on! Easy!"

Travis would no more stick his hands in there than break up a pit bull fight, but he patted Hoot's shoulder, talking gently, as if to a spooked horse. Eventually he got them to back off, and his zombie crew shuffled around the living room knocking doodads off little tables and spitting blood.

Eddy howled; Hoot huffed. Travis stood in the open doorway, ready to run if Trucker John recovered faster than expected. The ex-man was missing significant chunks of arms and belly. It turned Travis's stomach. Not as much as if he'd been the one eaten by Trucker John, but still, he felt bad.

The thing that cheered him up was knowing that it wouldn't last long. And even as he watched, Trucker John's flesh was growing in.

"He's going to be plenty mad when he gets up. Soon as you get washed, guys, let's get him tied down. Give him time to get used to the idea it's not his house. I mean, how can he own a house? He's not even alive."

Mercy twirled a finger in Freedom's hair and found a snarl, and another, and another. She hadn't sat her daughters down with a decent hair-brushing for three days. As soon as the evildoers were gone, assuming they ever arrived, she would put them all in nice tight braids. She sat with her back against a burlap bag stuffed with something lumpy and listened to them sleep. She worried about her home and her children. Jacob was on Satan's side but still her boy; Ezekiel was out there somewhere playing soldier, thanks to that Smokey. But the image that wouldn't leave her alone was a dusky, muscular body, uncomplicated and unsanctioned. The untethered sensation of being with him was like falling from a great height into a mapless forest.

On the top side of the floorboards, Bee and Cricket sat in front of the wood stove. They had opened the iron doors to better enjoy the crackles and heat and aroma of burning softwood. It was waste beyond luxury, but they agreed this was one time they might indulge themselves.

"Cold night," Cricket observed. "I wouldn't invade on a night like this."

"They like hardship. It's milk and honey to them."

"Do you think they'll come, then?"

"They might."

"It's a good thing we have the cellar," Cricket said.

Bee nodded.

Cricket said, "The children won't mind how small it is. They'll think it's fun. Children like to hide."

"I remember."

"Too crowded for us to shove in with them."

Bee nodded again.

"They have a lot of years left to live."

Bee said, "Of course we wouldn't leave Lacy."

"Well, sure. Lacy won't do well all on her own."

"I wish she'd come home," Bee said. "I don't begrudge waiting, but at the same time I wish she'd hurry."

"She lives by her own clock," Cricket said. "More to do with the stars wheeling around or magnetic pulsations than mere days and nights."

"But I wish she'd come."

The fire flared and spat an ember onto the oval hooked rug, next to Bee's feet. She flicked it onto the floorboards with her toe and rubbed it out.

"Vigilance," Cricket said.

36

Jackie said, "I've got a few ideas what to do with these fools. They've got mouths like a sewer and they never shut up."

"I guess you'll have to trust us," Markowski said.

"Yeah." Lucky snickered, then winced. "We'll be good. You can let us go."

Smokey ignored them and answered Jackie. "I'll think of something. You take care of you."

"And Birdie and Sue," Rey added. "There's nothing more to do here."

"We need me on deck, armed and pissed off," Jackie argued. "Let's hide the smut brothers here under six feet of dirt and we can relax and pick off their compadres."

"Actually," Rey said, "I would consider that. It has merit. It would make our lives easier and save time."

"That's against the Gevena Convention!" Markowski protested.

Smokey said, "It's *Geneva* Convention, and you're not in the military anyway."

"Yeah," Jackie said. "I got your Geneva Convention right here." She raised her gun.

"But for now, go hide," Rey told her. "We'll deal with the prisoners."

After a final perfunctory argument, Jackie went home.

Rey took Smokey out of earshot. "You go on home. This never was your fight. There's a decent chance we can disappear in the woods. They won't stay forever. You go back up the mountain, and thank you for your help." She swallowed. "You're a good man. A good neighbor."

"A decent chance you can disappear in the woods? Are you on crack? The few of you they don't find and kill will die of exposure or become zombie chow." He went back to check out a stealthy noise from the kitchen, but the prisoners were still bound securely.

"You come with me up the mountain," he whispered when he came back. "You know my sweat lodge?"

"I think so. Well, no, I don't."

"Yeah, it's pretty well hidden. In back of it there's a little dugout you can crawl into, nice and dry, relatively speaking, stocked with food and water and a catalytic stove. Come with me. We'll ride this out."

"It sounds perfect."

Smokey's face relaxed a little. "Good. Now, about the mercenaries in the kitchen—"

"For you, perfect. I'm not leaving my people. But I appreciate the offer."

He tensed up again. "Damn it, Rey—"

"You wouldn't leave them if you were me."

"What good is you dying going to do them? You've made them as safe as anybody can. Now put on your own oxygen mask."

"I haven't made them safe. I brought this down on them. Even if it weren't all my fault I wouldn't leave them. They're my family and I'm staying with them. You go. You've done enough."

"All right, I'll be running along now. Enjoy watching your village get torched. Been nice knowing you."

"See you later, Smokey." Rey leaned toward him, hesitated, then carried out the impulse and kissed him on the cheek. His stubble had grown out to a bear-like smoothness.

Smokey glowered at her. "I'm not going without you."

"I'm not leaving."

Smokey looked as mad as Rey had ever seen him. "God damn it," he said.

"Aww," said Lucky.

"Ain't love grand," Markowski said.

"Get a little sleep," Rey told him. "I'll wake you up in half an hour."

"I'll sleep when I'm dead."

"You hope."

Smokey smiled.

Rey couldn't sleep, either. Instead she left Smokey on guard duty and looked in at the Pear Sisters' house.

Cricket opened the door. The air inside was warm and fragrant with mint tea and cedar.

"Why aren't you in your root cellar?" Rey felt like an impertinent fool, bossing the elder Pears around. But somebody had to do it.

Bee answered from her rocker by the fire. A puffy quilt was tucked around her. "Sit down, Rey. You look about done in. We prefer to stay above ground while we can. There's a long time to be under the dirt, and it's so pleasant up here, isn't it?"

"They might murder you," Rey said gently.

Bee nodded. "I understand that. Then again, they might not. Sometimes elderly ladies are allowed to live. We don't appear threatening. We have a reputation for being feeble and fragile. And we are, we are. But we are not completely helpless."

She pulled her father's shotgun out from under the quilt across her knees. "We will fight. Mother and Daddy would have."

Rey saw a vision of Bee blowing away a camo'd man in an explosion of blood and buckshot, then of automatic gunfire ripping the women apart. She said, "Oh, Bee."

Cricket came in and handed Rey a steaming mug that smelled of mint and honey and canned milk. "Here you are. A little nourishment. You've been working so hard over this."

Rey bent her head into the wisps of steam. "Thank you."

"Don't blame yourself," Bee said.

Rey knew it was only fatigue and stress, but her eyes started stinging.

"Sugar Agate's murder aside, we all are allowed secrets," Bee said. "We on Cannibal Mountain especially. Any one of us could draw attention from outside. It's only a matter of time and happenstance."

"How did you know it was me they're after?"

"As the quip goes, I was born at night, but not last night. Who else could it be? I know Fiddlin' Sue's and Buck's secret: they stole their babies back. Jackie Tobasco can cure a bad hairdo but she's no doctor. Berry? There's a remote possibility she was a doctor of something, but Jackie would have bragged on her. Mercy doesn't believe in science. Sugar Agate? No. It had to be you. But the blame lies on whoever those bad men are, not on you."

Rey swallowed sweet tea. Bee rocked.

"Tell me about the cave," Rey said.

"You've been in it," Bee said.

"The Crack. I went inside it. I found skeletons."

"Oh, dear," Cricket said.

"I see," Bee said.

"Does that surprise you?"

"Were they ... was one of them ... new? Fresh?"

"Skeletons are not new or fresh," Bee said sharply, "by their very nature."

Cricket wrung her hands inside her sweater.

"Animals fell in and couldn't get out," Bee said. "That's why Daddy blocked the cave off."

Rey said, "There's a human skeleton in there."

"Only one?" Cricket blurted.

Bee placed a stick of cedar in the fire; it immediately blazed up.

"Don't use up all our cedar," Cricket warned.

"No matter," Bee said. She took a breath.

"We were young, or youngish. Lacey was a mere girl. Romantic and silly and happy. She was the one of us who wondered what life would be like in the valley. She wanted clothes and radio music, boyfriends, city life. Of course she didn't know anything about what city life was or what boyfriends were, but she was curious. She had so much love in her it poured out. But no idea of reality."

"No common sense at all," Cricket agreed.

"And in 1959 we had visitors. A couple hiked in on a camping trip. We welcomed them but Mother and Daddy didn't encourage them to overstay. They were a nice couple. Margaret was pretty and game for about anything to do with the outdoors. The man—"

"Kevin," Cricket put in.

"—had natural charm. Margaret adored him. He told wonderful stories. Even Daddy listened, in spite of his wanting them to leave. Lacewing was mesmerized by Kevin's stories. She followed the two of them around, making a pest of herself. She was too old to tag along behind a married couple, if they were married, and of course we assumed they were. Margaret got tired of it, but they were on our land so they put up with it. Kevin didn't seem to mind. He liked the company. I think he had grown tired of the way Margaret fussed over him."

"She was no challenge," Cricket offered.

Bee nodded. "Lacewing spent more and more time with them. She glowed. She danced on air. She couldn't go a minute without talking about how Kevin had climbed a mountain in Africa or Kevin sang like an angel or Kevin had carried her across a mud puddle. Cricket and I had never seen that phenomenon before, but Mother knew what it was and Daddy did too. Mother forbade her to visit them anymore. Daddy had a talk with Kevin.

"They should have packed up and walked away, but Margaret wanted to rub it in. She came to say goodbye to us and made a point of telling Lacewing how happy she and Kevin were and generally showing off how Kevin was her man and she had won.

"Even then, it all might have ended with nothing more than tears and a broken heart. Broken hearts mend, I'm told. But being a narcissist, Kevin was blind. He had to meet Lacewing by the top of the waterfall, where they had picnicked. He told her how lovely she was, how free; how she was a spirit of Nature, a wood nymph. Could they could have this one golden hour to hold close all the rest of their lives? Here by the pure, singing water, in the light of day and the clean air, mightn't they fulfill the spiritual meeting that God intended before the base world parted them forever, and other nonsense."

"And Lacewing said Yes," Cricket said sadly.

"Naturally. And immediately afterwards, he went back to camp to help Margaret pack."

"Leaving Lacewing alone."

"Her grasp of life's practicalities was fragile, her heart totally open."

"Kevin and Margaret walked past our house to the bridge," Cricket said. "Lacewing had been waiting in the trees for them. She rushed out and threw herself on him. Margaret pushed her off. They fought and Kevin separated them. He was laughing. Lacey told Margaret what they'd done up there by the waterfall. Margaret called Lacey some ugly names. It was really Kevin she should have been angry at, of course, but she loved him."

Bee's voice was soft. "From there we only know what we put together from happened afterwards. Margaret chased her into the trees and Kevin ran after Margaret. Cricket came to get Mother and Daddy, but by the time they got going there was no sign of Lacewing or the other two. Lacewing was fast on her feet and she knew the woods like her own name.

"That was the last we saw of Kevin or Margaret. They moved on, Lacey told us. She cried some, which Mother said was normal for this situation, and she was more distracted than usual for a long time after. She suffered a rude awakening to the ways of the world and of men. We did everything we could to make our little girl happy again. Spoiled her, and we knew it, but we didn't care. And eventually she recovered. She stayed distracted and vague, more than ever, but she was happy. We have always done all we could to make her happy. I hope she's happy now, wherever she is."

Cricket brought another cup and a slice of cornbread and watched until Rey ate and drank, then sat in a straight chair beside the stove. "She didn't kill them."

"Not technically," Bee said. "She must have known Kevin followed her into the cave. She would have been able to leap over the chasm easily; she knew exactly where it was even in the dark."

"So dark in that cave," Cricket said. "Nobody else would have seen it."

Seconds of silence went by in which the fire hissed over a pocket of trapped moisture. Bee said, "We never heard them. They must have died in the fall."

Cricket nodded emphatically. "I'm sure they died instantly. They couldn't have starved to death. We would have heard them calling for help." She darted a look at her older sister, but Bee didn't meet the question in Cricket's eyes.

Rey pictured the skeleton and skull she'd been face to face with. The skull had not been crushed. Had the cervical vertebrae been broken? The light had been so poor and fleeting.

"They were missed," Bee said. "It had started raining in earnest and we had a Chinook wind that lasted days, with the balmy, soaking miasma it brings. A sheriff came up asking about them. Everything was fine until Lacewing got the heebie-jeebies and started talking about Kevin. How he loved her until Margaret came between them and Daddy ran them off. She spun a splendid, romantic tale for the officer, complete with tears and fainting spells. That was the first time we saw her change right before our eyes into someone else.

"The sheriff went away and came back with two deputies. Then newspaper reporters came. Camped on our porch and in our back garden, taking pictures with their big cameras, shouting questions. Demanding we send Lacewing Pear out. She was a freak show to them. They stayed three weeks and made life hell. Mother fed Lacey calmatives and rocked her like a baby.

"The deputies searched the woods, probably the entire mountain. Daddy had hidden the cave well after the sheriff's first visit, and the search party never found it."

"They had some nerve," Cricket humphed.

"We ran them off with shotguns, which made them even more excited. Those stories must have been front page headlines all season long."

"Once the sheriffs gave up, the newsmen kind of drifted away," Cricket remembered. "And Lacey calmed down, and the whole thing was more or less forgotten."

Rey asked, "None of you ever looked down there?"

The sisters shook their heads, looking into the fire.

"No point in it," Bee said. "Leave the past in the past."

Rey swallowed the last of her tea. Real butter on hot cornbread was ambrosia. The women must have churned it themselves. Rey had never known they did that. Never had thought about anybody having butter, all these years. The warmth and hot tea and food worked on her brain, making her eyelids heavy and her thoughts languid. The Pear Sisters had the right idea—enjoy the fire and each others' company as long as it lasted.

She realized she had drifted halfway into sleep. Bee had been saying something. Rey opened her eyes wide and sat up straight.

" ... down there."

"It's just cold air and mist from the river," Cricket said. "I can't believe you think about that."

"You're right, but you've never explained those noises, and what came out of the cave."

"Nothing. That's what."

"A nothing that catches and talks. A nothing that kills."

Rey was fully awake again. "Something comes out of the cave? Who was killed?"

Cricket leaned against the ladder-back chair. "Nothing, really. Well, there was a death some years ago. Bee got spooked. The end."

"Hear the facts and you tell me, Rey. Twenty years after that couple left the mountain, and I mean twenty years to the day, we all heard talking from the cave." Bee pointed her eyebrows at Cricket with the word *all*. "And there was nobody in it."

"Talking." Cricket rolled her eyes.

"Echoing whispers that went on all night, growing louder as the moon set, and the mist clotted up thick and rolled out the cave mouth."

"Were you there?" Rey asked.

"I was."

"Tell her why," Cricket said.

"I was mad at Daddy. I camped out and it was raining so I slept in the cave."

"You drank half a bottle of wine first," Cricket reminded her.

"I was not drunk. If I had been drunk, it would not have made me hallucinate. It's the lack of alcohol that does that to the committed inebriate, not a glass or two of wine in a young, healthy person."

"Have you had our wine?" Cricket asked Rey.

Rey nodded.

"It kicks your ass," Cricket said.

Rey nodded again.

"Not mine," Bee said. "Not back then, anyway. I was minding my own business, sleeping peacefully even if the ground was hard and cold, and I heard people talking. Then the mist rolled up from the hole in the ground. I felt it like a wet bough, dragging over my face. It rolled out and out until I could barely breathe. The voices were talking all that time. I couldn't understand them, but it was a man's and a woman's voice, sounding like they were right beside me."

"That's how the cave does," Cricket said, patient but exasperated. "Fog carries sound better than dry air."

Bee ignored her. "The fog rolled over me, lingering as if it were feeling me, figuring out what I was. Then it folded and blew like a cloud out the cave mouth. I was drenched. I left my bedroll there and went home. I was afraid all the way home I'd run into that cloud on the way."

"And the death?" Rey asked.

Bee and Cricket both looked down at their laps. Bee pulled the lap blanket around the shotgun and tucked it around her legs, as if they weren't roasting distance from the fire. "That was the night Daddy died."

"Oh. I'm sorry," Rey said.

"It was unexpected," Cricket said. "We knew Mother was on her way out when she went before him, but we thought our father would be around for a long time more."

"Was it an accident? Or a medical crisis?" Rey asked.

"It was no accident," Bee said.

Cricket said, "He started coughing in the night and ran a fever. Chills shook him and broke him out into a cold sweat. He couldn't catch his breath. It was awful."

"Pneumonia, I suppose," Bee said. "It took him in one swoop." She looked at Rey. "You're a doctor. Pneumonia doesn't do that, does it? Not normally."

"Not usually, but I think it can."

Bee nodded. "So. You see. The mist got him."

Cricket rolled her eyes. "And I suppose the mist was really Kevin and Margaret having their ghostly revenge."

"Mist is mist. Fog is fog. Death is death. I don't know what it was. It had consciousness. It talked. It killed. Cricket can scoff until kingdom come, but I know what I know."

Rey asked, "Does Lacewing think it was ... alive?"

"Oh, we never told her," Cricket said quickly. "God, no."

"She'd think it was coming for her next," Bee said. "She was the last of us to see them alive. All Daddy did was try to end Lacewing's foolishness, and he died for it."

She killed them, but you don't like to think it out loud, Rey said to herself. Sisters stick together.

The fire blazed brighter. Sunset was two or so hours away, but the day was dim, the whole east side of the mountain in rain shadow. Time had passed, precious time before the next invasion.

"You should reconsider hiding," Rey said, standing up. She carried her cup and saucer to the kitchen and snapped her coat up to her neck.

It occurred to Rey she might not get another chance, so she asked, "Why is this called Cannibal Mountain?"

Bee raised an eyebrow, looking surprised that Rey didn't know. "Mother's mother was a Campbell. It was their land."

Rey waited, but Bee just smiled a little.

"There were no cannibals, I hope," Rey said.

"Oh, no," Cricket said. "But Campbell sounds so like Cannibal, and the folks figured Cannibal was a good name if we wanted to keep people away. Which we did. So we let officials and newspapermen and other snoops call it Cannibal Mountain and it got put on the maps."

"Good luck." Rey wanted to hug them, but she'd never hugged them before, and to start now could mean only goodbye.

37

Smokey opened one eye. "Can I get up now?"

"No. Go back to sleep."

"This is stupid. I'm not sleepy."

"Get sleepy. Stop being in control. Don't soldiers learn how to sleep whenever they get a chance?"

"Right before an attack is not a valid chance. And I wasn't a soldier."

"I'm serious, Smokey. Even ten minutes will keep you clear."

"I'm clear."

"Shut up and go to sleep."

"Yes, mommy. But first I want another story and a lullaby."

"A story. Once upon a time there was a big bad wolf. He came to the first little pig's house and the pig was out of his mind with sleep deprivation and the wolf blew down the house with a grenade and ate the little pig."

"I hate this story."

"Close your eyes and I'll tell you a different one."

Smokey obediently closed his eyes. Rey saw a little smile play over his lips. Nice, but she was looking for a slack jaw and eyeball movements behind his lids.

"The second little pig was smarter. She took a refreshing nap before the wolf got to her house, and when he tried to knock down her house with a battering ram, she shot him right between the eyes because *her* eyes were rested and her mind was sharp and she was an excellent sniper."

"Mm. I like a happy ending."

"I don't think stories are helping you sleep."

"Sing to me."

"I can't sing."

"My mother had the world's worst singing voice and I was the best-rested boy on the block."

Rey couldn't remember her mother singing to her. Her grandmother either. Her grandfather had sung to her sometimes, silly songs that were oldies even when he was a boy. "I don't know any lullabies."

"Then I'll sing to you." Smokey started, coughed, started again. "Toora, loora, loora, ... "

She stopped him. "I don't like it. It's too sad. That and the one about the circle and the dead mother and the hearse."

Smokey squeezed her hand gently and turned toward the wall.

Lullabies were for other people.

This was love: these Cannibalites, these children and parents and misfits, the old women and Smokey. He'd jumped in as if they mattered to him as much as they mattered to her. Why? True, they depended on each other, but Smokey could make it anywhere in the world. He didn't need these people, yet he was risking his life to help them.

That was more than romance or lullabies. That meant something.

The only thing in the world Rey wanted right now was to spoon up to Smokey's back, wrap her arms and legs around him, and drift away. Instead, she got up and quietly opened kitchen drawers until she found a pencil and a ledger book. *Don't look for me*, she wrote on the back of a page. *The others could use your help, but nobody will blame you if you go home now.*

What else? *See you later? Good luck?* She wrote *Thank you* and signed it Rey Nickel; tore the paper out of the book, folded it and laid it on the floor beside Smokey.

The rain drops fell far apart and heavy, like little water balloons. She hoped she would have a chance to dry out before the mercenaries killed her. The last time she'd been thoroughly dry had been last August. It seemed like a lifetime ago.

She deliberated over where to wait. She wanted them to find her right away and leave everyone else alone, but she didn't want Smokey to be able to find her, in case he tried. She figured four likely entry points: up the western cliffs or through the river, both of which would take skill and equipment; if they came by helicopter, they'd have their choice of the rocky peak or the clearing. The sites were far apart, and if she chose the wrong one, she wouldn't be in time to stop them searching houses.

A noise came from the house behind her and she scooted deeper into the trees. The way her stomach clutched, she knew she expected to see Smokey coming after her. Wanted him to come after her. But two men raced low around the house and straight up the road, out in the open, unafraid and in a hurry: Markowski and the man they called Lucky. Rey didn't see any weapons. She ran out from the trees and pointed Markowski's semiautomatic at their backs. The gun spat and pushed her backwards. The men didn't turn to look, just zagged opposite ways across the road into the bushes and shadows.

A shudder throbbed in the air over the mountain. It got louder fast, as if somebody had cranked up the volume. The wind carried the sound; it grew louder still as its source cleared the mountain crest.

The black helicopter hovered over the clearing, big and menacing and excruciatingly loud. Rey ran toward it, legs pumping, head down. By the time she got to the turnoff beyond the Pear Sisters' house she could see lines spinning down from the black roaring machine. They descended faster than she could run.

Rey ran full bore along the trail to the clearing. Without warning, something grabbed her by the arm and yanked her into the bushes. She kicked back and caused a grunt of pain in her captor.

"I'm giving myself up! I surrender!"

"Shut up." He pressed a hand over her mouth.

"Smokey?" she tried to say against his palm.

"Shh."

She kicked him again and he wrapped a leg around her shins. She yanked one arm free and elbowed him in the ribs.

"Quit it, you idiot," he hissed. "I'm saving you."

He pulled her to the ground and lay on top of her, capturing her limbs and covering her mouth. Rey was furious, but felt her traitorous body relaxing under him.

"I followed them." His mouth was an inch away from her ear and she could barely hear him.

Rey whipped her head from side to side, trying dislodge his hand.

He said, "Stay here."

She nodded. He took his hand off.

She said, "If you don't let me go now they'll kill everyone."

The look on his face told her she wasn't going to change his mind. She lay still, waiting to catch him off-guard.

Heavy footsteps approached, two or more men coming toward them from the clearing. Through the crowns of the bushes Rey recognized Markowski and Lucky, heads bobbing as they hustled to join their outfit. Abruptly, Markowski's head jerked down to the right and Lucky's jerked down to the left. They each emitted a strangled grunt. There was a cracking of branches, a brief thrashing, a pause—then Earl stepped out of the bushes on the right side of the trail and El Duane stepped out on the left. They bent low, hardly making any kind of effort, toward the edge of the clearing. As they passed, Earl turned his head and stared directly into Rey's eyes. He looked like the old Sasquatch video: insolent and imposed-upon.

With Smokey's attention diverted, Rey shoved him off and bolted through the undergrowth, keeping big fir trunks between herself and the clearing. Ten feet from the open ground she stopped and crouched down. Smokey came alongside. They looked up at men in black descending down the lines, swaying spiders spawned from the belly of the big arachnid in the sky. The men bristled with large guns but wore no packs. They weren't planning a long stay. In and out, search and destroy. Fast as spiders, they were on the ground, six in all. Enough to do the job.

The mercenaries unhooked themselves from the lines and stood clear while the helicopter rose straight up, unsteady in the wind over the treetops, and the lines were pulled up. The men turned toward each other. In the absence of deafening noise their voices carried clearly. Obviously they already had the lay of the land. One of them pointed, gave terse orders, and individuals turned outward from their scrum.

Rey shouted. "I'm Jillian Newhause! I'm the one you want!"

Six men whipped around to look in her direction. She emerged from the trees and raised her hands. Men flanked right and left as they moved on her.

Around the edges of the clearing, leaf-littered fallen trees and mossy boulders blurred as if wavering in the helicopter's backwash. The invaders, their eyes trained on their objective, did not seem to notice or care. Yeah, shit moved in the woods. Anyway, they had guns.

The tree trunks and rocks got taller. Moss peeled away. Leaves drifted to the ground and the pieces of forest stood erect. The mercenaries finally caught it and whirled around, pointing their guns, but the mobile forest moved fast. A couple of automatic fire bursts split the air, but it happened quicker than the mercenaries could comprehend. The look of surprise on the leader's face turned to horror. Before he went down with Buck on top of him he yelped, but the protest was brief, due to Buck ripping open his throat and twisting his head off. Buck made it look easy.

The undead dispatched the mercenaries and set to work on them. Berry burped and spat out a scrap of black fabric.

"Wow," Smokey said.

"Just like that," Rey said.

"Outstanding work. I should tell them."

"Maybe not just yet."

The scene reminded Rey of medieval debauches, back before table manners had been invented.

"Yeah," Smokey said. "Give them a little time to shift gears. They're fully engaged at present."

"Why don't we go now?" Rey suggested.

"I'm right behind you."

38

If any commandos had been alive to flush out hidden villagers, they would have found Sue and her friends-in-hiding right
away. Sue paced the hayloft, peering out the high window every
time she reached the end wall; she stuck her head out twice and
called Misty, long and loud, the way she called her home for dinner.

"Way to hide," Jackie said. "You're not stomping loud enough,
though. Try to push more hay dust down between the cracks, too."

"Get bent," Sue told her.

"Go take a long walk off a short pier," Jackie retorted. "They can
hear you a mile away."

"Not over the helicopter noise they can't."

The noise faded as the helicopter moved away.

"Okay, *now* they can hear you a mile away. Once they bust the
door down, you'll have about one second to regret all the goddamn
noise you're making."

"They won't have to bust down the door," Birdie said. "Sue didn't
put the bar across."

"What the hell? You left it open?" Jackie moaned. "Oh, god, why
am I here?"

"What if Misty comes home, or Crystal or Buck, and couldn't
get in?"

"Jeesum Crow, they're not coming home. Maybe Misty, once she gets done playing girl soldier. But the other two, they're running with the pack."

"Misty doesn't have to *play* soldier. She's an excellent shot and she's not afraid of anything."

Jackie said, "She's fourteen. She's just showing off for Ezekiel Alder, who is showing off for Misty. Remember hormones? They breed defiance and a false sense of having your shit together."

Sue backed up to the hole in the floor, climbed down the ladder, and opened the barn door. Jackie demanded to know where she thought she was going, but Sue wouldn't say. Gray light and fresh air rushed in. Hay dust drifted; Jackie sneezed.

The door slammed closed and bounced open again. Birdie looked out the window.

"She's headed up to the road." She wiped her glasses and brushed fingers through her hair, releasing wisps of hay. "I reckon I should go bar the door."

"Then when one of those men takes after her she'll run back here and pound on the door, beggin' us to let her in." Jackie huffed out a breath and spat dust. "I guess it'd be quieter if she just came on in without the pounding and begging. So let's leave the door be."

Birdie settled down into a soft pile by the window. "I don't feel so very safe up here."

"Good," Jackie said. "Because you're not safe, not one little bit."

Misty spat out a no-see-um and closed her mouth. She opened it again to say, "Whooa."

"Very cool," EZ agreed.

"We missed the action. I never even got to shoot anybody."

"Yeah, I guess it's over," EZ said.

They were whispering. Not because they were afraid. No, Misty told herself. Nothing to be afraid of now. But it was pretty weird: the not-dead sitting on the ground eating, some of them prowling through the bodies, snarling and grabbing at somebody else's piece of bad guy. Of course the revived wouldn't attack her or EZ, not right in front of Dad. They sure were going to town on those enemies, though.

"The Z's do like to eat."

"Hollow legs," EZ said. "Maybe they're growing."

"I guess they burn up a lot of food, the way they move and attack like that. Hard. Fast. Cougars eat a lot, right? Wolves? When they can get it, they chow down."

"But then they sleep for a few days. I never saw these guys sleep."

Misty remembered waking up in the night next to revived Crystal, before she'd run off with Dad. Crystal's eyes were always open, glowing in the dark. It had been neat, actually, like a night-light must be, just enough to keep you from stubbing your toe or seeing monsters in the corners.

"You know what," EZ whispered, "they remember what Smokey trained them to do, but they added their own stuff to it."

"Like eating their enemies."

"Yeah." He stopped staring at the carnage on the other side of the stickery Oregon grape and looked at Misty. "Maybe they *are* growing."

"Shut up."

"No, really. They got smarter. They got stronger. They got faster and hungrier. Maybe they'll get bigger. They're turning into giants."

"You better not say things like that," Misty warned.

"Hungry giants, searching for tender flesh, the kind that's easy to chew. Sweet girl meat." He broke off and felt his face redden. That had come out dirty.

"Weirdo."

"*Giants,*" EZ hissed.

Misty socked him on the arm.

"At least it's over," she said. "We're safe. I guess I should go tell Mom she can come out."

"Too bad we didn't get to help."

"Maybe next time. When the aliens land, we'll be there. Hey, we already got the black helicopters. Your dad was right about that. But right now I'm going to go throw up a little." Misty pivoted on her heels and hunched doubled-over into the woods.

39

"Thank God it's over. We can finally get my house put back together." Mercy scrubbed Heaven's hands harder and shot a meaningful look at Rey, sliding her eyes around Smokey, pretending, as usual, that he didn't exist.

"We'll all help," Rey reassured her.

"So you keep saying," Mercy said, starting in on Heaven's face.

Freedom and Liberty were already clean and waiting by the Pear Sisters' door. Mercy had washed her own hands but otherwise was still coated with a thin but visible layer of dirt. Cellar dirt was evidently more offensive than ordinary garden-variety outdoor dirt. The girls had been washragged half to death.

Bee and Cricket helped the older girls into their coats and gave them each a slice of bread and jam. The girls promised to milk their cow the minute they got home and have a big glass of milk before they got into bed. Rey watched them hurry along the road, Heaven riding on Mercy's left hip, Liberty leading the way, Freedom trailing behind. It was a different family now, without the men and boys: small and vulnerable and tenuous.

"Of course it's not over at all," Cricket said.

"Of course not," Bee agreed. "This isn't the olden days when people were allowed to drop off the face of the earth. They'll be expected to call in on their walkie-talkies and when they don't, something will happen. What do you think that will be?"

Smokey took the question.

"The helo will come back. There'll be more troops."

"Our revived soldiers can kill them, too." Cricket said.

Smokey shook his head. "It won't end until something ends it. We're outmanned and outgunned. There's really no way to win this. I'm sorry to say it so bluntly, but I think we all knew that. The best thing to do is leave, and I mean immediately."

"What's our timeline?" Rey asked.

"No way to tell. If I were base commander, I'd give them sixty minutes to sew things up, but I'd expect a status report before that."

"Then we've got to get their phone and call it in."

"They'll have codes."

"Garble it," Rey suggested. "Bad reception. Get the idea across that everything's good, but not too clearly."

"Worth a try. Let's dig their comm out before it's totally slimed."

Rey hoped they'd think of plan B before the third wave arrived.

The scene was two short of a Last Supper—if The Last Supper had been organized by a chimpanzee, catered by Hieronymus Bosch, and painted by Salvador Dali.

"Jesus," Smokey commented.

"Jesus is conspicuously absent," Rey said.

They moved cautiously between the diners. Six carcasses, ten picnickers. Fortunately, brisket was not as prized as round and shank portions, so Rey was allowed to search a few pockets for a radio or sat phone. Smokey picked through the debris on the ground.

"You're their leader," Rey told him. "Maybe they'll let you borrow their food. Try Jacob first. He's less likely to take your hand off."

Jacob and Crystal hunched side by side like teenagers sharing a diner booth. As Smokey got close, Jacob hissed at him.

"At ease, soldier. I just need to look at that shirt."

Jacob growled.

"Relinquish the shirt, son. That's an order." Smokey stood in front of the kid, standing like General Patton over some beaten-down dogface.

Jacob dropped the torso and backed off. Smokey nodded at him and stuck his hand inside the remaining rags of the camo jacket, came up figuratively, though not literally, dry.

"It's a mess in there," Smokey said. "But no phone. Resume eating, soldier."

It took the two of them to persuade El Duane to give up his rib rack, and some sweet talk from Rey to get Earl's out of his hands for the fifteen seconds it took to dig around in the gore and find nothing.

Rey walked the perimeter of the blow-dried circle the helicopter blades had made and found what they needed in a pocket of a bloody but empty pair of camouflage pants.

"Got it!"

Smokey dropped the empty trousers he'd been looking in and came over.

Rey handed it over. "It's pretty well slimed."

Smokey shook it; particles of clotted blood flew off. After wiping it on the shin of his pants he poked at an orange switch. Rey heard static. Smokey switched it off.

"What are you going to say?" Rey asked.

"I'm thinking I'll try to tell them all is well but we need to stay overnight. Sound good?"

"Won't they have a password or something? Some cute name for their operation? Project Get Newhause or something."

"We'll have to skip over that part."

He raised the radio to his face. Rey put a hand on his forearm. "Are you sure about this? I'm afraid it'll be a red flag. Maybe we'll have more time if we stay quiet."

"You might be right," Smokey said. "But there's even odds." He let the radio dangle. "Your call, Rey."

"My call was to give myself up, but you vetoed that. I feel like everything from here on is your responsibility. It would have been over and done with if I'd gone with them."

"Not for you. Probably not for any of us. I can't see them tipping their hats and saying Have a nice life, goodbye and good luck. I see them more as mowing down every living witness before they torture and kill you. Now what's your pleasure on the communication?"

Rey stared at the radio. "Tell them we need more time."

"That we do," Smokey agreed.

He scooped up a handful of ground litter, turned the radio on and covered the mike with the dead leaves and fir needles. A voice squawked. Smokey said some garbled things while he rubbed leaves against the mike. "Req- Overni- -stems Go-." He repeated it, added something military-sounding which he abruptly cut off, and shut off the power.

"Best I can do." He handed the radio to Rey. "I hope I didn't spook them."

Rey handed the radio back. "We'll keep an ear out for helicopters."

Before they left the clearing, Smokey assumed his Patton stance again and addressed his troops.

"Men, women," he intoned. "You did fine work here today. I'm proud of each and every one of you. If any more enemy come calling, I'm counting on you to finish them off just like you did this bunch. No hesitation, no mercy. It's kill or be killed. So kill."

He gave them a salute, which was unreturned, pivoted on his heel, and strode down the path.

"I'm inspired," Rey said.

"Don't let me inspire you. Inspire yourself," Smokey said.

40

Misty finished throwing up and spat. She hit a rhododendron leaf ten feet away, dead center. "You could have held my hair for me."

"I hate barf."

"Everybody hates barf. Friends hold each others' hair anyway."

"Then I'll pass on friendship." Just thinking about vomit made EZ's stomach crawl up his throat.

They were heading back to the Dollers' store even though he knew he should go home. Home made him feel like he was being smothered by a giant wool muffler. Even knowing his mother supposedly needed him—according to her and Smokey—he couldn't make himself go there.

"What a baby."

That wasn't fair. "Hey, you're the one who lost your lunch over a little blood."

"Massacres make me sick. Sorry."

EZ shrugged. "Doesn't bother me any."

"Then you're weird."

"Maybe I'm one of *them*." He held his arms out in front of him like a sleepwalker, lurching from side to side. That wasn't right, though. The Zs had started out lurchy, but now they were like animals. Smart, fast, tricky. Hungry. He put his arms down.

"Yeah, better not make fun of them. They're probably watching us right now. They'll eat you next. Sweet, tender boy flesh."

"Ha ha. Whatever." But she'd made him look behind them, and that made her laugh.

When an actual rustling came from behind a twinned doug fir, EZ and Misty both skittered in their tracks.

"Just a critter," Misty said.

"Yeah."

"It sounded kind of big." Misty whispered it.

"Yeah."

A bush jiggled, a shadow winked out, and there stood Jacob and Crystal. They stood forehead to forehead with their arms around each others' waists.

EZ's mouth dropped open. Misty didn't say a word, but EZ heard her stop breathing for a couple of seconds.

Crystal and Jacob didn't look up for the longest time. EZ was wondering if they were sick or something when Crystal turned her head and stared unblinking at her sister.

Misty took a breath. "Hey, Cryssy . What's up?"

Crystal made a noise like a murmur or a growl, or maybe a purr: definitely not words. She pressed her face against Jacob's. Jacob pulled her in tighter.

"So is he your, um, boyfriend now?" Misty ventured.

There was no answer.

"Dumb question," EZ said.

"Hey, I don't know. Maybe they're stuck together or something from all the blood and guts."

"Yuh-huh." To his brother, EZ said, "So, Jake, she never gave you the time of day before, even if she knew it, which she didn't. But now you're dead, Crystal's into you?"

Jacob glanced at him, then turned his back. Crystal's hand was wrapped around his. They stepped forward, away from their siblings. EZ knew exactly where they were, didn't take his eyes off of them, but they weren't there anymore. There were only green leaves and mossy tree bark and spotty gray light.

"Crystal!" Misty called. She craned her neck toward the place they'd been standing. "Where are you?"

The faintest of rustlings sounded from the undergrowth, then silence.

"They really are fast," Misty said. "I didn't even see them leave."

"I don't think they left," EZ said. "I think they disappeared."

"Well, that's a new one."

"Good one, too."

They waited a while, but it was impossible to know if Jacob and Crystal were still there or not without going over and feeling for them, but EZ didn't do that, and Misty didn't do that either, so they waited until it seemed like they were alone again.

"I don't get what she sees in him," EZ said.

"Have you seen him? He's built. I'd kiss him myself."

"No you would not."

"Almost."

"He's green."

"So's Crystal. She probably likes him green."

"You know, you two aren't identical anymore. She's got all these curves and muscles. Nice looking girl. Maybe I'll take her away from Jake."

"Shut up, perv."

EZ said, "She's like Wonder Woman."

"Shut up."

"Jealous?"

"I think I'll throw up again."

EZ walked away. It was good to hear Misty come after him.

"Great," she said. "They're in undead love. And they can disappear. That's not fair at all."

"I know," EZ said. "Zombies have all the fun."

The dapper little man pulled the woman close to his brocade-vested chest. "Sure they won't look for us up heah, Kitten?"

"Cloud Nine is our little secret." She smoothed his pencil moustache and curled the ends around her finger. His moustache was the cutest thing she'd ever seen.

"You are the most, you big hunk of heartbreak." She kissed him.

There wasn't a lot of room to move, but the privacy was prime. Forty feet above the ground, the tree house wrapped around the grand-daddy fir tree like a bobby soxer around Sinatra's leg. Jobert had about flipped his wig when she showed it to him.

"Ah love it!" he'd said. "But why? My house has heat and you don't have to climb a tree to get into it."

"Don't be such a square," she'd chided. "We don't need those clydes bugging us. Did you get a load of the walking dead action down there? It's strictly from nowhere. Whereas we are cool, high in the sky like an eye. Now haul up the blankets and grub, bub, before one of those sub-zeros catches wise."

Sure enough, he'd made with the happy faces ever since. It was terrific here, with the wind rocking them in a tree cradle. Once you got used to the amenities, you wondered why you'd ever pooped the party in flatland.

Jobert kissed her ear to make her giggle. "Warm enough, Kitten?"

"Warm for your form." She snuggled in closer.

Far, far below, an ant-person ran through the trees, then more ant-people followed with their heels on fire. From this angel's eye view, whatever they were chasing or running from was way too insignif for so much burning rubber. Once a whirly-bird rattled the treetop, but the half-walls held everything on deck, and pretty soon all was smooth again.

He slid his hands under her plaid wool jacket. "It's fun listenin' to them fuss around down theah."

"Only because we're together. I'm real, real gone on you, Heaven Sent." She leaned in to kiss his cheek, shaved smooth as baby skin.

"Me too, baby. I never felt so free. You are mah woodland spirit."

Lacewing nodded, making her puff of a ponytail bounce. "I have that effect on men."

"Did you hear something?"

Over the past years, Bee's hearing had gotten mixed up with intuition. Some of the sounds she heard weren't really there, according to other people. Her sisters looked at her sometimes like she was a simpleton, the same look she'd given her grandmother while her hearing was fading. Right 'til the end, Grandma had denied missing a word.

But I'm not deaf. I hear different things than other people. Like whatever that sound was.

"Nope," Cricket answered. "What was it?"

Bee looked east. "From down by the river, I think."

"Invaders?"

A crow yelled, birds chattered in the yard. The usual worry of high branches by the unceasing wind, a fir cone bouncing down the gauntlet of limbs. Nothing out of place.

Bee picked up the hatchet and her basket of kindling and went in the back door.

"What was it?" Cricket followed her inside.

"A thump. I heard it in my feet."

"Probably a boulder turning over in the riverbed."

"Yes, it was like that," Bee said. "It makes me uncomfortable."

"Well, you know what a rock sounds like. Was it a rock?"

Bee put out the fire and opened the damper wide to let the smoke dissipate into the rising air currents. She said, "Lock up."

They sat in the falling light, drinking scalding tea made on the kerosene stove, keeping an eye out to the road. Cricket had scattered twigs and matchstick kindling around the house.

"Those undead people won't make any noise on your alarm," Bee told her.

"Regular people will," Cricket said. "And it's not our undead I'm worried about."

"No." Bee sipped a mouthful of air and steam and tea. "They've turned out fairly well, all told. So far."

"So far," Cricket agreed.

Wind over tree boughs, wind in the window cracks. The old house creaking. Steam and herbs, sleep weighting the eyelids.

Every day measured, Bee thought, *yet the years tumble away. Once in a long while a boulder rolls, down deep. Between times, you watch it rush by, too swift to catch.*

"They eat a lot," Cricket said. "They like meat."

"And bones."

"Not old bones, I don't think."

"We don't know what they prefer, do we? Maybe old bones are the best. Easier to crack open to get at the marrow."

"Not so much marrow to get at," Cricket pointed out.

"Speak for yourself."

Voices carried up the hill from the river bank, low voices without words.

The sisters looked out the window without rising from their chairs. The wind was up a bit, as it usually was this time of day. The bass tones seeped through the walls, through the skin, strangers' voices echoing in the joints and prickling in the veins.

"That's them, then," Bee said.

"Who?" Cricket asked.

"Them. Whoever they are, that's them."

Cricket rose. "Shall we?"

"I see no reason in the world why not."

They gathered a few necessaries and crossed the kitchen.

"I don't look forward to this," Bee said. "I don't want to complain, but the immediate future is not going to be comfortable."

"We've had a pretty plush life up to now," Cricket said. "A bit of adversity will be bracing."

Fiddlin' Sue knew exactly where the drop-off was supposed to be, but the December rains had carved off a chunk of riverbank and before she could stop, her feet fell out from under her. In the two seconds it took to reach the rocks at the bottom, a fingernail ripped off below the quick and a skinny but vicious branch whipped a slice in her left cheekbone. She sat crumpled on the rocks, which weren't as smooth as they looked, and picked gravel out of her palms. The thump of a turning river rock didn't register until small, dry stones knocked against each other. Something was walking close by.

More than one something. The falls were a ways downstream, but their featureless noise fogged the ears even this far upriver. The river itself gurgled and rushed, never the same and never silent. It was impossible to pick out small sounds against all that. Sue listened hard, opening her mouth wide to quiet her breath. Tapping and clunking of small rocks ... and a whisper. Someone said *Shh*.

A whiff of wool and wood smoke found her nose, followed by the familiar scent of peppermint leaves.

Sue stood up. "It's me," she said. "What are you doing here?"

"What are *you* doing here?" Cricket sounded short on air.

"I'm looking for Crystal."

Bee stood up straighter, showing no weakness, but Sue saw that the hand she'd laid on Cricket's shoulder was clutching tight.

"Was that you making the thump?" Sue asked.

"I hoped it was you," Cricket said.

Their voices dropped.

"Just a rock turning," Sue said.

Bee turned her head, looking out at the blackening water. "Come this way."

Bee led them along the bank about twenty yards, past the low rapids where water humped over a wide stone ledge. She stopped a few times to peer through the vegetation at the steepening walls. Then she slipped between a brushy vine maple and a willow and was gone.

Cricket and Fiddlin' Sue groped after her. The brush closed behind them. Two big round river rocks and a chunk of log made stools in the shallow cutback.

"I haven't been here in years. Decades," Cricket said.

"It's just the same," Bee said.

They listened.

"The water's too noisy," Sue said.

"That helps us, too," Bee said. "But we should stay quiet."

"You think something's out there?"

"Oh, something's out there. What, is the question."

"Friend or foe," Cricket said.

"Foe," Bee said. "Definitely foe."

They listened some more.

Then Sue asked, "Why did you come down here? If you knew somebody was sneaking around, why head right for them?"

Cricket and Bee looked at each other. It was too dark to see their faces, but Sue could see their heads turn, then turn back.

"You didn't want to miss the show." Sue laughed, but quietly. "You gals take the cake. You know no fear."

"I know some fear," Bee said. "I choose not to let it push me around."

"And what have we got to lose?" Cricket whispered. Sue could barely hear her over the push of water.

"We want to live," Bee explained. "But evidently it takes a lot to kill us off."

"We're living in the moment," Cricket added. "Carpe diem."

"You gals," Sue said again.

She knew they were close to trouble. She knew the Pear Sisters wouldn't be any help against the undead, or invaders, or beasts prowling the riverbank. Yet sitting in the little den with them, she felt safe as a bear cub with two mothers.

The cozy feeling chilled in a hurry. Where were Crystal, and Misty, and Buck? Together, fighting an invisible enemy? Or were they each alone, fighting each other, unknowing, in the dark?

41

Stones clattered under Rey's boots. Two steps ahead of her, down the bank, Smokey reached the water's edge without making a sound. They had skirted the road's end in favor of a circuitous route through the brush. Smokey had argued for patrolling the west side of the mountain, but Rey said she would watch the shortest way in, which was across the river, and Smokey could watch the back cliff if he wanted to. He'd opted to stick with her. As they'd neared the river, the thump of a big rock turning over made her veer away from the road's end. It might have been nothing, but she didn't trust it.

Hadn't there been voices? It was easy to hear voices in the river. Easy to understand how people said the river was alive and talking, always saying something yet keeping its secrets.

She skidded and collided with Smokey's back under a tangle of willows. He felt solid and safe. She considered staying there tucked against him, but this wasn't the time. On the other hand, it might be the only time, the last chance. Maybe wisdom lay in spending your last minutes wrapped around somebody you cared about instead of fighting a losing battle.

Wisdom, maybe, but not sense.

Crouching at Smokey's side, she felt the water-chilled air tickle her face. It was almost as good as sleep.

His body tensed. She followed his stare.

She squinted and willed her pupils to dilate, tried to make her eyes see something other than what was there, but there it was. A black, oily shape emerged from the river, walking gracefully as a wraith out of the deep, icy river that had pulled the bridge off of its concrete foundations and had been known to bounce a pickup truck along like a leaf. Behind the thing more shapes rose smoothly up out of the dark water: twenty, maybe two dozen of them, standing like shadows, all facing the road.

Then she smelled the revived Cannibalites massing silently behind her at the road's end. How they had gotten so stealthy after such clumsy beginnings was something Rey was getting used to, even if she didn't understand it. She automatically started planning research protocol and writing up the summary before she remembered that, one way or another, her future held no research. Her raising of the dead would never be acclaimed by the scientific community, but it had produced unforeseen and amazing results, one of which was a squad of formerly dead humans materializing on the riverbank within growling distance of the bizarre strangers watching at the water's edge.

Water gurgled past, in a hurry to get out of there. One of the strangers moved to the front of his group. His gang stirred and spread out; the Cannibal Mountain fighters puffed up and spread out and advanced a step; the strangers moved forward to meet them. A standoff, Rey thought, holding her breath, until El Duane jumped on the point man-thing, knocking him flat into the rapids. Instantly the silence erupted in a chaos of howling and grunting.

Rey shrank down, feeling her neck trying to disappear into her coat collar while she cowered against Smokey. The sounds alone were enough to make her skin quiver. Under the staccato of rocks knocking together she heard bones snapping, the thud of fists, and the wet *mosh* of flesh tearing away. The inhuman armies clashed and clinched in a blur of shadows. Berry rode one of the invaders like a cowgirl. It charged for the water and they splashed in, smashing at each other's faces as the current swept them away.

Trucker John grabbed two invaders and smacked them together. They grabbed his massive arms and twisted his right arm, then his left, out of his shoulders. He retaliated by biting through the smaller one's neck and shaking it like a pit bull, then wiping the other one off against a tree and stomping his belly into mush.

There was more light at the river than in the trees, but individuals were getting harder to identify. Rey's stomach quivered. She wanted to run in and help her team kick invader ass, but even her own undead were in too deep a frenzy for her to discriminate between friend and foe.

They weren't necessarily winning the battle. Trucker John was still in it, using his tree trunk legs while his arms grew back—fingers had already sprouted from his armpits. Little Eddy, Crystal, and Jacob zipped around causing a lot of damage in the understory while the bigger troops tore off heads and stove in ribs. One disemboweled invader squirmed; its belly closed up and the thing got to its feet and lurched, head down, at Hoot, who reopened the wound, removed the thing's head, and stuffed it inside the gaping abdominal cavity.

Rey had performed many autopsies, but this carnage was too much. She looked at the ground, wishing she could shut out the sounds. She prayed for it to end, but what if the oily dark things won? And if the Cannibalite undead killed all the invaders, and somehow made them stay dead, would the friendlies stop killing? Could they stop, or had the attack triggered something, turned on a gene, engaged neuronal pathways that could never be turned off?

Smokey slipped an arm around her shoulder and gave her a morale-boosting shake. *Maybe we'll be all right after all. Stay alert.* She leaned into him and he kept her in his circle of protection.

A writhing clump of shadows moved toward their hiding place. Jacob and Crystal tangled with three outsiders and the snarling knot traveled past Smokey and Rey. The main battle jerked along behind, following them, as if they had received orders to relocate. The invaders were fewer than when they'd first appeared. A de-limbed, scooped-out carcass rose up on its bloody stumps and lurched with the grisly parade. They passed the thicket where Rey and Smokey hid, stumbling into the water, charging out again to drag an enemy down. Removing a victim's arms and drowning it was a favored tactic.

Weren't they regenerating faster now? If only she could isolate them and record the changes! God, for a video camera! Regeneration of arms and hands in minutes ... seconds! She knew they must metabo-lize gigaCalories to regrow limbs and organs and especially heads so rapidly. Perhaps that would be their Achilles heel: rapid depletion of energy. Instant starvation. Once they had eaten their enemies, they would die. But they weren't eating each other. Rey was postulating explanations for this—no time during battle; the enemy didn't taste good; the enemy was poisonous—when a new and terrifying sound ripped through her thoughts. A woman had screamed.

"Someone's down here!" she whispered to Smokey.

He shook his head. *Don't make a sound.*

The river masked the origin of the scream, but Rey felt the sound in her right ear. The scream came again, then a second voice shouted something angry.

"It's the Pear Sisters," Rey whispered. "And Sue, I think. Goddamn it!"

The voice shouted again in Fiddlin' Sue's famous five-mile hol-ler. Sue would have come to the river looking for her daughters, but why the Pear Sisters had come with her Rey couldn't imagine. It sounded as if they'd been discovered now, and if they weren't already being torn apart, there were only seconds to try to stop it.

Rey broke cover and stumbled toward the women. The revived Cannibalites chased the invaders up the rocky ground, too intent on destruction to notice the humans following them. Squelching sounds and violent grunts erupted from the melee. The local undead attacked like lions, double-teaming their victims and tearing them open. Earl crushed a head with a rock the size of a car engine. It was a redundant act he must have done for sheer joy because his victim's intestines and various organs were already strewn across the rocks.

Cricket cried out and Rey put on a burst of speed. She nearly ran into Eddy when he stopped suddenly. Ahead, the entire group had halted and several of the invaders had crowded up to the high bank. The women screamed. Sue shouted, "Get down!" and a gunshot blasted, then another.

Rey pushed past Eddy and through the revived, ignoring the mutilated corpses littering the ground. When two of the invaders whirled around to confront her she shot them in their hideous faces. While Cannibalite undead fell upon them eagerly she shoved through toward where the women's voices had come from.

"Sue! It's me!"

Another shot pounded her ears and the bullet parted the air next to Rey's temple. The battle intensified behind her.

"Rey?" Sue's voice said. "Get out of here!"

Rey was looking into a shallow cave where Sue stooped, flanked by the cowering Pear Sisters.

"Move out! I'm fixing to shoot a bunch of those ugly bastards right now!" Sue sighted along her rifle barrel.

Rey ducked, squatted beside Cricket, and aimed into the pressing invaders. Two of them moved forward in their creepy, laconic way. Rey shot it mid-face and it went down. She gave it another blast that vaporized its face. It would take a few minutes to regrow its brains and eyes—she hoped.

"Hold fire," Rey said.

The Cannibalites pummeled and disassembled invaders at the cave mouth.

Rey grabbed Cricket's arm and pulled. "Got to go."

"Bee!" Cricket said. "Get Bee!"

Rey dragged Bee to her feet. "Upsy-daisy. Come on, quick! Sue, cover us."

"Here they come," Smokey warned. "Go! Go! Go!"

His semiautomatic blurted bullets. The women half-carried Bee and Cricket, who pedaled their feet over the rocks.

Roars, clattering stones, and wet sundering noises pursued them. In her peripheral vision Rey glimpsed Hoot smashing two invaders into each other, once to get their attention and one more time to demolish their skulls. Something blurred on her other side. Its oily arm clutched her shoulder. Then it flew into the air with a squawk and sailed over her head into the river. Crystal shot a side-long look at Rey as she loped past, still clutching a handful of the creature's scalp. Jacob came up behind Crystal and side by side they kept pace a yard ahead of the five humans they protected.

They covered ground fast and made it to the defunct trolley crossing. As they started to climb the slippery, root-held steps to the road, Smokey let loose a barrage of bullets. At the same instant, something slammed Rey in the solar plexus. She flew sideways a dozen feet and landed hard, airless and dazed. Sue's rifle sounded once.

"Let go of her, you goddang mons—" Sue was cut off mid-word.

In an eye-blink two twisted figures snatched up Bee and Cricket Pear and leaped up the bank. One of them jumped right over Sue's prostrate body. Her hand snatched at its foot but it twitched her off and disappeared into the trees. Cricket's moans were ululations as she was roughly jounced over the creature's shoulder. From Bee there was no noise at all.

Jacob and Crystal howled and took off after the invaders. A wisp of cloth floated from Jacob's fist to the ground. The river breeze lifted it and sent it flapping and scurrying along the road toward Rey and wrapped itself around her legs. She kicked at it frantically and realized she could now inhale. She got to her hands and knees, panting for air. Stink oozed from the fabric. She tried to flick it away but it stuck to her hands with revolting persistence.

Smokey reached her. "You okay?"

"Yeah." She inhaled, gagged, turned her face up to get away from the rag. "They got the Pears."

"I know. Where's Sue?"

Rey struggled to her feet, felt her ribs for breakage, ran her tongue around her mouth to taste for blood. It hurt to breathe. "Sue's around here somewhere," she said. "They knocked her down, but they didn't take her."

Smokey said, "Let's get out of here."

She had lost her flashlight somewhere, but Smokey pulled one from his coat pocket and shined it, with the lens mostly covered, on the road and surrounding ground. Rey expected him to urge her to leave immediately, but instead he kept looking for Sue.

Rey scanned the ground as best she could in the twilight. Below, the battle raged on. She softly called Sue's name, sure she wouldn't be heard in the chaos, keeping an eye on the fighters. As she looked on, half the combatants vanished.

They were there, then they weren't.

"Smokey," she said.

"Find her?"

Then Smokey caught the silence and looked down.

"They disappeared," Rey told him.

"What?"

"Disappeared. Into thin air."

"They're fast."

She shook her head. "They didn't run. They disappeared."

Rey and Smokey stared at the Cannibalite undead, who were slowly turning, punching the air, huffing, searching for their enemy.

Berry let loose a wild karate kick and the sound of it landing was clear, even though what it had connected with was invisible. Berry lunged, grabbed armfuls of nothing, and landed on her face.

Growls rumbled. Unintelligible vocalizations rose; the revived were talking to each other in their own language. Then Crystal hooted. The others looked toward her. One—Trucker John, maybe—was yanked backward by an unseen hand and caromed, flailing, off the riverbank. Crystal disappeared. Jacob followed her into invisibility. One by one, like stars behind a cloud, the undead winked out and the riverbank was empty.

Empty of visible bodies, that was. The fight resumed with a vengeance. Ghost warriors punched and tore at each other. Splashes, stones striking stones and bone, and riverbank vegetation cracking mapped the direction of the battle as it surged downstream.

"Damn," Smokey said.

"Pretty good trick," said Rey. "Maybe they can teach us how to do that." She took the flashlight from Smokey and shined it deeper into the trees. Logs, bushes ... and the sprawled body of Fiddlin' Sue.

Rey rushed to her. Felt for a carotid pulse. Laid down the flashlight and covered Sue's mouth with her own, breathed.

Smokey came to them and started cardiac compressions.

At last Sue took in a tentative gasp, rasped an exhalation, and breathed on her own. In another minute she was conscious. Rey wasted no time, but hoisted her onto her own back and set off for the Dollar's store.

"I'll take her," Smokey said, but Rey told him to find the Pear Sisters.

Smokey didn't answer and didn't leave.

"I've got this. Get the sisters before the creeps eat them."

Smokey's voice was gentle but firm. "It's too late. Whatever they're going to do to them, they've already done it."

Rey stopped to catch her breath. Her chest hurt more from the exertion and her legs trembled. "Bullshit. You don't know."

Smokey lifted Sue from Rey's back.

"Get in the house. Weapon at ready. We don't know where they are now. They could be waiting for us in the store. They could be anywhere."

With Sue in a fireman's carry, he led the way to the store, turning constantly, looking for movement in the shrubs, listening for footsteps.

Rey said, "I hate this."

"Only because you're sane."

The door was no defense, but it didn't matter any more. Undead, friendly or otherwise, could be standing in front of them unseen. All they could do was stay defensive, re-board up the door, and hope the enemy had better things to worry about than three humans hiding in a half-demolished storefront. While Smokey checked the interior Rey sat with Sue in the bedroom. From time to time things crashed as he swung a broom around, feeling for bodies. After a little while he came to the bedroom door.

"No bogies in here as far as I can tell. 'Course, they might be good at bobbing and weaving. How's Sue?"

"Breathing and pulse are good. She's a little clammy. It could be mild shock."

"You should try to sleep a little."

"I'll sleep—"

"—when I'm dead. Right."

Rey said, "We've got maybe a few hours, and that's if they bought our little broadcast. We still don't have a place to hide everybody. And now the Pear Sisters ... "

"Yeah."

"We're screwed, aren't we?"

"Could be. But it's not over 'til it's over." He smiled. It was a smile without much humor in it, but it made Rey feel better.

"Never say die, chin up, stiff upper lip, and all that." Rey smiled back.

Something scraped the outside wall. Smokey slipped around the foot of the bed and peered through a gap in the boards over the window.

"What is it?" Rey whispered.

"I don't see anything."

"It's one of them, then."

"But which them, is the question."

"Does it matter?" Rey said.

"It does." Smokey looked at her, glanced at Sue, back at Rey. "Have faith in our team. I think we can count on them."

He looked through the window again just as something shuffled against the front door. The something knocked.

42

The front window revealed nothing. Smokey moved to the corner between the door hinges and wall.

"Who is it?"

He heard a soft, polite cough, like a gorilla huffing. *Does that mean "In five seconds I'm going to rip your head off,"* he wondered, *or "I wish to share my bananas with you?"*

"Show yourself."

He felt rather than heard a body lean on the door.

It said, "L-p-pllp."

One of the undead troops, Berry or Crystal. Or one of the enemy, doing a good imitation. They could disappear; why couldn't they do impressions?

He hadn't bothered teaching them a password because they couldn't talk. It would have come in handy right about now.

"What's your favorite food?" Smokey asked.

Without hesitation, whoever it was replied, "Ohnz!"

From the bedroom, Rey asked, "Who is it?"

"Somebody who likes bones. Sounds like a female. I'm thinking one of ours."

"Let her in. I'll cover you from here."

"There could be a dozen more of them behind her."

"I know."

Smokey hesitated, then pried two boards loose and crouched behind the door. Something pushed, the space between the door and frame widened, then the something pushed the door closed again.

"Show yourself," Smokey ordered, "or I'll shoot!"

The air wavered, the wall in the background stammered out, back in, and out of existence. A humanoid form seemingly made of wall took shape and in a couple of seconds turned into Berry.

"Are you alone?" Smokey asked.

"Aahhh." Berry spread her arms to show there was nothing to bump into. Her muscles had split open the sleeves of her shirt, and she—or someone—had torn off her fatigue trousers above the round bulge of her quadriceps.

"Berry, what's going on?" Rey asked. "Where are the others?"

Berry took Rey's hand.

"Hey," Smokey warned.

"It's all right," Rey told him. "She needs something."

"Pelehp, plep!" Berry tugged Rey toward the door.

"What?" Rey said.

Berry pulled Rey's arm. "Pah-lep!"

"Jeez, it's like talking to Lassie," Smokey said. "Trouble in the old abandoned well, girl?"

Berry whirled on him, her jaundiced eyes wide and urgent. "Aahhh!"

"I think you hit it," Rey told Smokey.

"Is there a well?"

"Not that I know of."

"Then what's she talking about?"

"Oh," Berry urged. "Oh!"

She pointed west, her arm following the road as it climbed the hill. She pulled Rey.

"She's developed phenomenal strength," Rey observed, following Berry.

Smokey blocked the door, aiming his weapon at Berry's face.

"No, it's okay," Rey said. "I'm going with her."

"No way."

"It's important. Berry, is it about the Pear Sisters?"

"Aahhh! Oh! Ohl." Berry leaned in and articulated carefully, as if speaking to the hard-of-thinking. "Ho. Ho-ohl."

With Fiddlin' Sue conscious and safely, relatively speaking, barricaded in the Dollers' store, Rey and Smokey followed Berry through the trees toward the cave. Rey had two flashlights and a coil of rope; Smokey carried his semiautomatic and a pistol, another flashlight, and a small tarp. They each carried one of Birdie's jackets.

Something bit at Rey's heart as she approached the hole in the ground; something more than fear. Her adrenaline had overpowered fear and good sense, which was adrenaline's job one. What tore at her emotions was worse than fear. It was tenderness, a wide, quaking protective feeling for the old women: their fragile bones, their tissuey skin, their knowledge that everything would not necessarily end happily. They were suddenly intensely precious.

The updraft of clammy air wavered for a moment at the cave mouth and in the pause Rey caught a whiff of fug. It smelled familiar. It smelled like decay and death.

"Who's here?" Rey asked the darkness.

Feet shuffled. Somebody coughed, raising the stink level. The gloom wavered and indefinite, then translucent, then solid reanimates stood crowded around The Crack.

"Quit that," Smokey said. "Be here or don't be here. Make up your minds."

Rey addressed Berry. "What's going on?"

All the revived gibbered at once, pointing downwards, excited about something.

"The bad guys took the Pear Sisters down there?" Rey asked.

The gibbering rose in pitch.

"Okay. I'll go get them. Anybody with me?"

Every revived raised his or her hand and crowded in, pushing Rey uncomfortably close to the hole in the floor.

Smokey said, "I'll go down first."

"It's my fight. They're my family. I'll go first."

"Better chance of living through it if I take point. Besides, tripping over your bloody, lifeless body will slow me down." He took the rope and started coiling it, efficiently tying knots at intervals.

"So you think the bad guys are down there with the sisters?"

"Seems like a reasonable assumption." He said, "Some of you have to stay up here and hold the rope. Trucker John, Earl, El Duane, wrap it around you like this." He started them out and they got the idea disturbingly fast, even though they grumbled about staying above ground.

"You'll be the second group down. I'll make sure you get there."

Belayed by the three big guys, Smokey rappelled down. Rey lay on her stomach, shining a light beside his disappearing form. The light revealed nothing. She listened for an attack, elderly cries for rescue, anything. The rope went slack and she felt two sharp tugs on it.

"What's happening?" she called as she hauled the rope up.

"Nothing. I'm at the bottom." A dim light flicked on; impossible to tell by the light and his faint voice if Smokey was twenty feet away or a hundred. Rey estimated the rope length at thirty or forty feet.

She harnessed herself in and walked down the uneven vertical wall. Berry held the third flashlight; Rey had the small one in her mouth. Glimpses of black and ochre rock passed through its beam. Everything was slick, thoroughly and eternally wet. Rock facets glistened close up, zoomed out as Rey pushed off from the wall, then rushed toward her again. Dozens of pale sticks jumbled on ledges and in crevices, tangled in dirty white masses. From a nest of ribs, a human skull gaped at her. Years of dissection and post-mortems didn't stop her from flinching.

The graveyard slipped up past her head. Another pile of bones on another ledge appeared. Large animals of some kind: a skull, probably of a deer; the dome of a larger skull, but not human; thick femurs and racks of ribs and rubble mounds of scattered vertebrae. Everywhere she looked, every place a rock or crack could stop gravity's work, another broken skeleton rested.

The floor jolted her own bones.

"Smokey?"

"Shh. Right here."

Their flashlight beams found each other. Rey untied the rope harness and suppressed a surge of panic as it snaked up and away.

"Did you see anything?" she whispered.

"Not yet. We'll have a recon when the rest of them get here. What the hell are all those skeletons doing here?"

Rey shrugged, remembered he probably couldn't see it, and said, "Mostly animals. They've been here a long time. And one or more humans."

"That's pretty weird."

"Yeah. I suppose the animals fell in."

"And the humans?"

That was a subject for another time. "How do we get back up again?" She hoped to God Smokey had thought that through.

"There'll be at least one person left above. Can't come down without somebody up there to hold the rope." He clapped her on the shoulder. "No worries. I booked us a round trip."

Breathing came with a weight of pea soup fog. Good for the skin, hard on the lungs.

Rey took a lungful of the atmosphere and called, "Bee! Cricket!"

"Shut up," Smokey said.

"You shut up."

"If the bad things are down here, they'll come for us. At least wait 'til our odds are upped a little."

A form lowered through the chute. Eddy.

"Great," Smokey muttered. "The spindliest one of the crew."

Spindly and evidently hungry. Eddy had snagged a radius of some species on the way down and cracked it open; he sucked at the marrow and licked his lips. He made it sound delicious.

The next to join them was Hoot. Smokey cheered up. Then Berry, and Jacob followed by Crystal. There was a short wait during which muffled sounds of an argument drifted down with the dust and debris. The argument gave way to sounds like meaty fists on thick skulls. A minute after the ruckus died down Buck Hill swung in.

Smokey had to persuade him to untie the rope. Buck had a pissed off set to his face that said *Damned if those yahoos are gettin' the rope.*

"I wonder why the guys didn't just drop Buck," Rey whispered. "I suppose that wouldn't have been sporting."

"I really am so proud," Smokey said. "Sporting zombies. They owe it all to your civilizing influence."

"Too true," Rey agreed.

When Buck saw what everybody else had he wanted some, too. Without hesitation, he grabbed Jacob's short-rack of ribs. Jacob, barely up to Buck's armpit, barked and wriggled out of his grip, taking the ribs with him. Buck's long arm snatched the boy's shredded collar and yanked him back. Jacob swatted Buck across the face with a rib.

"No fighting!" Rey ordered. She swung the light across the cave walls until she found a heap of fractured bones. As she grabbed at them she brushed against something yielding and skin-like; a multitude of small, smooth, round things slid under her palm. Skeletal remains were one thing; unknown soft tissues were another. Recoiling, Rey pressed the bones into Jacob's arms. He snarled at Buck one more time and settled back to gnaw alongside Crystal.

Rey felt like a teacher with a class of hyperactive kids on a field trip to a candy store. "Control yourselves, people," she told them, but they paid her no mind.

"Walk and chomp, folks," Smokey quietly ordered. "Let's rescue some maidens and kill some bad guys."

"Do we still have to be quiet?" Rey asked.

"Wouldn't hurt, but I think they know we're coming by now, what with the fighting and the torchlight procession."

It was a three-torch procession. Those orange eyes seemed to possess goggle-grade night vision, so Smokey volunteered Berry and Hoot—the lithest and the strongest—to lead the way, then followed them with the brightest flashlight. Behind him filed the rest of the troops with Rey in the middle. The cave floor sloped downward over treacherous steps that held a grudge against pedestrians, with particular malice toward ankles.

A thin yodeling sound set the hairs on Rey's arms standing at the alert. She froze. The walker behind her bumped into her and caught her by the shoulder. His hand was broad and hard. She instinctively jerked away. He grunted softly, an unmistakable warning.

"Was that one of the ladies?" Smokey asked quietly.

"No," Rey said, thinking, *God, I don't want to know what could make them emit that sound.* "Where did it come from?"

"Hard to tell."

The blood-curdling noise came again—from ahead, behind, echoing off the rocks.

Then, horribly, one of the undead between Rey and Smokey answered in a perfect imitation. Others joined in, ululating nightmare calls that filled the cave with howled threats. Rey's shoulders hunched toward her ears for safety.

"Shut that shit up!"

The warbling drowned out Smokey's bark. Then the risen surged forward, carrying Rey and Smokey along like deadwood in a flood. Rey shuffled and hopped trying to keep her footing; she would have gone down under the big undead feet if steely hands hadn't snagged her and held her upright, dragging her along. In the din it was impossible to tell how many invaders there might be or how close they were. Somewhere ahead a glint of pale light shot across Rey's eyes. Daylight, flashlight, or a new reanimate capability: generating light. And why not? They regenerated body parts better than any salamander; they might as well emit light better than any firefly. Nothing about them could surprise her now.

The ululations crescendoed and stopped. In the silence, bursts of dull light revealed the black, elongated shapes of the invaders and the Cannibalites charging into each other. Rey dived for a spot where she could get a clear shot and out of the corner of her eye saw Smokey doing the same. Gunshots echoed in the fine bones of her ears. Strobed images seared her retinas: a head flying into the darkness. An invader riding Hoot's neck like a nightmare orangutan. Berry clasped in a deadly dance with two blue-pulsing invaders. Rey got off some good shots and some risky ones. A couple of the spectral black forms fell and were ripped apart by the beefier home-dead.

Got him! The armed undead shot, too, blowing the enemy into dark mists that stuck to Rey's cheeks. In a dull green pulse she watched a killed invader wobble up on new legs and attack one of the littler Cannibalites, ripping his or her arm off and flinging it backward in a perfect arc. The Cannibalite countered with some unseen move, and in the next oxblood-tinted pulse of light the invader was a stack of limbs topped by a head. Rey shot a dozen holes in the stack.

Reassemble that, *motherfucker.*

43

A burst of red hazed the air and hit Rey's face in a cold, sticky spray.

The ululations came from everywhere. A chillingly human scream pierced the caterwauling.

Cricket.

To reach the sisters they would have to go through the monsters.

What were these half-visible things? Rey dreaded admitting that she knew the answer, but she did; of course she did. Just as the Cannibalite revived were her own creations, these were Everett Roberts'. But somehow she did not believe they were evolving toward humanness and beyond, the way hers were.

Mine. My monsters. A hot pulse of something protective and narrow-eyed ran through her.

I'll be damned, she thought. So that's what a maternal impulse feels like.

A flash of yellowish light glinted off a gold earring as Crystal's head sailed past. Rey shouted. Two of the monsters leaped at her. Rey fired twice and hit them both. They flew backwards and in a second a cluster of the revived tore them into a rough dice. Jacob ran past her and snatched up Crystal's head. Already a muscular neck had sprouted from Crystal's jaw line and below the jaw, shoulder buds swelled. Jacob cradled the head on his thigh and smoothed Crystal's hair back from her forehead.

Crouching low, Rey waited for a clear shot at one of the blackish forms. The pulses of light came less frequently now and the vivid colors were duller. If the lights stopped altogether, the humans would be easy pickings, with their flashlight beams drawing fire.

Cricket screamed again.

"Goddamn it, leave them alone!" Rey shouted.

From somewhere ahead, Smokey called, "We've got 'em! Cover me!"

"I can't see you. How can I cover you? "

"If anything moves that isn't me, shoot it."

Rey moved toward his voice.

She could smell him, a woody cleanish smell inside the funk of gunpowder and walking dead and mildew. A hand steadied her shoulder.

"Is that you?" she said.

"Is that *you?*"

"I asked you first."

Smokey said, "Stay low. Follow me."

Rey grabbed a handful of jacket and let him lead her down the tunnel. Once he whirled around and shot over her head. Her ears rang. Something heavy and nasty fell on her backside and she bucked it off. They moved on again.

In front of her, Smokey said, "Ladies?"

Silence.

"Where are they?" Rey asked him.

"Put your hand out. No, here."

Bee's voice whispered, "Rey? It's you?"

"Come on. Let's get you out of here!" They turned back toward the thick of the battle.

"Oh, no, sir." Cricket stopped. "We can't go in that. We'll get shot. I'll wait in that little hole you took me out of."

Smokey's voice was firm. "We'll be fine. Stay low, ladies. Cricket, hold onto Rey's coat. Bee, hold onto your sister. I've got your back. Feel it? I've got you."

"Great gods," Bee said, and they moved low up-tunnel toward the Crack.

Even though all the soldiers were deader than any dead thing EZ had ever seen, he kept looking behind him as they threaded through the brush and trees.

"Somebody following us?" Misty asked, letting a rhododendron branch fly backwards and slap him with cold rainwater.

He shook his head. "Nobody's there."

"Quit looking, then. You're making me nervous."

"Just hurry up."

They were headed to Rey's. Nobody was at the Pears' house and they hadn't wanted to chance exposing themselves on the open road. Demolished Hoochville was of course deserted. If Rey's house was deserted, too, the plan was to go back north to Joe Bear's. EZ wouldn't say it even to himself, but he wanted a grown-up. He was tired of handling things. He tried to remember a line, any line, of poetry he'd written, but there wasn't any poetry in his head. Only blood and a picture of his father and brother gnawing on human arm bones. Not very poetic. Although maybe you *could* write poems about that stuff. Maybe he'd be the first. After all, what else could you do with memories like that?

They rounded the big grown-over stump where the path turned left toward Rey's cabin. Something crashed in the bushes and Misty dove for the ground. EZ stumbled backwards and landed on his butt. He clawed for his gun but before he got hold of it a goat shoved through the salal and skittered up to him, straddling Misty's legs. It said, "Blaaaaa."

"You scared the crap out of me, stupid," he accused.

"Blaa," the goat repeated.

"Get it off me," Misty said. She wiggled forward, kicking the goat in the knees. It kicked back, but not hard, then leaned in and nibbled at EZ's ear.

"It's Patches. You hungry, girl?" EZ rubbed the bony head and the goat turned her face sideways in contentment.

"She's hungry. I'll give her some food when we get to the house."

"I'm hungry, too," Misty said. "I'm about ready to eat some goat stew. Hear that, goat? Are you tender? She doesn't smell tender, but I'm so hungry I could eat her raw."

"I think you caught the zombie fever," EZ said. "And don't look at me like that!"

The low roof of Rey's little house showed above the undergrowth. The goat bounded ahead, bleating. An answering bleat came from the porch. From a hundred feet away EZ heard the hooves dancing on the boards. Then he heard the door slam open and a stranger said, "Shut the fuck up with that racket! I'm comin' out there if I hear one more goat foot! Jesus H. Christ, fucking animals." The door slammed shut.

They looked at each other, both faces saying "Who is *that*?"

"Soldier?" Misty whispered.

Not replying, EZ made a get down sign with his hand and crept uphill, meaning to circle around the cabin. He wasn't all that surprised when Misty ignored his perfectly clear direction and followed him.

Unfortunately, the goats clattered off the porch and followed him, too, making no effort to be quiet. "Git! Go away!" Misty hissed and tried to shoo them off, but they paid her the same mind she had paid Ezekiel. The four wove through the trees behind the cabin as the front door banged open again.

"Who the fuck is it?" the voice demanded. "Never mind. You're fucking toast," he said matter-of-factly.

Patches and her companion stiffened their already stiff joints, jerked their heads toward the house, and bounded uphill in a panic, breaking branches all the way. EZ felt his neck hairs stand at attention. Misty dug her fingers into his arm. He eased his gun out of his coat pocket and Misty let go of his arm and did the same. After a minute a fir cone crunched and a man in a black overcoat came around the corner. He steadied himself with his left hand on the goat pen rail. His right hand scanned a small, technical-looking assault rifle around the trees.

When nothing happened, EZ thought the guy had missed them in the shadows. But something caught his attention—a glint of light on a metal snap, a breath, something—and he focused on the kids like a hungry snake.

"Whatcha got there, kids? Real guns? Set 'em down and back away, hands up, all that shit." As they obeyed, he shook his head. "Kids with guns. What the hell kind of place is this?"

Misty made a sudden move and in a blink the guy's gun was on her. "You a girl? Come here, little girl. I ain't gonna hurt you." Misty didn't move, not even to breathe.

"I said come here. You wanna engraved invitation?" He raised his weapon. It was dull black and a whole different kind of machine from the guns on the mountain, like something from outer space. The way he handled it, it looked as if it didn't weigh an ounce.

Misty started to cry. EZ wanted to pat her back or tell her to stop it, but mostly he wanted to be out of there. Misty crying told him this was worse than the carnage in the clearing, worse than his close relations eating raw human flesh.

"All right, stay the fuck there, you little brat." The man aimed.

Misty crawled forward, puppy sounds squeezing out of her throat. EZ promised God, that mysterious reject, that he would pray for forgiveness for being glad Misty wasn't going to be right beside him when she got shot to pieces. Then he suffered a quick realization. It wouldn't matter. This was the end for him, too.

He heard a breaking voice—his!—half man and half scared-peeless kid, say, "Who are you?"

"I'm the man with the gun. Shut up."

"Let Misty go. We didn't do anything. Misty won't hurt you." He couldn't believe he was talking.

"Oh, okay. Gee, I was scared she was gonna hurt me. Sure, I'll let her go. Asshole." The man made a hooking motion with the ugly gun. "You come over here, too."

EZ thought he could probably get away. Trees would block most of the bullets. Most of them. And the guy seemed unsteady on the rough ground. EZ glanced at his shoes. Shiny, small. Everything about him was shiny somehow, even his soft black overcoat.

"Today would be fine, champ."

EZ stood up and walked toward the man and Misty. She was still crying but she'd stopped making noise except to sniff back snot.

"Who lives up here?"

"We do," EZ said.

"Who else?"

"My family. Misty's family. Some other people."

"Who are all the weirdos runnin' around in the woods? I never seen freaks like them. That your family?"

"Um, no. Well, one of them. My dad. My brother."

"That's two, genius." The man's eyebrow raised. "Oh, I heard about this shit. Your dad is your brother. That right, hillbilly?"

"No! My dad's my dad and my brother's my brother. And my uncle."

"Shocker. Your brother's your uncle."

EZ opened his mouth to clarify things but the man kept talking. "I don't really give a shit about your family tree. All I want to know is how do I get out of this freak show and back to my goddamn car."

Misty found a voice. It was thin, but it worked. "How did you get here?"

The man looked at her as if he was surprised she could talk.

"Can't you just go back the same way you came in?" she asked. Her sass worked even when she was scared to death.

"No, I can not go back the same way we came in, which is why I'm asking you." He gave Misty a cuff on the side of her head, not hard enough to knock her down but hard enough to shock her.

EZ twitched. "Hey!"

The gun leveled at his chest. It was some kind of automatic, that's all EZ knew about it, and it looked like it would spit out a hundred bullets in three or four seconds. Getting him off the mountain was a very good idea.

"You're taking me back to my car now." He used the ugly muzzle again to show them what to do. "Don't screw up."

EZ started uncertainly down the slope. Misty was behind him and the gangster was behind her. When EZ tried to turn around to see how Misty was doing and what the man in black was doing, the man put the gun right up next to Misty's head and EZ turned back around. His knees shook but he managed to walk.

"Where you headed, Boy Scout?"

"The only way off the mountain is on the trolley over the river. Isn't that how you came?" Surely the guy hadn't been lowered from the black helicopter in his shiny shoes and city overcoat.

"Where, at the end of the road? There ain't no trawler over the river. I looked."

Smokey and Rey had taken the trolley down to keep strangers out, but evidently it hadn't worked. The mercenaries had gotten in from the sky. The man—*We?* There were more than one of them?— had gotten in somehow. EZ had never done more than look down at the western cliffs where trees grew with their trunks in the sky.

Misty stumbled into EZ's back and he knew the man had shoved her. It made EZ mad. Fear rolled up out of his guts into a burning ball.

"I said tell me where you're going, and it's not to a trawler."

"Trolley." Misty corrected him and got another shove.

"The back trail. I don't know where your car is, but that's the only way off if we can't take the trolley. I'd be glad to pull you across, but I can't put it back together. Not even both of us could do it. We have to go down the west side."

"West, east, I don't care. Get me outta here." Either EZ was hearing fear in everything now, or the guy was genuinely scared. "I seen those freaks running in the woods. One of 'em was eating a fucking hairy white leg! Eating it like a turkey drumstick like it was fucking Thanksgiving. Everywhere I go they follow me until I found that little shit hole, and may I say you people live like animals. That's who I thought you were, more of those creeps. You're lucky I didn't shoot you then."

Then. As opposed to as soon as they got him down the mountain?

"This way," EZ said, turning west.

44

They waddled and hunched under bullets and bodies. Rey and Smokey, in front and rear positions, got smacked now and then with a flying arm or slapped by a disembodied hand, but they made it halfway back to the Crack entrance without much trouble. The revived were at least holding their own. Rey knew this because she saw mostly familiar figures and fewer eely invaders. The invaders, though, like her own undead, were good at regenerating tissue, even whole torsos, from spare parts. Rey wished she could get samples to study. *In a controlled environment I could grow another Crystal. Another Jacob. I don't know what we'd do with them, but the paper would practically publish itself.*

Then there was whooping and woo-hooing and more of the ululating and the army of revived Cannibalites passed the rescue party. In the slow strobes and yellowing flashlight beams the good guys circled the bad guys and herded them forward. One of the losers made a break for it and was ripped to pieces by Trucker John and scattered like wet confetti. Jostling and pumped up, the victors pushed on out of sight around a bend in the tunnel.

"Well." Smokey said.

"Did we win?" asked Cricket.

"I think so," Rey said.

"Catch up with them," Smokey ordered. "I'll cover our rear. Rey, lead on. Look out for partial survivors."

"Ugh," said Cricket. "I hope I never see another arm crawl across the floor."

They caught up with the group of fighters at the Crack entrance. Except for the animal and human bones littering the ground, it was a beautiful sight. Morning had come and a trace of clean daylight shone into the tunnel.

There were only four prisoners. They were docile as unwatered plants, but they climbed the rope easily enough. Rey refused to go up until everyone was out. This mess was nearly over now, all but figuring out what to do with the horrors that drooped inside the circle of their new masters. It would be wonderful to go home, to eat and sleep and forget for awhile. Rey grasped the rope and sandwiched it between her feet. Overhead, Buck and Hoot pulled and she rose upward, past the bones, back to the land of the living.

As first light touched her face there was a sudden rustling in the cave overhead, the sound of scuffling feet. The rope dropped, caught. Rey hung below the opening. "What's going on?" she called up. The rope dropped again and in the moment it took for her to fall to the tunnel floor pandemonium broke out.

Fiddlin' Sue woke with a headache skewering her skull. She knew she was forgetting something important. The place was wrong, the silence was unnatural, the air smelled like decay. When she sat up the skewer in her brain twisted and she heaved bile. Hanging onto the walls, she got to the kitchen and forced half a glass of water down her throat, wondering, before it all clouded over again, how she had come to be in the Dollers' store and where her husband and children were.

"I think we can go out now," Birdie said for the third time.

"Based on what?" Jackie answered for the second time. The first time she hadn't said anything. She had a strong feeling Berry was in trouble. She had a simultaneous feeling that Berry was somewhere out there kicking serious ass. Maybe it was Jackie herself that was in trouble. "I don't know what to think," she said aloud.

Birdie said, "Well, then, maybe I'll go. Just stick my head out. It'll be all right, don't you think?"

"Suit yourself," Jackie said. If she had to hide in a hayloft, she'd rather it was with Berry or Rey or about anybody except Birdie. The woman was driving her crazy. The only worse comrade-in-hiding would have been Sugar Agate. Or Trucker John. Or Dollar Bill.

Okay, maybe Birdie wasn't the worst fate that could befall her. "I just hope we're not going to die together," she said.

"What?" Birdie's steel-wire head jerked up. "We're not going to die yet! Nobody said anything about dying."

Jackie had closed her eyes, and she opened one to aim at Birdie. "Why do you think we're hiding?"

"But I don't want to die now. I've got things to do."

"Things to be, people to do." Aching for Berry twanged at Jackie's chest. Those first days after the revival had been so nice. Berry's body was falling apart, but she had stayed close. It had been so cozy, the two of them under the rain on the metal roof, a lantern each for reading, coffee steaming on the burner. The first blush of living deadness had answered Jackie's prayers. Where was her island girl now? Doing what, eating what—or whom? *If she comes back, if I live, I'll go with her. I'll learn to like hunting and prowling all night and if I can't like it I'll damn well fake it.*

Floors, walls, chairs scrubbed clean of blood and gore. Porch sluiced off and swept. Bed put back together. Mercy arched backwards to get the kinks out of her back and saw more gore on the ceiling. Why the first battle had to be in her home was one of the Lord's more mysterious moves. Sure: give the worst filth to the cleanest woman. It made a kind of Job-like sense.

The girls had stopped working and were on their bed playing dolls and monsters. Heaven whined about something unfair, Liberty placated her. They were clean and warm and they'd be fed within the hour, and that was the best Mercy could do for them. Keeping them safe from heathen marauders would happen at the point of her rifle.

As much of a relief as it was to have Earl out of the house, having the rest of her men and boys back would have been nice. Before all this apocalyptic business, Jacob and Ezekiel were just two more intrinsically lazy bodies to manage. She loved her boys, but they were always straining at the leash. It was a constant battle to get them to fall into step. With just the girls home, life felt lopsided and too easy. "I miss the little dickens," she thought. "Help them, Lord, and deliver Jacob from Satan's grip. Protect Ezekiel from his own foolishness. Bring El Duane back. Amen. Oh, and my husband, too."

El Duane. The warm pulse that invaded her blood when she thought of him made her feel good and dirty at the same time. A strange sensation, feeling dirty. Well, God wasn't anybody's fool. All the filth she'd scrubbed away had been put in her home for a reason. It was a sign, a clear message, wasn't it? Everything was God's hand moving.

Mercy cleared out the blasphemous picture of her brother-in-law's hand moving across her body.

The first rock hit Rey on the shoulder. A deluge of stones followed it. She scrambled to the edge of the hole, away from the barrage, but couldn't escape the choke of debris. When it was over, fading howls and snarls drifted down with the dust.

Rey looked into the enlarged Crack. The surface would not be easy to reach. The rope was gone or buried under boulders, which offered no way up. As she peered through the clotted air at the mess, a wraith-like silhouette leaned over the hole. Its smoky eyes stared at her, then retreated.

A second later a massive load of cave rock crashed down. When Rey could crawl forward again, breathing through her shirt-front, the light was gone. So was the Crack. The tunnel was a dark grave, as if the Crack, the cave, and the world had never existed.

It took a few stunned minutes to be sure the exit was impass-able, and less time than that for panic to grab her. Smokey would see she was missing, but how could he reach her? What was going on up there? It had sounded like another battle, which meant either more of Everett's experimental things had arrived, or another heli-copter full of mercenaries were here, or the revived had turned on the humans.

She clamped her jaw shut to stop hyperventilating.

Slow down. Stop and think. *Think.*

If the Cannibalites made it through the conflict, Smokey would get her out. If they couldn't excavate her by hand, he would get help. It was unlikely she would die before that happened. There was enough moisture on the tunnel walls to sustain her for days, and so much humidity in the atmosphere she would lose virtually none through respiration if she kept her adrenaline production low. It had been too long since she'd eaten a meal, but Smokey would get her out long before starvation damaged her organs.

If Smokey could get her out. If he lived through whatever was happening.

No one had ever died solely of darkness or solitude. *No, she had only felt as if she were dying then, in forever darkness, with no way back …*

In the deep silence Rey felt her way back the way they'd come. The palpable mist was a relief from the dust closer to the rock-fall and her breath came easier, which told her she hadn't pan-icked as badly as she'd thought. Dust had been the cause of her compromised respiration. There was a cause for everything, and a solution.

As long as you lived.

Even death, though, was a solution. She had presumed to solve death, and death was not willing to be solved. Death evidently did not consider itself a problem.

She fell once and took more care after that to feel for every step, to find low ceilings and jutting rocks with her hands instead of her head.

A sinister drumming excited weird fantasies until she realized it was her own heartbeat. The walls pressed in closer. Rey measured the horizontal span with her arms; it was still approximately six feet across. The ceiling was more or less where it had been the first time she'd come through. Claustrophobia was not a disorder she could afford to indulge now. First survive. Plenty of time later to pick a post-traumatic stress symptom. Breathe. Think. Find an exit.

She dismissed the shift of clammy air against her ankles until it tickled the hair on her arms. Speleology was not her field. Did enclosed caves have air currents? Rey spread her fingers, feeling for a direction. A cold stream brushed her fingertips. There was definite airflow. Its origin might be a way out.

The odor of rot curled into her nostrils. These foreign monsters smelled toxic in their dismembered state. She should be wearing a mask, full Hazmat. *I* should *have a flashlight. I* should *not be down here in the first place.*

The puffs of air shifted to the other side. Crosscurrents would make tracking the source more difficult. She stood very still, trying to exhale gently so as not to obscure the only trace she had of an escape route.

A sound made her heart jump. Something was behind her in the dark, something very quiet and very close.

She whirled around. The pinkish-brown gleam at her knees resolved into a shape: not the attenuated length of undead invaders, but a low, bullish animal. Thick white tusks curved upward from its grublike snout.

Rey shouted at it and waved her fists but it was no dog to be ordered away. It stepped closer. Rey's shifted her shoulder to bring her weapon within reach but there was no weapon. It was no doubt buried under the cave-in with her flashlight.

She had the incongruous thought that if it were friendly she could use its feeble light to get out. But it obviously did not have friendship in mind. It reared chest-high, aimed its tusks at her face, and gathered itself to charge.

The man in the city coat said, "Hey, I recognize that. That's the place that blew up. Burned Gecko all to hell. You kids do that?"

They were passing Hoochville, where the burned body had been found. "We don't blow up houses," Misty said.

"I ain't saying it's a bad thing. It's a skill. I'd admit it if I was you. I won't hold it against you for taking Gecko out. Guy could be a pain in the ass. 'Easy peasy,' he says. 'In, do the girl, out. Fresh air'll do us good.' What an asshole."

EZ led on, keeping trees between them and Joe Bear's house, making for the deer track. He said, "What do you mean, do the girl?" As soon as he said it he clenched his teeth together.

"Mind your own business."

Did they mean murder or something worse? Bringing it out in the open could only make it more real, get it into the gangster's mind, make him think of doing it again—whatever it was.

Misty asked, "Did your friend kill Sugar Agate?"

"I don't know any Sugar. Some hoochie took some trinkets off my boss, which he normally didn't mind, only one or two of them wasn't trinkets. They had great sentimental value, like his sentimental three kilos of powder and a large and very rare collection of sentimental one-thousand dollar bills. He took that as a personal, what, a heartbreak, poor guy. So he finds out where she's living, in some commune."

Misty stumbled into EZ and went to her knees; the gangster had tripped on a mossy rock and fallen on her. "Watch it!" he barked.

"Sorry," EZ said. "The green rocks are slippery."

"Then don't take us on the fucking green rocks, Scout."

'Sorry," EZ said again. They started walking again.

"Anyhow, imagine our surprise when the hippie dippies are out fucking hunting in the dark. I go looking for Sweet Little Susie and Gecko keeps an eye on the hunters. Then all fucking hell pops out. The deal is Gecko and me are supposed to come back together, so I go looking for him. I figure he'll be where the gunfire is since that's where you usually find him. He's shooting every which way into the trees.

" 'What the fuck?' I ask him, and he downs a couple of hillbillies. They're shooting at us so what can we do? We got a couple dozen of 'em and said, Good enough for govamit work and he took the fuck off and I take care of the girl and then like a jerk I wait for him and before I know it I'm hiding in the goddamn woods and can't find my way out of this crap, which if you had any brains you'd develop it into a casino. You got any Indians up here? You wanna make some money let me know."

"Thanks," EZ said.

He slowed and reached a hand back to get Misty's attention. The guy was watching his step and evidently didn't notice. To cover, EZ said, "Be careful here," although the going was pretty easy. The trail was the width of a deer's body and clear as long as you knew what you were looking at.

Misty asked, "Did you get your boss's stuff back?"

"You ever buy any blow?"

"Um, I don't think so."

"Then she sold it before she got here."

EZ said, "The real easy trail's right through those bushes and little trees there." He stopped and pointed ahead to a thicket of waving firs, much shorter than the towering trees behind them. Clouds of deciduous leaves waved among them. It was a gray spring day and no blue shone between the twenty shades of green.

" 'Bout fuckin' time." The guy was breathing hard after the half-mile hike. "I hate mountains." *Pant.* "I hate fucking trees. I'd like to kill a goddamn tree." *Pant.* "Okay, let's go."

Misty said "Ow! That's sharp," and EZ knew the man had prod-ded her with his gun.

EZ stopped and stared straight up. "Oh, my God, it's coming!"

"What?" The man stopped and his black outer-space gun swiv-eled to the treetops.

"Run!" EZ screamed and charged forward, yanking Misty along behind him. "Run, mister!" His voice was shrill and terrified.

Misty dove to the side and EZ forced himself into a salmonberry bush. The gangster lunged two steps forward, still staring into the swaying fir peaks, and ran into EZ's leg, which stuck out from the salmonberry far enough to cut the man off at the shin. The au-tomatic woodpeckered a line of holes across two wide fir trunks. The man flailed his arms but his gun's recoil stopped his forward momentum and pushed him backwards. He might have used the opposing forces to regain his balance if Misty hadn't shoved him hard from behind.

When he grabbed for a branch, anything, to keep him from going over the cliff that he could now see under his toes, Misty relieved him of his gun. EZ tried to get there to give him a firm send-off, but his boot laces got tangled in the salmonberry twigs and by the time he got loose, Misty was already braced against an alder trunk. Alder and vine maple like a lot of sun, and they grew well on the cliff edge where the sky opened up. The thicket of short trees was actually crowns of two-hundred-foot ancient firs growing from the mountainside that flattened out on a rock ledge far, far below. Just in case the man managed to grab hold of a branch or sapling on the way down, Misty held her finger on the trigger and perforated his flapping overcoat.

EZ lay on his belly and peered over the edge. "Give him a little more," he advised, and put his fingers in his ears.

They waited until the birds resumed their conversations, with something exciting to twitter and squawk over now, before taking the trail back to the east side of Cannibal Mountain.

"Let's get our moms," EZ said. "And the rest of them."

"There were two bad men," Misty said. "The Gecko must've been the man that got burned up."

"There's more bad out there besides hit men," EZ answered. "And now they've heard us, they'll be looking. I know a good place to hide."

"All of us?"

"Might be a tight fit, but it'll do."

Misty walked in front. "I never killed anybody before."

"I know it." He waited a minute. "You're not going to throw up again, are you?"

"Nope. Steady as a rock." She held her hand in front of her, palm down. It quivered. She shoved the hand in her coat pocket. "I'm good."

"Because I hate barf."

"Let's go get Mom."

45

"This is not at all necessary."

Hoot ignored Bee's protest and carried her like a baby in his leg-sized arms.

"I'm sure I can walk." Bee wasn't sure at all, but being snugged into Hoot's chest felt embarrassingly intimate. And there was the personal odor problem, as well. His, not hers—although she might well smell like a old skunk after what she'd been through. Hoot tucked the coat around her neck and the last of the wet chill slunk away, foiled again.

It wasn't easy to let someone else be in charge. But in the present situation, she had to admit, she was not in charge, not even of her own locomotion. She and Cricket were borne toward the cave entrance, blessed daylight, and home. She noticed the gate had been torn away and then the rhythmic rocking dragged her eyelids down.

Smokey sent three of his army with the old ladies, two to transport plus a guard, and waited for Rey to get her stubborn ass up the rope.

"Any time today," he shouted into the hole. A flicker of flashlight glanced off the invisible wall and the top of her head wavered into view. It was a nice top of a head; even after extended bug-hunting and sewer-crawling the brown hair was shiny and just tousled enough to make him wonder if he could get away with combing his fingers through it once she was on deck. That made him remember their shower and the way his stinging eyes had taken the edge off the attention his body was paying her ... naked and wet and clean and so close the water had to look for secret passageways between their bodies.

"You might try helping to pull the rope," she barked.

Smokey said, "You're fine." *Yes, she sure as hell was.*

This shit was all over but the mopping up. Count on one more skirmish with the mercs in the black helo. Then there'd be time for celebration, which if he had any say about it would be just him and Rey, in a high quiet place.

The cave, with its mouth opening away from the morning sun, was dim enough for the light pulses to show against the gloom. By the time they caught Smokey's full attention, the illuminated captives had started their ululations. They had a nasty, triumphant tone that gave Smokey enough warning to grab the rope just as the two revived soldiers loosened their grip on their burdens, growled, and ran for the cave mouth.

He heard Rey call but before he could answer or do anything at all, the cave was full of flailing and war cries, and something landed on him and dragged him backwards, the rope slipping out of his burning palms until the frayed end slithered away and over the lip of the Crack.

He got off a good shot at the mutant holding him and stomped its ugly face to pulp to slow it down. His soldiers were fighting hard but were being beaten back by the things that had turned on them. New ones had arrived, not many, but fast and organized and brutal.

One of the new undead got behind him and clamped his neck in an iron arm. Smokey kicked hard enough to snap both its legs and clawed out one of its eyes, but the vise grip didn't weaken. There was an explosion followed by a mighty rumble, then that and the screaming and gunfire faded as his brain used up its last oxygen, waiting for arterial supply that didn't arrive.

In Cricket's experience, strange men needed to be viewed with robust suspicion. Most of the time they brought trouble. Sometimes they straightened out, like the men on the mountain, but even they benefited from a dose of guidance now and then. The strange man silhouetted in the cave mouth didn't look as if guidance would make a dent in him. His posture reeked of arrogance and his gleaming handgun was aimed directly at Cricket's face.

The man said, "Drop them."

Buck didn't move. The man's gun bounced slightly and Buck staggered. A crease of heat bloomed on Cricket's cheek. The gun bounced again and with its boom Buck crumpled. Cricket slid out of his arms onto the ground and tried to look like an elderly dead woman. She peeked through the eye nearest the ground and saw her older sister being lowered none too gently. The next gunshot made both Cricket's eyes pinch shut. The ground trembled for a minute before everything went quiet again.

The man said, "Bring them outside and dispose of them, the reanimates first. Be thorough." He sounded bored.

Claws dug into Cricket's calves and yanked. She couldn't help shrieking. The claws dragged her over jagged ground.

Half a century had gone by since Cricket had last heard it, but she recognized the sound of her own big sister crying.

Cricket screamed. "You let her go, you beast!"

A voice answered.

It was the voice of an angel—an angel with a decided attitude and a Western twang. The angel said, "You heard the lady. You and your varmints let them ladies go. And I do mean now." A shotgun bolt slid and locked. Cricket had heard that shotgun bolt before. It was on her daddy's gun.

Cricket blinked hard to clear the blood and dirt out of her eyes. Standing behind and to the left of the man who had been giving orders was the ghost of Annie Oakley or a pretty good facsimile thereof. Boots, vest, neckerchief, and a halo of hair lit by pearly light, all backing up a gun that had looked huge even in her daddy's big paws. A cowgirl avenger from Heaven with a bead drawn on the bad man—not that a bead was necessary, with the maw of that big side-by-side an inch away from his vital organs.

"Tell 'em to throw their guns down, step up and lay down on the ground, hands up front. First one don't follow orders, city boy, you get it in the guts. Take you awhile to die that way, I reckon," the angel said.

A new voice said, "Bettah listen to huh. Ah know ah always do, and ah'm a bettah man for it." There were words inside the thick Mississippi mud of an accent. It wasn't easy to make them out, but N'Awlins gumboed through the vowels and washed away the consonants until only the general tone was left, and the tone said "The enemy of my friend is my enemy, and I, too, am armed."

Cricket didn't dare move, for she understood the ease of her daddy's shotgun's trigger action. She watched the taloned feet of the monsters pass by, slow now instead of eager. It took some minutes for it all to get settled; Cricket could only see a little of what happened but eventually the Cannibalites were standing and the horribles were trussed.

The angel said, "Go to it, boys, ladies," and there was a flurry of shredding and pounding, shooting and chopping, rending and stomping, followed by huffing that sounded like a lot of cougars coughing up hairballs.

Cricket ahemmed. "Lacewing?"

"Right here, honey." The cowgirl angel came over and kneeled down in front of her sister. "You makin' out all right?"

"I'm fine. How's Bee?"

"Bee's tougher 'n rawhide. Bein' bossy for eighty-eight years will do that to a person." She looked toward the cave mouth. "Keep that rattlesnake covered good, Joe Bear. He'll slither away if he gets a chance."

"Yes, dahlin'," her love and admirer answered. "You mahnd if I shoot him just a li'l bit?"

"Later, sweetheart. Then you can skin him out for all I care."

The bad man grunted hard, as if something had kicked him in a soft spot.

Lacewing's compadre asked, "How your sistahs, lovey?"

"Ready to go on home, I expect. That about right, Cricket?"

"Make ready the palanquin bearers and prepare a feast and a sumptuous divan while you're at it."

Everett walked as well as he was able, bound tightly and flanked close. The wounded Cannibalite soldiers had healed—would that all good soldiers healed as quickly, Cricket mused—and carried the older Pears and Smokey to the Pear Sisters' house. Lacewing fed them and cosseted them with Jobert's tender assistance.

"He's breathing," Cricket said, "but barely. Will somebody watch him?" She floated toward the sleep that had been waiting behind the scenery to carry her away.

Smokey and the strange man were watched with gimlet eyes, for different reasons. Lacewing kept three undead to watch for outliers; the rest went to roam the territory in search of incompletely killed enemies. Loading the bed-warmers with hot embers, Jobert said, "I hope theah ain't no more'a that dynamite."

"Nobody left to use it, I expect," Lacewing answered.

"Mm." Jobert tucked bed-warming pans at his love's sisters' feet and sat at the window looking over the bend in the road, his engraved mother-of-pearl-handled duelling pistols at the ready. "Blew up your cave, my deah. Blew it all to hell. I only hope theah was no one down below when it fell in."

It had no eyes.

Where eyes should have been, thin tissue covered the gelatinous vestiges of photosensitive nerves. A troglophile, and a big one. Maybe a singular one, but Rey couldn't count on that. If it hunted cooperatively she was in serious trouble.

It glowed brighter. Stimulation must affect the bioluminescent cells, Rey marveled. Some organisms exhausted their luminescent abilities when captured, but this organism absolutely had to be extracted and examined—alive, if possible. Then she considered her predicament.

I need to be extracted. Alive, if possible.

Fascinating as this specimen was, it was clearly considering Rey as either threat or food. Being sightless, it would use sound, olfactory reception, or vibration to locate food. She couldn't do much about her smell, which was at the moment richly organic. But she could be quiet and still. That might be enough to make her invisible.

Failed hypothesis, she noted, when the thing moved closer.

Now run.

It was fast and it knew the tunnel well. Running in the dark was not going to work for Rey. If the light-generating thing had been in front she might have managed, but on her third step she fell. She rolled out of its path. It charged past her and for a second she hoped she was safe, but it snuffled and turned back, hearing or smelling or sensing her in some unknown way Rey could do nothing about.

It located her quickly and charged, head lowered to give its tusks the most efficient gutting angle. Rey scrambled but it snagged her sleeve. They both stopped, the animal wondering if it had speared her, Rey wondering how to keep it hung up on her sleeve so it couldn't use its other tusk to finish the job. It snorted. Its breath made her gag. Singed hair, rotten teeth, and decomposing intestines had never smelled that bad. It shook its thick neck and nearly tore her arm from its socket. Just as it ripped free Rey found a rock and delivered a hay-maker to one of its light receptors. It grunted and staggered back. Rey swung again and got its soft, blunt snout but the force of the connection knocked the rock out of her hand.

She drew her legs back and kicked it in the face with both feet, her ankle narrowly missing its right tusk. It seemed nonplussed, and Rey realized it was unused to living prey. It ate dead or dying meat, probably small living troglodytes, but it didn't know how to fight an opponent its own size. Rey jumped to her feet while the beast got its bearings. Fighting for your life was instinctive for both of them, and she had to assume the thing would catch on fast. It had the muscle, the weapons, and the hunger to win. Rey couldn't compete with those, but she had three possible advantages. She could see it, she was smart, and she was terrified of being eaten alive.

She risked another kick at the snout but the thing twisted away and brought her down with its curved left tusk. Something tore close to her achilles tendon and for a second she thought she was done for, but the ankle still worked. The beast had given her a measure of its strength when it threw her down. There was power in its heavy body and the tusks were formidable, but for all its bulk it was soft. In the cave it had become weaker than its ancestor, soft and repellent. Rey kicked it in the throat and her foot sank into yielding flesh. The air she knocked out of its lungs stank of vomit.

"That's what hiding underground does to you," she told it. "You need to get out more."

It paused when she spoke. The photosensitive spots turned toward her, but neither they nor the translucent ears tracked her when she sidestepped.

Half alive. Half a life. It ate and feared, cowering through a meager existence. The cave had changed it forever into something less than itself, an unwholesome, ugly, stunted thing.

Hiding deforms. I know all about that.

The beast charged again, Rey dodged; it rammed into the cave wall. Rey heard the snap of a tusk breaking off.

Rey crept further into the cave. A low-hanging rock banged her scalp and she scrubbed away the blood. She stumbled over something soft and big. Its odor was foul, more dead snake than rotting vomitus. The smell of the foreign mutants was unforgettable. This one, for some reason, had not regenerated.

Behind her, feet padded, gathering speed. Rey crouched and felt desperately for a loose rock or a weapon on the zombie's body. She prepared to kick again but in the split second before the animal reached her it veered away from her feet, aiming for her head. She pivoted on her seat but was too slow.

Her trapezius muscle tore with a searing pain. She cried out and rolled into a protective ball. The animal backed off and pawed the ground. Its light glowed brighter, bathing the tunnel walls in sickly pink. Rey tucked her injured arm across her chest and swept the floor for a rock, a bone, a skull, anything; dug into the rank folds of the carcass beside her and closed her fingers around something but the beast was already upon her. This time it tried to hook her but the broken tusk merely tore the skin of her hip and bruised her femur. She swung at it with her good hand and realized as the object in her fist glanced off its sloped forehead that she had found a flashlight. She pushed the ridged button and the light snapped on. She squinted against the light and aimed it at the beast's face.

It recoiled. *Functional photoreceptors.* She kept the beam on its face and it writhed away. It was a hideous animal: gelatinous flesh over blood vessels and pulsing organs, whitish skin backlit by pulsing bioluminescent nodules the color of sodium lights. The snout seeped pale, sanguinous fluid. It breathed hard. Possibly fatigue, possibly it had reached the limits of its adaptability. There had to be dentition; it presumably ate bodies that found their way through the Crack into the tunnel, so it would have canines and incisors. Even lacking one tusk it was capable of gouging, tearing, and ripping her to pieces.

Rey had the advantage for a very short time. Cautiously, she stood up. Her shoulder burned and her ankle throbbed. She shined the light on the carcass at her feet. The head sagged forward, showing a cavity at the base of the skull. The thing's spine had been torn out. Its plucked-out brainstem curled beside the neck like a fetus, trailing a fibrous tail of spinal cord.

Rey moved on, alternately shining the flashlight at the beast and ahead, marking overhangs and stones. The creature's light dimmed in the artificial light but did not go out. She stepped on a shoe-sized rock, tucked the flashlight between her hurt arm and ribs and took the rock in her right hand and moved on.

The tunnel bent in a shallow curve. As she rounded it, three things happened. The gray-pink light brightened, a wall of mist hit her face, and she heard the sound of trickling water.

Rey whirled and caught the animal as it lunged for her midsection, its single intact tusk centered on her belly. The rock connected with its jaw. Teeth crunched behind the yielding gums. The thing didn't make a sound except to inhale sharply. Pale blood dripped from its snout. It buried its mouth under its foreleg and backed out of reach. Its glow dimmed again. Rey still had the rock in her hand. She had skinned her knuckles on its teeth when she'd punched it, but her rigid fingers couldn't have let loose of the rock if she'd wanted them to.

She turned her back to the thing and hurried ahead. Her light bounced off the thickening mist and revealed nothing, but the trickling sound grew louder. She turned back every few steps but couldn't see or smell the animal through the obscuring fog. As the passage straightened out the trickle became definite splashing, and through the blood pounding in her ears Rey heard the white noise of rushing water.

46

Misty headed straight for her barn; EZ found his mother at home. She tried to put him to work fixing the back door, but he respectfully declined.

"You've got to come with us, Ma," he insisted.

"You don't tell your mother what to do."

"That thy days may be long upon the earth. Our days aren't going to be long upon the earth if you don't get hidden now. I know you won't go to the barn so I've got a better place. It's safe."

"There is no safe place," Mercy said. " 'They shall go into the holes in the rock and into the caves of the earth.' Isaiah two-nineteen. But the rock shall not hide them."

"It's not in the rocks or a cave. Please, Ma." EZ didn't wait for her, but brought his little sisters out from the bedroom and kitchen and led them outside. Mercy ordered them to come right back. They dared not look at her but trailed behind EZ, all holding hands. In front of the house Jackie Tobasco, Birdie, and Misty waited for the little Alders to join them.

Misty told EZ to go ahead, her mother wasn't in the barn where she was supposed to be. She ran to look for Sue. The rest of them took the cutoff trail up to Rey's cabin.

"We're not going up there!" Mercy called after them. "I'd sooner hide in the root cellar again!"

As the last of them disappeared into the bushes she made an angry but inarticulate sound through her clenched jaw, then carefully closed and latched the front door and walked briskly after them, head up, as if going to Rey's house were her own idea.

When Misty found her mother on the floor in the Dollers' kitchen she had to force herself to unfreeze. Her mother wouldn't have frozen up. She never had. No matter what happened, Mom did something about it. Misty sank to her knees and smoothed her mother's hair back from her face. She was so pretty, even though she was old, probably in her thirties, even forty, maybe. But Mom was beautiful. Misty told her so.

"You're alive, right? I'm sorry, Mom. I had to go and help. I did help, too. I—" Tears fell on her mother's cheekbone. Misty rubbed them away; they were warm against her mother's skin. "I killed a man, Mom. I had to." Misty scrubbed her eyes with her sleeve.

"He was going to kill us and it just came over me, like I wasn't even doing it, and I shot him. He killed them. Dad and Mr. Alder and all them, Hoot and Mr. Dollar, the man shot them. But I killed him. I'm sorry, Mom."

Misty scooched her legs under her mother's head for a pillow. "Please be all right, Mom. I'll stay here until you wake up."

Fiddlin' Sue winced. She opened one eye.

"Mom?"

"Misty? Or is that you, Crystal?"

Misty didn't think she looked anything like Crystal, especially now that Crystal had changed into a baby-poo-colored supergirl. "It's me, Misty."

"Oh, Misty honey. Help me up."

It was hard getting her started, but Misty got her on her feet and, after a few false starts, out the door.

"Where're we going, honey? Not far, I hope."

"Not very far. Someplace safe. EZ and them are waiting for us."

Sue looked around, suddenly panicked. "Where are those things? Those monsters?"

"I don't know. Let's get out of here, though, 'kay? Lean on me."

"I'm too heavy, honey girl."

"I'm strong, Mom."

"Did you say you killed a man or was I out of my head when I heard that?"

Misty didn't say anything, but the tension in her shoulder told her mother the answer.

"Well, we're okay, that's what matters." Sue pulled Misty closer and let herself lean on her daughter's shoulder. "God in heaven. You're just like me."

The thing had sneaked up on her, using the water noise and spray as cover. It snagged Rey's boot as she leaped sideways and dragged her into what felt like a pool of liquid ice. Rey grabbed at the ground for a handhold but it was slick with a thousand years of water and slime. A wash of light permeated the spray, not bright but white and clean. It was the outside world. It was, maybe, a way out.

Water closed over her mouth, then over her head. The shock of its cold stopped her heart until epinephrine gave it a kick-start; her surface blood vessels narrowed and her pulmonary passages opened in an effort to push death back until the brain figured out a way to get her body out of the crisis.

Rey kicked hard and kept kicking until her shoe came off and sank, still attached by the tusk to the animal. She clutched at every projection with her fingers; free of the murderous anchor, she did her best approximation of levitation and in a long ten seconds was out of the water. She caught her breath and then remembered to move hard and fast.

Running in place, slapping her arms across her body, she watched for the animal in the pool to surface. Her flashlight had gone to the bottom, but weak, early daylight leaked in from beyond the pool. The pool was apparently as wide as the tunnel, fed by dozens of streams trickling through the walls. Sock Creek must be overhead, Rey deduced; she was near the waterfall. If the light came through an opening big enough for her to pass through, and if the opening were reachable, she had a possible way out.

But the light came from beyond the pool, and the beast was probably in the pool. It could have drowned; it could have gotten out and was now waiting for her in the blinding fog. Fog that the dark-adapted animal knew intimately, fog that made no difference to its sightless eyes.

To willingly submerge herself in that frigid water was unthinkable. Her muscles were cramping. If she knew how long a swim was necessary and if there were an exit at the end, she would risk it. But she didn't know. It was more likely that there was nothing at the other side but cracks where water trickled out the way it trickled in. Rey herself had never seen a crevice behind the falls. But there were things on Cannibal Mountain undiscovered by her, perhaps by anyone, since the Campbells and Pears had settled here a century ago.

Stay and starve, hope to die of hypothermia before she became something's dinner, wait for rescue. Or swim the pool to a hypothermic and highly probable death by drowning or being eaten. *My money's on hypothermia first, then becoming dinner, then rescue. Rather, recovery. Not that there'll be anything to recover but bones.*

Her torn shoulder was throbbing again now that it had warmed a little, but she gathered an armload of small rocks and held them in the crook of her elbow. She lobbed a rock into the water. Nothing responded, but it was impossible to tell with the surface lost in mist. She aimed deep, close and far, hoping to disturb the beast if it was lying in wait down there, its jaws open for a sunlight- and chlorophyll-warmed foot to swim by.

No air bubbles broke that she could see. All she knew without a doubt was that she was getting colder and compared to this, the wettest, coldest winter day in the Coast Range would be an afternoon in Hawai'i.

"Goddamn it to hell," she said. "Goddamn, damn, damn it," and she eased into the water.

It sucked the life out of her the way a kid would blow out a birthday candle. Swimming wasn't a particular strength, but she thought she might now be breaking a national speed record. Remembering how the beast had avoided her kicks, she thrashed her legs violently. She felt it tasting her, malevolent and bottomless. She moved her arms faster. Every stroke was a mountain moved.

When the beam of light fell on her face she thought *Finally, a tunnel with light at the end. It looks so warm.* She gave herself up to it. Immediately her head bumped a rock on the same tender spot where the ceiling had opened her skin. Dazed, Rey thrashed randomly and by luck found a slope that let her get her chest out of the water, then her legs.

She hurried to the shaft of light. Behind her the water churned. Rey whirled around and saw one dripping white tusk curl up from the water. The bulbous head bobbed and gasped and the forefeet scrabbled for a grip on the slick ledge. It slipped back and submerged, then struggled out again.

Rey couldn't stand to watch. She might be able to pull it out by its remaining tusk—but with what result? Save it only to fight it again?

"Go back! Go!" She waved her good arm at it but it tried again futilely and weakly to get at her, or perhaps only to get out of the water. Soon it would succumb to the cold and drown.

Rey gathered a handful of pebbles in her blue-mottled hand and threw them at the creature. It barely flinched. Rey threw some across the pool. One or two made it and caught the thing's attention. It had intelligence, or good instincts. Hopeful, Rey threw more to tempt it to follow the sound and go back. Its translucent head dipped below the surface. It thrashed up, gasping; sank again.

"There's nothing I can do," Rey whispered. "I'm sorry."

Horribly, it bobbed up again. She lobbed one more pebble to the far bank. The troglophile turned its jelly snout toward the sound and Rey turned toward the streak of light.

It shined through a tall slit that looked no more than six inches wide. It was no exit, yet it admitted a deluge of noise and spray. Rey pressed herself against the rock and sighed, "Open sesame." Nothing magical happened. Rock was rock.

But how was so much water coming through? Without being artificially powered, it was physically impossible for that volume to pass through that aperture. Splash-back would deliver part of the necessary force, but that didn't explain all of it. Rey followed the tunnel end across its width until a blast of air raised her hair and the roar of falling water surrounded her. She walked through the cascade and found there were two overlapping walls, one behind the other. Between the inner and outer walls was a gap wider than her arm span; beyond the outer wall was the white exultation of Sock Creek plunging into the river. Dizzy and free and freezing, Rey watched the underside of the falls rush endlessly down. On one of the rare hot July afternoons when the wind blew in from the swollen valley and shouldered the marine air out to sea, she would have happily lingered in the chill.

The opening was lined with brilliant green moss. Ferns rooted in crevices swayed to the random rhythm of the water. The slick footing made her keep back from the edge, but Rey knew from gazing at the falls from the river that the cliff face was vertical, coated with ice-slick moss, and unclimbable.

The view was spectacular, one that few people got to see, and the moss was soft. She sank into a green cushion and closed her eyes against the dazzle just for a moment. Her entire body ached with cold and fatigue. Cold seeped into her deep tissues, rattled her bones, turned her breath blue. She didn't fight it. Why try? There was no way down and no way up. She was grateful to die in the light and to be spared further violence. The waterfall applauded with the enthusiasm of a distant, cheering crowd.

As she drifted on the featherbed of sound, something disturbed her. She mentally waved it away. She only needed a bit of rest. It was doing her good. Already she felt warmer. So pleasant to relax, to drift into earned sleep.

There was no light in the crawl space under the house. No time. There had been a man's voice, but now there was no sound at all. She curled into a ball and waited as her mother had told her to, quiet as a pill bug. Her lips cracked; after a long time her stomach stopped growling. The quiet and dark deepened and when she cried, she cried without making any noise in the perfect blackness.

Afterwards, her grandparents held the terror down with love and concerted jolliness, but that suffocating fear had knitted into her bones. She missed her parents.

Years of hiding: in the warren of the Summerland Mission labs, on Cannibal Mountain ... yet the longer she lived here, the less it felt like hiding and the more it felt like being home, with a family again after all the lonely years. The mountain people, strange as they were, filled her hollow places.

But death, blind and hungry, had taken too much. Death always won. It was winning now. She had fought it, thinking human knowledge could cripple it, but after all, death was only sleep, and she was cold and very, very tired.

Rock careening off rock cut through the white noise. The percussion ticked again, followed by stealthy silence.

Rey felt it rather than heard it. *Tock.* The vibration impinged on the temporal bones surrounding her ear, reverberated through the tiny holes in her skull, tickled the auditory nerve, delivered a message to the brain which reported to the mind: Something is walking behind you.

EZ took down Rey's blue chamois shirt from its wooden clothes hook, pulled the hook to the left, and the board wall opened. "In there."

Jackie Tobasco looked in over EZ's shoulder. Last fall she would have had a clear sight line over the top of his head. Boys seemed to grow that way: nothing, then a foot in six months. Kids, then men. Men, but still kids. They were hard to keep track of. She said, "What is it?"

"Obviously it's a secret room," Mercy said.

Jackie said, "Does Rey know this is in her house?"

"Oh, come on," Mercy said, snorting out exasperated air. "She's kept this secret all the time she's been here. I knew we couldn't trust her."

Jackie faced her, squared off. "We can trust Rey Nickel."

"Dr. Newhouse, you mean?" Mercy interrupted.

"—as far as the, the, the sky is wide. And you know it, we all know it, so shut the hell up about Rey."

"Don't curse at me." Mercy leaned in.

"Hell. Damn. *God* damn." Jackie leaned in closer.

EZ stepped between them. "Go inside. It's the safest place. See? You didn't know it was there until I showed you. Nobody'll find us there."

One by one they crowded in. Heaven, Freedom, and Liberty crawled under the workbench; EZ and Misty boosted themselves up and sat on its surface. Sue placed herself between Jackie and Mercy.

"It's her science stuff," Jackie observed. "Look at all this. Crap, there's a dead chipmunk. With wires in it."

"I told you. She's a witch." A droplet of spit flew from Mercy's tongue to Sue's cheek.

"I thought you said she was an evil scientist," Jackie retorted. "Now she's a witch. Here, this wall is made of gingerbread! Yummy." She broke off a splinter and nibbled it. "Have some witch candy, Mercy. You're looking a little bit boney."

EZ suggested that Jackie calm down, and said, "Mom, be nice."

Those were fighting words to Mercy Alder, but Sue looked down at her from her full height and told her to hush up so whoever was hunting them would have at least a bare chance of not hearing them. In the glare of Sue's still half-focused eyes Mercy hissed "Secrets!" and then clamped her lips shut.

"Oh, you don't have secrets?" Jackie said. "Nobody up here has anything *but* secrets. Anyway, I think you have a pretty big secret, Mercy. About a certain male relative of the undead persuasion."

Mercy pressed her lips together but the word of God would not be stoppered.

" 'Whoever goes about slandering reveals secrets, but he who is trustworthy in spirit keeps a thing covered.' Proverbs eleven-thirteen. Or thirteen-eleven."

Sue said, "That's what Jackie's trying to tell you, Mercy. Now you both keep quiet."

EZ turned to his mother. "Who? Dad? What's Jackie talking about?"

Finally everybody kept quiet.

47

Obediently, her heart thumped.

She knew she was hypothermic and exhausted. How long would it take to lose consciousness, succumb to the cold and slip away? The epinephrine pumped from her adrenal glands would last a few minutes. She wouldn't win at the waiting game.

She looked to the left and right of the sheet of whitewater, searched her memory for ledges or cliff-side bushes and saplings. She caught a glimpse of the leaves of a woody plant. Deep-rooted enough to hold her?

Only one way to find out, she decided, with insouciance she did not really feel; she sucked in a wet breath and stepped out.

She wrapped her arms around the plant and felt the deluge tear her off. Mountain smashed against her torn shoulder. Chaos whited out the pain. She grabbed at something, lost it, grabbed again and felt it being torn out of her fingers. But she used the tenuous purchase to hunch out of the main thrust of the falls and wrapped her arms around a tangle of roots. She scrambled until she found a toehold and worked her way out to a branch: a beautiful, thick, scaly hunk of tree that she hugged hard. She wrapped her legs around it and crawled to a trunk that grew from thirty jagged feet below. Below her were three more branches, and she climbed and half-slid from one to another until she was ten feet above solid ground. Too solid, she found when she landed, but the only parts of her in excruciating pain were the ankle and the shoulder the beast had ripped. Close ahead the riverbank dropped away. Rey kept to the trees and limped up the slope, away from the river. Every step hurt, but she promised herself dry clothes as soon as she found the Pear Sisters and Smokey.

All that water and she had forgotten to drink.

The dark hole in the forest where Trucker John's trailer slowly decayed was empty of menace. Rey had seen bodies ripped apart, heads exploded into mush; it would take more than Trucker John and shadows to frighten her after all this. Anyway, the man was less disturbing in his present state than he had been when fully alive. Undeadness suited him. Overhead, birds chucked and trilled. Trucker John had probably heard in Sugar Agate a voice like that, sweet and out of reach. If he had killed Sugar Agate, Rey could hardly blame him. She preferred to believe he killed out of unrequited love, not to get his house back—but it was a lovely house, and even Trucker John knew the difference between a hovel and a home.

Rey paused behind the Pear woodshed and listened to a creaking cedar branch, a chair scraping across the wooden floor, the wind in the treetops.

When a hand gripped her shoulder she twisted and jumped aside, but there was nothing there. The disembodied hand grabbed her wrist and its owner materialized, staring into her eyes as he appeared. The eyes had turned from jaundiced to dried-blood brown, and there was an intelligence in his face Rey hadn't seen when he was a living teenager. He said, almost clearly, "Rey. Come on." And, incredibly, he smiled.

"Jacob! Don't scare me like that. I could have hurt you."

The boy's smile held a disconcerting pity for the human in front of him. "No," he said. "You can't."

At first look the Pear Sisters' house was a step back in time. Everything was in place, mint and the usual mystery herbs perfused the air. Small smokeless flames nibbled on dry wood in the stove, and in front of the stove a wool blanket warmed in the old rocking chair. On a closer look, however, everything had changed. In the kitchen Jobert, of all people, sat on a chair squarely on top of the trap door over the root cellar. He sipped from a china teacup, adding a hint of whiskey to the herbal atmosphere. In Bee's bedroom, the two older sisters were bundled together in Bee's double bed for warmth. Lacewing sat on the little boudoir chair, tenderly watching over them with a five-foot-long shotgun cradled in her lap.

Rey asked, "Are they ... ?"

"Just a mite tired, poor dears. It's been quite a trial, but they'll come along. Rest and food and good hot tea do the job every time." Lacewing was swathed in several shawls, her hair pulled into a bun centered on the crown of her head. Rey recognized the British war nurse.

"You're back." Rey was glad to see her. "We didn't know if you were okay."

"Fit as a fiddle. Bit out of tune, perhaps, but right as rain. The gentleman's in Cricket's bed. He'll come around directly."

Smokey's head was propped up on two pillows, a red quilt pulled to his chin. Eddy and Hoot flanked the bed, a mismatched but effective pair of guards. Rey touched his forehead. Smokey didn't react.

"Oh, Smokey." Turning to Eddy, she asked, "What happened?" and wondered why she bothered asking him.

Eddy's cracked lips croaked something unintelligible. A combination of death, revival, and forty years of hard boozing hadn't done his mental acuity any good.

From the doorway, Lacewing said, "Overpowered at the end. Good man. Fought valiantly. A spot of bad luck, but don't fret yourself. He's a strong soul. Be up and about before you know it."

"Is it a head injury?" Rey pulled the quilt down and quickly inspected Smokey's body. There were no open wounds or palpable broken bones. When she pulled his eyelids open, his pupils contracted equally but he slept through it.

Lacewing said, "You're in need of care yourself. Come along, love. We've everything you need in the kitchen."

For an untrained nurse, Lacewing did an efficient job of disinfecting and dressing Rey's wounds. She gently rubbed salve that smelled of lavender onto the unbroken skin and wrapped Rey's ankle with soft cloth. She gave her a cup of meaty pea soup and a mug of cocoa, and then led her to her own unused single bed across the small room from Smokey.

"No, I can't," Rey protested.

"Best thing for you, dear. We'll need you in good fighting trim, not the worn-out rag you are at present. In you go." And before Rey knew it she was tucked in with warmed stones at her feet, and her eyes closed on Smokey's stubbled, slack face.

The jellyfish in the closet sprouted tusks and bleated at her. Her mother fitted herself into her red coat and fell to the floor and the lights went out. Rey's brain, starved for REM sleep, plowed through a million images and made haphazard connections. The bleating persisted as Rey woke up in a soft bed, watched by two semi-dead men, four feet away from an unconscious but attractive, worse-for-the-wear man.

"Blaaa."

"Patches," Rey said, and tried again so actual sound would come out. "Patches?"

"Blaaaaa," Patches said, and rubbed her knobby forehead against the windowpane. Her friend Midnight said "Behhh," which meant the same thing as "Blaaa." Different goat voices, same goat message. Somehow they had lived, had found her, and now demanded she go home where she ought to be and get on with the business of feeding them. Bushes and leaves were all well and good, but Rey had the good stuff and they had waited long enough.

Rey raised her head, flopped back down to take the pain out of her shoulder. She muttered, "Chickens," and sat up.

She washed herself and checked on Smokey one more time. He was breathing evenly but was still unconscious. Rey rolled up a tube of paper and listened to his heart and lungs as best she could; his lungs were clear and his heart pumped strongly. There was nothing she could do but watch him, and Lacewing assured her he would not be neglected.

Rey cut a slice from a whole wheat loaf and put it in her now-dry jacket pocket.

"I've got to see to the animals," she told Lacewing. "Where are the others?"

Lacewing didn't know. Rey asked Jobert to round up as many re-vived as he could find for a scouting party and meet back here.

The goats bounded ahead of her, frisky now that life was getting back to normal. They didn't like strangers, gunfire, and enforced grazing.

After she left, Lacewing thought to ask Jobert, "Did you tell her about the man in the cellar?"

"No, dahlin, she didn't ask."

"Should we feed and water him, do you suppose?"

"He's fine and dandy. 'Bout knocked me off my chayeh poun-din' on the trap door. Says he's got money if I'll let him go."

"What would you do with money?" Lacewing asked rhetorically.

"Buy you something lovely." Jobert took Lacewing onto his lap and kissed her tenderly and long. Blows from below caused the chair to jump and skitter, but the couple was not bothered in the least.

All present and accounted for. The goats had gotten fresh vegeta-bles, the chickens happily pecked the ground, but somebody had been in her home and made a mess.

"Are you sure you weren't in here?"

The goats looked innocently in through the window, their teeth full of greenery. It was the kind of mess two goats would make. Food was spilled, the bed was tossed, all the boxes and cupboards emptied. Goats couldn't have reached the high cupboard, though. That had been tossed by a human. Rey got on her knees and looked under the bed. The platinum box was where she had left it inside the bed frame. Not that she would ever use it again—never!—but it was still in her possession, and that was a very good thing.

Whoever had been here and whatever they had been looking for, they were gone and nothing important was missing. Rey picked up her things, saving ruined food for the animals, and set her one-room house in order. She shook out the blankets and as they drifted to the bed she heard a discrete and singular creak. She waited. She imagined she heard breathing. A small voice lisped, "I have to go potty."

By now reaching for her pistol was a habit. She opened the door to her hidden lab.

Nine faces stared at her.

"Rey!" some of them said.

"How did you—who let you in here? *Why* are you in here?"

EZ's sisters each pointed at their brother. EZ looked down, away, at his mother, and finally to Rey. He said, "It seemed like the safest place."

Flummoxed, Rey stared at her guests. Heaven hopped up and, holding her hand between her legs, waddled out the door.

"You might as well come out." Rey stood back.

"I thought we had to hide," Birdie said. "I'm so confused."

"It's all right," Rey told her. "Just keep your weapons handy. Mercy, you'd better go keep an eye on the baby."

"I don't need you to tell me how to mind my own—"

Rey shut the front door on her. She asked enough questions to get everybody's story and told them what had happened at her end and how things stood at the Pears' house. When the pottying was completed they all crowded together in the little main room. Rey and Ezekiel stood in the doorway to watch. According to Lacewing, there was nothing left to bother them, but Rey couldn't shake her unease.

Conversation stopped. They were all worn out and sick of hiding and, being misfits and introverts, except perhaps Jackie Tobasco, were sick of each other. A single thought balloon might have captioned their collective thought: I just want to go home and close the damn door.

Jackie said, "I was thinking."

"Good," Sue said. "It's about time."

Jackie ignored her. "I'm lonely without Berry. I never liked being alone."

"She's around," Rey said. "She's just busy. She'll be back, probably tonight."

Jackie shook her head. "Tonight she'll be running with the pack. She was wild before, but now, you know ... "

"Yeah," Sue said. "I know."

"Well, we all miss our folks," Mercy said. "They'll settle down. Nobody wants to live like a wild animal forever. When the novelty wears off they'll come back wanting to be fed, and you'll wish they'd run off again for a few days and give you some peace."

"Me?" Freedom asked her.

"No, not you. Not you either." Mercy preempted the questions on Liberty's and Heaven's lips.

Jackie sounded lost. "At first I was so happy with the way things turned out. Rey had done me a solid favor, turning my girl into a sweet little homebody. But it didn't last." She turned a sorrowful face to Rey. "She's gone from me now. I know it."

"The thing is," Rey said slowly, thinking about it, "we don't know what they'll do next. They seem to be getting more human. Not their old selves, but more something. More, for sure."

"You're wrong. Berry's getting farther and farther away. She might as well be on her old island for all I have of her. I can't lose her, Rey. I can't. So I decided I'm going to join her."

"That won't be easy," Rey said. "She's stronger and fast and she can do things you can't do. I'm sure she still loves you, though. You won't lose her."

Jackie stood up and walked onto the porch and stared into the woods. "I already lost her. But that's not what I mean. I'm going to go with her." She faced Rey. "I'm going to kill myself and you're going to revive me and I'll be with Berry forever or for as long as we both shall live."

Rey was speechless.

"In sickness and in health, in life and death," Jackie went on. "We promised. Always. Berry can't help herself, so it's up to me to keep our vows. I'm doing it today."

"The hell you are," Rey managed.

"The hell I'm not," Jackie said, her stubbornness set at full power. "If you can't stand to revive me you can let me stay dead. I don't care to live without love."

"You idiot! Christ, I never heard anything so histrionic. Maybe I'd be more convinced if you could swoon or something."

"At dark, I think," Jackie said. "She'll be roaming. Do you think she's ready to take care of somebody while they evolve? I hate to impose on anybody else, especially not you, given your attitude, which sucks."

Rey leaned over Jackie, her best and oldest friend, and said, "I'm not taking care of you if you commit s—use your own hand. I'm not, Jackie, I'm not going to aid and abet your nutso fantasy. What good would it do? Even if it worked, you'd starve in your own filth unless Berry figured out how to take care of you and decided to do it. Who knows what's in their minds? You don't know if she can still love anybody. The whole bunch of them are fighting machines with special nonhuman abilities, but that doesn't make them superhuman. Plain and simple, they're zombies. You'd be killing yourself for nothing."

"I doubt if she'd starve," Sue put in. "You know how they hunt."

Jackie put the flat of one hand on Rey's solar plexus. "I'm doing it. I'm lonesome. I've thought about it. I'll be at my house if you decide to wake me up." She walked out the door.

"Mom?" Misty looked at Sue for an explanation. "Jackie's not going to ... ?"

"It's what you call a grand gesture, honey. Grown-ups usually know better. Don't worry." Sue patted Misty's hair.

Rey loped across her clearing and caught Jackie's arm. "How do you propose to off yourself?"

"Gun, of course. That worked for Berry and the others; it should do all right for me."

"You know, all you people make a good case for gun control."

Jackie shrugged and reclaimed her arm. "They're just tools. Like your suitcase full of science tools. You can use it for good or bad, and good and bad's a matter of personal opinion."

"My opinion is you're going off the deep end. Jackie, you're my very best friend. We've talked about some hairy stuff and you've pounded sense into me when I needed it and I've done the same for you. I can't let you do this. I can't."

"You can't stop me."

Rey withdrew her pistol from her waistband and aimed it at Jackie's feet. "I can't let you go. You know I'll stop you somehow."

There was so much distance in Jackie's eyes it seemed to Rey that she was already in her bed waiting for resurrection.

"I've always been a little jealous of you, being so in love. I thought with half a brain—the half between my legs—that I might love Travis, but I was in love with love. Plus, you know how cute he is."

Jackie half smiled.

"Don't throw your life away for romantic love, is all I'm trying to say. There's more to life than one person. We need you, Jackie. You need us and Berry needs you; the real you, the full crazy red-hot

Jackie Tobasco. You're stressed and overtired and I bet you haven't had a good meal in awhile. Don't decide right now. Give it a couple of days. Please."

Jackie looked at the sky. It wasn't exactly raining, but a squadron of drops kamikaze'd to earth, testing the terrain.

"I'll wait," Jackie agreed. "But I need to see Berry now." She slipped out from under Rey's arm and ran down the path to the road.

48

Jackie asked for Berry, but Berry was out patrolling. Jackie spilled her plan to Lacewing. Lacewing's eyes got big and she pursed her lips together.

"This is a matter for Bee to resolve," she said, and went to Bee's room.

"It's a done deal. Don't bother Bee with it."

But Lacewing woke up her sister and told her an exaggerated version of what Jackie had said: people were going to die on purpose so they could join the revived and live forever.

"What?" Bee said. "That's absolute nonsense."

Lacewing said, "Jackie Tobasco said so. She's their leader."

"That's not what I said," Jackie protested.

Bee sat straight up. Her hair fell in a braid down the front of her nightshirt. Lacewing had tied the end in a blue ribbon. "Do they live forever?"

"I don't know," Jackie said. "They're doing pretty good so far."

"They seem to be quite healthy, and they grow more robust daily," Bee mused. "Whereas I feel less like my old self and more like a plucked scarecrow every day. It is not a pleasant feeling." She pulled the ends of the blue ribbon and let it fall on the quilt.

"We are one breath away from death every moment. We know this. And when you have breathed a million or more breaths, you breathe by the grace of Death, by his lenience, and you have used more than your allotment of moments. I will die soon. I nearly died today, and have come closer than I liked earlier this week. Close calls don't exhilarate me. For an old woman I'm unusually resilient, but adventure takes its toll."

Bee jostled Cricket and Cricket's snores broke off.

"Get up, Cricket. We're going to Rey's house."

"Snrff?"

"You want to live forever, don't you? I think we should put on several layers of clothing and set out what food we have already pre-pared to get us through the first difficult days."

"Rey won't let you do it," Jackie told her.

Bee toddled to the tall bureau and tossed several pairs of un-derwear, trousers, and shirts onto the bed.

"Hey, I didn't mean you should do it!" Jackie stuffed the clothes back in the bureau drawer. Bee pulled them out again. Jackie yelled, "Rey won't do it, I'm telling you. I'm taking a big chance myself. I'll probably wind up completely dead. And so will you. Stop that!"

Cricket rolled out of bed. Lacewing pulled her into the kitch-en and bustled around with the big box of herbs and vials while Cricket, yawning and creaking, prepared food for the imminent time when cooking would be beyond their newborn powers.

"Fine. Don't listen to me. Just don't say I didn't tell you so when you're laying on the ground deader than smelt."

Bee paused, turned to Jackie Tobasco, and said, "You are not the only person suffering loss. Your gesture of tragic sacrifice is noted. If you wish, I shall record it in the journal. If you would be so kind, prepare whatever physical memorial you want before you gather your skirts and sweep off the stage in your grand exit."

"Exit stage left," Cricket sang out from the kitchen.

"Exuent all," Lacewing intoned.

"Oh, hell. You're all abso-freakin-lutely nuts." Jackie backed out of the bedroom, leaving the old lunatics to prepare for their personal apocalypses.

Like a fireman at an arsonists' convention, Rey thought. Limping down the road to Jackie's trailer, she remembered nostalgically the old days when corralling the villagers had seemed like herding cats. That had been kid stuff.

Smokey was on her mind, but at least he was safe in bed, whereas Jackie was not to be trusted. She'd wait, as promised, but she hadn't said for how long. It would be nice if Jackie was home, setting her hair and smoking and re-reading a trashy novel; then Rey wouldn't have to hobble all over the place looking for her. But if that's what it took, that was what she would do. Her grandfather's voice gruffed up from a locked and dusty brain file: *Damn it, I can only piss on one fire at a time.*

Bee led the way, as usual. Lacewing trailed behind, pleading with the older sisters to wait up. She carried her medicine chest, which if they didn't believe was heavy they could come and lug themselves, and she was tired, too, and what was the big hurry anyway since they were all going to wind up at the same place?

Jobert watched his darling leave. Leaving was an event he had performed for many an inamorata, sometimes as he jumped out her bedroom window, sometimes as he pulled out of the station on the evening train. He was not accustomed to being on this side of parting and it did not sit well with him.

"Lacey! Come back, dahlin'!" But Lacey didn't look back.

Something in his brocade-covered heart shrank as his sweetheart, so lately found and too soon lost, rounded the corner and vanished in the ferns.

"Wait! Wait for Jobert!"

He shoved a pearly duelling pistol in each side of his waistband and ran after her. His vacated chair quivered, stilled, then bumped rhythmically, sending some kind of message, but Jobert was long gone.

By the time Jackie Tobasco got back to Rey's place, the little front yard was full of people. Jackie had looked everywhere for Berry, and wouldn't you know it, here was Berry with the whole mountainful of people, standing around listening to Bee and Rey argue.

"You have more sense than this, Bee. You're the chief. It's up to you not to let everybody run off a cliff." Rey was toe to toe with Bee, half a head taller but a full head less willful.

Bee turned away from Rey and faced the gathering. "I'm going to explain it again, because the doctor makes a good point. I've made decisions for others, and I always had a reason beyond my own convenience, although I don't necessarily put my convenience last. For what some of you will think is the first time, I don't expect anyone to follow my lead.

"In the past few days my sister and I have come closer to death than anyone ought to. When you reach our age, you can't pretend that death won't find you. Death is your footprint. We breath death. We eat death, and death eats us. Death holds our hand while we sleep. It—I was going to say, death will find you, but that's not right. Death doesn't need to find you. It has been in you since you were conceived. It infected you from the sperm and egg that came from your dying father and mother. You are made of death."

Liberty pulled her mother's skirt. "What's sperm?" Mercy told her it was nothing at all. It goes with eggs? Liberty wondered, and Mercy said yes and hush up.

"Unfortunately," Bee said, "it's our endless chore in life to evade death, and any job is easier when we think we might succeed. But now my age compels me to admit that I won't succeed much longer. Death is not my shadow. I am death's shadow. The exciting events since the shootings—"

Here Bee turned to look at Rey, but there was no recrimination in her look. She held out an arm and beckoned Rey to come to her side. Bee spoke the rest of her piece with her arm around Rey, who looked helplessly at the attentive circle of her living and semi-living friends. Even the dead paid attention when Bee talked.

"Since that fateful night, my sisters and I have trod on death's coattails too many times. We have pushed our luck."

Cricket was nodding her head. Lacewing took Cricket's hand. They both had a basket at their feet, each covered in an embroidered tea towel. Rey noticed one was a red and yellow flower basket pattern, the other was a bluebird with leaves in its beak.

"I say all this because I want to be clear: I don't want to die. I know how close it is, how hungry it is, and that death always gets its way. But I aim to beat it if I can. This doctor is my weapon against that greedy glutton."

Bee raised Rey's hand like a referee proclaiming the winner after a boxing match. Rey cringed.

"She is our weapon against that bitch Death. To Death, I say, 'You'll never take me alive!' "

The villagers clapped. Cricket and Lacewing whistled.

"How do you like them apples, Death?" Cricket jeered.

Sue Hill stood with Zombie Buck and Crystal, who now looked no more like her twin sister than a lioness looks like a schnauzer. Sue kept scanning the darkening woods for Misty, who had taken her own leave to patrol the perimeter with Ezekiel Alder. What a bad influence that boy had turned out to be.

Mercy stood back a little with her stairstep daughters on one side and Jacob on the other, standing with El Duane. Earl was behind El

Duane, a camo cap twisting in his hands. Mercy's lips moved with prayers or lamentations.

Jobert, as close as he could get to Lacewing, said, "Well, I don't know ... it appeahs a powerful gamble."

"I do know." Birdie cleared her throat, getting it primed to speak up. "I been through some things, myself. Right up here on this mountain, and nobody never noticed. I never asked them to. But I'm done with that." She looked at Zombie Bill, who glowered back at her. Birdie didn't even quiver. "I like what I seen so far, and I'll throw in my ticket with Berry and Crystal and the rest of them. Count me in."

That was where Jackie had to speak up, too. "I don't understand why you throw yourself into this for no good reason. I've got a good reason. She's right here." Jackie opened her arms to Berry, who looked at her with a pleasant expression, but didn't run into the embrace. Jackie slowly lowered her arms.

"It's not a philosophy thing, it's for real. For love. I mean true love, which I don't guess everybody here has had the chance to know like I and Berry have. Bee never thought of it until I told her that's what I was doing, so she has to do it, too, because she has to own all the good ideas."

"Somebody stole your thunder," Cricket said.

"There's plenty of thunder and lightning to go around," Bee said.

Rey tore a fistful of leaves off a salal bush and ripped them to particles. "I can not believe it." Louder, she said, "I'm not doing it! Not Doing It! Can anybody hear me?"

Apparently no one could.

Lacewing sat on the wet ground and unfolded tier upon tier of tinctures, vials, and potions. "Well, then, Rey dear, I recommend a whopping big bonfire, as you won't be able to bury all this lot. We've a bag of pitchwood and plenty of seasoned wood at the house. I'm sorry you won't be able to simply chuck us all in the Crack. It's made burials far easier over the years." Lacewing looked up, smiling. "It seems Sugar Agate was the last to have the honor of the Crack as her final resting place. I didn't realize that when I put her in, but it goes to prove one never knows."

There was a collective silence.

"You threw Sugar Agate in the Crack?" Sue said.

"Of course. Where else would I put her?"

"Oh, my God," Rey said.

"It's not pleasant, is it?" Lacewing said rhetorically. "With that thing down there and its foul fumes. Poor Daddy never came back to himself after he trapped it and lowered it in. Did we ever find out how it got out in the first place, Bee?"

"Daddy never said," Bee answered. "I don't think he knew."

"He was just out hunting and there it was, trying to gore him to death. He should have shot it then and there," Cricket said. "It still makes me mad, what it did to him. Ugly brute."

Unable to help herself and half-demented by this conversation, Rey asked, "What did it do to him?"

"Made him sick, of course. Pneumonia. That's how he died. Saving the thing. Taking it home." Cricket sat next to Lacewing and opened the basket she had brought. "It was white and sickly was all he really told us, and never would speak another word about it. Just put that gate across the cave and locked it. We only found the key years and years after he died. He'd hidden it in a bottle of castor oil."

"He knew we'd never look there," Lacewing said. "Ugh."

"No, we never took another dose after he and Mother were gone." Bee said to Rey, "I wish you had come along before Daddy and Mother left us. I would dearly love to see them again."

Cricket said, "I think what killed him was going there so much, feeding it. He felt guilty locking it away after it had taken so much trouble to get free. I'm sure it was starving, and when he locked the gate of course no more animals could go down the chute, so he fed it himself."

"With what?" Rey asked, after a pause.

"Oh, you know. Deer. Departed souls."

Cricket said, "Those hikers."

"Whoever," Lacewing said airily. "You were inside, weren't you, Rey? There must have been some remains left. Did you see Sugar Agate?"

Rey recalled the beads rolling under her hands and the white beaded Indian princess dress Sugar Agate looked so pretty in, wearing it with aplomb as if it were not an affected stereotype but her birthright. Rey wouldn't have been surprised if Sugar Agate had stolen it from an actual Native American Plains chieftainess, if there was such a thing.

"Jackie, don't be angry with us," Bee said, changing the subject to more immediate matters. "If you were the first to think of it, thank you. We all want to be together, you see. No one wants to be alone."

"Not even underground." Lacewing had been mixing liquids in a small pot, and now poured the solution through a funnel into the wine bottle Cricket drew out of her basket.

"I took a few swigs already, to make room," Cricket said to the assemblage, "but I guarantee no backwash."

"Because backwash is your big health concern right now," Rey said.

"So who all's coming on this here ride?" Cricket asked. The few swigs had been perhaps more than a few. "Me and my sisters, Jackie. Birdie. Who else? Sue?"

"I couldn't leave Misty." Sue looked worried. "I don't like her out there."

"She's with Ezekiel. My boy will watch out for her," Mercy said.

"Oh, he will?" Sue retorted. "When does that start?"

Bee took Rey's hands in hers. "No one thought to ask if you wanted to come, too, Rey. But I don't see how you could. I'm so sorry."

"It's good to be needed," Rey said, but she was unable to load her words with enough sarcasm to make a dent.

"Mercy?" Cricket asked.

"Don't be ridiculous. I'll die when the Lord says Die, and I plan to end up in Heaven, so I guess this is goodbye forever." She let that innuendo sink in, then murmured, "I won't take a unborn baby's life, anyway."

Sue said, "What unborn baby?"

"Oh, my God." Rey blurted, "You're pregnant! Is it human?"

Mercy blushed and raised her chin. "It's El Duane's child, and I'm not ashamed to carry it. He's my husband now."

"But Ma, you're married to Daddy," Liberty pointed out.

"We vowed before God Till Death Us Do Part, and death us did part, and I became a widow. It's Biblical custom to marry your deceased husband's brother. They did it all the time in Bible days."

"So we get a baby sister?" Freedom asked.

"Or brother," said Liberty.

"Or other," Rey said. "None of the above."

Mercy held her chin up and linked her arm through El Duane's.

Bee said, "Well. My goodness. A new ... er, *baby* ... on the mountain. Congratulations, Mercy, El Duane."

Cricket took up where she'd left off. "I guess that makes up our little expeditionary party." She lined up a set of emerald-green, cut glass cordial glasses and Lacewing poured two fingers of the Pear Sisters' homemade sweet blackberry wine, spiked à la Lacewing Pear, in each. Cricket pushed herself to her feet. Her joints cracked audibly. She and Lacewing served, starting with Bee and ending with Birdie.

"A toast, then." Cricket raised her glass.

"To a sweet slumber," Bee said, "and a happy life."

"To lunacy," Rey said, raising an imaginary glass.

"It'll be interesting to be someone new," Lacewing mused. "A change is as good as a rest, I always think. One does grow so tired of being the same old person all the time." She raised her glass.

Birdie looked at her husband and raised her glass a fraction without changing her expression or taking her eyes off him.

Jackie held the emerald glass in front of her eyes. "It's so pretty. Will I still like pretty things? Oh, well. Doesn't make no never mind." She put the glass to her lips.

"Jackie, no!" Rey lunged for her.

Jackie raised the glass to her lips. "Rey, honey, don't worry. Just do your best. No blame." She swallowed. Rey grabbed for Jackie's feet and yanked. Jackie landed on top of her. The cordial glass rolled across the dirt and spring grass.

Jackie rested her head against Rey's and gazed up at the trees. "Don't they look like a big crown up there, Rey? Like sky inside a big crown. It's too late, sweetie. I already drank it."

Bee said, "Gather up, quickly. Form a wheel, as we did with the first batch. That will make it easier on Rey."

The sisters, Jackie Tobasco, and Birdie Dollar lay heads together on the soft ground, feet pointing out like the spokes of a wheel, a reprise of a Busby Berkley floor show staged under the wide lens of the sky. Jackie took Birdie's and Lacewing's hands. She found Berry with her eyes. "Take good care of me, sweetheart. I'll be with you real soon."

Cricket held Lacewing's other hand and Bee's on her other side. "It's good to be in the middle spot. I've secretly always liked being in the middle."

"Am I supposed to feel something?" Birdie asked. "Because I don't feel anything."

"A bit of a tingle in the tongue, perhaps," Lacewing said. "And your eyes are growing heavy. Heeehvy. So sleepy. Sleeeepier and sleeeepier." She giggled.

Cricket laughed. Bee laughed out loud. Rey didn't remember Bee ever laughing out loud.

Birdie shrieked, "I feel the tingle! I never felt the tingle before! Ooh, I like the tingle," and howled at an invisible moon.

Bee giggled, then let loose a belly laugh that tolled out of her like stones rolling over in a riverbed.

Subliminally, then audibly, the pulse of a helicopter blade neared. The revived turned to the sound. Some ran toward it; some vanished.

The pulsing slowed.

From behind Rey's cabin, Misty screamed.

Rey ran, but Sue got there first. There were three people, two standing, one on the ground. One of the standing ones held a long bread knife, red at the serrated edge. Misty Hill lay on her back, red cloaking her throat and running into the moss and leaf litter. Her eyes stared beyond the trees into the sky and beyond that into nothing.

Sue Hill hugged her daughter to her chest, pinched together the skin at the edges of her torn throat, talking to her soft and fast.

Standing beside the girl's bleeding body, Everett Roberts smiled at Rey.

"Doctor Newhause, I presume." He grinned. "Good to see you again."

49

Beside Misty, Ezekiel Alder stared, his mouth useless from shock, his eyes wild.

Dr. Everett Roberts held up the bloodied knife. "I was trying not to make a fuss."

Rey pointed her gun at his chest. "What did you do?"

"I see you have a modern weapon. When I came here, I didn't really know what to expect. Stone Age technology, possibly."

Rey's finger snugged against the trigger. "You cut Misty's throat!"

"You don't expect me to let her kill me."

Sue struggled upright with Misty in her arms. "Shoot him."

"I will. Ezekiel, go in the house."

Roberts flicked his free hand and Rey saw in it one end of a leather belt. The other end cinched EZ's neck. Roberts knitted his eyebrows together in a look of concern. "If your subjects move an inch I slit the boy's throat. I wonder if you care, though." Into Ezekiel's ear, he confided, "Dr. Newhause has killed hundreds of people."

Rey said, "No—"

Roberts shrugged but kept the dripping knife hard against Ezekiel's throat. "Kill, utilize, harvest. I concede it's a matter of semantics."

"We'll tear you apart if you don't let EZ go right now."

He ignored her threat. "We're leaving together. Bring that." He meant the metal case at Rey's side.

Rey hoped at least some of the revived had stayed, gone invisible, and were moving toward Roberts and EZ. Whether they could plan and execute a take-down, or had really left the scene for some unfathomable undead reason, she wanted the knife as far from the boy's throat as possible. If they grabbed Roberts' arm, the blade was positioned to slice through EZ's hyoid cartilage and jugular vein. "Put your hands on top of your head. I'm detaining you for murder."

Roberts made a sour nasal explosion which Rey recognized as his laugh. "Put the gun down, Dr. Newhause."

EZ sucked in air as a trickle of his blood slid over the knife blade.

Roberts looked around. "Where are your subjects, Jillian?" As usual, he answered himself. "They seem to have deserted you. You realize if they try to stop us, someone's child dies."

"They'll stop you if they choose to, and someone's child already died."

Rey didn't care for the irony of the situation. Any other time since the invasion started she would have gladly given herself up. Now that she finally had the opportunity, surrender was unthinkable. Her foolish people had twenty minutes, thirty at most, before the window for revival slammed shut. Rey's options were to sacrifice EZ with his mother and sisters watching and maybe put Everett Roberts out of action, or go with him and probably let the people on the ground die before Roberts killed EZ anyway.

"I want you alive," Roberts assured her. "You're in no danger. I need you physically and mentally fit." Monstrously, he dug the point of the bread knife into EZ's throat again. "And since I don't want to carry you out, I prefer you retain the ability to walk under your own power. So you have nothing whatever to worry about."

Nothing to worry about. Rey would have laughed if she'd been capable of laughing. She had no kind of odds, only the desperate wish that her company of revived would rescue her, that Smokey would wake up and take control, that she would think of something.

"Let's go, Dr. Newhause. Lead the way to the trolley."

"It doesn't work." Rey caught a flicker of hope. No trolley meant she might have an advantage somehow. Then she wondered aloud, "How did you get here?"

"Ah. The hand trolley is functional. My subjects reassembled it. The trolley's an awkward and dangerous contraption, but I know you'll manage to pull us across. Let's not waste any more time. Go."

As she led the way to her unfinished walkway to the road, Rey saw Sue upend the wine bottle into her mouth, then jostle herself and her daughter into the circle. Rey heard Sue croon to Misty, "We stay together, girl. We're stayin' together."

Disorientation was nothing new to Travis. In the good old days, he'd woken up half the time not knowing where he was. No problemo. He just went back to sleep. This was weird, though, only not in a fun way. He didn't know where he was *plus* there was some important reason he should get up, pronto.

Travis groaned and looked around for a clue as to his location. Wood as far as the eye could see. Wood to the left, wood to the right, different wood overhead. He was uncomfortable.

He was on a floor.

It was easy after that. He was on his own floor, looking at the underside of his bed. This had happened before, but never had he slept under a bed with a pillow and blanket. It had been a spur of the moment deal in the past, not something planned out, as the blanket and pillow suggested.

Someone had left a pair of ogre boots on the floor beside his bed. Weird. Flashes of beer-goggled bar pickups scared him for a second, but there were no bars and nobody to pick up. He poked a finger gingerly at the toe of one collapsing, encrusted boot. Heavy sucker. He shoved the boot. The boot shoved back.

Travis yelped. He wormed backwards and rolled out from under the bed and peeked over the mattress. Trucker John stood looking at him. In his arms he cradled an old rifle. Trucker John's face, the rifle, and the boots looked like they were made out of the same stuff and the stuff was basically dirt. Travis didn't doubt that the boots could move fast, the gun could shoot hard, and the face could do some serious damage beyond just staring at him, which felt pretty damaging all by itself.

"Dude, what's up with the bedside vigil? Could you like come back later and we'll turn over a brew, okay? Jeez."

Trucker John said, "My house. You go."

"Seriously?"

Trucker John moved his feet and made a bad-sounding rumble in his throat.

"Okay, don't get all twisted." Travis eased his feet into his own boots, grabbed his vest off the bedroom door latch, and sidled through the main room. Sugar Agate's crystals hung in the window, the colored glass bottles tinkled in the breeze from the open door, which had a newly-busted latch; her hairbrush and silver necklace lay on the table waiting for her come home and brush her shiny hair and fasten the chain around her little neck. His bear claw pin lay next to a bowl of sucked-out honeycomb. He grabbed it. Hell if he was going to leave it for the old zombie. Everybody else was willing to let a little theft slide, but Trucker John was the repo man from Hell.

Down at the bottom of the road, past Jackie Tobasco's house, where Travis imagined he would find coffee and sympathy, a knot of people swarmed around the hand trolley holder-upper. *Cool,* he said to himself. *We're hooked up again. Welcome back to the 19th freaking century.*

One of the people at the river's edge was Rey, looking uber cool in her muddy clothes. Even without a gun—why wasn't she wearing a gun? Was the crazy shit over?—she looked like a warrior princess. Hot, wicked, and dangerous. Travis wondered why he had fooled around with Sugar Agate. Not to speak ill of the dead, but as cute as she was with her hair and her figure, she was a devil. But that soft skin ... Travis got lost in the thought, then remembered Rey. God, she was something, and not just to look at. Matter of fact, she looked dirty and sweaty and beat to shit, but on her it was hot as hell. Maybe it wasn't too late to get back with Rey. The old sleepy, sweaty days and nights meandered through his mind again; then Sugar Agate got into his memories and the three of them were together, which was interesting, and Travis lost track of what he was doing.

The trolley stanchion was a gallows-shaped construction with a long cable stretching over the river. Roberts' servants had figured out how to string the cable across, and the trolley hung from it on its two big pulleys. It looked as sturdy as it ever had: heavy weathered boards bolted to make a shallow box about six feet long with a bench seat at each end, the thick cable sagging slightly over the middle of the river so whichever way you crossed, the beginning of the ride was easy and the end was hard work.

When they got to the stanchion Rey said, "I've been trying to give myself up since your things got here. You don't need Ezekiel. You've got me."

Behind her, Everett said, "You'll give yourself up now?"

"I've been trying to."

"But your priorities have changed. I couldn't help noticing all your dying friends. They're waiting for you to perform the protocol you developed. I assume you'd be unwilling to leave them at this critical time."

"Not so. I already administered the reversal. We're only waiting for them to wake up."

"The mother of the girl I disarmed hasn't undergone any treatment."

"She's the only one," Rey said. "I'm sorry she'll have to die, but the rest are fine. I can leave them. You don't need a hostage. Let EZ go."

"EZ. That's your nickname, son?"

EZ wheezed.

"Let him go, Everett. I won't fight you." She couldn't tell if he knew she was lying. "I'm done here."

EZ's face was grey. He smelled of urine; sweat dripped down his forehead.

"You'll be okay," Rey told him. "Hang in there." Into his ear, she whispered, "Stay alert, EZ."

"No talking," Everett ordered. He looked at the stanchion where a short rope tied the car to the timbers; he looked in turn at Rey and at EZ and back at the rope.

Years of working with Everett had taught Rey to read his thoughts as clearly as if he'd spoken them. He was figuring out the logistics involved in getting them all into the trolley without Rey or EZ running off into the woods or crossing the river without him. If Rey got in first, she could escape. If Roberts got in first, Rey would take EZ and run. If Roberts put EZ in first, he would lose his hostage and Rey would attack him.

Rey's hopes rose. But only for a moment. Roberts pursed his lips and emitted a thin whistle. Two of his monstrosities slithered out of the undergrowth, gleaming like oiled lizards.

"Take her," he ordered, then changed his mind, still not sure of how to organize things. "No, take the boy." He shoved EZ at his minions, letting go of the belt but not the knife.

"Let Ezekiel go," Rey pleaded again. "He'll untie the trolley and you and I can go."

Everett Roberts eyed Rey speculatively, but it didn't take him long to reject her proposal. "Since I don't want to get shot, we'll do it another way."

"Ezekiel's not armed."

"I have no doubt the trees are full of your cohorts waiting for a clear shot at me."

That was exactly what Rey wanted to believe. But Roberts credited the mountain revived with more volition than she did. They were good at fighting and following Smokey's directions, but Rey hadn't seen much evidence that they could figure out how to manage a hostage situation.

Facing the road, Rey saw Travis as soon as he started toward them, but Roberts wouldn't look away from her long enough for her signal him. If Travis could creep silently behind Roberts, Rey thought she could grab EZ and get him away. But Travis grinned and ran toward her, oblivious to Rey's fingers over her lips, the only signal she thought she might get away with.

Sure enough, Travis hollered, "Whoo-hoo! Trolley's up!"

Dr. Roberts lunged with the speed and agility of a more athletically inclined man and aimed the knife at Rey's heart. He knew without thinking how to hold a knife so the tip would slide between the ribs, the serrated edge rip through the pericardium and penetrate the left ventricle.

"What's—?" Travis stared from thirty feet away, trying to figure out what the stranger was doing to Rey and where and why she and Ezekiel were going with him.

When Smokey opened his eyes he was in a strange bed. His head hurt. Smokey had little tolerance for being disoriented. He'd stayed alive, free, and solvent as long as he had by controlling his brain and his senses. *Shape up,* he commanded himself, but objects in the room wobbled in duplicate. Something was wrong with his ears, too, an uneasy throbbing. The combination made his muscles tighten up the way they did when something bad was trying to happen to him.

The throbbing got clearer; his eyes settled into tenuous monovision. The headache stayed put, but through the ache and haze he put it together. Yep, something bad *was* trying to happen to him. A helicopter was landing. That sound had burned permanent circuits into his brain. The only spot a helicopter could land was the clearing. He was in a squashy bed under a puffy quilt. Ergo, he was in the Pear Sisters' house by the clearing and the merc's helo was back.

He had to hang onto the bedposts and walls, but he stayed upright well enough to lurch through the house. He was alone. If an invasion was in the immediate future a company of his own soldiers would have been nice, but at least there weren't any helpless civilians around. In the kitchen the door in the floor was opened out and a straight chair lay beside it. Smokey poured a glass of water, felt his stomach fist up in response, and forced himself to drink the rest of the glass. Half a loaf of brown bread rested on the wooden counter, but although he knew he would need fuel, he couldn't make himself eat, and there wasn't time, anyway. The beat of the single rotary blade slowed; he heard the engine whining and the beat shift to the *whash* that said the bird had landed.

His knife poised over Rey's chest, Everett Roberts took a moment to savor the way things were working out. Rey grabbed for EZ, but the undead things pulled him away. Roberts reflexively bent his elbow and the knife etched a slit down Rey's chest. She felt the sting but grabbed for the knife, kicking at Roberts' knee, feeling her boot connect with his patella.

Travis yelled, "Hey! You! You, asshole! Knock it off!" He ran toward Roberts.

"You harshed everybody's mellow, you crazy dingo! You and your trained monkeys can just back your shit up."

The trained monkeys threw their captive into the trolley and slunk toward Travis. Rey shouted, "Run, Travis!" and tried to leap into the trolley bed to grab EZ.

Travis wound up and aimed a roundhouse at the dingo's jaw. He came close to connecting, but the scientist's servants were on Travis before his arm completed its trajectory. Travis thrashed like a wildcat, but with no effort at all they put him on the ground and looked at their master for the go-ahead, their hideous faces blank and patient.

Dr. Roberts said, "At will, boys."

Rey shouted, "Get the brainstem! Rip out the brainstem!"

"Brains have stems?" Travis said. "Huh." He shoved the bone pin he'd been holding in his fist, the pin Sugar Agate had tried to tell him was goat bone when it was obviously ivory or at least grizzly bear fang, into the nape of one monster's neck, gave it a convulsive twist, and yanked. The undead thing flopped off of him, its fragile bulb of frayed nerves seeping gray fluid into the dirt. Then the other undead thing removed Travis's head.

It sounded to Rey as if one of the monsters had its nasty face in her ear, but the sound she heard was her own howl. She cleared the trolley side rail; stood up and pulled hard against the cable, got nowhere and remembered they were still tied up.

Roberts folded manicured fingers over the rail. "Help me up." He sounded entitled to Rey's assistance, the way at the lab he had always assumed she was there for his convenience. It pissed her off.

"Go fuck yourself," Rey told him.

"Don't be an ass," Roberts said. "You're a professional. Help me aboard before you cause me serious harm and jeopardize our entire mission."

"We're not going anywhere."

Roberts narrowed his eyes. Then it dawned on him the car was tied to the stanchion. "Untie us," he told the remaining undead thing. It stared at him uncomprehendingly.

"You forgot to put the brains in," Rey said.

He made the thing hold the car still while he untied them, and got it to boost him in. Then he kicked it away. "Jesus, I hate to touch those things." He shuddered. Even with the help of the undead lackey, he'd had to let go of the belt to get himself over the rail and into the trolley.

Rey captured the free end and worked at the blood-stiffened knot around EZ's neck. "EZ, are you okay?"

"My face hurts."

"I bet. It's killing me," Rey kidded, her fingers frantic to get the belt off of him in case Roberts or the monster overpowered her.

"Ha," EZ said. "Good one."

"Pull us across!" Roberts commanded.

"Go screw yourself," Rey said.

"The world is yours, don't you comprehend that? Summerland Mission makes the rules from now on. What was your work for? This hillbilly commune? For Christ's sake, Newhause, I'm not trying to hurt you. We need each other."

Rey asked EZ, "Can you help pull us across?" If they got away from the thing on the ground, she could deal with Everett Roberts. She'd hoped EZ wouldn't have to witness her kill a man, but considering the man in question, seeing him murdered might do EZ a world of good.

The cable car bobbed, then rocked. Rey looked up. The dark zombie was walking the wire from the riverbank, balancing gracefully with its long arms outstretched, moving fast.

We have company," Roberts observed.

"Pull!" Rey and EZ worked in sync, reaching overhead and forward to grip the cable, moving their arms back to slide the car forward, releasing alternately so the car did not slide backwards, grabbing cable again: work they had done a hundred times but never so urgently.

The walker was closer. It stepped confidently, its expressionless face focused on Rey. EZ started jumping up and down, bouncing the cable, creating as much movement as he could. Rey coordinated with him, pushing up and pulling down, amplifying the motion. The little car rocked and bounced violently. Roberts screamed at them to stop before they all fell out, were they crazy? He wrapped an elbow around the top rail but was slammed against the floor.

"You're bruising me!" His voice broke with every lurch.

"Tell your helper to go away," Rey said. "We'll quit."

"Go back!" Roberts waved a hand in the direction of the wire walker, who had been forced to crouch down and hold the cable in its hands. It ignored him.

"Not so good at following directions," Rey said.

Roberts flapped at it halfheartedly. Obviously he wanted it to reach the car, where it would save him. But the worried look on his face revealed conflict. He wanted Jillian Newhause's secrets, he needed his creation to control her, but he had no confidence he could deploy the thing without it eating her. He hung on.

Rey worked the cable harder. They had slowed the beast, but it was very close, and once it got to them they were dead. And her death meant the death of the circle of people in her front yard. The fools. They had insisted on putting their lives in her hands. They thought she had some superpower that could make them live forever, but she was nobody special. Save them? It was looking like she couldn't even save herself.

50

From the cover of a Douglas fir, Smokey watched the men in crisp digital woodlands camo jump out of the settling helicopter. They hadn't bothered with rappelling this time. Maybe they'd decided nothing on the ground could hurt them. Maybe they were better armed. Maybe they ran out of rope. There were six of them, plus a pilot. Somebody had to stay and guard the craft from wily woodsmen.

If I'd a known you was coming I'd a baked a cake, he sang softly. There was no chance anybody would hear him. *But I did know you were coming. If I hadn't been busy with rescuing elderly ladies and being unconscious I'd a baked you a nice cake. One with four and twenty zombies jumping out of the top.*

Where were the zombies, anyway? They should be all over the clearing, ripping and munching and making a nice mess. It was just about too late now. The mercs had spread out, waving their expensive weapons into the trees, jumping at every moving brush and branch, of which there were many, with the blades kicking turbulence around. A limb made the mistake of cracking off a cedar at the clearing's edge and got chewed into sawdust by nervous automatic fire. They advanced across the clearing to the three trails leading out: one up to what used to be Hoochville, one the other direction toward the cave and Sock Creek, and one directly past the Pear's house. *Damn good thing helos make noise,* Smokey thought. *Otherwise I would have been caught napping in the first place they came to.*

One stocky guy passed within two arms' lengths. The merc stepped on every possible twig and broke all available branches as he passed, peering fearfully into the thick shadows. All Smokey had to do was hunker down, keep his face pointed at the dirt, and hold still while Noisy Mercenary passed in a cloud of cologne.

Uphill a ruckus broke out. A radio crackled: the noisy smelly one squelched it. Seconds later shouts closed in on the clearing, followed by two camo'd men running like the hounds of hell were chasing them, which was pretty near the literal truth. One made it to the helicopter but the slower one went down under little Eddy, who flew through the air like a cat and caught the poor sucker's back in both hands. Eddy landed with both feet on his prey's back and jerked the head neatly to the side, twisted it off its stem and tossed it aside, and settled down to enjoy the fruits of his victory.

Gunfire spattered from behind the helo. Bits of ground around Eddy and his dinner exploded but Eddy didn't seem to notice. Hoot stepped out from behind a tree, or appeared beside a tree, it was hard to tell. The Norse Force dashed to the source of the assault and did something to make the gunman shriek like a peacock. Smokey heard the door shut. The pilot had shut himself inside. The motor picked up speed and the skids began to slip the surly bonds of earth. The machine roared up. Then it tilted to the right and wobbled, wagging its tail. It lost altitude and turned 180 degrees and plopped down again. Through the windshield Smokey saw the pilot's face contorted in horror and confusion.

The smelly mercenary ran by Smokey toward his ride out. All Smokey had to do was reach out and grab a leg. The rifle popped a few rounds into the undergrowth before Smokey lifted it from the downed merc's hands and used it to prod him hard in the ribs.

"Get in the bird," Smokey ordered.

The merc kept his eyes on Smokey as he got up. "What are you?"

"Hope you don't find out." Smokey ushered him to the helo and had him open the door.

"What the hell—" the guy said.

The pilot's eyes rolled wide in his head. He resembled a spooked horse. Smokey said, "Hoot?"

The shotgun seat darkened and revealed the bulk of the Norseman. His hair had grown in red-blond ropes and a rusty beard bushed out on his chin. All he lacked was a horned helmet.

"Shee-it," the merc said.

"Lookin' good, Hoot," Smokey said.

Hoot said, "Eat?"

"Not now. Let's gather them up and then you can have a snack."

"Roger that," Hoot said. "I get 'em." He got out and let loose a bellow. In less than a minute more zombies loped to meet him: Jacob and Crystal, Earl and Trucker John, and Dollar Bill. Eddy wiped his mouth on his sleeve with a new fastidiousness and joined his undead comrades.

The pilot found his voice. "What are they?"

"Your worst nightmare. The important thing is, where's your boss?"

"I don't know."

Crystal said, "Bad man. Kill Misty. Knife. Eat face."

"You ate him?"

"Gonna."

She meant the monsters' boss, who was out of the root cellar and on the loose, committing atrocities. "Where is he now?"

Jacob hugged Crystal. She didn't have any tears, but her eyes were red and the muscles in her forearms knotted into hard burls. Jacob said, "EZ. Rey." He buried his face in Crystal's bleached hair. "Sister. I kill him for you."

"So," Smokey told the pilot, "sounds like your boss is out of luck. I doubt he'll be writing you any checks. Unless you work for free, your job is over as of now."

The pilot nodded. The smelly merc swallowed. The stench of urine mingled with the cologne. One of them had pissed his pants.

"There are three others," Smokey said. "Where are they?"

"I don't know."

"What was the plan?"

Neither merc said anything.

"You had a plan, right? Or don't you do business that way? You just land and expect your firepower to solve all your tactical issues?"

"Find the doc, neutralize the locals, bring back the female alive if possible."

Smokey interpreted for his troops. "They're going to kill everybody they see unless you kill them first."

Trucker John acted immediately. He ripped the smelly mercenary into three pieces, setting a speed record for zombie-on-human dismemberment.

"Wait for my command," Smokey told him.

Trucker John ignored that and shouldered the legs and pelvis of the mercenary. He and rest of the undead warriors took off except for Hoot, who liked the helicopter too much to leave it, and Eddy, whom Smokey tagged to stand guard with his friend.

He asked the pilot, "Whose machine is this?"

"It's company aircraft. Ironman Services."

"Radio them now and tell them there was nobody here. You're bringing them back their property, but the client didn't pay off, so your guys quit. End of mission. Tell them now."

The pilot said, "I'm only the pilot. They want to hear it from Mitch."

"They'll hear it from you instead. They get their toy back in one piece. Make them listen."

The pilot complied. "Asshole disappeared on us ... don't work for free ... yeah ... estimate two twenty." He signed off. "Can we go now?" He tried to sound frosty but couldn't control the jitter in his jaws.

"When I say go, you'll go. First I need to know how you plan to keep this place a secret for the rest of your life."

"I won't tell." The pilot's eyes rounded with innocence. "None of us will say anything."

Smokey regarded him coolly.

"We're professionals. Secret is what we do, brother." He cracked a tight smile. "No worries on that front."

"Okay. You're a trustworthy soldier."

"Word on that."

"Scout's honor," Smokey said. "I just need some kind of assurance. Some kind of collateral besides your code of honor."

The pilot looked puzzled. Then he said, "I'm the one who should be asking for collateral, man. How do I know you and those jolly green giants won't shoot me in the back? The big one here wants to fuckin' eat me right now."

Smokey nodded. "That's true. He does. But I told him to wait."

"What do you suggest? I leave you my driver's license or something?"

"Good idea. Then I'd know where to find you. My only reservation is that a top secret operative like you probably has false ID. Maybe you got a whole wardrobe of licenses and documents, one for every day of the week, like underpants."

"Look for yourself." The pilot shrugged. He had soulful brown eyes and long eyelashes. He kept the calf eyes on Smokey's face as he slowly reached into his inner pocket, saying, "Here's my ID, boss."

"Hands up!" Smokey barked.

"It's all right. Just my pilot's license. I'm pulling it out now for you." The pilot hesitated, not acting as confident as he wanted to on the business end of a gun barrel.

Smokey watched the guy's hands and face, seeing the signs and tells but thinking about Misty and EZ and Rey and what the mercenaries' client had done and would do. Smokey thought about the Pear Sisters, too proud to admit they hurt. The shit the kids had been through and what was in store for them when Roberts and his goons were done; about the forest and how nice it was left alone; about his own horticulture operation. The quiet on the mountain without helicopters and assholes and especially without officials and publicity. His thoughts circled back to Rey: her face and the muscles and skin of her shoulders were as clear in his mind as if she was pressed up against him.

He said, "Can't do it."

The calf eyes widened. His hand burrowed deeper into his jacket. "No, man, I won't—"

Smokey shot a burst into the man's chest, waited a second and fired one more into his forehead. The body blew back against the door, the hand flopped out of the inner pocket, dragging out a small automatic pistol.

"Sorry," Smokey told him. "You'd tell. Who wouldn't?"

He left the pistol where it lay. Hoot or Eddy could take it if they wanted it.

Leaving the moonshiners in control—"No joyrides!"—Smokey slung the smelly mercenary's weapon over his shoulder, and with his own gun ready ran to the road, wondering if he would find Rey before the crazy bastard who'd snatched her decided she wasn't worth the trouble of keeping alive.

51

It looked like an oversized, wingless bat clinging upside down to the cable, its flat eyes staring hungrily at the humans.

"Make it go away!" EZ aimed a backwards kick at Roberts.

"Stop whining," Roberts said. "Be still, for Christ's sake."

EZ kicked again and landed it. Roberts grunted.

The monster crawled closer.

"I can protect you." Roberts' enunciation lacked its former crispness. "I control it. But I can't control it under torture!"

The thing was close enough now to smell its oily rot. Rey wondered exactly how Dr. Roberts had created it and if it had been chance, design, or carelessness that made it so hideous. He needed her to create what he hadn't been able to. As a god and a scientist, he had failed and he knew it. If this monster was the best he could do, it was no wonder he had pursued her to this secret place; no wonder he didn't think twice about killing children. He would do anything to harness—more precisely, steal—Jillian Newhause's knowledge. He had entered into contracts, made promises to powerful and ruthless entities, incurred nonnegotiable obligations. All his talk of the Summerland Mission saving humanity from death had been more than egomaniacal. He might have started out as Jesus Christ in a lab coat, but he had turned into Satan, with bigger, meaner Satans prodding him with their sharpest, best-funded pitchforks.

Roberts' creation slipped and for a moment Rey thought it would fall into the river, but its prehensile toes gripped the cable and it swung once, twice, and on the third swing launched itself at the trolley bed.

Roberts screamed, "Kill them!"

The thing scrabbled over its creator's body and turned its blind gaze from Rey to EZ. Its jaws opened. Saliva oozed in mucoid ropes from the red mouth.

"Yes, eat the boy!" Roberts smacked it on the back of the knees.

In slow motion, seeming to enjoy the anticipation, the thing raised an arm. Long fingers uncurled and it gathered itself to spring.

EZ stared, frozen.

"Jump, EZ," Rey said quietly. "Jump now."

EZ was young and resilient and quick, but today had emptied him out. He didn't move. Rey grabbed him by the waistband and toppled him over the rail into the river. EZ didn't make a sound on the way down. The white water boiled over his head and cartwheeled him away.

Once he put some distance between himself and the helicopter, Smokey followed the shouting. Rey's yard was full of people, but all of them were dead, undead, or doing a good imitation of being dead. The undead were agitated. It might have been a form of crying. It could have been fury, too, or confusion or some other uncharted living dead emotion. They howled and huffed. They barked and gargled, circling and patting their humans and fretting.

Rey's cabin was empty except for goats and chickens making themselves at home. An interior door revealed a room Smokey hadn't known was there. The equipment on the workbench piqued his curiosity, but Rey wasn't there, so he went outside again and got Buck Hill's attention. Buck didn't know where Rey was or if he did he didn't know how to convey that information; neither did Berry or Joe Bear. Smokey glanced again at the wheel of dead and the milling undead. To Buck he said, "Take care of them, brother," and ran down Rey's unfinished boardwalk.

With his gun ready for business, he turned right to the Alder and Hill homes and was rewarded with kids' voices inside the Alders' house. He announced himself at the door so as not to get shot and one of the little girls let him in. Right behind her loomed El Duane, who gave Smokey a comradely punch on the shoulder that staggered him. Mercy sat on the front edge of a kitchen chair, quietly and insistently speaking to nobody.

He interrupted Mercy's monotone. "Where's Rey?"

" ... the breastplate of righteousness, the shield of faith by which I will extinguish all the flaming missiles of the evil one."

"Mercy." Smokey shook her elbow.

"The belt of truth and the sword of the Spirit! Amen."

"Where is Rey?"

"Walking in the shoes of Satan."

"Which is where?"

"The girls are under armor, but my last boy is taken in the Devil's snare."

"Jacob said the doctor took EZ and Rey. Do you know where?" He spoke as if to a child, hoping to pin her to the here and now for a minute. But it was El Duane who answered. He pointed a tree trunk arm east and down.

At the top of the road Smokey heard shouting. He saw the trolley bouncing in midair. Something big and dark hung from the cable. As he ran, it swooped into the trolley bed. More shouting, then a human arced over the side and vanished in the spume.

EZ vanished in the boil of water. Rey felt pulled down with him. Then the thing was on her.

"No, no! Leave that one alone!" Dr. Roberts shouted at his creation.

It slowed down enough for Rey to dig her fingers into its neck, probing for a place to get under its cervical vertebrae. The thing knocked her hand away, slamming it into a wooden brace. It exhaled fumes of decayed mold. She gagged. The thing grabbed her hair and shoved its nightmare face in hers. Its iron grip constricted her throat.

I missed my chance. She had meant to jump after EZ but she had been too slow and now there was no one to help him, no one to help the fools up on the hill. It was over, because she was too slow. Blue dots of light gathered across her eyes. *Couldn't save EZ, couldn't save my family. Already too late, already too slow.*

The blue closed in. It made a noise like rushing water.

Choppy water ... torrents rolling down a tin roof. Buffeted by surf over hard sand ... Rey came back. Everett Roberts was hitting her. He spoke very sternly.

She put up her hands to defend herself. He pummeled her anyway. "Wake up, you bitch! You're not dying."

Rey grabbed one of his thin wrists in her fists and shoved him back. He didn't go far, but she used him to push herself backwards. She felt the trolley rail at the backs of her knees, cold air on her back.

Don't be too slow again. Now!

She flung out her arms and jumped backwards. The leap was liberating, but it ended too soon. Something had grabbed her ankle and she hung upside down, the stormy river pouring by overhead. "Let me go," she heard herself say. It seemed a reasonable request, the only reasonable solution to an intractable problem.

The hands that gripped her ankles pulled her away from the rushing water, scraping her against the rough wood. Through her pants legs the hands felt like vise grips.

"Hurry, get her up." Roberts' voice.

The monster hauled her up as neatly as if she were a stuffed toy and bent over her. Its face was unreadable, flat, inhuman, but Rey knew hunger when she saw it.

Apparently Roberts recognized it, too. He barked, "Leave her alone, goddamn you. How many times do I have to tell you not to kill this one? What a failure you are." He swatted at the creature's legs.

It whirled on him, snarling.

"Do you want to be recycled into feed? Follow orders!"

The thing growled, a thick, moist sound. Rey shrank back, putting as many inches as possible between herself and her enemies. They had forgotten about her for the moment. Rey wondered who would claim her, and whom she was rooting for. Not being eaten alive had much in its favor, but the human monster in front of her would only delay her death, and the wait would not be pleasant.

On the riverbank something caught her eye: Smokey, crouched in the scrub. Rey raised a hand. Smokey stood up and beckoned to her. What could he mean? Of course she'd be only too happy to go to him. Maybe he hadn't noticed that a couple of obstacles were in the way.

He made more of those mysterious signs that were supposed to mean something, then climbed on the tripod and grabbed the cable, swung his legs over it, and hunched toward the trolley car. Hardly thinking, Rey hooked her ankles over the cable and inched to meet him.

A vicious claw yanked her down and she landed askew on the boards. The foul beast snarled at her, then jumped up to walk the line toward Smokey.

She yelled. The monster closed the distance fast. It teetered once and hung by one knotty hand. Smokey quickened his pace, trying to get to it while it was vulnerable, but it was too fast and too agile.

"Give up," Roberts drawled.

Rey swung up again; got herself wrapped around the cable. "Here I am, creep! Back here!"

It turned toward her long enough for Smokey to make a couple of good passes along the cable. "I'm comin' for you, dirtbag! Afraid of me? Running away?"

It turned toward him gracefully. Spittle sprayed from its jaws. Its body had greased the wire and Rey had to wipe her hands one at a time on her pants. Her shoulder ached, her injured foot threatened to give out.

Underneath her, Roberts said, "You fool. All I ask is that you come back to work."

The thing was almost within striking distance of Smokey.

Roberts said, "Come down, Dr. Newhause. I'll protect you."

The cable trembled. Smokey's gun fired twice. Smokey grunted. Rey hugged the line in the crooks of her elbows and kept going.

"Smokey!"

She glimpsed the sharp outline of his weapon falling out of sight. The dark monster and Smokey, intertwined, dangled on the wire. Then the two fell together to the river.

Roberts dug his fingers into Rey's shoulders and dragged her down. "It's over. We are the important ones, and we survived." He leaned toward her and pushed a clump of sweaty hair back from her forehead. "We have our work. That's all that matters to people like us. But there are no people like us, are there?"

Rey stared at him, listening for sounds from the water, for Smokey's voice. She said, "Get your hands off of me."

Roberts held up his hands in a surrendering gesture. "I apologize. *In extremis*, you know, I felt we shared something."

"We share nothing." Rey stood to pull the trolley back to the village bank.

"That's the wrong way," Roberts said.

Rey pulled, reached out for a double handful of cable, flexed her arms until her hands were over her head and the trolley moved forward a foot-and-a-half. Three feet. Five.

Roberts stood up, fought for balance, and grabbed the cable. The forward motion stopped. He smiled, and the smile was a lie.

"It's over, Jillian," he said. "Come back to the real world. No hard feelings."

She gave him a moment's consideration, then raised her legs and rabbit-kicked him in the solar plexus. He lost his grip and fell backward. His backbone cracked against the boards. Rey pulled again. The shoreline was closer now. There were no voices rising over the rush of the water. The riverbank was empty. She pulled, in a hurry but sure she was too late.

Roberts wheezed.

She moved without volition, plodding forward. Like a zombie. Unstoppable.

The doctor found his breath. "My spine is fractured, I think. I need medical help."

"You'll have to wait your turn, doctor."

"My spine—I can't move. I need help!"

"Take a number."

"You know," he rasped, "your experiment has created the worst result of all. You created an unfeeling monster, inhuman, cold, dead inside. You created the perfect soldier. But one undesirable outcome is that your unfeeling monster also thinks she's God."

Rey pulled. She didn't know what waited on the shore, but she would get there somehow.

"You played God on your little commune so long you believed you really could create life. But you're not God."

"No."

Rey pulled.

The wind that rode the river rocked the little trolley. Rey had spent an evening suspended over the river one breezy summer night with Jackie Tobasco and Berry, drinking sweet fruit wine and laughing. Berry had fallen asleep, rocked in the cradle; they had covered themselves with a blanket and told stories under the stars.

A frog sang on the riverbank.

"Maybe I am God," Rey said.

"That's what I'm telling you. You've developed an unhealthy—"

"I was forced to be a god here. I didn't want to, but they made me do it."

"The natives made the white woman their god. Such a cliché."

Rey said, "I didn't like it and I don't like it now, but here I am with the power of life and death in my hands."

She moved closer to Roberts, who was arched backwards over the wooden bench. His eyes crossed as she pushed her face close to his. She said, "If I have to be God, I'm going to be the first *just* God in the history of God."

Roberts had no response except to crease his forehead.

"Justice," Rey said. "It'll be a refreshing change. Goodbye, Everett." Rey's hands were cramped, frozen into the perfect shape. She fitted them around his neck. He slapped at her but her knees pinned his arms and he couldn't fight her off. Once he lost consciousness it was easy to finish him. When the last exhalation left his chest, Rey felt a weight leave her shoulders. The open river looked wider, the sky higher, the coiled, urgent water faster.

She clamped her hands around the cable and pulled.

52

"Stop that." Mercy turned from the bower arch to glare at Fiddlin' Sue. "Undead or not, you'll keep to the plan."

Sue grinned. In her opinion "It Wasn't God Who Made Honky Tonk Angels" was perfect for the occasion, but it was Mercy's wedding and Mercy wanted a hymn, so hymn it would be. Mercy never had owned much of a sense of humor. El Duane, though, turned around and winked. Buck and the girls joined Sue in "Give Me Oil In My Lamp, Keep Me Burning." It was overly rousing and not serious enough for Mercy's taste, but she let it slide. Misty's bowing skills were still wobbly, but she was coming along real good; if Buck and Crystal were anything to go by, Misty would soon play like the devil with his hair on fire.

Mercy's white dress was made out of stiff taffeta that crackled as it dragged over the ground. Trucker John had picked it out at the Corvallis Goodwill. God knew what the clerks had thought of him in there, buying a bridal gown. He'd wadded it up in a sack to bring it home and Mercy had spent hours ironing it, but it had a high neck and long sleeves and an accommodating empire waist, all of which Mercy had painstakingly explained to Trucker John, with sketches. Her wedding, her rules.

Once the major remains of the mercenaries had been collected, Hoot and Smokey—Hoot as pilot; he'd refused to get out of the pilot's seat—flew them fifty miles down the coast and laid the machine and its contents down in the Pacific Ocean. Hoot made sure Smokey didn't drown on the swim to shore, although Smokey's weed-filled flotation device made his help unnecessary. Trucker John picked them up and Smokey conducted his business alone. They met at the Goodwill, bought books and a wedding gown and other useful items, then made a canned food run and drove home in the dark.

Like large, hairy fairy godmothers, they had tidied up the human mess. Some had toted the pieces of Travis up the hill; one had pulled EZ off the boulder he'd been clinging to, waterlogged but fully alive; two more had separated Smokey from the invader, which they had gleefully pulverized, brainstem first. Everett Roberts' body went into the pile on the helicopter floor. Now, with the village cleaned and mostly back to what it had been, there was a wedding and music and a trestle-full of food, and before long a new baby. Judging from the size of Mercy Alder's belly, it was going to be a big one.

The wedding dress was going to get a lot of use. Crystal was already sharpening her mother's scissors in preparation for cutting it off to a miniskirt. Then Berry would use the cut off skirt and Jackie T. planned to dye the bodice hot pink and wear it for their wedding. Lacey, having declined Jobert's proposal—which he offered in a hot sweat of passion on bended knee, with flowers—said she had her own mother's wedding gown if she should ever need it, but she had no plans to settle down just yet. After all, there was plenty of time. Maybe eternity.

"How about you?" Jackie asked Rey. "You better claim your piece before all that's left is a hanky."

It was bittersweet, all the celebrating and singing. Even the praying and the drizzle had a poignancy that made Rey drink more moonshine than she ever had before. New Hoochville was already a going concern in her goat shed, and the three moonshiners hung around like porch hounds, being fairly obvious about their readiness to move inside. Hoot and Eddy fussed over zombie Travis as sweetly as he had fussed over them, making him eat and teaching him how to set up a still and brewery. In undeath Travis was as spaced out and carefree as ever; his hair grew out even more golden and he stood straighter. Was he taller? Broader? Rey caught herself wondering what it would be like ... in his changed condition ... but there was a limit to the weirdness she could tolerate.

EZ had helped Rey dismantle the chicken coop board by board, making his case one more time for going with her. He dismantled her refusals one by one with his teenaged superpower of spinning magical thinking into logic.

"I like your creative reasoning, buddy."

"Thank you."

"And I admire your persistence."

"I admire your, um, butt-kicking," EZ returned.

"We do what we have to do. I admire *your* butt-kicking."

"And Smokey's. And the rest of them. Of course, the other ones had special zombie powers, so it was easier for them." EZ pulled bent nails out of a floorboard and tossed them on the growing pile. "You want me to try to straighten these out?"

"It's not worth it. They never get really straight again."

"Yeah. Some things you can't put back the way they were." He said, "Like me. I was a poet, and then I was a soldier, and now I'm nothing again."

"You're not nothing, EZ."

"I need to be in the real world. It's obvious. I've outgrown this place. I'm older than Jake, really. In maturity, I'm his big brother now."

Rey didn't argue.

"Let me go with you, Rey! I swear to God I'll die here. I don't want to live with a bunch of dead people. I can help you."

"I have to go alone," Rey told him again.

They'd gone around like that for days, ever since EZ understood Rey was planning to leave. If he thought he could wear her down, he was almost right.

"I thought you liked me," he said. He sounded angry, but Rey saw him rub his arm across his eyes.

"I like you lots.

He stopped pulling nails. "Did you know Misty and Crystal can read minds now? They can. They know what I'm thinking. It's creepy."

"Well, twins can do that sometimes."

"Yeah, but they do it with other people. They're all going to be tele, tele ... "

"Telepathic."

"I can't take it."

"EZ," Rey said, setting her crowbar down on a dry board, "your sisters need you. And your mother. If you're the oldest human being except for your mom, that's exactly the reason you have to stay. You have a responsibility."

"But—"

"If I didn't have responsibilities, I would stay. You don't realize how great it is here. It's Eden. The outside world is a wasteland, and if somebody doesn't step up it's going to get even worse."

"Let me help!"

"It'll happen. You're going to be twice as awesome as you are now. You take care of your people. That's all you've got. It's not all adventure, just like it's not all poetry or shooting. Some of it's shoveling cow shit and being human for your family."

He rubbed his shirt sleeve over his eyes hard. "You left your family when you moved here."

"I didn't have any family." Rey looked at the boy until he looked back. She said, "I gave my life to bringing people back because I couldn't get my family back. I made a new family on this mountain and it hurts to leave it, but there are bigger problems out there. That's my road for now. Your life is going to be more amazing and strange and powerful than you can imagine. If you came with me you'd miss it all."

"I could be your sidekick. I know stuff nobody else knows. I'll cover for you."

Rey went to him and hugged him. He pulled away at first but then burrowed into her shoulder and let her hold him. She said, "I know what it is to feel alone. But we make this sacrifice to keep everybody else from having to feel that." He let her smooth his hair. It was gritty with forest dust. Rey flicked out a fir needle. "This is when the real man stuff happens. Look here."

She made him look at her again. "Be the leader, not the side-kick. You know, in the movies, the sidekick always gets killed."

His eyes still looked miserable.

"I promise, when you're eighteen, if you still think you should leave, you can, and you'll find me. But wait until you've done your duty here. Deal?"

He pouted, shrugged, and said, "I guess."

"That's what I like. Enthusiasm."

After the reception Rey and Smokey hiked up to his place. His bob-cat was a proud mama of four fierce, round cubs. Smokey called himself Uncle Grandpa and gave them the run of his dugout.

At what passed for sunset in the Coast Range he and Rey sat at the cliff's edge and watched a pair of osprey circle over the hollow between mountains. Smokey offered Rey a toke.

"I still don't like it," she said.

"You don't mind if I do?"

"Knock yourself out."

He pulled her close. Rey said, "If you don't shave pretty soon, you're going to turn back into a Sasquatch."

"You wouldn't like that?"

"Not much."

"Sasquatches are virile. They're the macho men of the mythical forest."

"I don't know if I believe in myths anymore. Reality has gotten kind of mashed in with myth."

Smokey made the blunt's edges glow red. When he finally exhaled, he said, "Reality is for people who can't handle myths."

The ospreys hunted, circling in spirals.

"Do you think you'll come back?" he asked.

"Maybe. Yes."

"Should I come with you?"

Rey slipped her arms around his waist. "I'll be feeling my way along. I don't know what will happen. I guess I have to do the next part alone." He felt solid and warm. Rey couldn't imagine not feeling him again, ever, but there was work to do.

"You know I love it here," she said. "This is my family. You. The forest, the rain, everything. Maybe it'll turn out there's somebody else who can save the world. I sure as hell don't feel like it."

"Yeah." Smokey exhaled a fragrant cloud. "I don't know what'll happen either. This legalization has pretty much put me out of business. Either I'm going to have to join the system and get inspected and regulated and pay taxes and take a serious pay cut, or learn how to grow organic ginseng. Or I guess I could keep growing but stay outside the law, with a seriously devalued product. But it might be time to quit farm life completely."

"You love it here."

He nodded. "I'd better stick around awhile. EZ and his mother aren't going to be able to handle everybody on their own.

They watched the ospreys ride the thermals under fat nimbostrati rolling in from the Pacific.

"I'll adopt your chickens."

"And the goats?"

"Sure. Uncle Grandpa's home for wayward goats and hens."

They went inside and lit a fire. Toasty let Rey pet her cubs and accepted a head rub for herself, purring and liquid-eyed with furry joy.

Later, while they watched shadows flicker on the earth and log ceiling, Rey said, "*Morte Morietur.*"

"Hmm?" Manlike, he'd already drifted off.

"If you look for me on the outside—"

"I will."

"Write this down."

While he wrote Rey looked at the reflected ember-glow on his skin. Both of them had scars fading from red to pink; someday they would be thin white lines, memoirs written in invisible ink.

"*Morte* ... Latin?"

She repeated it for him. " 'Death will die.' I could be a little off. My Latin's rusty. But I'll post it somehow. I'll show you how to find me."

"Right you are, Double Oh Seven."

She kissed him and more time passed. Rey felt herself go liquid-eyed and purry with satisfaction. They slipped again into warm sleep.

Later still, Rey said "Smokey."

"Right here."

"I will want you to find me."

"I'm like a Northwest Mountie," he sang, rasping an ancient oldie in her ear, his herb-scented breath tickling her hair. "You know I'll bring you in someday."

Cricket and Lacewing walked Rey to the trolley. Bee hadn't recovered enough for walking yet, but she was quickly growing more robust, motivated toward recovery by Mercy acting like she ran the whole mountain. She had sent bread and jam tied in a cloth for Rey's trip out.

From behind the Dollers' store clacked the merry sound of bones hanging on Birdie's dooryard tree. Birdie came out onto her repaired front porch to wave Rey goodbye. Bill's boots flopped on her feet. Nobody had seen Bill since the second revival, and if Birdie didn't seem to mind, and as she ran the store fine without him, nobody else was going to worry much about him, either. Across the road, Trucker John's old trailer was a cinder pile that could hide about anything, including a large body, but no one sifted through the remains.

Jackie met the younger Pears and Rey at the trolley and waited while they said their goodbyes. Then Jackie and Rey pulled the trolley down the cable to the midpoint. Temporary deadness hadn't affected Jackie's ability to talk. They talked a long time, sitting above the rushing water, saying what hadn't been said and things that had been said before but felt good to say again. Then they hauled themselves and Rey's ditty bag along the uphill half of the line to the far bank.

"Don't get out," Rey told her. "I love you, Jacks. Be happy."

"I love you," Jackie echoed. She watched Rey get in the old pickup truck and listened to it grind and squeak until the sound was replaced by river and birds. Jackie pulled the trolley back across the river. It was easy now. She would go home and give herself a set and style, she thought, and tonight she would run the woods with Berry, just the two of them in the cold wet moonlight.

THE END

www.ingramcontent.com/pod-product-compliance
Lightning Source LLC
Chambersburg PA
CBHW051312250626

47155CB00007B/2288